W9-CGO-853

Harlequin Man of the Month Collection

Passionate, honorable…and a little arrogant—
these men are always sexy and completely
irresistible.

Whether heading an international empire,
saving a family's legacy or leading a kingdom,
our heroes live life with undeniable passion.
And within the pages of this special collection
they meet their match in beautiful, intelligent
and determined women who are up to the
challenge of winning the hearts of these
formidable men!

Wherever you find them—at the office, on an
island or in the bedroom—these heroes are
sure to seduce, because above all else they know
that love is the greatest goal.

If you enjoy these two classic Man of the Month
stories, be sure to check out more books
featuring strong, captivating heroes from the
Harlequin Desire line.

USA TODAY Bestselling Authors

Michelle Celmer
and
Yvonne Lindsay

THE TYCOON'S
CHARM

HARLEQUIN® MAN OF THE MONTH

Recycling programs
for this product may
not exist in your area.

ISBN-13: 978-0-373-60108-0

The Tycoon's Charm

Copyright © 2015 by Harlequin Books S.A.

The publisher acknowledges the copyright holders
of the individual works as follows:

The Tycoon's Paternity Agenda
Copyright © 2010 by Michelle Celmer

Honor-Bound Groom
Copyright © 2010 by Dolce Vita Trust

Printed in U.S.A.

CONTENTS

THE TYCOON'S PATERNITY AGENDA   7
Michelle Celmer

HONOR-BOUND GROOM   207
Yvonne Lindsay

THE TYCOON'S
PATERNITY AGENDA

Michelle Celmer

To my dad

One

There was no doubt about it, the man was insufferable.

Yet here she was sitting in her pickup truck in the visitors' lot of the Western Oil headquarters building in El Paso, the ruthless, Texas-afternoon sun scorching her face through the windshield.

Katherine Huntley hadn't seen her brother-in-law, Adam Blair, CEO of Western Oil, since her sister's funeral three years ago. His call asking to meet her had come as something of a surprise. It was no shock, however, that he'd had the gall to say he was too busy to meet on her own turf in Peckins, two hours north, and asked her to come to him. But he was the billionaire oil tycoon and she was a lowly cattle rancher, and she was guessing that he was used to people doing things his way.

But that's not why she agreed to come. She was long

past overdue for a trip to the warehouse store for supplies anyway, and it gave her the chance to visit the cemetery. Something she did far too infrequently these days. But seeing Rebecca's grave this morning, being reminded once again that Katy had gone from baby sister to only child, brought back the familiar grief. It simply wasn't fair that Becca, who'd had so much to live for, had been taken so young. That her parents had to know the excruciating pain of losing a child.

Katy glanced at the clock on the dash and realized she was about to be late, and since she prided herself on always being punctual, she shoved open her door and stepped out into the blistering heat. It was so hot the soles of her boots stuck to the blacktop. She swiftly crossed the lot to the front entrance, and the rush of icy air as she pushed through the double glass doors into the lobby actually made her shiver.

Considering the suspicious looks the security guards gave her as she walked through the metal detector, they must not have gotten many women dressed in jeans and work shirts visiting. And, of course, because she was wearing her steel-toe boots, the alarm began to wail.

"Empty your pockets, please," one of them told her.

She was about to explain that her pockets were already empty, when a deep voice ordered, "Let her through."

She looked up to find her brother-in-law waiting just past the security stand, and her heart took a quick dive downward.

Ex-brother-in-law.

Without question the security guards ushered her past, and Adam stepped forward to greet her.

"It's good to see you again, Katy."

"You, too." She wondered if she should hug him, but figured this situation was awkward enough without the burden of unnecessary physical contact, and settled for a handshake instead. But as his hand folded around her own, she wondered if he noticed the calluses and rough skin, not to mention the short, unpainted fingernails. She was sure he was used to women like Rebecca, who spent hours in the salon getting pedicures and manicures, and all the other beauty treatments she neither had time nor the inclination for.

Not that it made a difference what he thought of her nails. But when he released her hand, she stuck them both in her jeans pockets.

In contrast, Adam looked every bit the billionaire CEO that he was. She had nearly forgotten how big he was. Not only did he look as though he spent a lot of time in the weight room, he was above average in height. At five feet nine inches, few men towered over her, but Adam was at least six-four.

He wore his dark hair in the same closely cropped style, although she could see strands of gray peppering his temples now. Of course, as was the case with men like him, it only made him look more distinguished. There were also worry lines at the corners of his eyes and across his forehead that hadn't been there before. Probably from the stress of dealing with Rebecca's illness.

Despite that, he looked good for a man of forty.

Katy was only seventeen when her sister married Adam ten years ago, and though she had never admitted it to a soul, she'd had a mild adolescent crush on her gorgeous new brother-in-law. But neither she nor her parents would have guessed that the charming, handsome man intended to steal Rebecca away from them.

"How was your trip down?" he asked.

She shrugged. "The same as it always is."

She waited for him to explain what she was doing there, or at the very least thank her for making the long drive to see him. Instead he gestured to the shop across the lobby. "Can I buy you a cup of coffee?"

"Sure. Why not?"

Other than the shop employees, everyone seated inside wore business attire, and most had their nose buried in a laptop computer, or a cell phone stuck to their ear. But when Adam entered, everyone stopped what they were doing to nod, or greet him.

Good Lord. When the man entered a room, he owned it. But he was the boss, and it was obvious people respected him. Or feared him.

She followed him to the counter and he spouted some long, complicated-sounding drink to the clerk, then turned to Katy and asked, "What would you like?"

"Plain old black coffee," she told the clerk. She didn't care for the frou-frou blends and flavors that had become so popular lately. Her tastes were as simple as her lifestyle.

With drinks in hand, he led her to a table at the back of the shop. She had just assumed they would go up to his office, but this was okay, too. A little less formal and intimidating. Not that she had a reason to feel intimidated. She didn't know why she was here, so she wasn't really sure what she should be feeling at this point.

When they were seated, Adam asked, "How are

your parents? And how are things at the ranch? I trust business is good."

"We're good. I don't know if you heard, but we went totally organic about two years ago."

"That's great. It's the way of the future."

She sipped her coffee. It was hot and strong, just the way she liked it. "But I'm sure you didn't ask me here to talk about cattle."

"No," he agreed. "There's something I need to discuss with you. Something…personal."

She couldn't imagine what personal matter he might have to discuss with her as anything they might have had in common had been buried along with her sister. But she shrugged and said, "Okay."

"I'm not sure if Becca mentioned it, but before she was diagnosed, we had been having fertility issues. Our doctor suggested in vitro, and Becca was going through the hormone therapy to have her eggs extracted when they discovered the cancer."

"She told me." And Katy knew that her sister had felt like a failure for being unable to conceive. She had been terrified of disappointing Adam. Her entire life seemed to revolve around pleasing him. In fact, Becca spent so much time and energy being the perfect high-society wife that she'd had little time left for her family. Adam's schedule had been so busy, they hadn't even come for Christmas the year before she got sick.

If it had been Katy, she would have put her foot down and insisted she see her family. Even if it meant spending the holidays apart from her spouse. Of course, she never would have married a man like Adam in the first place. She could never be with anyone so demanding and self-centered. And especially someone who didn't share her love for the ranch. But according to her parents, practically from the instant Becca left the womb, she had been gunning to move to the city, to live a more sophisticated lifestyle.

Sometimes Katy swore Becca was a doorstep baby.

"She was so sure she would beat it," Adam continued. "We went ahead with our plans, thinking we could hire a surrogate to carry the baby. But, of course, we never got the chance."

"She told me that, too," Katy said, pushing down the bitterness that wanted to bubble to the surface. Harvesting the eggs had meant holding off on treating the cancer, which just might have been the thing that killed her. Katy had begged Becca to forget the eggs and go forward with the treatment. They could always adopt later on, but Becca knew how much Adam wanted a child—his own flesh and blood—and as always, she would have done anything to make him happy.

It would have been easy to blame Adam for her death, but ultimately, it had been Becca's choice. One she had paid dearly for.

"I'm not sure what any of this has to do with me," Katy said.

"I thought you should know that I've decided to use the frozen embryos and hire a surrogate to carry the baby."

He said it so bluntly, so matter-of-factly, it took several seconds for the meaning of his words to sink in.

Baby? Was he saying that he was going to hire some stranger to have her *sister's* child?

Katy was beyond stunned…and utterly speechless. Of all the possible reasons for Adam asking her here, that particular one had never crossed her mind. How could he even consider doing this to her family?

She realized her jaw had fallen and closed her mouth so forcefully her teeth snapped together. Adam was watching her, waiting for her to say something.

Finally she managed, "I…I'm not sure what to say."

"So we're clear, I'm not asking for your permission. Or your approval. Out of courtesy—since it's Rebecca's child, too—I felt I should tell you what I plan to do."

He wasn't the kind of man to do things as a "courtesy." He did nothing unless it benefited him. She was guessing that he'd consulted a lawyer, and his lawyer had advised him to contact Becca's family.

"I also thought you could give me some advice on the best way to break the news to your parents," Adam added, and Katy was too dumbfounded to speak. As if losing their daughter wasn't heartbreaking enough, now they would have to live with the knowledge that they had a grandchild out there with a father who was too busy to even give them the time of day? How could he even think about doing this to them? And then to ask her *help*? Was he really so arrogant? So self-absorbed?

"My advice to you would be don't do it," she told him.

He looked confused. "Don't tell them?"

"Don't use the embryos." She was so angry, her voice was actually shaking. "Haven't my parents been through enough? I can't believe you could be selfish enough to even consider putting them through this."

"I would be giving them a grandchild. A part of their daughter would live on. I'd think that would please them."

"A grandchild they would never see? You really think that's going to make them *happy*?"

"Why would you assume they wouldn't see the baby?"

Was he kidding? "I can count on one hand how many times you and Becca came to visit the last three years of your marriage. My parents were always making the effort, and in most instances you were too busy to make the time for them." She became aware, by the curious stares they were getting, that the volume of her voice had risen to a near-hysterical level. She took a deep breath, forced herself to lower it. "Why not get remarried and have a baby with your new wife? You're a rich, handsome guy. I'm sure women would line up to marry you. Or you could adopt. Just leave my family out of this."

Adam's voice remained calm and even. "As I said, I'm not asking your permission. This meeting was simply a courtesy."

"Bull," she hissed under her breath.

Adam's brow rose. "Excuse me?"

"I'm not some simple, stupid country girl, Adam. So please, don't insult my intelligence by treating me like an uneducated hick. I'm here because your lawyer probably warned you that my parents could fight this, and you want to avoid any legal entanglements."

His expression darkened, and she knew she'd hit a nerve. "Your family has no legal rights over the embryos."

"Maybe not, but if we decided to fight you, it could drag on for years, couldn't it?"

His brow dipped low over his eyes, and he leaned

forward slightly. "You don't have the financial means to take me on in court."

Not one to be intimidated, she met his challenge and leaned toward him. "I don't doubt there's some bleeding-heart attorney out there who would just love to take on a case like this pro bono."

He didn't even flinch. Did he know she was bluffing? Not only did she know of no attorney like that, she didn't think her parents would ever try to fight Adam. They would be miserably unhappy, but like Becca's defection from the family fold, they would accept it. And learn to live with it. They didn't like to make waves, to cause problems, which is why they allowed Becca to drift so far from the family in the first place. Had it been up to Katy, things would have been different.

Adam's expression softened and he said in a calm and rational voice, "I think we're getting ahead of ourselves."

"What do you even know about being a parent?" she snapped. "When would you find the time? Have you even considered what you're getting yourself into? Diaper changes and midnight feedings. Or will you hire someone to raise the baby for you? Leave all the dirty work to them?"

"You don't know anything about me," he said.

"Sad, considering you were married to my sister for seven years."

He took a deep breath and blew it out. "I think we got off on the wrong foot here."

Actually, what she had done was reverse the balance of power so that now she had the upper hand. It was the only way to deal with men like him. A trick Becca had obviously never learned.

"Trust me when I say, I have given this consider-able thought, and I feel it's something I *need* to do. And I assure you that both you and your parents will see the baby. My parents are both dead, so you'll be the only other family the child has. I would never deny him that."

"And I'm just supposed to believe you?"

"At this point, you really don't have much choice. Because we both know that the chances of finding a lawyer who will represent you for free are slim to none. I've been in business a long time. I recognize a bluff when I see it."

She bit her lip. So much for having the upper hand.

"I'm not doing this to hurt anyone, Katy. I just want a child."

But why did it have to be *Becca's* child? "We may not be as rich as you, but we can still fight it."

"And you would lose."

Yes, she would. But she could put up one hell of a fight. And put her parents through hell in the process. Not to mention decimate them all financially.

The sad fact was she had no choice but to accept this. She was going to have to take him on his word that they would see the baby. What other recourse did she have?

"Can I ask who the surrogate will be?"

He was gracious enough not to gloat at her obvious surrender. "I'm not sure yet. My attorney is looking at possible candidates."

She frowned. "How will you know they're trust-worthy?"

"They'll go through a rigorous interview process

and background check. If they've ever been arrested, or used illegal substances, we'll know about it."

But there was no way to know everything. Katy watched the national news and knew situations like this had a way of going horribly awry. What if the woman smoked, or did drugs while she was pregnant? Or took some other physical risk that might harm the baby? Or what if she decided she didn't want to give the baby up? Would it matter that it was Rebecca's egg?

Or even worse, she could just disappear with Rebecca's child, never to be seen again. For Katy's parents—and probably Adam, too—it would be like losing Rebecca all over again.

"What if you think the woman is trustworthy, but you're wrong?" she asked him, growing more uneasy by the second.

"We won't be," Adam assured her, but that wasn't good enough.

She took a swallow of her coffee, burning her tongue. If she let him do this, she could look forward to nine months of being on edge, worrying about her niece or nephew's safety.

There was only one person she trusted enough to carry her sister's baby. It was completely crazy, but she knew it was the only way. The only *good* way. And she would do whatever necessary to convince him.

"I know the perfect person to be the surrogate," she told Adam.

"Who?"

"Me."

Two

Adam had imagined several possible scenarios of what Katy's reaction would be when he told her his plans. He thought she might be excited. Grateful even that a part of Rebecca would live on in the baby. He had also considered her being upset, or even indignant, which proved to be much closer to the truth.

But not a single one of those scenarios included her offering to carry the baby herself. And as far as he was concerned, that wasn't an option.

Admittedly he had approached Katy first because he figured she would be easily manipulated, but sweet little Katy had an edge now. She was a lot tougher than she used to be. And she was right about his lawyer's advice. If there were a legal battle over the issue of the embryos, he would win. But it could drag on for years. He didn't want to wait that long. He was ready now. And though allowing her to be the surrogate would significantly ease any opposition from her family, he could see an entire new series of problems arise as a result.

"I can't ask you to do that," he told her.

"You didn't ask. I offered."

"I'm not sure if you fully understand the sacrifice it will be. Physically and emotionally."

"I have friends who have gone through pregnancies, so I know exactly what to expect."

"I imagine that knowing a pregnant person and being one are two very different things."

"I *want* to do it, Adam."

He could see that, but the idea had trouble written all over it. In every language.

He tried a different angle. "How will your... 'significant other' feel about this?"

"That won't be an issue. I see Willy Jenkins occasionally, but he isn't what I would call significant. We're more like...friends with benefits, if you know what I mean."

He did, and for some ridiculous reason he wanted to string this Jenkins guy up by his toes. To him she would always be Rebecca's baby sister. Little Katy.

But Katy was a grown woman. Twenty-seven or -eight, if memory served. It was none of his business who she was friends with.

Or why.

"The process could take a year," he told her. "Longer if it takes more than one try. What if you meet someone?"

"Who the heck am I going to meet? Peckins has a population of eight hundred. Most of the men in town

I've known since kindergarten. If I was going to fall madly in love with one of them, I'd have done it by now."

He tried a different angle. "Have you thought of the physical toll it could take on your body?"

"Look who you're talking to," she said, gesturing to her casual clothing, the ash-blond hair pulled back in a ponytail. "I'm not like Rebecca. I don't obsess about my weight, or worry about things like stretch marks. And you won't find anyone more responsible. I don't smoke or take drugs, not even over-the-counter pain relievers. I have an occasional beer, but beyond that I don't drink, so giving it up isn't a problem. Not to mention that I'm healthy as a horse. And my doctor never fails to point out at my annual physical that I have a body built for childbearing."

She certainly did. She had the figure of a fifties pinup model. A time when women looked like women, not prepubescent boys. In his opinion Rebecca had always been too obsessed with her weight and her looks, as though she thought he would love her less if she didn't look perfect 100 percent of the time. Even during chemo she never failed to drag herself out of bed to put on makeup. And when she could no longer get out of bed, she had the nurse do it for her.

The familiar stab of pain he felt when he thought of her that way pierced the shell around his heart from the inside out.

Katy surprised him by reaching across the table and taking his hand. What surprised him even more was the tingling sensation that started in his fingers and worked its way up his arm. Her hands were a little rough from working on the ranch, but her skin was warm. Her nails were bare, but clean and neatly trimmed. Everything about her was very…natural.

Which was more than he could say for this situation, and the odd, longing sensation deep in his gut.

"Adam, you know as well as I do that despite all the background checks you can do, there's no one you could trust as much as me."

He hated to admit it—she was right. Despite their very complicated past and feelings of resentment over Becca, Katy would never do anything to put her sister's child in harm's way. But she could use the opportunity to try to manipulate him, and he never put himself in a position to lose the upper hand. Not professionally, and especially not personally.

Not anymore.

But this was the welfare of his child they were discussing. Wasn't it his obligation as a father to put his child first, to make its health and well-being his number-one priority?

Katy squeezed his hand so tight he started to lose sensation in his fingers, and they were beginning to get curious glances from his employees.

He gently extracted his hand from hers. "Look, Katy—"

"Please, Adam. Please let me do this." She paused, her eyes pleading, then said, "You know it's what Becca would have wanted."

Ouch. That was a low blow, and she knew how to hit where it really stung. The worst part was that she was right. Didn't he owe it to Becca to let Katy do this for them? For the baby? Wasn't he partially to blame for Becca losing touch with her family in the first place?

"Though it's against my better judgment, and I

would like to run it past my attorney before I give you a definitive answer...I'm inclined to say yes."

Her expression was a combination of relief and gratitude. "Thank you, Adam. I promise, you won't regret this."

Impossible, since he regretted it already.

Katy left soon after, and Adam headed back up to his office, feeling conflicted.

On one hand he could see the benefits of choosing Katy as a surrogate. In theory, it was an ideal arrangement. But he knew from experience that things did not always go as planned, and what may seem "ideal" one day could swiftly become a disaster the next.

Before he made any decisions, he would speak with his attorney.

His assistant, Bren, stopped him as he walked past her desk to his office. "Senator Lyons called while you were gone. He said he'll be out of the office the rest of the day but he'll call you back tomorrow."

"Did he say what he wanted?"

"My guess would be a campaign contribution. Isn't he up for reelection?"

"You're probably right."

"Also, Mr. Suarez needs to see you when you have a minute."

"Call down to his office and tell him now would be good," he told her. It was doubtful he would be able to concentrate on work anyway. Too much on his mind.

He stepped into his office, stopped at the wet bar to pour himself a scotch, then sat behind his desk and booted his computer.

"Hey, boss."

He looked up to find Emilio Suarez, Western Oil CFO, standing in his open doorway.

Western Oil was in dire financial straits when Adam inherited it from his father, and Emilio's financial genius had brought it back from the brink of ruin. Though he was from a Puerto Rican family of modest means, through grants and scholarships Emilio had graduated college at the top of his class, which was what had caught Adam's attention when he was looking for a management team. Emilio had become an irreplaceable employee—not to mention a good friend—and worth every penny of his ridiculously exorbitant salary.

Adam gestured him inside. "You wanted to talk to me?"

He came in, shutting the door behind him, and stopped to pour himself a drink. "I got an interesting call from my brother today."

"The federal prosecutor, the one in Europe or the other brother?"

The "other" brother was the family black sheep. A drifter who only called when he needed something. Money usually. For bail, or to pay off loan sharks.

"The prosecutor," he said, taking a seat opposite Adam's desk. "And if anyone asks, you did not hear this from me."

"Of course."

"You know Leonard Betts?"

"By reputation only." He was a financial wizard and according to Forbes, the richest man in Texas. It had been said that everything he touched turned to gold.

"You ever invest with him?" Emilio asked.

He shook his head. "He always seemed a little too

successful, if you know what I mean. Either he's extremely lucky—and luck can run out—or he's shady."

"You've got good instincts. According to Alejandro, he's been under investigation by the SEC, and it's looking like he and his wife will be arrested and charged for a Ponzi scheme."

Adam shook his head in disbelief. "His wife, too?"

"And her parents. Or at least, her mother. Her father died a few years ago."

"So it was a family business."

"I guess. I just thought I should warn you that, although it's unlikely, there's the slightest possibility that when the media gets wind of this, my name may come up."

Adam sat straighter in his seat. "You've invested with him?"

"No! No, my market is real estate. This is more of a personal connection."

Adam frowned, not sure he was liking what he was hearing. It would be in the company's best interest to stay as far removed as possible from this scandal. "How personal?"

"In college, I was engaged to Isabelle Winthrop. Betts's wife."

Adam's jaw nearly fell. Emilio had never mentioned knowing her, much less being engaged to her. Or anyone for that matter. He was so fiercely against the entire institution of marriage, Adam wouldn't have guessed that he would have been planning a trip to the altar with any woman. "I had no idea."

"She dumped me for Betts two weeks before we planned to elope."

"Damn. I'm really sorry, Emilio."

Emilio shrugged. "Honestly, she did me a favor. We were young and stupid. We would have been divorced in a year."

Something in his eyes told Adam he was making light of an otherwise painful situation. But he didn't push the issue. If Emilio wanted to talk about it, he knew Adam was there for him.

"There's no doubt she was a gold digger, but I'll be honest, I never imagined her capable of helping Leonard bilk his clients out of millions of dollars."

"Well, if your name does come up, we'll use Cassandra."

Cassandra Benson was Western Oil's public relations director. For her, media spin was an art form. If properly motivated, she could make climate change sound environmentally beneficial.

"So," Emilio said, leaning back in his chair and taking a swallow of his drink. "What's this I hear about you and a mystery woman?"

"Wow, good news travels fast." He should have taken Katy up to his office. It was just that the coffee shop seemed more…neutral. He should have known better and met her somewhere off campus and far from the building. Like California.

"The CEO can't sit in the company coffee shop holding hands with a woman no one has seen before, and expect it to go unnoticed."

"Well, she's not a mystery woman. She's my sister-in-law. And we weren't holding hands. We were talking."

"I thought you didn't see Becca's family any longer."

"I haven't in a long time. But something has come up."

"Is everything okay?"

Up until today, Adam hadn't talked to anyone but his attorney and the fertility doctor about his baby plan, but he knew he could trust Emilio to keep it quiet. So he told him, and his reaction was about what Adam would have expected.

"Wow," Emilio said, shaking his head in disbelief. "I didn't even know you wanted kids. I mean, I knew that you and Rebecca were trying, but I had no idea you would want to be a single father."

"It's something I've wanted for a while. It just feels like the right time to me. And since I don't plan to get married again..." He shrugged. "Surrogacy seems to be my best option."

"Why the meeting with Becca's sister...I'm sorry, I don't recall her name."

"Katherine...Katy. I called her as a courtesy, and on the advice of my attorney."

"So, what did she say?"

"She wants to be the surrogate."

One brow rose. "Seriously?"

"Yeah. In fact, she was pretty adamant about it. She claims that she's the only person I can trust."

"Do you trust her?"

"I believe that she would never do anything to harm Becca's baby."

"But..."

"Katy seems very...headstrong. If I hire someone, I'll be calling the shots. Katy on the other hand is in a position to make things very complicated."

"Correct me if I'm wrong, but if you tell her no, she could make things complicated, too."

"Exactly."

"So you're damned if you do and damned if you don't."

"More or less." And he didn't like being backed into a corner.

"So what did you tell her?"

"That I had to talk to my attorney."

"You hear so many horror stories about surrogacy agreements going bad. Just a few weeks ago Alejandro was telling me about a case in New Mexico. A couple hired a surrogate to carry their baby. She was Hispanic, and halfway through the pregnancy moved back to Mexico and dropped off the map. Unfortunately the law is in her favor."

Adam had heard similar cautionary tales.

"I think, if you have someone you can trust, let her do it," Emilio said.

He would make the call to his attorney, to check on the legalities of it and his rights as the father, but Emilio was right. Choosing Katy just made the most sense. And ultimately the benefits would outweigh the negatives.

He hoped.

Three

What the hell was he doing here?

The limo pitched and swayed up the pitted, muddy gravel road that led to the Huntleys' cattle ranch, and Adam lunged to keep the documents he'd been reading on the ride up from sliding off the leather seat and scattering to the floor.

His driver and bodyguard, Reece, would have to take a trip to the car wash as soon as they got back to El Paso, Adam realized as he gazed out the mud-splattered window. At least the torrential rain they'd encountered an hour ago had let up and now there was nothing but blue sky for miles.

As they bounced forward up the drive, Adam could see that not much had changed in the four years since he'd last been here. The house, a typical, sprawling and rustic ranch, was older, but well maintained. Pastures with grazing cattle stretched as far as the eye could see.

The ranch had been in their family for five generations. A tradition Becca had had no interest in carrying on. As far as she had been concerned, Katy could have it all.

And now she would.

The limo rolled to a stop by the front porch steps and Reece got out to open his door. As he did, a wall of hot, damp air engulfed the cool interior, making the leather feel instantly sticky to the touch.

This meeting had been Katy's idea, and he wasn't looking forward to it. Not that he disliked his former in-laws. He just had nothing in common with them. However, if they were going to be involved in his child's life, the least he could do was make an effort to be cordial. According to Katy, the news of his plan to use the embryos had come as a shock to them, but knowing Katy would be the surrogate had softened the blow. And since a meeting with his attorney last week, when he and Katy signed a surrogacy agreement, it was official. With any luck, nine months from her next ovulation cycle she would be having his and Becca's baby.

After months of consideration and planning, it was difficult to believe that it was finally happening. That after years of longing to have a child, he finally had his chance. And despite Katy and her parents' concerns, he would be a good father. Unlike his own father, who had been barely more than a ghost after Adam's mother passed away. Adam spent most of his childhood away at boarding schools, or in summer camps. The only decent thing his father had ever done was leave him Western Oil when he died. And though it had taken several years of hard work, Adam had pulled it back from the brink of death.

"Sir?"

Adam looked up and realized Reece was standing by the open car door, waiting for him to climb out.

"Everything okay, sir?" he asked.

"Fine." May as well get this over with, he thought, climbing from the back of the car into the sticky heat.

"Hey, stranger," he heard someone call from the vicinity of the barn, and looked over to see Katy walking toward him. She was dressed for work, her thick, leather gloves and boots caked with mud. Her hair was pulled back into a ponytail and as she got closer he saw that there was a smudge of dirt on her left cheek. For some odd reason he felt the urge to reach up and rub it clean.

He looked her up and down and asked, "Am I early? I was sure you said four o'clock."

"No, you're right on time. The rain set us back in our chores a bit, that's all." She followed his gaze down her sweat-soaked shirt and mud-splattered jeans and said apologetically, "I'd hug you, but I'm a little filthy."

Filthy or not, he wasn't the hug type. "I'll settle for a handshake."

She tugged off her glove and wiped her hand on the leg of her jeans before extending it to him. Her skin was hot and clammy, her grip firm. She turned to Reece and introduced herself. "Katherine Huntley, but everyone calls me Katy."

He warily accepted her outstretched hand. He wasn't used to being acknowledged, much less greeted so warmly. Adam recalled that the hired help had always been regarded as family on the Huntley ranch. "Reece Wilson, ma'am."

"It's a scorcher. Would you like to come inside with us?" she asked, gesturing to the house. "Have something cold to drink?"

"No, thank you, ma'am."

"If you're worried about your car," she said with a grin, "I promise no one will steal it."

Was she actually flirting with his driver? "He's fine," Adam said. "And we have a lot to discuss."

Her smile dissolved and there was disapproval in her tone when she said, "Well, then, come on in."

He followed her up the steps to the porch, where she kicked off her muddy boots before opening the door and gesturing him inside. A small vestibule opened up into the great room and to the left were the stairs leading to the second floor.

The furniture was still an eclectic mix of styles and eras. Careworn, but comfortable. The only modern addition he could see was the large, flat-screen television over the fireplace. Not much else had changed. Not that he'd been there so often he would notice small differences. He could count on two hands how many times they had visited in the seven years he and Becca were married. Not that he hadn't wanted to, despite what Katy and her parents believed.

"My parents wanted to be here to greet you, but they were held up at a cattle auction in Bellevue," Katy told him. "They should be back within the hour."

He had hoped to get this business out of the way, so he could return to El Paso at a decent hour. Though it was Friday, he had a long workday ahead of him tomorrow.

"Would you like a cold drink?" she asked. "Iced tea or lemonade?"

"Whatever is easiest."

Katy turned toward the door leading to the kitchen and hollered, "Elvie! You in there?"

Several seconds passed, then the door slid open several inches and a timid looking Hispanic girl who couldn't have been a day over sixteen peered out. When she saw Adam standing there her eyes widened, then lowered shyly, and she said in a thick accent, "*Sí,* Ms. Katy."

"Elvie, this is Mr. Blair. Could you please fetch him something cold to drink, and take something out to his driver, too?"

She nodded and slipped silently back into the kitchen.

Katy looked down at her filthy clothes. "I'm a mess. I hope you don't mind, but I'm going to hop into a quick shower and get cleaned up."

"By all means." It wasn't as if he was going anywhere. Until her parents returned he was more or less stuck there.

"I'll just be a few minutes. Make yourself at home."

She left him there and headed up the stairs. With nothing to do but wait, Adam walked over to the hearth, where frame after frame of family photos sat. Adam had very few photos of his own family, and only one of his mother.

In his father's grief, he'd taken down all the pictures of Adam's mother after her death and stored them with the other family antiques and keepsakes in the attic of his El Paso estate. A few years later, when Adam was away at school and his father traveling in Europe, faulty wiring started a fire and the entire main house burned to the ground. Taking whatever was left of his mother with it.

At the time it was just one more reason in an ever-growing list to hate his father. When Adam got the call that he'd died, he hadn't talked to the old man in almost five years.

He leaned in to get a closer look at a photo of Becca that had been taken at her high school graduation. She looked so young. So full of promise. He'd met her only a few years later. Her college roommate was the daughter of a family friend and Becca had accompanied them to his home for a cocktail party. Though Adam had been a decade older, he'd found her completely irresistible, and it was obvious the attraction was mutual. Though it had been against his better judgment, he asked her out, and was genuinely surprised when she declined. Few women had ever rejected his advances.

She found him attractive, she said, but needed to focus all her energy on school. She had a plan, she'd told him, a future to build, and she wouldn't stray from that. Which made him respect her even more.

But he wasn't used to taking no for an answer, either, so he'd persisted, and finally she agreed to one date. But only as friends. He took her to dinner and the theater. She hadn't even kissed him goodnight, but as he drove home, he knew that he would eventually marry her. She was everything he wanted in a wife.

They saw each other several times before she finally let him kiss her, and held out for an excruciating three months before she would sleep with him. He wouldn't say that first time had been a disappointment, exactly. It had just taken a while to get everything working smoothly. Their sex life had never been what he would call smoking hot anyway. It was more…comfortable. Besides, their relationship had been based more on respect than sex. And he preferred it that way.

They were seeing each other almost six months before she admitted her humble background—not that it had made a difference to him—and it wasn't until they became engaged a year later that she finally introduced him to her family.

After months of hearing complaints about her family, and how backward and primitive ranch life was, he'd half expected to meet the modern equivalent of the Beverly Hillbillies, but her parents were both educated, intelligent people. He never really understood why she resented them so. Her family seemed to adore her, yet she always made excuses why they shouldn't visit, and the longer she stayed away, the more her resentment seemed to grow. He had tried to talk to her about it, tried to reason with her, but she would always change the subject.

Elvie appeared in the kitchen doorway holding a glass of lemonade. Eyes wary, she stepped into the room and walked toward the sofa. He took a step in her direction to take the glass from her, and she reacted as if he'd raised a hand to strike her. She set the drink down on the coffee table with a loud clunk then scurried back across the room and through the kitchen door.

"Thank you," he said to her retreating form. He hoped she was a better housekeeper than a conversationalist. He picked up the icy glass and raised it to his lips, but some of the lemonade had splashed over and it dripped onto the lapel of his suit jacket.

Damn it. There was nothing he hated more than

stains on his clothes. He looked around for something to blot it up, so it didn't leave a permanent mark. He moved toward the kitchen, to ask Elvie for a cloth or towel, but given her reaction to him, he might scare her half to death if he so much as stepped through the door. He opted for the second floor bathroom instead, which he vaguely recalled to be somewhere along the upstairs hallway.

He headed up the stairs and when he reached the top step a grayish-brown ball of fur appeared from nowhere and wrapped itself around his ankles, nearly tripping him. He caught the banister to keep from tumbling backward.

Timid housekeepers and homicidal cats. What could he possibly encounter next?

He gave the feline a gentle shove with the toe of his Italian-leather shoe, which he noticed was dotted with mud, and shooed it away. It meowed in protest and darted to one of the closed doors, using its weight to shove it open. Wondering if that could be the bathroom he was searching for, he crossed the hall and peered inside. But it wasn't the bathroom. It was Katy's room. She stood beside the bed, wearing nothing but a bath towel, her hair damp and hanging down her back.

Damn.

She didn't seem to notice him there so he opened his mouth to say something, to warn her of his presence, but it was too late. Before he could utter a sound, she tugged the towel loose and dropped it to the wood floor.

And his jaw nearly went with it. He tried to look away, knew he *should* look away, but the message wasn't making it to his brain.

Her breasts were high and plump, the kind made

just for cupping, with small, pale pink nipples any man would love to get his lips around. Her hips were the perfect fullness for her height. In fact, she was perfectly proportioned. Becca had been rail thin and petite. Almost nymph-like. Katy was built like a *woman*.

Then his eyes slipped lower and he saw that she clearly was a natural blonde.

It had been a long time since he'd seen a woman naked, so the sudden caveman urge he was feeling to put his hands on her was understandable. But this was Katy. His wife's baby sister.

The thing is, she was no baby.

A droplet of water leaked from her hair and rolled down the generous swell of her breast. He watched, mesmerized as it caught on the crest of her nipple, wondering if it felt even half as erotic as it looked.

Katy cleared her throat, and Adam realized that at some point during his gawking she had realized he was there. He lifted his eyes to hers and saw that she was watching him watch her.

Rather than berate him or try to cover herself—or both, since neither would be unexpected at this point— she just stood there wearing a look that asked what the heck he thought he was doing.

Why the hell wasn't she covering herself? Was she an exhibitionist or something? Or maybe the more appropriate question was, why was he still looking?

She planted her hands on her hips, casual as can be, and asked. "Was there something you needed?"

He had to struggle to keep his eyes on hers, when they naturally wanted to stray back down to her breasts. "I was looking for the bathroom, then there was this cat, and it opened your door."

"Right."

"This was an accident." A very unfortunate, wonderful accident.

"If that's true, then I think at this point the gentlemanly thing to do would be to turn around. Don't you?"

"Of course. Sorry." He swiftly turned his back to her. What the hell was wrong with him? He never got flustered, but right now he was acting like a sex-starved adolescent. She must have thought he was either a pervert, or a complete moron. "I don't know what I was thinking. I guess I *wasn't* thinking. I was…surprised. I apologize."

"Try two doors down on the right," she said from behind him, closer now. So close he was sure that if he turned, he could reach out and touch her. He pictured himself doing just that. He imagined the weight of her breast in his palm, the taste of her lips as he pressed his mouth to hers.…

He nearly groaned, the sudden ache in his crotch was so intense. What the hell was the matter with him? "Two doors down?"

"The bathroom. You were looking for it, right?"

"Right," he said, barely getting the word out without his voice cracking. He forced his feet forward.

Since Becca's death he'd barely thought about sex, but now it would seem that his libido had lurched into overdrive.

"And, Adam?" she added.

He paused, but didn't dare turn back around. "Yes?"

"For the record, if you wanted to see me naked, all you had to do was ask."

Four

Oh, good Lord in heaven.

Katy closed her bedroom door and leaned against it, heart throbbing in her chest, legs as weak as a newborn calf's. The sudden and unexpected heat at the apex of her thighs…heaven help her, she might actually self-combust. It was as unexpected as it was mortifying.

The way Adam had looked at her, the fire in his eyes…she couldn't even recall the last time a man had looked at her that way. Hell, she wasn't sure if anyone *ever* had.

She pinched her eyes shut and squeezed her legs together, willing it away, but that only made it worse. An adolescent crush was one thing, but this? It couldn't be more wrong. Or inappropriate. He was her brother-in-law. Her sister's *husband*. The father of the child she would eventually be carrying.

Not to mention that she didn't even *like* him. He was overbearing and arrogant, and generally not a very nice person.

At least she knew that he wasn't lying about seeing her being an accident. Her bedroom door didn't latch correctly and her cat, Sylvester, was always letting himself in. If she had known Adam was going to be wandering around upstairs she would have been more careful. And maybe making that crack about Adam only having to ask wasn't her smartest move, but she refused to let him know how rattled she was.

Not that she was ashamed of the way she looked. As bodies went, hers wasn't half-bad. She just never planned on Adam ever seeing it. Not outside of the de-livery room anyway.

She just hoped he never took her up on her offer.

Of course he wouldn't! He was no more interested in her than she was in him. Not only were they ex in-laws, but they were polar opposites. They didn't share a single thing in common as far as she could tell. Except maybe sexual attraction. But that was fleeting, and superficial. Like her on-again off-again relation-ship with Willy Jenkins used to be. He was a pretty good kisser, and fun under the covers, but he wasn't known for his stimulating conversation. As her best friend Missy would say, he was nice to visit, but she wouldn't want to live there.

Not that Katy would be "visiting" Adam. She would have to be pretty hard up to sleep with a man she had no affection for. She couldn't imagine ever being that desperate.

She heard a vehicle out front and peered through the curtains to see her parents' truck pull up in front of the barn. Well, shoot! Now she had to go out there and act like nothing happened. Which technically it hadn't.

She yanked on clean jeans and a T-shirt and pulled her damp hair back in a ponytail. As she tugged on her cowboy boots she heard the side kitchen door slam, then the muffled sound of voices from the great room below. She had talked Adam into this visit, so it didn't seem fair making him face her parents alone. And at the same time, she was dreading this. She didn't like to play the role of the mediator. That had always been her mother's thing.

In the week since she had talked Adam into letting her be the surrogate, Katy had been working on convincing her parents that she was doing the right thing, and that they were going to have to trust Adam. She just hoped that seeing him face-to-face didn't bring back a flood of the old resentment.

At first, when they learned that Becca was engaged, besides being stunned that she'd never mentioned a steady man in her life, her parents had been truly excited about having a son-in-law. But from the minute they met Adam it was obvious he came from a different world. And as hard as they tried to be accepting, to welcome him to the family, it seemed he always held something back. Her parents interpreted it as Adam thinking he was better than them, even though he had always been gracious enough not to condescend, or treat them with anything but respect.

At first Katy had given him the benefit of the doubt. She wanted to believe that he was as amazing as her sister described. But when he and Becca visited less and less, and Katy realized just how hard Becca had to work to keep him happy, she'd had to face the truth. Adam was an arrogant, controlling and critical husband.

But Katy wasn't doing this for him. She was doing it for Becca, and her parents, and most of all the baby. Which made what just happened between them seem wholly insignificant. It was a fluke, that's all. One that would never happen again.

She headed down the stairs to the great room. Her parents sat stiffly on the sofa and Adam looked just as uncomfortable on the love seat opposite them. When she entered the room everyone turned, looking relieved to see her.

"Sorry to keep you waiting," she told Adam, and his expression gave away no hint of their earlier...confrontation. Although he might have snuck a quick look at her breasts.

"Your parents and I have had a chance to get reacquainted," he said, and from the vibe in the room, Katy could guess it hadn't exactly gone well.

So as not to be antagonistic and give anyone the impression she was taking sides, she sat by neither her parents nor Adam, but instead on the hearth between them.

The contrast was staggering. Adam looked cool and confident in his suit, like he was ready to negotiate a million-dollar deal, while her parents looked like... well, like they always had. Her father had gotten a little paunchy over the past few years, and his salt-and-pepper hair was thinning at his temples, but he still looked pretty good for a man of sixty-two. And as far as Katy was concerned, her mother, fifty-nine on her next birthday, was as beautiful as she'd been at sixteen. She was still tall, slender and graceful with the face of an angel. She wore her gray-streaked, pale blond hair in loose waves that hung to just above her waist, or at times pulled back in a braid.

She was a perpetually happy person, always preferring to see the glass not only as half full, but the ideal temperature, as well. But now creases of concern bracketed her eyes.

"I was just telling Adam how surprised we were when we heard of his plans," her father said, and his tone clearly said he didn't like it much.

Katy's mom rested a hand on his knee then told Adam, "But we're hoping you can convince us that you've thought this through, and taken our family into consideration."

Katy bit her lip, praying that Adam's first reaction wasn't to get defensive. What had he told Katy that day in the coffee shop? That he wasn't seeking anyone's approval or permission? But he had to expect this, didn't he? He had to know her parents would be wary. That was the whole point of his visit. To set their minds at ease.

Or maybe he didn't see it that way. Maybe he truly didn't give a damn what they thought.

"As I told Katy, I have no intention of keeping the child from you," he assured them, in a tone that showed no hint of impatience, and Katy went limp with relief. "You'll be his or her only grandparents. In fact, I think that spending time on the ranch will be an enriching experience."

"I'm also not sure I like the idea of Katy being your surrogate," her father added, and suddenly everyone looked at her.

"I have my concerns as well, Mr. Huntley. But she wouldn't take no for an answer."

"I think we all know how stubborn she can be," her father said, talking about her as though she wasn't sitting right there. "I'd like to see her concentrate on finding a husband, and having kids of her own."

She was so sick of that tired old argument. Just because practically every other woman in her family married young and immediately started squeezing out babies, that didn't mean it was right for her.

"I'm not ready for a husband or kids," she told her father. Or more accurately, they weren't ready for her. Every time she thought she'd found Mr. Right, he turned out to be Mr. Right Now, then inevitably became Mr. Last Week. She was beginning to suspect that these men who kept breaking her heart knew something she didn't. Like maybe she just wasn't marriage material.

"You might feel differently when you meet the right man," he countered. "And besides, I don't think you realize how hard this will be. And what if, God forbid, something happens, then you can't have kids of your own? You could regret it the rest of your life."

"What if I walk out the door and get hit by lightning?" she snapped. "Do you expect me to stop going outside?"

He cast her a stern look, and she bit her tongue.

"Gabe," her mother said gently. "You know that my pregnancies were completely uneventful. And Katy has always been just like me. She'll do fine. You have to admit it will be nice to have a grandbaby." Moisture welled in the corners of her eyes. "To have a part of Rebecca with us."

"I assure you that Katy will have the best prenatal care available," Adam told them. "We won't let anything happen to her."

The way he hadn't let anything happen to Becca?

The question hung between them unspoken. It was hard not to blame Adam for Becca's death. Though he had done everything within his power to save her. She had seen the best doctors, received the most effective, groundbreaking treatment money could buy. Unfortunately it hadn't been enough.

If she hadn't insisted they harvest the damned eggs...

"What about multiples?" her father asked. "She's not going to be like that octo-mom and have eight babies."

"Absolutely not. The doctor has already made it clear that for a woman Katy's age, with no prior fertility issues, he won't implant more that two embryos at a time. And if Katy is uncomfortable with the idea of carrying twins, we'll only implant one. It's her call."

"But the odds are better if they implant two?" Katy asked.

"Yes."

"So we'll do two."

"You're sure?" Adam asked. "Maybe you should take some more time to think about it."

"I don't need time. I'm sure."

"Could you imagine that?" her mother said. "Two grandbabies!"

"I still don't like it," her father said, then he looked at his wife and his expression softened. "But it wouldn't be the first time the women in this family have overruled me."

"So it's settled," Katy said, before he could change his mind, with a finality that she hoped stuck this time.

"When will this happen?" Katy's mom asked.

"We have an appointment with a fertility specialist next Wednesday," Adam told her. "First he has to do a full exam and determine if she's healthy enough to become pregnant. Then he'll determine the optimal time for the implantation."

"So if everything looks good, it could be soon," Katy said, feeling excited. "I could be pregnant as soon as next month."

"And if it doesn't work?" her father asked.

"We try again," Adam said. "If we do two embryos at a time, we can do three implantations."

"It sounds so simple," her mother said, but Katy knew things like this were never as simple as they sounded. That didn't mean they weren't worth doing.

"And if none of them take?" Katy asked.

"I'll consider adoption."

"We appreciate you coming all the way out here to talk to us," her mother said. "I know it's eased my mind."

Adam looked at his watch. "But I should be going. I need to get back to El Paso."

"But you just got here," Katy said, surprised that after such a long drive he would want to get back on the road so soon. Was he really so uncomfortable there that he couldn't stick around for a couple of hours? What would he do when the baby was born? Would they always be coming to him?

"The least we can do is feed you supper," her mother said.

"I appreciate the offer, but I have an important meeting Monday that I need to prepare for. Maybe some other time."

They all knew those were just polite words. There wouldn't be another time. He wouldn't be coming back if he could possibly avoid it.

Katy rose to her feet. "I'll walk you out."

He said a somewhat stiff goodbye to her parents, then followed Katy out the front door. The moist heat was almost suffocating as they stepped out onto the porch. Adam's driver had taken refuge in the limo and was reading a newspaper, but when he saw them emerge he swiftly opened his door and got out. Katy turned to Adam, thinking that he had to be roasting in his suit and anxious to get back into the cool car.

"Thanks again for coming all the way out here. And thanks for being so patient with my father." It had to be doubly weird for him, trying to convince her parents she would be a good surrogate, when he himself still had doubts.

"It wasn't quite as bad as I thought it would be. Knowing your father holds me responsible for Becca's death, I realize it can't be easy for him to entrust me with the care of his only living child."

"Why would you think that?" she asked, although for the life of her she didn't know why she gave a damn what he believed.

He gave her a "spare me" look. "Not that I blame him. I should have been able to save her."

"Sounds like maybe it's *you* who holds you responsible."

If her words bothered him, he didn't let on. "I've made my peace with Becca's death."

"Your actions would suggest otherwise, Adam."

He looked at her for a second, like he might say something else, something snarky, then he seemed to change his mind. He turned and walked down the steps. Reece opened the rear car door, but before he got in, Adam turned back to her.

"By the way, I wanted to apologize again, for what happened upstairs."

She folded her arms under her breasts. "You mean when you stared at me while I was naked?"

Reece's eyes widened for an instant, before he caught himself and wiped the surprised look off his face. And if she'd embarrassed Adam—which was the whole point—he didn't let it show. Was he a robot or something? Devoid of human feelings?

"Yes, that," he said.

She shrugged. "I've been stared at before."

"Don't forget we have an appointment with Dr. Meyer on Wednesday at 3:00 p.m."

She snorted. "Like I could forget that."

"I'll see you Wednesday," he said and she could swear he almost smiled. She found herself wishing he would, so he would seem more…human. Maybe he forgot how.

He may have been an overbearing, arrogant, narcissistic jerk, but that didn't mean he deserved to be unhappy. Although he hadn't looked unhappy earlier, when he was standing in her bedroom doorway. He looked like he wanted to throw her down on the bed and have his way with her, which, let's face it, was never going to happen.

He got in the car, and Reece closed the door. Katy waved as they pulled down the driveway. The windows were tinted so she couldn't tell if Adam was watching, but she had the feeling he was. When they turned onto the road and disappeared out of sight, she crossed the porch to the side door around the corner…and almost plowed into her mom, who was pulling on her mucking boots.

Katy squeaked in surprise and skidded to a stop, hoping she hadn't heard that comment about Adam seeing her naked.

"Going out to the barn?" she asked brightly. A little *too* brightly if her mother's wry expression was any indication.

"Be careful, Katy," she said and it was obvious she *had* heard. "When you fall, it's hard and fast."

Fall? *For Adam?* Ugh. Not in a million years. She had clearly taken what was said *completely* out of context. "It's not what you think. He was looking for the bathroom and saw me getting dressed. It was an accident. What I said just now, that was only to embarrass him."

She didn't look convinced. "I know you always had a bit of a crush on him."

"For pity's sake! When I was a *kid*. Not only do I not have a crush, but I don't even *like* him."

"He's not like us, Katy."

Didn't she know it. "You're preaching to the choir, Mom."

"I just want you to consider this carefully. When you're pregnant, and your hormones are all out of whack, those emotional lines can get…fuzzy."

"I'm not going to fall for Adam. It's not even a remote possibility."

She didn't look like she believed Katy, but she let it drop.

The idea of her and Adam in a relationship was beyond ridiculous. Her mother had to know that.

Or was she seeing something that Katy wasn't?

Five

Adam met Katy at the doctor's office Wednesday as planned. She got there first, and as he walked into the lobby he was a bit taken aback when he saw her. In fact, until she smiled and waved, he didn't even realize it *was* her. Dressed in a white-cotton peasant blouse and a caramel-colored ankle-length skirt, she looked like…a woman. She'd even traded in her usual ponytail for soft, loose ringlets that framed her face and draped across her shoulders. Even he couldn't deny that the effect was breathtaking.

He had always considered her attractive, but now she looked…well, frankly, she looked *hot*.

It was only the third time in his life that he'd seen her wear anything but jeans and boots. The first was his wedding, and the second Becca's funeral, but neither time had he been paying attention to how she looked.

Was it possible that she'd always looked this blatantly sexy and he'd just never noticed?

And today, he wasn't the only one. Heads were turning as she walked past, eyes following her with obvious appreciation. But he knew something they didn't. He knew that as good as she looked in her clothes, she looked even better out of them.

A fact he'd been trying to forget all week.

Katy on the other hand seemed oblivious to the looks she was getting, as though she didn't have even the slightest idea how pretty she was. Or more likely, didn't care either way. He'd never met a woman so casual about her self-image. As evidenced, he realized with a tug of humor, by the fact that under the skirt she was wearing cowboy boots.

He could take the woman out of the country, but not the country out of the woman.

"You're early," he said as she approached him.

"I know, I didn't want to risk being late," she told him, then added, as if she thought he wouldn't notice on his own, "I wore my girl clothes."

"So you did."

"I'm *really* nervous."

"I'm sure everything will be fine." He looked at his watch and said, "We should probably get upstairs."

Though he had resigned himself to the idea of her being the surrogate and had for the most part convinced himself it was for the best, deep down he half hoped the doctor would find some reason to deem her an inappropriate candidate for the procedure. But after a thorough examination, Katy was given a clean bill of health. And like her own physician, Dr. Meyer even went so far as to comment that her body was ideal for childbearing. So there was definitely no turning back now.

It was a done deal.

After a consultation with the doctor in his office, where he explained the procedure in great detail, they made an appointment for the following week to have two embryos implanted.

"Are you nervous?" Katy asked him as they walked back down to the lobby together.

He shrugged.

"Oh, come on, you have to be at least a little nervous."

"I guess." After waiting so long for this, the process did seem to be moving very quickly. "How about you? Are you having second thoughts?"

"Not at all. I'm just really excited. I can hardly believe it's next week. I thought it would take months."

"It won't be a problem, you leaving the ranch for a couple of days?"

"They can get by without me. But I was thinking, because I'll be on bed rest for twenty-four hours after the transfer, maybe you could recommend a hotel."

Did she honestly think he would let her stay alone in a hotel? Not only would that be rude and insensitive of him, he wanted her close by, so he could keep an eye on her and make sure she followed the doctor's orders to the letter. They had three shots at this. He didn't want anything going wrong.

"Nonsense," he told her. "You'll stay with me."

"Are you sure? I don't want to impose."

They pushed out the door into the blazing afternoon heat where his car sat at the curb already waiting for him. "Of course I'm sure."

"In that case, thanks. It's been years since I've been to your house."

Three years to be exact. The day of Becca's funeral.

They stopped on the sidewalk near the limo. He really should get back to work, but she'd driven all this way and the least he could do was feed her.

"Why don't I buy you lunch?"

"I really need to get going," she said apologetically. "I'll probably just swing into the drive-through on my way home."

She would decline his invitation for something as unpalatable as fast food? Not to mention unhealthy. "Are you sure? There's a café just around the corner."

"I promised my folks I would make a few stops for them on the way home, and I don't want to get back too late. Can I take a rain check?"

"Of course," he said, though her casual refusal puzzled him. When it came to women, he was usually the one declining offers. And lately there had been plenty of them, no thanks to one of his coworkers who thought Adam had done enough grieving and needed to get back into circulation.

Not that Adam considered Katy a woman. In the relationship sense, that is. In his eyes she was a business associate. One who was looking at him curiously.

"What?"

"If it means that much to you, we can go," she said.

"Go?"

"To lunch. You looked…I don't know…disappointed."

Had he? "No, of course not."

"You're sure? Because I can make the time."

"Of course I'm sure."

She didn't look as though she believed him. "I know this has to be tough for you. I mean, as much as you want a child, they're Becca's eggs. It must stir up a lot of feelings." She took a step toward him, reached out and put a hand on his arm. Why did she have to do that? Be so…physical? "If you need someone to talk to—"

"I don't," he assured her, his gaze straying to her cleavage. Probably because there was so much of it, and she was standing so close that it was right there, inches from his face. Okay, more than inches, but still.

"Hello!" she said, snapping her fingers in front of his eyes, until he lifted them to hers. "I'm trying to be nice, and all you can do is stare at my boobs? And people wonder why I dress the way I do."

She was right. That was totally inappropriate. He was acting like he'd never seen breasts before. When not only had he seen breasts, he'd seen hers.

"I apologize," he said, keeping his eyes on her face. "And no, I don't need to talk."

"I just figured you asked me to lunch for a reason."

"I did. I thought you might be hungry."

She sighed heavily. "Okay. But I'm here if you change your mind. Just call me."

"I won't."

"You know, it wouldn't kill you to lighten up a little. You're so serious all the time. That can't be healthy."

"You've never seen me at work. I'm a party animal."

She rolled her eyes. "Sure you are."

"So I'll see you next week?" he asked, anxious to end this nightmare of a conversation. She seemed to have an annoying way of getting under his skin.

"See you next week."

She turned and sashayed to her truck, hips swaying,

curls bouncing. Anyone looking at her would know, just from the way she walked, that she had attitude.

And suddenly he was picturing her naked again. Wondering what she would have done if he'd stepped into her room, if he had reached for her...

"Sir?" Reece said, and Adam realized he was standing there holding the door open, and he'd heard their entire exchange. "She's something, huh?"

She was *something* all right. He just hadn't quite figured out what.

"She's really quite beautiful, isn't she?"

"I guess."

Reece didn't say a word, but his expression said he knew his boss was full of it. That any red-blooded heterosexual male would have to be blind not to think she was totally hot. But the last thing Adam needed was for his driver to think he had a thing for his surrogate. Not that he didn't trust Reece implicitly, but there were certain lines a man did not cross, even hypothetically.

This was definitely one of them.

Katy assumed the week would crawl by, but before she knew it, she was on her way back to El Paso. Adam had called a few days earlier, suggesting she come to stay the night before, so she wouldn't have to make the two-hour drive before the appointment, but she told him no. As nervous and excited as she knew she would be, sleeping would be tough enough without being in an unfamiliar room, in a strange bed. And for some reason, the thought of sleeping in the same house with Adam made her nervous. Not that she thought he would try something. It just felt...weird. But tonight she didn't have a choice. She physically couldn't drive home.

Her mother had offered to drive her to El Paso and stay for the procedure, then drive her directly back. She wasn't too keen on Katy staying at Adam's place, either. But the doctor said bed rest, and she couldn't exactly sack out in the truck bed for the two-hour drive.

Adam still lived in the sprawling, six-bedroom, seven-bath, eight-thousand-square-foot monstrosity Becca had insisted they needed. They could have had a whole brood of children and still had space to spare. And though she loved her sister dearly, and was sure that she had been a very accomplished interior designer, her personal tastes were excessive to say the least, and bordering on gaudy. She didn't seem to understand the concept of less is more.

Katy pulled up the circle drive and parked by the front door, next to the concrete, cherub-adorned fountain, realizing how utterly out of place her truck looked there.

She grabbed her duffel from the front seat, climbed out and walked to the front entrance, but before she could ring the bell the door swung open. Standing there was Adam's housekeeper, whom Katy vaguely remembered from the day of Becca's funeral, an older woman with a gently lined and kind face.

Though Adam seemed the type to insist his staff wear a formal uniform, she was dressed in jeans and a Texas A & M sweatshirt.

She smiled warmly. "Ms. Huntley, so nice to see you again! I'm Celia."

Katy liked her immediately.

"Hi, Celia."

"Come in, come in!" She ushered Katy inside, taking the bag before she could protest. The air was filled with the scent of something warm and sweet. "Can you believe how hot it is and it's barely 10:00 a.m.? Why don't I show you to your room, then I'll get you something cold to drink. Are you hungry? I could fix you breakfast."

"I'm fine, thanks." She'd been too nervous to force down more than a slice of toast and a glass of juice before she left home. "Is Adam here?"

"He went into the office for a few hours. He's sending a car for you at ten-thirty."

She'd been under the impression they would ride to the appointment together, but she should have known he would squeeze in a few hours at the office first. Hadn't that always been Becca's biggest complaint? That Adam worked too much. Which begged the question, when would he have time to take care of a baby? But it was a little late to worry about that now.

Celia led Katy across the foyer and either Katy had a skewed recollection of the interior, or Adam had made changes to the decor because it wasn't nearly as distasteful as she remembered. Considering she had only been here twice before, it was difficult to be sure. In any case, it was very warm and inviting now.

They walked up to the second floor and Celia showed her to one of the spare bedrooms. If Katy was remembering right, the master was at the end of the hall not twenty feet away. She didn't like that Adam would be in such close proximity, but what could she do, ask to sack out on the living-room couch? At least Celia would be there to act as a buffer.

Besides, she was being silly. She was only staying there because it was convenient. And because, she suspected, Adam didn't completely trust her to follow the doctor's instructions, if left to her own devices. She had to admit that being flat on her back for twenty-four hours sounded like the worst kind of torture. She was not an idle person. She didn't have the patience to sit around doing nothing. But this time she didn't have a choice.

"This is nice," Katy said, looking around as Celia set her bag down on the floral duvet. The room was tastefully decorated in creamy pastels. Feminine and inviting without being too frilly.

"There are fresh towels in the bathroom. And if you need anything, anything at all while you're here, don't hesitate to ask. I think it's a very generous thing you're doing for Adam. Since he decided to do this, it's the happiest I've seen him since he lost Becca. He would deny it if you asked, but the last few years have been very hard on him. I was starting to believe he would never get over her."

If he loved her that much, why did Becca have to work so hard to keep him happy? she wanted to ask. Why was she always terrified that he would grow bored and leave her for someone else? Maybe Celia wasn't seeing the whole picture, or hadn't known Adam long enough to realize what he was really like.

Katy sat on the edge of the bed. "How long have you worked for Adam?"

"Ever since his father passed. But I've known him most of his life. I practically raised him. When he wasn't off at boarding school, that is."

"Oh, I didn't realize you'd been with the family that long."

"Going on thirty-two years now. Since Mrs. Blair,

Adam's mother, took ill. I lost my own boy in the Gulf War, so Adam has been like a son to me."

"I'm so sorry," Katy said. Losing a child was a sorrow her parents knew all too well.

"I still consider myself blessed. I have two beautiful daughters and five grandchildren between them."

"What do you think of Adam having a child? If you don't mind my asking."

Celia sat down beside her. "I think Adam will be a wonderful father. He lets my grandchildren come over and use the pool, and he's so good with them. He's wanted this for a very long time."

Celia was probably biased, but Katy wanted desperately to believe her. Although, wanting a child, and being good with someone else's grandchildren, didn't necessarily make someone a good parent.

"When you get to know him better, you'll see," Celia assured her.

"But how am I supposed to get to know him when he's so closed off. So uptight."

"That's just a smoke screen. Though he doesn't let it show, he feels very deeply. He's been hurt, Katy. It takes him time to trust. But he's a good man." She laid a hand on Katy's knee. "I know it's been hard for you and your parents. And probably nothing I can say will totally reassure you. But I promise you, Adam would never do anything to deliberately hurt anyone. Especially family."

"I want to believe that." But she didn't. Not for a second. Because that would mean everything her sister had told her was a lie. And believing that wasn't an option.

Six

On a normal day, Adam was an active participant at the informal weekly management team briefing they held in his office, but today he couldn't stop looking at the clock.

Nathaniel Everett, their Chief Brand Officer was explaining the new campaign his team had been developing to promote their latest, ecologically friendly practices. Groundbreaking upgrades that would not only keep them in line with future federal guidelines, but no doubt result in record profits.

On a normal day that would have filled Adam with a thrilling sense of accomplishment, but today his heart just wasn't in it. In fact, for a while now, six months at least, work didn't hold the same appeal as it had in the past. And that fact hadn't escaped his team.

At first he'd written it off as a temporary slump,

but when he didn't go back to feeling like his old self, he began to suspect it was something deeper. Clearly something was missing. There was a void in his life, in his very soul that work would no longer fill. It was when he knew it was time to have a child.

"So, what do you think?" he heard Nathan ask, and realized he had completely zoned out.

"Good," he said, hoping he could fake his way through.

Nathan smiled wryly. "You haven't heard a damn thing I've said, have you?"

He could lie, but what was the point? "Sorry. I'm off my game today."

"Rough night?" Nathan's brother, Jordan, their Chief Operations Officer, asked, his tone suggestive. He'd been asserting for months that Adam's major problem was he needed to get laid. And while Adam wouldn't deny he'd been...*tense* lately, random sex with a woman he barely knew was Jordan's thing, not his. In fact, common knowledge of Jordan's sexual prowess was what had endeared him to the roughnecks on the rig. Despite his Ivy League education, they related to him somehow. Looked up to him even. He managed to fit in, yet still hold his own in the boardroom without batting an eye. He was like a chameleon, changing color to suit his environment.

Adam envied him that sometimes.

"Only because I didn't sleep well," he told Jordan. "Maybe we can reschedule for tomorrow."

Jordan shrugged. "Fine by me."

"I have a meeting with Cassandra anyway," Nathan told him, rising from his chair. "Should we say 10:00 a.m.?"

Everyone agreed, then gathered their things and left. Emilio, who had been quiet through most of the meeting, hung back.

"Everything all right?" he asked. He obviously didn't buy that a simple lack of sleep could leave Adam so distracted.

"Katy and I have an appointment today. In fact, I have to leave soon or I'm going to be late."

"The fertility doctor?" he asked.

Adam nodded. "She's having the embryos transferred today."

"I didn't realize it would be so soon. Congratulations."

"That doesn't mean it will work, but Katy is young and healthy and the doctor seems hopeful."

"I'll keep my fingers crossed for you. I guess I don't have to ask if you're nervous."

It took a lot to set him on edge, but today the pressure was getting to him. "It shows, huh?"

"Hey, who wouldn't be? This is a big step you're taking."

Adam looked at his watch. "And I have to meet Katy."

Emilio turned to leave, but stopped in the doorway. "I meant to ask the other day. This is probably none of my business...."

"What?"

"Well, since Becca had cancer, and that can be genetic...I just wondered if that would put your child at risk. It runs in my family, too. On my father's side."

"I've spoken to a geneticist and the fact that cervical cancer doesn't run in either of our families reduces the risk of predisposing the baby."

Emilio grinned. "So you've done your research. That's what I figured. Well, good luck."

When he was gone Adam grabbed what he needed and headed down to the parking garage. Since Reece had gone to get Katy, he took the company limo to the doctor's office. When he got inside, she was already there in the lobby waiting for him. And this time he had no trouble spotting her. She stood by the elevator bank, her face flush with excitement, dressed in her "girl" clothes again. This time it was a yellow sundress with a fitted bodice and A-line skirt, and instead of boots she'd worn strappy, flat-soled sandals.

Though he would never admit it to anyone, she looked sexy as hell. And if she were anyone but his sister-in-law, or his surrogate, he just might put an end to his three-year dating freeze and ask her out to dinner.

But no matter how attractive he found her, she was who she was, which kept her strictly off-limits. Not that she would agree to go out with him if he did ask. Knowing her, she would refuse on principle alone, just to irritate him.

"Early again, I see," he said as he approached her.

"You can thank Reece for that. He was worried about traffic."

He stabbed the button for the second floor. "Did you get settled in at the house?"

"I did, and Celia seems wonderful."

"She is."

"She really adores you, you know. You're lucky to have someone like that in your life."

She didn't have to tell him that. After his mother died, and his father took a permanent emotional vacation, Celia was the only "parent" he'd had. She wasn't just his housekeeper. She was family. He couldn't imagine what his life would be like now if it hadn't been for her.

"How can you look so calm?" she asked as the doors slid open and they stepped in. "I don't think I've ever been so nervous in my life."

"I don't do nervous." Katy must have put on perfume, too, because she smelled really nice. Flowery and feminine, but not overpoweringly so. In fact, the scent was so faint, yet so intoxicating, he had the urge to lean in closer and breathe her in. Bury his nose in the silky curls tumbling like silk ribbons across her shoulders.

Silk ribbons? Jesus, he needed to get his head examined.

"How could you not be nervous?" she said, clearly unwilling to let the subject drop.

"Okay, I'm a little nervous. Happy?"

"Well, if you are, you sure don't look it. I guess you're just really good at hiding your feelings."

"That comes as part of the outdoor plumbing package." The doors slid open and they stepped out, but when he turned to Katy she had a funny look on her face. "What?"

"Did you just make a joke?"

"I guess so. Is that a problem?"

"The ability to joke suggests you have a sense of humor. Adam, I had no idea."

He tried to looked indignant, but the corners of his mouth twitched upward.

She gasped. "Oh, my gosh! You just smiled! Do you know that since I met you at Western Oil that day I haven't seen you smile a single time? I didn't even realize you still knew how."

In spite of himself, he smiled wider. "All right, you've made your point."

She gave him a playful poke. "Better be careful, or God forbid, people might start to think you have feelings."

What she didn't realize was that he felt very deeply. Too much for his own good, in fact. And look where it had gotten him.

Which is why he expended so much effort to feel as little as possible now. Or at the very least, not let it show.

They walked down the hall to the fertility suite and were immediately shown into the doctor's private office for a quick consultation, in case they had any last-minute questions—a courtesy Adam was sure he reserved for only his special patients. In other words, the ones with the thickest wallets. Dr. Meyer had a fund for lower-income couples with medical conditions preventing them from conceiving, and understanding their pain, not to mention the perks it would include, Adam had donated generously.

After a brief chat, they were taken to the room where Katy would change into her gown.

"I guess this is it," Adam said. "I'll see you afterward."

"Afterward?" she asked, looking confused. "You're not going to come in for the procedure. I thought you would want to be there."

"I do. I just…I thought it would make you uncomfortable."

"Call me old-fashioned, but I believe a father should at least be in the room when his child is conceived. Even if he's not actually…you know…doing the work."

Leave it to Katy to be absolutely blunt. "If you're comfortable with it, then sure, count me in."

"The doctor knows the situation. I'm sure he can be discreet. And if not…" she shrugged. "It's not like you haven't seen me naked. And you'll be seeing it all again when the baby is born. Right?"

He had hoped she would allow him to be in the delivery room, but he figured he would wait until later in the pregnancy to ask. Now he didn't have to worry.

He didn't doubt that if he'd hired a surrogate, a stranger, she might not be as open to him being so involved in the entire process. And he appreciated it. More than Katy would ever know.

"Well, I better go change," she said. "Don't want to keep the embryos waiting."

"Thank you, Katy."

She smiled, then she did something totally unexpected. She rose up on her toes and pressed a kiss to his cheek.

Her lips were soft and warm and just the slightest bit damp. And though it didn't last long, just a second or two, something happened. Something passed between them, although he couldn't say for sure what it was. If it was physical or emotional. But whatever it was, he felt it straight through to his bones. And clearly, so did she.

She stepped back, looking puzzled, lifting a hand up to touch her lips. And something must have been wrong with him because his first instinct was to take her in his arms and draw her against him, bury his face against her hair and just…hold her. He wondered what she would do if he tried.

But he didn't, and after a few seconds the moment, whatever it was, seemed to pass.

"I guess I better go," she said, glancing back to the nurse who was waiting for her, looking apprehensive, as if the gravity of what she was about to do had suddenly taken hold. "You'll be there?"

Maybe she just didn't want to feel as though she was in this alone. "I'll be there," he assured her, and realized that his heart was beating faster. Maybe he was more nervous than he'd thought. Or could it have been something else?

She started to turn, and before he realized what he was doing, he reached out and grabbed her arm. Startled, she turned back to him, looking at his hand as though she was surprised he would touch her. And honestly, he was a bit surprised himself.

"You're sure you want to do this," he said. "It's not too late to back out."

The apprehension seemed to dissolve before his eyes and she smiled. A really sweet, pretty smile that he was sure he would remember for the rest of his life.

"I'm sure," she said, placing her hand over his. "I want to do this."

He let his hand slip out from under hers and fall to his side.

"You can sit in the procedure waiting room," the nurse said, pointing it out to him. "They'll call you in when she's ready."

The waiting room was blessedly empty, but after twenty minutes passed he began to worry they had forgotten about him. He was about to get up and ask someone what was taking so long when another nurse appeared in the doorway. She led him to an exam room where Katy was already in position with her feet in the stirrups, ready to go. And other than a bit of bare leg, she was very discreetly covered.

She looked relieved to see him.

"Is everyone ready?" the doctor asked, looking from Katy to Adam.

Adam nodded. Katy took a deep breath, exhaled and said, "Let's do it."

She reached for his hand and he took it, holding firmly as the doctor did the transfer. The procedure itself seemed pretty simple, and if Katy's occasional winces were any indication, involved only minor discomfort. Within ten minutes it was over.

"That's it," Dr. Meyer said, peeling off his gloves. "Now comes the hard part. The waiting."

Per his orders Katy had to lie there for two hours before she would be allowed home, so after the staff cleared the room Adam pulled a chair up beside her and sat down.

"I think it worked," she said, looking contentedly serene. "I can almost feel the cells beginning to divide."

"Is that even possible?" he asked.

She shrugged. "Probably not, but I have a good feeling about this."

He didn't want to get his hopes up, but he had a good feeling about it, too. Something about the day, the entire experience felt…special. Like it was meant to be. Which was strange, since he'd never been superstitious.

She looked over at him and smiled. "If someone had told me a month ago that I would be here today, having fertilized embryos injected into me, I would have told them they were insane."

Boy, could he relate. He always knew that someday he would use the embryos, but not with Katy as the surrogate. "If it's unsuccessful, are you still willing to try again?"

"Of course! I'm in this for the long haul." She yawned deeply, her eyes overflowing with tears. "Well, goodness, all of the sudden I feel exhausted."

She must have slept as fitfully as he had last night. Plus she'd had that long drive this morning. "Why don't you close your eyes and rest."

"Maybe just for a minute," she said, her eyes slipping closed. Within minutes her breathing became slow and deep and her lips parted slightly. He sat there looking at her and had the strangest urge to touch her face. To run his finger across her full bottom lip…

He shook away the thought. He hoped this was a one-shot deal. He hoped the test came up positive, not only because he wanted a child, but because he wanted to get the emotionally taxing part of the process out of the way. This entire experience was doing strange things to his head.

He sat there for a while, checking messages and reading email on his phone. Then he played a few games of Tetris.

After an hour, when she was still out cold, he decided to make a few calls. Careful not to disturb her, he stepped out into the hall and called Celia on his cell, asking her to have lunch ready when they got back, then he checked in with his secretary and returned a few other calls that couldn't wait until he got back to the office. When he finally returned to the room, Katy was awake.

"Oh, there you are," she said, looking anxious. "I thought maybe you'd left."

Did she really think he would just up and leave her

there alone? "Of course not. I just had a few calls to make and I didn't want to disturb you." He reclaimed his seat. "Did you have a good nap?"

"Yeah. I must have gone out cold. All the stress probably. At least now, if we have to do it again, I'll know what to expect." She touched his arm. "I wish it could have been Becca here with you."

Emotion caught in his throat. "Me, too."

There was a knock at the door, then the nurse stuck her head in. "You can get dressed and go now."

"Already? I guess I slept longer than I thought."

"And don't forget, strict bed rest for the next twenty-four hours," she said sternly.

"Like I could forget that," she muttered, sitting up.

Adam waited in the hall while Katy put her clothes on, then they went to the reception desk to make an appointment for her blood test in ten days.

"Can you believe that ten days from now we'll know if I'm pregnant?" she said excitedly as they walked down to the limo. His only concern right now was getting her home and back into bed. Although he was sure, the next ten days might just be the longest of his life.

Seven

It was official. Katy was starting to dislike Adam a lot less.

She had just assumed that when they got back to his place he would get her settled, pat her on the head and say good job, then motor off to the office for a shareholders meeting or something equally important sounding. In reality, he had barely left her side all day. She watched television and Adam sat in a chair beside the bed with his laptop.

He must have asked her a hundred times if there was anything she needed, anything he could do for her. And here she had honestly believed the only person he cared about was himself. He'd even smiled a few times.

And that kiss back in the doctor's office? What was up with that? It had been an impulse on her part. After all, what they were doing was pretty personal. It just seemed like the right thing to do. She'd never expected to *feel* it. Although to be honest she still wasn't sure what it was exactly that she'd felt. It was an odd sort of...awareness. Not sexual exactly, but not completely innocent, either. It was as if some deeper part of each of them had risen to the surface and collided, causing a sort of cosmic friction or interference or something. And she could tell, by the look on Adam's face, that he'd felt it, too.

It had been a weird, but not unpleasant experience. In fact, it felt sort of nice. But that didn't mean she wanted it to happen again. Unfortunately the more she tried to forget it, forget how smooth his cheek felt, the tangy scent of his aftershave, the more it consumed her.

She couldn't help sneaking looks his way, wondering if he was thinking about it, too. But she wasn't being as sneaky as she thought because he finally looked over at her and asked, "Is there a reason you keep looking at me?"

"Am I?" she asked, as if she'd had no clue. "I didn't realize. I guess I must be doing it unconsciously."

"Okay," he said, although he didn't look as though he believed her. But he didn't push the issue, either. And she was glad. She made a conscious effort not to look at him again.

Around six when Celia brought them supper on a tray, it was a relief to be able to sit up for a while. Celia set her tray over her lap, then gestured Adam to the opposite side of the bed.

"You, sit," she ordered.

"I am sitting."

"Now, *niño pequeño*," she said sternly. "Little Boy."

A holdover nickname from when he was small, Katy was guessing.

"Why can't I eat here?" He sounded like a little boy arguing with his mother.

"Because I said so, that's why. Now move, before your supper gets cold."

"You're seriously not going to let me eat here? In a chair, I might add, that I *own?*"

"And you honestly think I'm going to let you eat spaghetti on *Persian silk?* Becca would roll over in her grave."

He seemed to get that it was a losing battle, because he shoved himself up from the chair and mumbled, "The way you boss me around, a person would think this was your house."

He rounded the bed, kicked off his shoes and climbed on, sitting cross-legged next to Katy. "Happy now?"

"Good boy," Celia said, setting his tray in front of him, stopping just shy of patting his head. He looked more than a little annoyed, which Katy was guessing was the whole point. He may have *owned* the house, but Celia was clearly in charge.

It was one of the sweetest, most heartwarming things she had ever seen. The big powerful billionaire was really just a pussycat.

"Can I get you anything else?" Celia asked.

"A double scotch if it wouldn't be too much trouble," Adam said.

She smiled and said, "Of course. Katy?"

"Under the circumstances, I should probably lay off the booze. But thanks for asking."

"I didn't mean…" She sighed and shook her head,

as if they were both hopeless. "Heaven help us, you're just as bad as he is."

She walked out mumbling to herself.

"Niño pequeño?" Katy asked, unable to stifle a smile.

"I swear sometimes she thinks I'm still ten years old," he grumbled, but there was affection in his eyes. He loved Celia, even if he didn't want to admit it.

"I think everyone needs someone to boss them around every once in a while," she said. "It keeps you grounded."

"Well, then, I should be pretty well-grounded, because she bosses me around on a daily basis."

And she could tell that though he wanted Katy to believe otherwise, he wouldn't have it any other way.

Celia returned several minutes later with his drink, then left them to eat. Katy just assumed that when they were finished, Adam would sit in the chair again. Instead he fluffed the pillows and leaned back against them. It was probably the most laid-back she had ever seen him. In fact, she'd never imagined he could be so relaxed.

She couldn't help but wonder if it had anything to do with the scotch. Maybe the alcohol had lowered his inhibitions. She recalled Becca telling her once, a long time ago, that if she wanted something, all she had to do was give him a drink or two and he was about as staunch as a wet noodle. And while Katy didn't necessarily believe it was ethical to take advantage of an intoxicated person, if it made him open up to her a little…well, what was the harm?

When Celia came back for their dishes, Katy asked

her for a glass of orange juice. "And I think Adam could use another drink."

He looked at his watch, then shrugged and said, "Why not?"

Around nine, after he'd drained his second glass and was clearly feeling no pain—he'd even laughed during one of the shows—she used the bathroom and changed into her pajamas, then climbed back into bed. The program they'd been watching had just ended, so she switched off the television, rolled on her side to face him and asked, "Adam, can we talk?"

He looked down at her and frowned. "Is something wrong?"

"Oh, no, nothing," she assured him. "It just only seems right that I should get to know the father of the baby I'll be carrying. Don't you think?"

His brow dipped low. "Oh, you mean you want to *talk*."

"What have you got against talking? It's how people get to know each other."

He looked uncomfortable. "That wasn't part of the deal."

"Maybe it should be."

"You know, my life isn't really all that interesting."

"I doubt that." She gave him a playful poke. "Come on, tell me something about you. Just one thing."

"Let me think. Oh, I know. I don't like talking about myself."

She laughed. "Adam!"

"What?" he said with a grin. "You said one thing."

"Something I don't already know. Tell me about… your father."

He shrugged. "There isn't much to tell."

"Were you close?"

"There were times, when my mom was still alive, that he would occasionally notice me. But then she died, and he checked out."

That was the saddest thing she'd ever heard. If they were all the other had, they should have stuck together. They could have leaned on each other. The way she and her parents supported each other when Becca died. She supposed that sort of tragedy could either pull a family together, or rip them apart.

"You must have been very lonely."

He shrugged again. "Celia was there for me."

He said it so casually, but she had the feeling that losing his mother had scarred him deeper than he would ever admit. How could it not?

"How did your mother die?"

"Cancer."

Which must have made learning about Becca's cancer all the more devastating. And scary. "How old were you?"

"Young enough to believe it was my fault."

She sucked in a quiet breath. That was probably the most honest thing he had ever said to her. Her heart ached for him. For the frightened little boy he must have been.

He looked over at her. "Everyone has bad things happen to them, Katy. You get through it, you move on."

Was he forgetting that she had lost someone dear to her, too?

"Have you?" she asked. "Moved on, I mean." She knew the instant the words were out, as the shutters on his emotions snapped closed again, that she had pushed too far. So much for getting to know one another.

He looked at his watch and frowned. "It's getting late."

He got up and grabbed his shoes from the floor.

"You don't have to go," she said. "We can talk about something else."

His expression said he'd had just about all the conversation he could stand for one night. Maybe a dozen nights. Maybe he was only in here to keep tabs on her. To be sure that she followed the doctor's instructions. "You need your rest and I have an early meeting tomorrow. I probably won't see you in the morning, but Celia will get you whatever you need."

Like the turtles she and Willy used to catch in the grass by the riverbank when she was a kid, he'd sensed danger and retreated back into his shell. God forbid he let himself open up to her, let himself *feel* something. Would it really be so terrible?

He hesitated in the doorway, like he might change his mind, but instead he said, "Have a safe trip back to Peckins," then he was gone.

Adam had actually started acting like a human being today, which she couldn't deny intrigued her. And now that she'd had a preview of the man hiding behind the icy exterior, she wanted to dig deeper. She wanted to know who he was.

But when had this ever been about getting to know Adam better? And why would she bother? When it was over, and the baby was born, they would just go back to being strangers. Seeing each other occasionally when he brought the baby around.

She laid a hand gently across her belly, wondering

what was going on inside, if the procedure had worked and the embryo was attaching to her womb. Her tiny little niece or nephew, she thought with a smile. Even knowing that there was only an average 10 percent success rate, she had a good feeling about their chances.

She switched off the light and lay in the dark, thinking about everything that had happened since she left Peckins that morning. The ease of the procedure, and the way Adam had stayed with her all day. She thought that they had shared something special, that they were becoming friends, but it was clear he didn't want that. And for some stupid reason the idea made her inexplicably sad.

It had only been seven days since the procedure, and would be three more days before she would even know if she was pregnant, and Katy had already determined that she agreed to have a child with the most demanding and obstinate man on the face of the earth.

Adam had called her about a *million* times.

Okay, so it was more like fifteen or twenty, but it sure felt like a million. She had only been back to Peckins an hour when he phoned to check on her, which, in light of his cool attitude the night before, she found sort of touching. He reminded her that the doctor said to take it easy for several days, meaning no heavy lifting or strenuous activity. Which she, of course, already knew. She assured him she was following the postprocedure instructions to the letter, and he had nothing to worry about.

Thinking that she'd made herself pretty clear, she was surprised when later that evening he'd called *again*.

Was she eating right? Drinking enough water? Staying off her feet?

She patiently assured him that she was *still* following the doctor's orders, and when they hung up shortly after, assumed that would be the last she heard from him in a while. But he called again the next morning.

Had she gotten a full eight hours sleep? She wasn't drinking coffee, was she? And since country breakfasts were often laden with saturated fats, she should consider fruit and an egg-white omelet as a substitute.

She assured him again, maybe not quite so patiently this time, that she knew what to do. And she was only a little surprised when he called later in the day to say he'd been doing research on the internet and needed her email address so he could send her links to several sites he thought contained necessary information about prenatal health. And had she ever considered becoming a vegetarian?

If he was this fanatical before there was even a confirmed pregnancy, what was he going to be like when she was actually pregnant? Two to three calls a day, *every* day, for nine months?

She would be giving birth from a padded room in the psychiatric ward.

It wouldn't be so bad if the phone calls were even slightly conversational in tone. As in, "Hi, how are you? What have you been up to?" Instead he more or less barked orders, without even the most basic of pleasantries.

On day seven, he called to say that he'd been giving their situation considerable thought, and he'd come to the conclusion that he would feel more comfortable if she came to stay with him in El Paso for the duration of her pregnancy. So he could "keep a close eye on her."

It was the final straw.

"I will not, under any circumstances, drop everything and move two hours from home. The ranch is my life. My parents need me here. And all the phone calls and emails…it has to stop. You're *smothering* me and we don't even know that I'm pregnant yet."

"But you could be, so doesn't it make sense to start taking care of yourself now? This is my child we're talking about."

"It's also my life."

"If you were here with me I wouldn't have to call. And you wouldn't have to do anything. Celia would take care of you."

She liked Celia, but honestly, it sounded like hell on earth. She wasn't an idle person. Most days she was up before dawn and didn't stop moving until bedtime. "I *love* working, Adam."

"But obviously you'll have to quit."

"Why would I do that?"

"Because you'll be pregnant."

Oh, he did *not* just say that. "What century are you living in? Pregnant women work all the time."

"At a desk job maybe, or as a clerk in a store. I seriously doubt there are pregnant women out there roping cattle on horseback and mucking stables."

"Is *that* what you think I do?"

"It's not?"

"Not *just* that. And, of course, I wouldn't do those things when I'm pregnant. Do you really think I would be that irresponsible? And for your information, I spend a *lot* of time behind a desk."

"I didn't mean to imply that you're irresponsible. And I guess I just assumed your responsibilities were more physical in nature."

"So you assumed I got a business degree just for the fun of it?" she snapped. "Next you'll be telling me that I'm wasting my education staying on the ranch." As if she hadn't heard that enough from Becca over the years.

"I'm just worried about the health of my child."

"We obviously need to get a few things straight here. One, I am *not* moving to El Paso. There is no reason why I can't have a perfectly healthy pregnancy in Peckins. And two, I am definitely not quitting work. My parents depend on me, not to mention that I love what I do. I understand that you're worried about the baby's health, but you're just going to have to trust me. And lastly, if you insist on calling to check up on me, could you have the decency to not treat me like a…a *baby factory*. Maybe we could even have a conversation. You do know what that is, right?"

"Yes," he said curtly. He obviously didn't like what he was hearing, but when she signed the contract to be his surrogate, nowhere did it say she had to comply to his every demand.

Move in with him? Was he nuts?

"Even though Becca is gone, we're still family. Would it really be so terrible if we were friends?"

"I never said I didn't want to be your friend."

"You didn't have to. I'm sure you've heard the phrase, *actions speak louder than words*. And maybe you haven't considered this, but if you get to know me a little better, it will be easier for you to trust me."

"I suppose you're right," he said grudgingly.

At least it was start. But she had the sinking feeling that it was going to a really *long* nine months.

Eight

Since their phone conversation three days ago, Adam had cut off all contact with Katy, and it had been surprisingly difficult. Since the procedure he'd been thinking about her almost twenty-four/seven. The more he read up on pregnancy, the deeper home it hit just how many things could go wrong with not just the baby, but Katy, as well.

He had accepted responsibility for Becca's death, and learned to live with the guilt, but the idea that her sister's life was now in his hands had him on constant edge. It was his responsibility to make sure she was healthy.

It was something he should have considered before he put this baby plan into motion. But it was too late now. Katy was due to arrive any minute so they could go for her blood test. In a few hours they would know if the procedure worked.

He was both excited and dreading it. Hopeful but conflicted. From his home office, where he'd been working while waiting for her to arrive, he heard the doorbell. Even though he was sure it was Katy, he let Celia answer it.

After a minute, Celia knocked on his door. "Katy is here, and I think something is wrong. She ran straight upstairs to the spare bedroom. And it looked like she'd been crying."

He bolted up from his chair, his heart in the pit of his stomach.

With Celia close behind Adam rushed up the stairs to the spare room. The door was open, so he stepped inside. The door to the bathroom was closed. He knocked softly and asked, "Katy, are you all right?"

"Give me a minute," she called.

He walked back over to the bedroom door to wait with Celia. After several minutes the bathroom door opened and Katy emerged. She was in her girls' clothes, and her red-rimmed eyes said she probably had been crying.

Ridiculous as it was, his first instinct was to take her in his arms and try to comfort her, which was exactly why he didn't.

"What's wrong?" he asked.

"I had some light cramping this morning before I left, but I thought it might just be a fluke." She sniffled and swiped at the tear that had spilled over onto her cheek. "But it wasn't."

The disappointment was all-encompassing. "You're not pregnant?"

She bit her lip and shook her head. "I was so sure it worked. I really expected to be pregnant."

Celia crossed the room and gathered Katy in her arms, and Adam couldn't help thinking that it should be him comforting her. But he was glad Celia had stepped in for him.

"You'll have more chances," Celia assured her, rubbing her back soothingly. "I know it's disappointing, but it will happen." She looked over at Adam and gestured to the box of tissue on the nightstand.

He plucked one out and brought it to her. Celia took it and pressed it into Katy's hand. "Why don't I make you a soothing cup of chamomile tea?"

Katy sniffled and nodded.

Celia turned and gave Adam a look, then jerked her head in Katy's direction, as if to say "Console her, you idiot." But he couldn't seem to make himself do it.

Katy stood there dabbing her eyes. "I was so sure I was pregnant."

"The doctor said it could take a few times."

"I know, but I had such a good feeling." She took a deep, shuddering breath. "I'm so sorry, Adam."

"Sorry for what?"

"I feel responsible."

She looked so damned…forlorn. And Katy never struck him as the kind of woman to cry on a whim. He recalled that even at Becca's funeral she'd held it together. And how could he just stand there, like a self-ish bastard, when he was the one who put her in this situation? Had he really grown so cold and unfeeling?

Or was it that he felt *too* much?

"I'm sorry," she said in a wobbly voice. "I'm acting stupid."

Another tear spilled over and rolled down her cheek, and he cringed. The gene all men possessed that made them wither at the sight of a crying female kicked into overdrive. Besides, if he didn't do something, she would probably just interpret it as him being mad at her, or something equally ridiculous.

Feeling he had no choice, he stepped closer and tugged her into his arms. She came willingly, leaning into the embrace, hands fisted against his chest, head tucked under his chin.

There it was again, just like when she'd kissed his cheek, that feeling of awareness. As if every touch, every sensation was multiplied tenfold. The softness of her body where it pressed against his. The flowery scent of her hair. The flutter of her breath through his shirt and the warmth that seemed to seep through her clothing to his skin.

His body began to react the way any man's would. Well, any man who hadn't been this physically close to a woman in three years. Or intimate in closer to four. Until recently he couldn't say he'd missed it. He'd barely given any thought to sex. It was as if his body had been in deep hibernation, unable to feel physical pleasure.

But he sure as hell could feel it now. And if he didn't get a hold of himself, she would feel it, too.

"I'm sorry," she said again.

"Would you *stop* apologizing."

"I just feel like, maybe if I had done something different, if I had been more careful."

Beating herself up over this wasn't going to change anything. "It was nothing you did."

"But you only have embryos for two more attempts. What if those fail, too?"

"I knew going into this that there was a chance it wouldn't work. I do have other options."

"But then the last of Becca will be gone forever."

"Katy, look at me." She didn't move, so he cradled her chin in his palm and lifted her face to his. Big mistake. Her eyes were wide and sad, and so blue he could almost swim in their depths, and when they locked on his, the sensation was so intense he felt it like a physical blow. Whatever it was he'd been about to say to her was lost.

Her lips parted, like she might speak, and his eyes were drawn to her mouth. Though he knew it was wrong, never had the idea of kissing a woman intrigued him this way. And clearly whatever craziness was causing this, it was doing the same to her. He could tell, by the sudden shift in her demeanor, by the look in her eyes, that she was going to kiss him again. And he wasn't entirely sure he wanted to stop her.

Not only did he not stop her, but as she rose up, he leaned in to meet her halfway.

Their lips touched and whatever was left of his common sense evaporated with their mingling breath. His only coherent thought was *more*. Whatever she was willing to give, he would take.

So thank God Celia chose that exact instant to call up from the base of the stairs, "The tea is ready!"

Katy pulled away from him, eyes wide with the realization of what they had just done.

"We'll be down in a minute," he called to Celia.

"Oh, my God," she whispered, reaching up to touch her lips. "Did you *feel* that?"

Feel it? His heart was about to pound out of his chest. And he couldn't stop looking at her mouth.

He needed to get a hold of himself.

"Okay, this is not that bad," she said, trying to rationalize a situation that was completely *ir*rational. "We're both disappointed, and upset. That's all. This doesn't mean anything. Right?"

Leave it to Katy to take the situation and blow it wide open.

"Right. We're just upset." He didn't know if he actually believed it, but it seemed to be what she needed to hear. Why couldn't she be one of those women who was content to pretend everything was fine. Like Becca. It had been like pulling teeth to get her to admit when there was a problem, or she was upset about something.

Of course, that had been no picnic, either. Was there no happy medium?

"We need to call the doctor's office," Katy said. "Find out what we should do."

He was glad one of them was thinking clearly. Because the only clear thought he was having right now was how much he'd like to see her naked again.

They had opened a door, and he couldn't help wondering if it was only a matter of time before someone stepped through.

She had kissed Adam. On the mouth.

One minute Katy had been racked with guilt that the procedure hadn't worked, and the next she was practically crawling out of her skin, she was so hot for him. And thank God for Celia and her timing, or who knows what *might* have happened. The possibilities both horrified and intrigued her. Though Becca was gone, he would always be her brother-in-law. Her sister's husband. To Katy *and* her parents, who would kill her if they had any clue what had just happened.

Sure, she'd hoped she and Adam could get to know each other, but she'd never meant in the *biblical* sense. Talk about going from one extreme to another.

Like her mom had so eloquently put it, he wasn't like them. So whatever was causing these weird feelings was going to have to stop.

Despite the fact that they both seemed determined to forget it happened, their trip to the doctor's office later that afternoon had been tense. But at least the appointment with Dr. Meyer had been encouraging. He assured her that she'd done nothing to cause the implantation to fail. He wrote her a prescription for hormone shots that she would begin taking a week before the next scheduled implantation. He explained that it could make her womb more hospitable and increase their chances for success.

She wasn't sure what the shots were actually doing for her womb, but as she drove back to El Paso the morning of the second procedure, her emotions were in a hopeless tangle. What if things were completely awkward between her and Adam? He had emailed her a few times in the past week to check on her, but they hadn't actually talked since her last visit.

Like last time, she drove straight to Adam's house, then Reece took her in the limo to the clinic. She assumed Adam would already be waiting in the lobby, and she was so nervous about seeing him again her hands were trembling. But he wasn't there yet. She waited in their usual spot by the elevator, wringing her hands. He sent her a text message a few minutes later that said he was running late, and to go on up without him.

What if he didn't make it on time? Would they wait for him? The idea of doing this alone made her heart race.

She took the elevator up to the clinic. She checked in, hoping they would make her wait this time, but the nurse called her back right away. She took her time changing into a gown, her anxiety mounting, waiting for a reply saying that he'd arrived. But when the nurse took her to the procedure room, she had no choice but to leave her phone in her purse.

He wasn't going to make it, she realized. Was he really held up at work, or avoiding her? Had that kiss done more damage than she'd realized? This was starting to become a familiar cycle for her. Get close to a man, let her guard down, then inevitably drive him away. What other conclusion could she draw, but that there was something seriously wrong with her? She was like a human deflector. Men got close, then bounced off the surface.

Most of her friends were already married and starting families. And here she was having a baby for someone else, because she was so unappealing, so unlovable no one wanted her.

The nurse got her situated on the table and ready for the transfer. She must have sensed Katy was upset because she put a hand on her shoulder and asked, "You okay, honey?"

Tears welled in her eyes. "I don't think Adam is going to make it."

"Mr. Blair is already here, in the waiting room."

"He is?"

She nodded and smiled. "I was just about to go get him."

She was so relieved, if she hadn't been lying down, her knees probably would have given out.

The nurse slipped out into the hall, returning a minute later with Adam. She was so happy to see him she had to bite down hard on her lip to keep from bursting into tears, but they started leaking out of her eyes anyway.

Looking worried, Adam grabbed a chair and sat down beside her. "Katy, what's the matter? Why are you crying?"

"I thought you weren't coming," she said, her voice wobbly.

"I told you I'd just be a few minutes late."

She wiped her eyes. "I know. I don't know what's wrong with me."

"It's probably the hormones you've been taking," the nurse said, handing her a tissue. "It makes some women weepy."

In that case she hoped it worked this time, so she didn't have to take this emotional roller-coaster ride again. For someone who barely even suffered PMS, this was the pits.

"Is there anything I can do?" Adam asked, looking so adorably helpless, she could have hugged him. Or kissed him. He was sitting awfully close. If she just reached up and slipped a hand around his neck, pulled him down...

Ugh. Had she really just gone from weeping, to fantasizing about jumping him? As if things weren't weird enough already.

She really was a basket case.

The door opened and Dr. Meyer came in, asking cheerfully, "Are we ready to make a baby?"

Katy nodded and held her hand out to Adam. He took it, cradling it between his, holding tight while the doctor did the transfer. Just like the last time it was quick, and mostly painless.

"You know the drill," the nurse told them when it was over. "Two hours on your back."

The nurse stepped out into the hall and it was just the two of them. Alone. Last time Adam had let go of her hand as soon as the procedure was finished, but not now. Maybe he didn't think she was so terrible after all.

"I'm really sorry about earlier," she said. "I *never* cry. Not even when I was thrown from a horse and busted my collarbone. But it seems as though every time I see you now I'm blubbering about something."

"Katy, I understand."

"I just don't want you to think I'm a big baby." Because that's sure what she felt like.

"I don't. The same thing happened to Becca when they were getting her ready to harvest the eggs. Then they found the cancer and, well, suffice it to say that didn't help matters."

It was hard to imagine Becca crying about anything. Even the cancer. She had always been so strong, so determined to beat it. Even near the end, when all hope was lost, she was tough. Around Katy and their parents anyway.

"Sometimes I feel guilty that I don't miss her more," she said. "That we drifted so far apart."

"It happens, I guess."

"It's really sad. She was my sister for twenty-four years, but I don't think she ever really knew me."

That seemed to surprise him. "In what way?"

"She always thought that by staying on the ranch with our parents, I was settling—giving in—or something. She must have told me a million times that I was wasting my education. And my life. She said I should move to the city, try new things. Meet new people. And no matter how many times I told her that I loved working on the ranch, that it was what made me happy, she just didn't seem to get it. If it wasn't good enough for her, then it wasn't good enough for anyone. It was so...*infuriating*."

"What she thought shouldn't have mattered."

But it did. She had always looked up to Becca. She was beautiful and popular and sophisticated. Of course, she could also be self-centered and stubborn, too.

"I felt as though she never really saw me. The *real* me. To her I was always little Katy, young and naive. I think she expected me to be just like her. And not only did I not give a damn about being rich and sophisticated, I could never pine for a man the way she did for you. It's like she was obsessed. Everything she did was to keep you happy. To keep you interested. It just seemed...exhausting."

Adam frowned, and Katy felt a stab of guilt. What had possessed her to say something so insensitive?

"Oh, shoot. Adam, I'm sorry." She squeezed his hand, wishing she could take the words back. "I didn't mean to imply—"

"No, you're right. She was like that. But for the life of me I could never understand why. She didn't need to work to keep me interested. I loved her unconditionally. She was so independent and feisty."

Katy smiled. "She was definitely feisty. Full of piss and vinegar, my grandma used to say."

"She lost that. I don't know why, but after we got married, she changed."

"Maybe she loved you so much, she was afraid of losing you. Maybe she was worried that once you were married, you would get bored with her."

"That's ridiculous."

"When she met you, she seemed truly happy for the first time in her life. She was never happy at home. She never came out and said it, but we knew she was ashamed of where she came from. You'll never know how much that hurt my parents."

He surprised her by turning his hand and threading his fingers through hers. "I tried to get Becca to visit more. I told her I would make time. I had no family, so I knew how important it was. She just…" He shrugged helplessly.

That should have hurt, but mostly Katy just felt disappointed. Especially since Becca had led them to believe that it was Adam who never had time for them.

"It was like that with the fertility treatments, too," he said. "They found the cancer, and wanted to do the surgery and start treatment immediately. She flat-out refused. She wanted to harvest her eggs. I begged her to reconsider, but she knew it was our last chance to have a child that was biologically ours. There was no reasoning with her. The doctors warned her that she had a particularly aggressive strain, but she wouldn't budge."

Becca had always led Katy and her parents to believe that Adam had been the one to make that decision, that he insisted they wait and harvest the eggs first, and they had believed her. Had it all been a lie, to shelter herself from her parents' disapproval?

Why did she portray him to be so unreasonable and demanding?

"You want to hear the really ironic part of all this?" Adam said. "I don't think she really even wanted kids."

It was true Becca had never been much of a kid person. Katy had been a little surprised when she mentioned they were trying to get pregnant. But when it didn't happen right away she'd been devastated. Because when Becca wanted something, she didn't like to wait. After that, it was as if she was obsessed. "For a year that's all she talked about," she told Adam.

"Because she knew it was what *I* wanted."

"Why wouldn't she want kids?"

"I think...I think she was afraid that if we had a child, I might love it more than her. She wanted to be the center of my universe, and I think she believed that the baby would replace her."

Was she really that insecure? She was smart and beautiful and talented with a husband who loved her. Why couldn't she just be happy? Why did she have to make everything so complicated?

"I loved Becca," Adam said, "but I don't think I ever completely understood her. But that wasn't her fault. I should have tried harder, made more of an effort. I'll regret that for the rest of my life."

It occurred to her suddenly that she and Adam were talking. Having an honest conversation. And she hadn't even been trying. It just...happened.

She and Adam were from totally different worlds. So why, at that very moment, did he feel like an equal? Not a billionaire oil man, but just a man.

Nine

Something was off.

Katy jolted awake and opened her eyes, expecting to be in her bed at home, but as her eyes adjusted she realized she was in the spare room at Adam's house.

For a second she was confused, then she remembered they'd had the embryos implanted that morning.

She must have fallen asleep during the movie they were watching. She would check the time on the digital clock on the dresser, but that would necessitate her rolling over, and she was too comfortable to move. She must have conked out a while ago because the television had gone into sleep mode. She wondered why Adam hadn't switched it off when he left.

She usually slept pretty light, so she was surprised she hadn't felt him get out of bed. He'd sat there beside her almost the entire time they had been back from Dr.

Meyer's office. She hadn't even cared that he'd spent part of the time working on his laptop. She was content to just sit beside him reading the novel she'd brought with her. She even told him it was okay if he would be more comfortable working in his office. His reply was that they were in this together, and if she had to lie around all day, it was only fair he did the same. He was turning out to be a lot nicer than she ever expected. Still a bit dark and mysterious, but at least he'd opened up to her a little today.

She thought about her mother's warning, how Katy always fell hard and fast. Maybe she did have the slightest bit of a crush on Adam, but she knew better than to think it would amount to anything. She was finished with one-way relationships. And men like Adam didn't get serious about women like her. They had absolutely *nothing* in common.

Was she attracted to him? Of course. When they kissed had she practically burst into flames? She sure had, but all that meant was that they were attracted to each other.

And was she tempted by the thought of taking that attraction out for a quick spin? *Hell, yes!* But she knew that would only lead to getting her heart crushed, and who needed that? The trick was to keep herself out of temptation's way.

And what was the point of lying here in the dark obsessing about it when what she needed was a good night's sleep?

She closed her eyes, willing herself to relax. She was just starting to drift back off when she felt the bed move. If she were at home she would just assume

Sylvester had jumped into bed with her. But as far as she knew Adam didn't have a cat.

Maybe it had been her imagination.

Curious, she reached back, patting the covers behind her, her hand landing on something warm and solid. She yanked it back and looked over her shoulder. The reason she hadn't felt Adam get out of bed was because he never had!

Oh, good Lord.

Was it a coincidence that she'd just been thinking about avoiding temptation, and here it was, lying right beside her? Maybe it was fate. Or a sign.

It was a sign, all right. A sign that she needed to wake him up and get him the hell out of here.

She rolled over. He was lying on his side facing her, one arm under his head. She reached out to shake him awake, then stopped just shy of touching his arm. He was so serious all the time. Even when he smiled there was an undercurrent of tension, as if he was always plotting, always planning his next move. Now he looked so…peaceful.

As if it possessed a will of its own, her hand moved to his face instead, but until she felt the rasp of his beard stubble against her fingers, she didn't think she would be bold enough to actually touch him. And now that she had, she couldn't seem to make herself stop.

There was a small white scar just below his lip where the skin was smooth and she couldn't resist tracing it with her finger. The mouth that sometimes appeared so hard and unrelenting looked soft and tender while he slept. She wanted to touch that, too. With her fingers. And her lips.

The idea of actually doing it, touching her lips to his again, made her scalp tingle.

This is a bad idea, she told herself, but knowing that didn't stop her. In fact, it made doing it even more exciting. Because honestly, when did she ever do anything that was bad for her? As long as she could remember, she'd been the good girl. The obedient daughter. Didn't she deserve to take something for herself? Just this once?

Heart pounding, she leaned close, touching her lips to his chin. He didn't wake up, didn't even stir, so she moved up a little, to the corner of his mouth, and pressed her lips there, quickly, then pulled back to check his face. His eyes were still closed. The man slept like the dead.

Trembling with anticipation, she closed her eyes and very gently pressed her lips to his…and almost moaned it felt so nice. And there it was again, that curious feeling, just like before. *Awareness.* Like a magnet pull, drawing her closer to him. She wanted to curl herself around his body, sink into his warmth. She would crawl inside his skin if she could.

She realized her lips were still pressed to his, and without meaning to, she'd gotten a little bit carried away. She opened her eyes, to make sure he was still asleep, but Adam's eyes were open, too, and he was looking right at her.

She sucked in a surprised breath, and backed away, sure that she must have looked like a deer in headlights.

She waited for him to berate her, to ask her what the hell she thought she was doing. Instead he blinked several times, eyes foggy from sleep and asked in a gravelly voice, "Did you just kiss me?"

Okay, so maybe he wasn't as awake as he looked. Maybe she could lie and say it had been an accident. She had just leaned too close and accidentally bumped lips with him. He would buy that, right?

He was asleep, not stupid.

"Katy?" he said, waiting for an answer.

"Yes," she choked out, shame burning her cheeks. Not only for what she'd done, but for the fact that she wanted to do it again. "I'm sorry. I don't know what I was thinking."

She braced herself for the anger, but instead Adam touched her face…so tenderly that shivers of pleasure danced along her spine. Then he looked her right in the eye and said in a voice thick with desire, "Do it again."

He *wanted* her to kiss him?

Katy was too dumbfounded to move, but Adam apparently didn't want to wait, because he leaned in and kissed her first.

She discovered the instant their lips touched that it was a heck of a lot more fun kissing him when he was actually participating. It was exciting and terrifying and confusing and…wonderful. And it was obvious, after several minutes of making out like sex-starved teenagers, when he rolled her over onto her back and tugged her pajama top up over her head, this was going way beyond kissing. She may have started this, but it was clear that Adam intended to finish it.

What are you doing? the rational part of her brain demanded, that part that wasn't drowning in estrogen and pheromones. *This is* Adam, *your* brother-in-law. *Your* sister's *husband. This is wrong.*

But it was hard to take her rational self seriously when Adam was kissing her senseless and sliding his hand inside her pajama bottoms. She moaned as his fingers found the place where she was already hot and wet.

Already? Who was she kidding? Since she started the hormone shots she'd been walking around in a near-constant state of sexual arousal. It wasn't unusual for her to feel heightened sexual awareness when she was ovulating, but this was horny times fifty.

Maybe this had been inevitable. And maybe it made her a lousy sister, or just a terrible person in general, but she didn't care. She wanted him. She had never done a truly selfish thing in her life, but she was going to do this.

And she would *not* fall in love with him.

She fumbled with the buttons on Adam's shirt, her fingers clumsy and uncooperative, until she got fed up and just ripped the damned thing open. If he cared that she'd just ruined his shirt he didn't say so. Of course, he was a little preoccupied driving her crazy with his fingers and his mouth.

She shoved the shirt off his shoulders and down his arms, her eyes raking over his chest. Swirls of black hair circled small dark nipples then narrowed into a trail down the center of his lean stomach, disappearing under the waistband of his slacks.

Breathless with excitement, she put her hands on him. His skin was hot and she could feel the heavy thump of his heart. She wanted to touch him everywhere.

She half expected him to be as controlled and closed off as he always was. Hadn't Becca confided to her that sex with Adam was "nice," but sometimes she wished he would be a little more passionate, more adventurous? But Adam must have changed, because if he were any more passionate than he was now, they would set the sheets on fire. He was reckless and impulsive and…crazy.

They kissed and touched, tore at each other's clothes. There was barely a second when his mouth wasn't somewhere on her body. Her lips, her breasts, the column of her throat. He licked and nibbled as if he wanted to eat her alive. Until the sensations all started to run together, and her entire being quivered with the need for release.

And when she didn't think she could stand much more, when she felt she would go out of her mind if he didn't *take* her, he said, "I have to make love to you."

Not he *wanted* to, but he *had* to. As in, he wanted it so badly, he couldn't stop himself. And she felt exactly the same way.

As he centered himself between her thighs, his strong arms caging her, she considered fleetingly that maybe they shouldn't be doing this, but as he thrust inside her, her brain could do nothing but feel. Feel his hands and his mouth. Feel the slow, steady rhythm of his body moving inside of hers, connecting in a way she had never imagined. It felt as if she had been working up to this moment her entire life. Every man who had come before him…they hadn't come close to making her feel what she did now. Excited and humbled and terrified all at once. And as she cried out with release, felt Adam shudder and then go still inside of her, she was terrified that no one ever would again.

Because as earth-shatteringly wonderful as this had been, this was Adam, her brother-in-law. He was a billionaire oil man and she was a rancher. He wore thousand-dollar suits to work and she spent her days wading through cow manure.

They were worse than oil and water. They were gasoline and a lit match. And she could tell, by the way he rolled over and lay silently beside her, the only sound his breath coming in sharp rasps, he was probably thinking the same thing. He was probably afraid that she had just fallen head over heels in love with him, and was wondering how he was going to let her down easy.

Well, he didn't have to worry about her. She was firmly rooted in reality.

She took a deep breath, blew it out and said, "Despite what you're probably thinking right now, this was not a big deal."

Not a big deal?

Adam lay beside Katy, trying to catch his breath, after what was by far the best sex of his entire adult life.

Despite the fact that it was over *way* too fast. But it had been almost four years since he'd been with a woman, so the fact that he'd lasted more than thirty seconds was, in his opinion, a small miracle.

Then he had a thought, one that just about stopped his pulse. "Were we supposed to do that?"

"Well, given the nature of our relationship—"

"No, I mean, was that on the list?"

"List?"

"The things you're not supposed to do after the embryo transfer."

He heard her inhale sharply, then she jolted up in bed. "I don't know."

"I don't recall the doctor mentioning anything about

sex, but I could swear there was something on the list."
He might have thought of it sooner, but when he woke
to discover her kissing him, his brain must have shorted
out.

"Do you still have the list?" she asked. "I think I
left it here the last time."

"I think Celia put it on my desk."

She swung her legs over the side of the bed and he
grabbed her arm. "You're on bed rest. I'll go."

She looked at him like he was an idiot, since she was
probably thinking that the damage had already been
done. But technically she was still on bed rest, and
since she hadn't actually gotten out of bed, maybe they
were okay. He switched on the lamp, blinking against
the sudden bright light. He found his pants on the floor
beside the bed and yanked them on. Then he turned and
saw Katy sitting there naked, fishing her panties from
between the covers, her skin rosy, her breasts covered
with love bites, and almost took them back off again.

He actually paused for a second and reached for his
fly, then thought, *What the hell are you doing?* They
shouldn't have slept together the first time, but once
could at least be written off as sexual curiosity. Or
temporary insanity. The second time, though, showed
intent. It implied a relationship, and he sure as hell
didn't want that.

He didn't care how fantastic the sex was. There was
no way it was going to happen again.

He left Katy wrestling with her undergarments and
headed down to his office. He found the list buried
under a month's worth of miscellaneous papers. He
switched out the lights and took the stairs two at a time
up to the bedroom.

Katy was sitting in bed, wearing her pajama top and panties, looking anxious.

"Got it," he said, sitting beside her.

"What does it say?" she asked, leaning close to read it with him.

He saw it right away, at the bottom. He pointed to the line. "No intercourse or orgasms."

She closed her eyes and cursed. "So what does this mean?"

"That it might not work, I guess."

"And if it did work, could what we did have hurt the baby?"

"I don't know. I wouldn't think so. We'll just have to wait and ask, I guess. I wonder, though, maybe intercourse alone isn't that bad, maybe if you didn't..." He looked at her hopefully.

She looked confused, then she realized what he was implying. "Of course I did! You couldn't *tell?*"

He shrugged. She wouldn't be the first woman to... embellish. "I thought it couldn't hurt to ask."

"I'm so sorry," she said miserably, drawing her knees up to her chest and hugging them. "This is all my fault."

"No, it isn't."

"I started this. If I hadn't kissed you..."

Why did you? he wanted to ask her, but he had the feeling he'd rather not know. Besides, it didn't even matter. It happened. The damage was done. "I could have stopped you, but I didn't."

She buried her face in her hands. "How could I let this happen?"

"It's been an emotional couple of weeks for both of us. We made a mistake."

"We definitely can't do this again," she said.

"I agree."

"I mean, it was great, but…well…you know."

He was a little curious to know what she meant. What he was supposed to know. If for no other reason than to see if they had the same reasons, but at this point it didn't seem to matter.

They sat there in awkward silence for a minute or two. What was left to say at this point? "I should leave you alone, so you can get some rest."

She fidgeted with the edge of the blanket. "I do have a long drive tomorrow."

He got up and grabbed his shredded shirt from where it had landed on the floor. "Try not to worry. If it doesn't work, we'll try again."

"And we're never doing *this* again," she said, gesturing to the bed, as if he wasn't already clear on that point.

"Like you said, it's not a big deal. It doesn't change anything. It happened, and it won't happen again."

He couldn't tell if she looked relieved or disappointed, and the truth was, he really didn't want to know.

Ten

The next ten days were the longest in Katy's life. She tried to keep herself busy with work, but even putting together the ranch's quarterly taxes wasn't enough to distract her from the guilt that she might have completely blown their chances to conceive. And she didn't care what Adam said. It was her fault. He never would have made the first move.

Though she tried to put on a good face for her parents, they could tell she was upset. She told them she was just worried that it wouldn't work, but she didn't tell them why. How could she?

By the way, Mom and Dad, did I mention that I seduced and slept with my dead sister's husband? They would never forgive her. And she couldn't blame them. She wasn't even sure if she could forgive herself.

She did try to talk to her mom about Adam, and

how he wasn't the man they thought he was, and her mom got that, "Oh, no, here we go again, Katy has a crush" look, so she didn't even bother. Maybe because she was too ashamed to admit that her mom had been right. Although it was obvious by how readily Adam agreed it was a mistake, that he hadn't spontaneously fallen madly in love with her.

She wished she could say the same. But that was her own fault. Still, he was all she could think about lately. She probably wouldn't have minded him inundating her with calls and emails this time, but he seemed to know instinctively that it was better to back off. He'd text messaged her a couple of times, to see how she was feeling.

She kept waiting for some sort of sign, to start *feeling* pregnant.

"I knew right away," her best friend Missy told her as she fixed a bottle for the three-month-old strapped to her chest, while balancing a toddler on one hip and dodging the groping hands of the three- and five-year-olds. "My mood changed and my hair started falling out. Not like I was going bald," she added at Katy's look of horror. "But it got thinner during all my pregnancies."

"I don't feel anything," Katy told her.

"Oh, sweetie," she had said clucking sympathetically. "I'm sure it will work. And if it doesn't, you'll just try again. The doctors can only do so much. You have to trust your body to do the rest."

But she had betrayed her body. She didn't give it a chance to do the rest. And talking to Missy only made her feel worse because she was even more convinced that she wasn't pregnant. Because she didn't feel *any* different than before. Other than the crushing guilt that she had set Adam's baby plan back at least a month, not to mention that he only had two more viable embryos. Then the only thing left of her sister would be gone forever.

How would she live with herself if she had ruined this for him?

This had been so much easier when she didn't like him. When she thought he was a cold, arrogant jerk.

The morning of their next appointment, Katy drove to El Paso feeling like she had a boulder in her chest, convinced the transfer didn't take. If it had, she would have felt something by now. Some subtle sign that her body was changing. But there was nothing. Not a twinge or a flutter, no weird food cravings or morning sickness. She was so sure her period would start she almost hadn't bothered to come, but it would be her only chance to see Adam for at least another few weeks, when they did the final transfer.

And if that didn't work? Well, there was a good chance she might never see him again. And who knows, maybe it would be for the best.

She had herself so worked into a lather that when she stepped through the doors to the lobby of the medical building and saw Adam standing by the elevators waiting for her, she immediately burst into tears. Mortified beyond belief, she turned right back around and walked out.

She heard the door open behind her, and hurried footsteps in her direction, then she felt his hand on her shoulder. "Katy, what's wrong?"

She shook her head, unable to speak.

His arms went around her, pulling her against his

chest. And even though she knew she was only tortur-ing herself, she sank into him. Clung to him. Why did she do this to herself? Why did she fall for men who didn't want her?

He stroked her hair, her back. "Talk to me, Katy. What's wrong?"

Only *everything*.

"I'm not pregnant," she said miserably, burying her face against his chest.

"You started your period?"

"No, but…I just know. It didn't work."

"You don't know that," he said patiently.

"I do, and it's all my fault."

"Listen to me. You have to stop blaming yourself. And what's the point in getting so upset if you don't even know for sure?"

"I told you, I just know. I don't *feel* pregnant."

"That doesn't mean you aren't." He took her by the shoulders and held her at arm's length. "Calm down, and let's go inside and get the test. Then we'll know definitively if you are or aren't."

"And if I'm not?"

"Let's worry about that when the time comes, okay?"

She nodded and wiped her cheeks.

With a hand on her back, as if he thought she might try to make a run for it, Adam led her back through the door and up to the clinic.

They had to sit in the general waiting room this time, with half a dozen other couples, several of whom were clearly expecting. Happy couples who loved each other. Which of course only made her feel worse.

When the nurse finally called them back Katy was

on the verge of tears again. Adam must have realized because he took her hand and gave it a reassuring squeeze. The nurse drew blood, slapped a bandage on, and said, "I'll send this right to the lab and we'll call later this afternoon with the results."

"How much later?" Adam asked.

"Usually between three and four. Sometimes earlier. It just depends how busy they are."

"That's it?" Katy asked. "We don't see the doctor?"

"Not until after you get your results."

They stopped at the front desk on their way out, and Adam was able to get them an appointment for seven that evening, so she wouldn't have to make the long drive out again.

"I'm not letting you drive home that late," Adam said when they met back at his house and she mentioned leaving straight from Dr. Meyer's office. He opened the front door, disengaged the alarm, and gestured her inside. "You can stay with me."

"I'm not sure if that's a good idea."

"You don't trust me?"

She didn't trust herself. Especially not when he'd been so touchy-feely with her. Hugging her and holding her hand. It was torture. What would he do if she made the first move again? Would he give in and make love to her? Or would he push her away this time?

She wouldn't be finding out, because the possibility that he would reject her would be more than she could bear.

She followed him into the kitchen. "It's not that I don't trust you," she said. "It'll just be…awkward."

He stopped and turned to her. "Katy, if we're going

to make this surrogacy thing work, we have to get past what happened. If you can't do that—"

"Of course I can." It was obviously just a little harder for her than it was for him. "You're right. I'll stay here."

He pulled two bottles of water out of the fridge and handed her one. "So, what would you like to do until the doctor's office calls?"

"Don't you have to go back to work?"

He leaned against the edge of the counter. "Nope. I'm yours all day."

Oh, didn't she wish.

"We could go for a swim," he said.

"I didn't bring a suit." Or pajamas, or clothes for the next day, she realized.

He shrugged. "Who needs bathing suits? It's not like I haven't seen it before. Right?"

Her heart slammed the wall of her chest. She was too stunned to reply. Hope welled up inside of her, then fizzled out when she saw the corner of his mouth tip up and realized that he was kidding.

"That was a joke," she said.

"Yeah. It was a joke."

Not only did he have a sense of humor, but it was warped. And he obviously had no idea what he'd just done to her. Why would he? She was the one who'd said it meant nothing. Right? He had no idea how conflicted she felt. And she intended to keep it that way.

"Celia has a whole cabinet full of bathing suits in the cabana. There's bound to be one that will fit you."

Since they didn't have anything better to do, and they could take their cell phones with them by the pool, why not? But of course she found out *why not* when she walked out of the cabana, in the modest one-piece she'd found in her size, to find Adam standing by the pool, bare-chested, his bronze skin glistening in the sun, making him look like a Greek Adonis. He looked *really* good for forty. In fact, he could totally put to shame most of the twenty-something guys she knew. His body was truly a work of art. And she was stuck looking at it for God only knows how long.

Hey, it could be worse, she thought. He could be wearing a Speedo.

Since she didn't want to be away from her phone, she only waded around for a few minutes, then she laid back in one of the lounge chairs, sipping iced tea and watching Adam do laps. She recalled Becca telling her once that he'd been on the swim team in college. He'd been so good that later he had a shot at making the Olympic team, but had to drop out when his father died so he could take over Western Oil. She would have to ask him about that some time.

Or not. Probably the less she got to know him, the better. Why make it harder on herself?

Around one Celia brought out a tray of cheese enchiladas and homemade tamales, and though Katy was hungry, and the food was delicious, she was too nervous to eat much. She kept looking at the cell phones sitting side by side on the table, willing them to ring. And at the same time she was dreading it.

An hour later Celia left to do some shopping, and at three Katy and Adam had had enough sun and decided to go in. She was in the kitchen refilling her iced tea, and he was about to go take a quick shower, when his cell phone started to rumble on the counter. Then it started to ring.

For a second they both just stood there looking at it, as though it were some deadly venomous insect neither wanted to touch. Then Adam sighed, grabbed it off the counter and answered.

"Yes, this is he," he said to the caller, and though she could hear someone talking, she couldn't hear what they were saying. She stood there with her heart in her throat, waiting. He said, "uh-huh" twice and "we'll be there," then he hung up.

She was gripping the edge of the counter, hands trembling, and her heart was thumping out about a thousand beats per minute. "Well, what did they say?"

Adam shook his head, looking shell-shocked, and her heart plummeted. She was right. It hadn't worked. They blew it. Then he said, "Positive."

It took a second to process, then she repeated, to be sure she hadn't heard him wrong, *"Positive?"*

He nodded.

"This isn't a joke? It's really positive? It worked?"

A grin spread across his face. "It worked. You're pregnant."

All the stress and grief, and every other emotion that had been building for the last ten days welled up like a geyser and erupted in a whoop of joy that her parents probably heard all the way in Peckins.

In one minute she was across the room, and the next she was in Adam's arms and he was hugging her tight.

"I guess you're happy," he said, and though she couldn't see it, because she was plastered against him, she could hear the smile in his voice.

More than just being happy that she was pregnant, that at least one of the embryos had attached, she was relieved that she hadn't screwed things up for him. She could stop feeling guilty. She could stop thinking back to that night and berating herself for kissing him in the first place, and for not stopping him when he kissed her back, and started undressing her.

Touching her.

Sort of like right now, she realized, as she became aware that her breasts were crushed against his bare chest, that his hands were on her bare back. He smelled like chlorine and sunblock, and his skin felt hot to the touch. And it took exactly two seconds to realize that hugging him had been a terrible mistake.

But why wasn't he letting go? And why were his hands sliding farther south, dangerously close to her behind.

"Um, Adam?"

"Yeah?"

"Maybe you should, you know…let go of me."

"I probably should," he said, nuzzling the side of her throat.

Oh, good Lord.

"Okay…*now,*" she said, but he didn't let go. But to be fair, neither did she. Then she felt his lips on her neck and her legs nearly gave out.

"Katy?"

"Huh?"

"I think I have to kiss you again."

There it was again, that "have to" line.

"I really wish you wouldn't," she said, but his hands were already sliding up her back, tangling through her hair.

Oh, hell, here we go again, she thought as he eased her head back and crushed his lips down on hers. It was so hot she was sure she would melt into a puddle on the kitchen floor.

Did the man have to be such a good kisser.

"Hey Adam, are you two—oops!"

They both jumped a mile and swiftly untangled themselves from each other. Celia stood in the kitchen doorway, her arms filled with reusable canvas grocery bags.

"I'm sorry," she said, looking embarrassed. "I didn't mean to…interrupt."

Everyone seemed at a loss for words, so Katy said what she could to fill the awkward silence.

"We just heard from the doctor's office." As if that brought logic to their passionate embrace. "I'm pregnant!"

Eleven

According to the ultrasound Dr. Meyer performed at their appointment later that evening, she was pregnant with a single embryo.

After a brief examination, he showed them to his private office and explained just about everything she and Adam needed to know about her pregnancy—she was honestly, truly *pregnant!* What changes to expect in her body, and the things she should and shouldn't eat. The kind of activity that was safe and what medications weren't. And her due date, which they learned was early the following spring.

But now the appointment was almost over and neither had mentioned the one thing they both needed to know. It was the huge pink elephant in the room. And since Adam didn't seem inclined to ask, it was up to her to put it out there.

"If you have any other questions for me—" the doctor started to say, and Katy said, "I have one."

She looked over at Adam and he had a slightly pained look on his face. "Suppose, *hypothetically,* that a surrogate were to have sex right after the transfer. Could that hurt the baby in any way?"

The doctor looked up sharply from the notes he'd been jotting in her file. "You didn't, did you?"

His reaction startled her.

It couldn't be that bad, could it? "Even if we did, the embryo latched on," she rationalized. "So no harm done. Right?"

"Successful implantation is only part of the reason. For surrogates like yourself, who have no known fertility issues, there's also the problem of conception."

"But didn't we want her to conceive?" Adam asked, before she had the chance.

"In all likelihood, because the embryos were implanted at the most fertile stage in her cycle, her body also released its own healthy and viable egg. And I'm sure I don't have to explain to either of you what happens if you introduce sperm with an egg."

Katy's stomach bottomed out, and Adam went pale.

The doctor looked from Adam to Katy. "Gauging by your reactions, should I assume this might be the case?"

"So what you're saying," Adam clarified, as if it wasn't crystal clear already, "is that it could be Katy's own fertilized egg, and not one of the embryos."

"It could be."

Katy felt sick to her stomach. This could not possibly be happening.

Under the circumstances, Adam sounded unusually calm and detached when he asked, "Is there any way to tell?"

"Only though a DNA test. Either after the birth, or through amniocentesis."

"How soon could the amnio be done?" Adam asked.

"At the earliest, fourteen weeks, but I do have to warn you that there are risks involved."

"What kind of risks?"

"Infection, miscarriage."

Katy stared at him, slack-jawed, feeling as though she had just taken the leading role in the world's most horrific waking nightmare.

"So what kind of odds are we looking at?" Adam asked. How could he be so *calm?* Panic was clawing at her insides. It was all she could do not to get up and pace the room like a caged animal.

"Of course, I can't be certain, but I would put the odds at somewhere in the ball park of five to one."

She felt a slight tug of relief. As far as odds went, that wasn't *too* bad.

"Five to one that it was one of the embryos?" Adam clarified.

"No. That it was Katy's own egg."

Oh, crap.

Katy felt light-headed, like she might faint. What the *hell* had they done? Having her sister's baby was one thing, but to have her own baby, and with Adam of all people? This was crazy!

She wasn't ready to have a child yet, especially not with her sister's husband! A man she loved, whose only interest in her was to produce his offspring.

She had a sudden and disturbing vision of her family up on the stage during a *Jerry Springer* episode.

Her family. Oh, God. How was she going to explain this to her parents? They had been so excited when she called to tell them the good news earlier. They would be furious enough if they knew she had slept with Adam, but to learn she could be having her own baby, not Becca's? They might never speak to her again.

Adam put his hand on her arm. She looked up at him and he gestured to the door. She realized the appointment was over. There was nothing else the doctor could do for them at this point. From now on it would just be a waiting game. At least twelve more weeks.

It sounded like a lifetime.

Her legs felt unsteady as Adam led her out. She only half heard him as he stopped to make next month's appointment, then he ushered her out of the office and to the elevator. He was taking this awfully well.

"I can't believe this is happening," she said, as the elevator doors slid closed. "This is all my—"

"If you say it's your fault one more time, I swear to God I'm going to make you *walk* home," he said sharply, his eyes flashing with anger.

Whoa.

So much for him taking it well. Apparently he was as freaked out as she was. He was just better at hiding it.

He took a deep breath and blew it out. "I'm sorry. I didn't mean to snap. I just think that blaming each other, or ourselves, isn't going to get us anywhere. It's happened, and now we have to figure out the best way to deal with the situation."

She nodded.

Reece was waiting for them when they walked out

of the building. After they got in the limo, Adam asked, "Would you like to stop someplace and get dinner?"

The thought of food made her stomach roil. "I'm really not hungry right now."

"You've hardly eaten a thing all day. It's not healthy to skip meals."

Nor would it be healthy to eat a meal, then barf it back up, which is what would probably happen. "I'll have something later. I promise."

They were silent for the rest of the drive back to his place. She figured they would talk later that evening, after they'd each had a chance to process it, but as they walked inside she was hit with a wave of fatigue so intense she knew she needed to rest first. She was so exhausted she tripped on the foyer step and would have fallen on her face if Adam hadn't caught her by the arm.

"You okay?" he asked, brow creased with worry.

"Just really tired. I think I need to lie down."

"You know we need to talk."

"I know. And I'm not trying to avoid it. Maybe if I sleep for an hour or so, I'll feel better."

"Of course," he said, leading her upstairs to the spare room.

"Would you possibly have an old shirt or something that I can sleep in? I didn't know I would be staying over so I didn't bring extra clothes." She felt uncomfortable enough sleeping here, where this nightmare of a situation had been conceived, she couldn't imagine doing it in her underwear.

"I'm sure I can dig up something." He left for several minutes, then reappeared with a long-sleeved, button-down silk pajama top. "Will this work?"

"That's perfect. Thanks."

"I'll be in my office if you need me." He hesitated by the door, like he wanted to say something else, then he left, closing the door behind him. A second later she heard the muffled sound of him walking down the stairs.

It took all the effort she could muster to change into the pajama top, and though it was way too big for her, it was cool and soft against her skin. And even though it was freshly laundered, it smelled like Adam. That might have excited her if she hadn't been so dead on her feet. It was as if it was all just too much to take in and her body was shutting down. She crawled into bed, under the covers, and must have been out before her head even hit the pillow.

She woke later, feeling drugged and disoriented, not sure where she was, or if it was day or night. She recalled the doctor visit and for a second thought maybe it had all been a terrible dream.

But she was at Adam's house, and it hadn't been a dream. It was very, very real. She looked over at the digital clock, blinking to clear the sleep from her eyes. It read 1:15 a.m.

One-fifteen? She shot up in bed and swung her legs over the side, instantly awake. She and Adam were supposed to talk. He was waiting for her!

Then she realized, he had probably gone to bed already, and their conversation, critical as it would be, would have to wait until morning. She was disappointed, but at the same time relieved. She needed time to think this through, to wrap her head around it, and knowing Adam, he would want to make a decision right away. He would want to begin planning their next move.

She got up and used the bathroom, then brushed her teeth with a spare brush she found in the cabinet. Since she would have to wear the same clothes tomorrow for the drive home, and there was nothing she hated more than not feeling fresh, she washed her panties in the sink and hung them on the towel bar to dry.

She was about to climb back into bed when her stomach let out a hollow rumble, and she realized that she was famished. She recalled how delicious the enchiladas were that they'd had for lunch and wondered if there were any leftovers. She should really eat something. Because as Adam had pointed out, she shouldn't be skipping meals. Cliché and silly as it sounded, she was eating for two now.

She opened the door and peeked out into the hallway. The house was quiet and dark, just as she'd suspected. She felt her way down the stairs and tiptoed through the living room to the kitchen.

"Going somewhere?"

At the unexpected voice she let out a squeal of surprise, and whipped around. Adam was sitting slumped down on the couch, holding something…a drink, she realized. He was sitting in the dark drinking. Not that she could blame him. If alcohol wasn't bad for the baby, she would be drowning in it by now.

"I woke up hungry," she said. "I was going to get something to eat."

As her eyes adjusted, she could see that he was shirtless, and wearing what looked like a pair of pajama bottoms.

Oh, my.

"I thought you'd gone to bed," she said.

"Couldn't sleep."

Well, that was understandable. She wondered if he was upset, or even angry with her. It was too dark to see his individual features so she really couldn't get a read on him.

"I'm sorry I slept for so long."

"S'okay."

"I wasn't trying to avoid you."

"I know."

She took a step closer. "Are you okay?"

"What do you think?"

Fair enough. "Do you want to talk?"

"Actually, I think I'd prefer you take off your clothes."

She actually jerked backward. Was that another joke? "E-excuse me?"

"I want to see you naked."

"N-naked?"

"You said before that if I wanted to see you naked, all I have to do is ask. So I'm asking."

She may have said it, but she didn't actually *mean* it. And never in a million years did she believe he would actually ask. It had to be the alcohol talking. "You're drunk."

"So what if I am?"

"So, you're clearly not thinking straight."

"Isn't that the point of drinking?" He downed the contents of his glass and set it on the table beside him. "Besides, it's not like I haven't seen you naked before."

"Yes, but don't you think it will inevitably lead to something else?"

"Again, that's kind of the point."

Her heart started to hammer. "But we said we wouldn't."

"We said a lot of things, and look where it got us. So get naked, now."

He was only doing this because he was upset and intoxicated. He didn't really want her. Not the way she wanted him. "No. I'm upset, too, but this isn't going to solve anything."

"No, but it'll feel good, and that's enough for me right now. Don't you want to feel good?"

Maybe feeling good wasn't enough for her.

But what if it was? Maybe she could have him just one more time.

No. Bad idea.

"Adam, I'm serious. Stop. We can't do this. I don't want to do this."

"Making love to you again is all I've been able to think about," he said, and his words warmed her from the inside out. Even though she knew he was only saying them because he'd been drinking and his inhibitions were compromised. And even if he had been thinking about it, it was just sex to him. It had nothing to do with love. That's the way it was for men.

The men she knew anyway.

"We shouldn't," she said, but with a dismal lack of conviction. He was starting to wear her down.

"Come here, Katy," he said, in a low growl that set every one of her nerve endings ablaze.

He reached out to grasp her wrist. She put up only the slightest bit of resistance before she let him pull her down into his lap. She was straddling his thighs, his silk pajama pants feeling unbelievably erotic on her bare bottom. Then he kissed her, tangling his fingers through her hair. Tenderly, his lips soft, his mouth sweet and tangy as his tongue slid against hers.

Wait a minute…*sweet?*

She broke the kiss and pulled back to look at him. Where was the alcohol taste? She grabbed the glass he'd been drinking out of and sniffed it. "What was this?"

"Orange juice."

"With vodka?"

"Nope. Just plain old orange juice."

"But…you said you were drunk."

"No, *you* said I was drunk. I just didn't correct you."

"But I thought—"

He didn't let her finish. He covered her lips with his and kissed away whatever she'd been about to say. He stroked and caressed away her doubts, until there was nothing left but raw need. When he pulled the pajama top up over her head and saw that she wasn't wearing panties, he growled low in his throat. "I think you forgot something."

"I didn't have a clean pair for tomorrow, so I washed them out in the sink."

"Lucky me," he murmured as he dipped his head to take her nipple in his mouth. Her entire being shuddered with ecstasy.

Adam lifted her off his lap and laid her down on the cushions, settling beside her, then he was kissing her again. Her lips and her throat, her breasts. He tortured her with nips and love bites, until she was burning up with need. He worked his way downward, across her stomach, then lower still.

She was no stranger to oral sex, although she wasn't usually the one on the receiving end. And on the rare occasion she'd been in the hot seat, the truth is it hadn't really been that fantastic. More clumsy and awkward than arousing. But as Adam slipped down onto the floor beside her, spreading her thighs to make room for himself, as his tongue lashed out to taste her, she was so close to unraveling she couldn't see straight.

Then a light switched on in the kitchen, dimly illuminating the room. She and Adam froze as they heard Celia shuffle out of her room. The couch was facing away from the light, so the only way she would know they were there was if she walked into the living room, which wasn't entirely impossible.

She heard Celia get a glass out of the cupboard, and fill it with water. She was frantically trying to recall where Adam had thrown the pajama top when she felt his tongue on her again. She was so surprised she gasped, slapping a hand over her mouth to smother the sound. What the heck was he doing? Did he *want* to get caught?

Getting caught kissing was one thing, but this? This would be absolutely mortifying.

She tried to push his head away, to close her legs, but that only seemed to fuel his determination. He pressed her thighs open even wider, devouring her. Could this possibly be the man her sister claimed wasn't *adventurous* enough? And maybe it was the element of danger, or the sheer stupidity of what they were doing, but the more she tried to fight it, the more turned on she was getting. Then Adam entered her with his fingers, thrusting them deep inside of her, and her control shattered. She buried her face in the cushion to muffle the moan of pleasure she couldn't suppress.

She'd barely had a chance to catch her breath when

the light suddenly went out, and Celia shuffled back to her room behind the kitchen.

The second Katy heard the door close she gave Adam a good hard whack on the top of his head.

"Ow! What was that for?" he said, ducking away from a possible repeat attack.

"Are you crazy?" she hissed, sitting up. "She could have walked in here and seen us."

He was grinning. "But she didn't. And you can't deny that the idea of being caught was arousing as hell."

No, she couldn't deny it. But it wasn't a chance she was willing to take again. "Maybe we should move this party upstairs."

"That's probably not a bad idea."

No, it was. This whole thing was a horrible, horrible mistake. But it was too late now. He'd pleased her, and it was only fair to reciprocate. Right?

And if they were going to do this, they might as well have fun. And worry about the consequences in the morning.

She located the pajama top on the floor and pulled it on, just in case, then turned to Adam, grinning wickedly, and said, "Last one there is a rotten egg."

Twelve

Katy darted up the stairs, and Adam took off after her, catching up just outside the bedroom where she'd been sleeping. He hooked his arms around her waist, trapping her against him, and tugged in the direction of his bedroom. She pulled away from him, looking hesitant.

Confused, he asked, "What's the matter?"

"Where are we going?"

"My bedroom."

"Not there."

Because it wasn't just his bedroom, he realized. It was Becca's.

He didn't try to explain that while it was Becca's room, too, the bed itself had to be replaced due to her illness. And that even before that, he and Becca hadn't exactly shared a lot of passionate nights there.

But he didn't want to make Katy uncomfortable,

so when she took his hand and led him into the spare room, he let her.

She pulled the pajama top off and walked backward toward the bed, summoning him with a crooked finger. And when he got there she shoved him backward onto the mattress. The sheets were cool against his skin and smelled like her. He tried to pull her down beside him, but she straddled his legs instead. Her skin was flush with arousal, her nipples puckered tight. Her hair hung down in mussed curls that grazed the tops of her breasts. He'd never seen anything so sexy in his life.

She ran her hands down his chest, raking his skin with her nails. "I want to see you naked."

"All you had to do was ask," he said with a grin, and she tugged his pajama bottoms down and off his legs. Then she just stared at his erection in awe, as though she'd never seen one before.

She must have noticed his curious expression, because she said, "I didn't get a good look the other night." She reached out and wrapped her hand around him, slowly stroking from base to tip, then back down again. "I've never seen one this big. Not that I've seen a lot of them. Only three, besides yours."

That surprised him. Not that he thought Katy was the kind to sleep around, but she had a way about her that was blatantly sexual. Like the way she was casually running her thumb over the head of his erection, making it really tough to concentrate on the conversation. "That's not many," he said.

"You know, I didn't lose my virginity until I was nineteen."

Another surprise. "Really?"

"I had done a lot of fooling around before then, but

I planned to wait until I was married to actually seal the deal."

She gave him a gentle squeeze and his breath caught. "So why didn't you?"

"Because it occurred to me around then that it could take a long time to find Mr. Right, and I figured if fooling around felt good, actual sex would feel even better."

"Did it?"

She shrugged. "Not at first. But then sometimes it did, depending on who I was with. But that never really mattered because I'm completely capable of taking care of my own needs if necessary."

He didn't know who these men were she was sleeping with, but it would be a cold day in hell when he let a woman he was with "take care of her own needs."

"Is it weird that I'm telling you this?" she asked.

"Oddly enough, no." Even though he was having an increasingly difficult time concentrating on what she was saying. His gaze was fixed on her hand, sliding slowly up and down his shaft.

"When did you lose your virginity?" she asked.

"I was sixteen."

"Seriously?"

"She was eighteen."

"Ah, an older woman. Did it last?"

"About fifteen seconds."

She laughed. "I meant the relationship."

"That *was* the relationship." And he wouldn't last much longer than that now if she kept stroking him that way. "We hooked up at a party. I never saw her again."

"I've never had a one-night stand. Unless you count ten days ago." Letting go of his erection, she ran her hands up his stomach, over his chest. "But I guess after tonight we'll have to relabel it. Is there such a thing as a two-night stand?"

He didn't see any reason to slap a label on it. It was what it was.

She gazed down at him, lids heavy, cheeks rosy. "I like talking to you. And I like that you're willing to open up to me. I know that's not easy for you."

Not only did she like it, he realized that talking like this was turning her on. Like verbal foreplay.

A woman who got off on conversation. Who would have imagined? But he needed more. Less talk and more action. He needed to get his hands on her body, to be inside of her. It was all he'd been able to think about since that first time ten days ago. Looking back on it now, he should have realized that this was inevitable. That once was never going to be enough. "Why don't you make love to me," he said.

Her honey-dipped smile said she thought that was a pretty good idea. "Like this? With me on top?"

"However you'd like." On top, on the bottom. Upside down or sideways, he didn't really care.

She rose up onto her knees, flush with anticipation and centered herself over him, then she sank down, taking him inside of her, inch by excruciating inch, until he was as far as he could go. She was hot and wet and tight.

She looked down at him, and smiled. "Hmm, that's nice."

She took the words right out of his mouth. She started to move, riding him slowly, as though she had all the time in the world. Her eyes drifted closed, head rolled back. She looked completely lost in the sensation, and he was so fascinated watching her, his own pleasure seemed almost insignificant. He was content to let her use him as long as she wanted, stroking everything he could reach. Her thighs, her stomach, her breasts. Every part of her soft and feminine.

She took one of his hands and guided it between her legs, where their bodies were joined. He rubbed her there, and she started whimpering, making soft breathy sounds. She began to tremble all over and he knew she was almost there. Then her body clamped down hard around him, clenching and releasing. Watching her come was the most erotic thing he'd ever seen, and just like that he lost it. It was sexual release like he'd never felt before, hot pulsations that robbed him of the ability to do anything but feel.

Katy crumpled into a heap on his chest, curling herself around him. He could feel her heart hammering just as hard as his own. As much as he hated to admit it, sex with Becca had never been like this. She had always been too uptight, too worried that she would disappoint him to just let loose and have fun. And when they were trying to get pregnant, sex became a job. Then she was diagnosed and that put an end to their sex life altogether.

Maybe he should have felt bad comparing the two, and guilty knowing that, as much as he loved Becca, Katy was everything he'd always hoped his wife would be in the bedroom. But he didn't. Everything else was so screwed up, this seemed to be the only thing that made any sense. Even though it made no sense at all.

Maybe this was wrong, and he would regret it someday. All he knew was that for the past three years since Becca died he'd barely been able to look at another woman. Not a day passed that he didn't ache from missing his wife. But when he was with Katy he could forget for a while. He finally felt…at peace.

It was too bad that it had to end.

Katy woke the next morning and reached for Adam, but he wasn't there. She sat up and looked at the clock, surprised that it was almost nine-thirty. She was usually up at the crack of dawn. Of course, it had almost been the crack of dawn when Adam finally let her go to sleep.

The man had an insatiable sexual appetite, not to mention the stamina of someone half his age. After the third time she even started to wonder if he'd swallowed a couple of Viagra. Until he mentioned that, before their first night together, it had been *four* years, and suddenly it made sense. She didn't even know men could go that long without sex. She had just assumed he'd been with women since Becca died. But he was sure making up for lost time.

Now it was that dreaded morning after, and as exciting and, for lack of a better word, *magical,* as it had been, they had to face reality. Not to mention the situation with the baby.

She rolled out of bed and took stock of the room. Blankets askew, sheet pulled off the mattress in one corner. Celia was going to walk in and know instantly that they'd had wild sex all night. Of course, they hadn't exactly been quiet, so it was possible she'd figured it out for herself already.

Just in case, Katy spent a few minutes straightening things up, then took a long, hot shower. She half hoped that Adam had gone to work, even though she knew delaying the conversation they needed to have wouldn't make it any easier. But he was sitting at the kitchen table drinking coffee and reading the *Wall Street Journal.* She'd expected him to be dressed for work, but he was wearing chinos and a polo shirt with the Western Oil logo on it. His hair was damp, so he must have gotten up not long before she did. It was the first time she had seen him wear anything but a suit or slacks and a dress shirt. In fact, she had begun to question whether he even owned any casual clothes. Apparently he did, and damned if he didn't look delicious in them.

When he heard her enter the room he looked up and said, "Good morning."

"Mornin'."

"There's coffee," he said.

"I can't. You know, the baby."

"I made decaf."

"Oh. Thanks."

"Sit down. I'll pour you a cup."

She took a seat across from his, while he got up and poured her coffee. She couldn't tell if she should be uncomfortable or not. She was having a tough time reading him.

He set a steaming cup of black coffee in front of her and asked, "Are you hungry? I could make eggs or something."

"I didn't know billionaire oil men cooked."

"They do if they're hungry and their housekeeper is running errands. Or if you don't trust my cooking, I could take you out."

"I think maybe we should just talk instead."

He sat across from her. "Okay, let's talk."

She sat there for a minute and realized, they had so

many things to cover, she wasn't even sure where to begin. "Where should we start?"

"Why don't we start with us."

She grimaced. She had really hoped that was the one part they wouldn't have to talk about. And she knew that as much as she wanted there to be, there was no "us."

"I think we both know that this has the potential to get very complicated," he said.

It already was. "Look," she said. "Last night was great, but it never should have happened. Things are just so…jumbled up. We let our emotions get the best of us."

He looked relieved. "I'm glad you feel that way."

She knew he would be. She was letting him off easy. Giving him an out. Of course he would take it.

"But I want us to be friends," he said.

The "let's still be friends" speech. How many times had she heard that one? She gazed into the inky depths of her cup, so he wouldn't see how much this was hurting her.

And let's face it, even if he suddenly decided that he wanted a wife, that he wanted *her,* she would never cut it as the future Mrs. Adam Blair. He was way out of her league. Not to mention that he was here, and she was in Peckins. It was an impossible situation.

"Katy?"

"We could be having a baby together. That means we're more or less stuck with each other."

He arched one brow. "You make it sound pretty awful."

Because for her it would be. For a while anyway. But it was imperative he didn't know that. Because then he would feel guilty, and things would get uncomfortable. That was the last thing she wanted.

She forced a smile. "That's not what I meant. And of course we'll be friends."

"After talking to Dr. Meyer, I think we have to face the fact that it probably is ours."

"I know I said that I wasn't ready for a child of my own, but now that it's a possibility...I could never just hand it over to you."

He reached across the table and curled his hands over hers. She wished he would stop doing that. Stop touching her. He was only making it harder. "Katy, I would *never* expect you to do that. If it's our baby, we'll figure out a way to make it work."

Our baby. Hearing him say that gave her shivers.

She pulled her hands from his, before she did something stupid, like throw herself in his arms and *beg* him to love her. To at least try.

"What about the surrogacy agreement?" she asked.

"Null and void, I guess. We'll have to work out some kind of custody agreement and child support. But I don't want you to worry. Financially, everything will be taken care of."

Custody and child support? What a nightmare.

"I don't want to wait for the birth for the DNA test," she told him. "I want to do the amnio. As soon as possible."

"The doctor said there are risks. Is it really that critical to know so soon?"

Not for him, maybe. But it was for her. "I need to know what to feel."

He frowned. "I don't understand."

"Either way, this is your baby. You're the father.

But what am I? The baby's mother or just the aunt? I can't bear spending nine months thinking I'm going to have my own child, only to find that I have no maternal rights."

"I guess I never thought of it like that. Of course we'll do the amnio."

And until then she would just have to try to stay partial, try not to get too attached. Just in case. Because having her heart broken again so soon would be more than even she could bear.

"I also think we shouldn't talk about this with anyone but the doctor," she told him. "Not until we get the results. I can't put my parents through that."

Although, ironically, they were in the same situation as Adam. Whether it was Becca's baby or Katy's, it was still their grandchild. Only Katy's dilemma was unique.

"Whatever you want," Adam said. "I know this isn't what either one of us signed on for, but we'll make this work, Katy. Everything will be okay."

Eventually, she hoped.

She looked up at the clock, saw how late it was getting and said, "I really need to get home."

"You don't have to run off."

Oh, no, she did. The longer she stayed here, the more her heart hurt. "I have to get back to the ranch, and you probably have to get to work."

"I have been taking a lot of time off lately."

She took a swallow of coffee then got up and dumped what was left in the sink.

Adam got up, too. "I'll walk you out."

It was another scorcher, and she found herself looking forward to the cooler weather of autumn. She opened the truck door and turned to say goodbye, and Adam was right behind her. Startled, she stumbled backward and hit the front seat with the small of her back. He stepped closer, caging her in, and suddenly she couldn't breathe, couldn't think straight. And he knew it.

"One last kiss?" he asked, but he was already leaning in, taking charge.

No, no, please don't do this, she begged silently, but then his lips were on hers, and Lord help her, she couldn't deny him. His arms went around her, crushing her against the solid wall of his body. His fingers tangled in her hair. And she melted.

"Come back inside with me," he whispered against her lips. "Just one more time, and I promise I'll never ask again."

She wanted to, more than he would ever know. But she couldn't. Her heart was already splitting in two. He thought they'd had really awesome, no-strings-attached sex. But the strings were there, invisible to the naked eye, and she had to back away, before she became hopelessly entangled.

Adam watched Katy drive away, feeling…conflicted. Which was not a familiar feeling. He didn't want her to leave, and at the same time, he knew it was for the best. He cared about Katy. And though she was trying to hide it, he could see that she had pretty strong feelings for him. The last thing he wanted to do was hurt her. Especially now.

"I hope you know what you're doing."

He spun around to find Celia standing in the front

doorway watching him. "Your note said you were running errands."

"I was. Then I got home."

Great. "You could have said something."

"But then I wouldn't have been able to eavesdrop, would I?"

At least she wasn't shy about admitting it. "How long have you been here?"

She folded her arms across her chest. "Long enough."

Long enough to hear something that was putting that disapproving look on her face. The look that, since he was a small boy, always preceded a firm lecture.

He really wasn't in the mood.

"I assume you don't plan to marry her," she said.

"That would be a correct assumption. We don't even know for sure that the baby is hers."

"And if it is?"

He wouldn't marry her then, either.

She stared at him, tight-lipped.

"Don't do that," he said, walking past her into the house. "I'm not a kid any longer."

She slammed the door. "Then stop acting like one."

Wow, he hadn't seen her this angry in a long time. Not since the time he stole the headmaster's keys, took his Beamer for a spin, then crashed it into a tree. His father, whose attention he'd been trying to get, had been too busy to come get him, so he'd sent Celia. And boy was she pissed. Just like now.

And for what?

"I really don't see why you're so upset," he said.

"I'm upset because I like Katy, and you're breaking her heart."

"That's ridiculous." He walked to the kitchen and she followed him. This had nothing to do with Katy's heart. "She's understandably upset. It's a complicated situation."

"She's upset because she loves you, *estúpido*. And you're too much of a chicken to admit what you know is the truth."

He took a sip of his coffee, but it was cold, so he dumped it in the sink. When he turned back to her, she was staring at him. He sighed. "Okay, I'll bite. What *is* the truth?"

"That she could very well be the best thing that has ever happened to you! She's your soul mate."

An unexpected surge of emotion had him turning toward the window. "I buried my soul mate three years ago."

She stepped up behind him, touched his shoulder. "You buried your wife," she said softly, "but not your soul mate."

That wasn't the way he saw it.

"How long are you going to keep her up on a pedestal, pretending everything was perfect? I cared for Becca, and I know you loved her in your own way, but you were never half as happy with her as you are with Katy. You have this light in your eyes when you talk about her, and you probably don't realize it, but you talk about her a lot. And when you're with her…it's just so obvious that you two are meant to be together."

Celia was obviously seeing things that weren't really there. It was no secret that she hadn't been crazy about the idea of him marrying Becca. She never thought they were a good match. But she had been good to Becca nonetheless. Even when Becca sometimes hadn't been so nice to her. Becca wanted to be his entire universe and she'd been jealous of his relationship with Celia.

And yes, they'd had difficult times, and marital troubles, and instead of facing them he'd buried himself in work instead. But that wasn't her fault. He hadn't given their marriage a chance to be better.

And if he had, if they'd had a perfect marriage and had been blissfully happy, losing her would have been even more unbearable.

"I won't bury another wife," he told Celia.

"You don't get to choose who you love. The question is whether or not you accept that love."

"I'm content with my life just the way it is, and when the baby is here, it will be perfect."

"You really believe that?"

"I *know* that." He looked at his watch. "Now, I need to get to work."

She frowned and shook her head, as if she was thoroughly disappointed in him. But the last thing he needed was her playing matchmaker.

Did he have feelings for Katy? Of course. Could he love her? Without a doubt, but that didn't mean he should allow it. He wouldn't make that mistake again.

Thirteen

Though he planned to hold off until their regular manager's meeting, Adam couldn't wait to announce his good news. And after speaking with the rest of the board of directors, it was agreed that the sooner he set things in motion, the better. Though it meant shuffling a few meetings around, he gathered everyone in his office later that afternoon.

"I have a bit of good news," he said, then added, "Personal news," gaining the rapt attention of everyone. "I'm going to be a father."

Emilio grinned, while Nathan and Jordan just looked stunned.

"I wasn't even aware you were seeing anyone. Much less seriously enough to father a child," Nathan said, obviously anticipating a public-relations nightmare on the horizon. "Tell me she isn't the daughter of anyone important. Or, God forbid, underage."

Adam laughed. Leave it to him to expect the worst. "There's no scandal here. It's mine and Rebecca's child."

Nathan blinked. "Oh."

Jordan looked confused. "How is that possible?"

Adam told them about the embryos, and Katy's offer to carry the baby. For now, that was all they needed to know.

A lot of backslapping and handshakes followed, but he wasn't finished yet.

"There's something else. Something I'll be announcing formally in a few months. But I wanted to tell you all first. After the baby is born, I'm stepping down as CEO of Western Oil."

Three mouths fell open in unison.

"Stepping down?" Nathan asked. "You live for this company."

"I'll still be on the board. I just won't be as involved in the day-to-day operations. I want to be there for my child."

"Had you considered hiring a nanny?" Nathan asked.

"I could do that," Adam said. "But I promised myself a long time ago that when I had children, I would be there for them. Not a ghost, like my father. Especially since I'm raising this child on my own."

"Which raises the question, will you look outside the company for a replacement, or promote from within?" Emilio asked, getting to the heart of the matter.

"I've already spoken to the board. It was agreed that we would promote from within."

The three men exchanged glances. That meant that for the next eight months they would be under a veritable microscope, their every decision and act used to judge them. Three friends—two of them family—in competition for the brass ring. It had the potential to get very ugly. How they all handled the stress would be a determining factor to the board's decision.

"So who would you choose?" Nathan asked, knowing that the board would most likely follow Adam's lead.

"I won't make a choice until the board votes," he told them. "Until then everyone has an equal shot at the position. In essence, my choice will depend on your performance for the next eight months."

"No pressure there," Jordan said wryly.

"This position *is* pressure," Adam told him. "And as you all know I have a lot vested in this company. We all do. If not for each one of you, it wouldn't be what it is today."

"I think we all know who will get it," Nathan said. "You and Emilio are good friends. He's obviously got the advantage."

"This is business," Adam said. "Friendship has nothing to do with it."

"Not to mention that I'm going to leave you guys in the dust," Jordan said smugly, with a smile that said he was as good as in. His brother glared, but was smart enough to keep his mouth shut.

"Any questions?" Adam asked, but everyone seemed pretty clear on the way things would be until the decision was made.

When the meeting was over, Emilio hung back. "I

just wanted to say congratulations again. I know this is something you've wanted for a long time."

Adam gestured for him to close the door. He'd promised Katy he wouldn't tell anyone the truth, but Emilio was one of his closest friends. He knew he could trust him to keep their secret.

Emilio shut the door and sat back down.

"What I said about the baby being mine and Becca's, that might not be the case."

He frowned. "Whose is it, then?"

"Mine and Katy's."

"You slept with her?"

"The day the embryos were transferred the second time. The doctor says there's a five-to-one chance Katy's egg was fertilized."

Emilio shook his head and muttered something in Spanish. "Maybe this was inevitable."

Inevitable? "What do you mean?"

"A man doesn't talk about a woman constantly unless he's attracted to her."

Had he really talked about her so much that both Celia and Emilio took notice? Without even realizing it?

"What are you going to do now?" Emilio asked.

"The only thing we can do. Have a DNA test, and if it is Katy's, share custody."

"You won't marry her?"

Emilio had no business lecturing him on marriage. "I'm surprised you would even ask that. Especially when you're so against marriage."

Emilio shrugged. "I'm not the marrying type. You are."

He *was*. But not anymore. "You know damn well I'm never getting married again."

"I know you've said that."

"But you obviously don't believe it."

"I believe you have a responsibility to the child. And its mother."

"And if you were in my position? Would you ask her to marry you?"

"Of course."

Adam was stunned. "You don't believe in marriage."

"No, but in my culture it's a matter of pride for a man to take responsibility for his actions," he said, then added sheepishly, "And if I didn't, my mother would probably disown me."

"So you think I should marry her."

"What I think doesn't matter."

Then why all the unsolicited advice? What the hell was with everyone lately? First Celia, now Emilio?

"This is getting really complicated."

"You slept with your deceased wife's sister and you're having a baby. At what point did you think it *wouldn't* be complicated?"

He had a point.

"Look," Emilio said. "You've had a rough couple of years. I just think that you deserve to be happy." He looked at his watch and pushed himself up from his chair. "And speaking of being happy, I have a date with a lovely *older* woman."

"Older?"

"My mother," he said with a grin.

"You have my sympathies." Monthly trips to the opera were one part of his marriage Adam didn't miss.

Becca insisted they keep box seats. He used the time to either check email on his phone, or take a nap.

Emilio chuckled. "Not all men hate opera."

No, but he was betting more than half were only there for their wives. Although he had come to suspect that Becca favored the social aspect of the experience over the actual performance. She was big on flaunting their wealth, and always obsessed with wearing clothes from whichever up-and-coming designer was in favor at the time. She routinely spent the entire day in the salon getting her hair and nails and makeup fixed. He could never figure out why she couldn't be content to just be herself. Like Katy.

He did not just think that. Maybe he *was* too preoccupied with her.

Emilio was at the door when Adam asked, "Before you go, can I ask you a question?"

"Of course."

"Before Becca got sick, did I seem happy?"

Emilio frowned. "I'm not sure what you mean."

"Did you think we had a good marriage?"

He considered that, as though choosing his words carefully. "I recall thinking that if you were happy, you would have spent less time at work, and more with your wife."

"You work as much as I do."

"But I don't have a wife at home."

Another good point.

"Out of curiosity, why do you ask?"

"Celia said something this morning…" He shrugged. "You know what, never mind. Have fun tonight."

Emilio looked like he wanted to say more, but he knew Adam well enough not to push.

When he was gone, Adam glanced at the phone. Talking about Katy made him want to pick it up and call. She'd text messaged him earlier to say that she had gotten back home safely, so he really had no reason to call her. Maybe all he wanted was to hear her voice.

Which was exactly why he didn't do it.

Adam managed to hold out a week before he stumbled across a legitimate excuse to call Katy. He was reading an article on the internet about prenatal DNA testing, and a safer, less invasive method was mentioned.

He called her cell but it went straight to voice, so he tried the ranch phone instead. Katy's mom answered.

"Well, hello, Adam. What a pleasant surprise. How have you been?"

"Good. Busy."

"You know, we didn't get a chance to congratulate you. We were so pleased to hear that it worked the second time. I did some reading on the subject online and it sounds as though you and Katy were quite lucky."

Not as much as she might think.

"Is she there?" he asked.

"She's out running errands for her father, but she has her cell with her. Do you have the number?"

"I tried her cell but it went right to voice mail." He hoped the errands didn't involve any heavy lifting. She had to be careful not to overexert herself.

"There are a lot of holes in the service out here. She was probably driving through a dead zone."

What was the point of even having a cell phone if there was no reception? What if she got into an accident, or broke down? He would have to look into getting her a satellite phone.

"Don't forget, we still owe you that supper," she told him. "We'd just love it if you came up to see us. It's only right we celebrate together. We could make a day of it."

"I'd like that," he said, surprised by the realization that he actually meant it.

"You're welcome anytime. You know we don't stand on formality here. You just jump in your car and head up whenever the mood strikes."

"I'll do that."

"You're family, Adam. Don't ever forget that."

He had a sudden and unexpected lump in his throat. Her parents had every reason to think the worst of him, yet they still considered him one of them.

It was sad that Becca never understood what an extraordinary family she had, and he regretted not insisting she make more of an effort to keep in touch.

He regretted a lot of things about their marriage, and only recently had he begun to realize that.

"When Katy gets in could you tell her I called?"

"Will do, Adam. You take care."

He hung up and tried her cell again, this time leaving a message. "Hey, Katy, it's me. I found some interesting information about DNA testing that I want to discuss with you. Call me when you get this."

He answered a few emails while he waited for her to call him back. But after an hour passed, he began to wonder if she'd gotten his message. He dialed her cell, once again getting her voice mail.

"Me again," he said. "I just wanted to make sure you got my last message. Call me."

She was probably on the road, he figured, and wouldn't check her messages until she got home. Which was fine, since she shouldn't be driving and talking on her phone at the same time anyway. No point in taking chances.

He immersed himself in work, and before he knew it, it was nearly five o'clock. Katy hadn't called yet, but he was sure she had to be home by now. He tried her cell, but again it went straight to voice.

He dialed the ranch, and her mother answered again. "She's here, Adam, but she's out in the north pasture with her father. As soon as she gets inside I'll tell her you called. It shouldn't be more than an hour."

He waited one and a half, then he got caught up in an overseas call that ate another hour. When he was finished Bren buzzed him.

"Ms. Huntley called."

"Why didn't you tell me?" he snapped, and realized he'd just bit her head off unjustly. She had strict instructions that unless it was a dire emergency she was not to interrupt overseas calls.

"Sorry," he said. "Long day."

He picked up the phone and called Katy back again.

"You mean she didn't call you?" her mother said, sounding surprised. "I gave her your message."

"No, she did. But I was on an overseas call. Is she there now?"

"No. She left about ten minutes ago. She went to see a movie with her friend Willy."

Willy? "Willy Jenkins?"

"That's right."

He felt his hackles rise. She was with Willy "Friends-with-Benefits" Jenkins? The idea of what they might do after the film made his blood pressure skyrocket.

"I'll probably be asleep when she gets in, but I'll leave a message that you called."

Meaning she was expecting Katy to be late. "I'd appreciate that," he told her, jaw tense. He hung up and shoved himself back from his desk. As long as she was pregnant with *his* child she had no business sleeping with *anyone*. Who knows what kind of diseases or viruses this Willy person could have contracted? The way she made it sound, he wasn't one to turn down a casual roll in the hay. He could have slept with dozens of women.

He distinctly recalled that when she offered to do this for him, she agreed to practice abstinence.

The only exception to that particular rule was if the man she was sleeping with was *him*.

After playing phone tag for the better part of the next day, Katy finally got a hold of Adam around seven. Her parents were outside so she curled up on the couch with the cordless phone.

Though she had tried hard to keep him off her mind, she'd missed him. Missed hearing his voice.

"Hi, it's me," she said when he answered.

"Well, you're a tough woman to get a hold of," he said sharply.

She was so taken aback she was speechless. And hurt. They hadn't talked in almost a week, and when they finally did he was a jerk. He was clearly upset with her, but she couldn't imagine what she'd done.

"I've been calling you for two days," he said. "I guess you've been busy."

"Busy?"

"Going on dates with Willy Jenkins."

Dates? Is that what this was about? Her mom must have mentioned she went to the movies last night when she talked to him. Although she would hardly call it a date. "You have a problem with me going to the show with a friend?"

"I do if you're sleeping with him."

Sleeping with him? Where the heck had that come from? Her mom sure hadn't told him *that*. "Who told you I was sleeping with him?"

"You did."

"I did? When?"

"That day in the coffee shop. You said you were 'friends with benefits.'"

Yes, but that was years ago, and… Oh, good Lord. She slapped a hand over her mouth to stifle a giggle.

Was he jealous? Of *Willy?*

The billionaire oil man was threatened by a lowly ranch hand? Adam must have been sitting around all day stewing in his own juices.

It was such a ridiculous notion, and he had himself in such a lather, she couldn't resist poking the lion with a stick.

"What makes you think it's any of your business *who* I sleep with?" she asked him.

"As long as you're pregnant with my child, it's my business."

"How do you figure?"

"We had an agreement that you would practice abstinence while you were pregnant."

They did? She didn't recall agreeing to that. But since she'd had no plans to sleep with *anyone*—not even him—it never seemed relevant anyway. "So I should be practicing abstinence, unless I'm having sex with you? Is that it?"

There was a pause, then he said, "That's different."

Behind her someone cleared their throat, and she snapped her head around to find her mom standing in the kitchen doorway. The woman was stealthy as a damned cat. And it was clear, by her expression, that she'd heard what Katy said about sleeping with Adam.

Well, damn it all to hell.

Fourteen

"Adam, I need to call you back," Katy said.

"Why?" he demanded.

"Because I do."

"We need to discuss this," he barked, like he was issuing an executive order.

"I know we do. It'll just be a few minutes."

"What's so important you can't talk to me right now?"

At the end of her patience, she said, "Willy is here for a quickie, that's what!"

She hung up on him and dropped the phone on the couch beside her.

Her mom stood in the kitchen doorway, arms folded, shaking her head. "That was real mature."

Not one of her finer moments, but he was sort of asking for it.

The phone immediately began to ring. Her mom walked over to the couch, picked it up and answered. "Well, hello, Adam." She paused then said, "She's not feeling too well. Morning sickness, I'm afraid."

Another pause, then she said, "Yes, I know it's not morning. They just call it that, but it can happen anytime of day. I'll have her call you back when it passes."

She hung up and sat down beside Katy.

"I fell hard and fast, just like you said I would," Katy admitted. "So go ahead, say I told you so."

"Would it make you feel better if I did?"

She sighed and collapsed back against the couch cushions. "Probably not."

"Are you…*seeing* him?"

"He didn't want me." She shrugged, suddenly on the verge of tears. "What else is new, right?"

"Oh, honey." She gathered Katy in her arms and hugged her.

"I guess I should have listened to you."

"At least now I know why you've been moping around for a week." She paused, then asked, "Did he… seduce you?"

"He was a perfect gentleman," she admitted, as if she wasn't ashamed enough. "This was my fault. I don't know what I was thinking. I guess I *wasn't* thinking."

"It'll be easier after you have the baby. You won't have to see him at all if you don't want to."

Now that her mom knew about the affair, not fessing up to the rest of it felt like lying. "Actually, I might be stuck seeing him a lot. For at least the next nineteen years."

"What do you mean?"

"There's a pretty good chance that my own egg was fertilized."

She braced for the fireworks, but instead her mom hugged her tighter. "Oh, Katy. Why didn't you say something?"

"I thought you would be angry. And I was embarrassed that I screwed things up so badly."

"How does Adam feel about this?"

"He's been wonderful. Besides breaking my heart, but that isn't his fault. I know how you and Daddy feel about him, but he's not the person you think he is. Rebecca lied to us, Mom. About a lot of things."

"Katy—"

"I know you don't want to believe it. I didn't, either. But Adam told me things, and he has no reason to lie."

"I don't find that so hard to believe," she said, sounding sad.

"We don't have to tell Daddy about the baby, do we?" Katy asked.

"Your father and I don't keep secrets."

"He's going to be furious. And he's going to want to kill Adam."

"Give him a little credit. He may be upset at first, but he'll be reasonable. I do think it will be easier to swallow coming from me."

She was so relieved she felt limp. "When are you going to tell him?"

"I'll talk to him tonight, when we go up to bed. That way he'll have all night to mull it over before he talks to you."

She threw her arms around her mother and hugged her. "Thank you. For being so understanding. I thought you would be so disappointed in me."

"Oh, sweetheart, you've been the best daughter a mother could ask for. It would take an awful lot to disappoint me."

Katy rested her head on her mother's shoulder, breathed in the scent of her perfume. Avon Odyssey. She'd worn the same fragrance as long as Katy could remember. It was familiar and comforting.

"So, does Adam know how you feel about him?"

"What's the point? Even if he felt the same way, it would never work. We're too different."

"Different how?"

"He's rich and sophisticated, and I'm not."

"So, you think he's better than you?"

"Not better, but we want different things out of life. Not to mention that he's in El Paso. And I'm happy right here, where I am." She sat back and looked at her mother. "Aren't you the one who told me that he's not like us?"

"I guess I did." She touched Katy's cheek. "I just don't like to see my baby unhappy. And like you said, maybe he's not the man we thought he was. He must be pretty special if you fell for him."

"Well, it's all a moot point because Adam said himself that he'll never get married again. And even if he did, if he wanted me, I would always feel as though I was competing with Rebecca. I don't think she had a clue how lucky she was."

"Probably not. Your sister took a lot of things for granted."

She sat snuggled up to her mom, like she had when she was little, and found herself wishing she could go back to those days. When things were so much less complicated, and her life actually made sense.

"You should probably call Adam back," her mom said.

Yeah, and she should probably apologize for the "quickie" remark. In all fairness, if their roles were reversed, she wouldn't be too keen on the idea of the mother of her child sleeping around.

It wasn't Adam's fault that she'd fallen for him, so it wasn't right to take out her frustrations on him.

"I'll call him right now."

Her mom gave her one last firm squeeze, then got up from the couch. Katy hit Redial, expecting Adam to be fuming by now, but when he answered he sounded humbled.

"Are you okay?" he asked.

"I'm fine."

"I owe you an apology," he said, totally stunning her. "I overreacted. I'm used to being in charge, being in control, and with you so far away, I'm feeling a little…well, helpless, I guess."

She knew that hadn't been easy for him to admit. "I'm sorry, too. That remark about Willy was uncalled for. Of course you have every right to be concerned. And for the record, I'm not sleeping with him or anyone else. Nor do I intend to."

"I don't suppose you would reconsider moving here until the baby is born."

Good Lord, what a nightmare that would be. As if this wasn't complicated and heartbreaking enough. "I can't, Adam."

"Just thought I would ask."

"And, just so you know, I wasn't sick. My mom overheard what I said about us sleeping together, and I could tell she wanted an explanation."

"How much did you tell her?"

"Everything."

She could practically feel him grimacing. "I thought you wanted to wait until we knew for sure."

"I did, but not telling her started to feel like lying. And she took it surprisingly well."

"What about your dad?"

"She's telling him tonight. He may not take it so well."

"He doesn't happen to keep firearms around?"

She smiled. "Yeah, but he hasn't pulled his rifle on anyone since I was sixteen and he caught me behind the stable kissing one of the ranch hands."

"You are kidding. Right?"

"Nope. Not only did the guy get fired on the spot, I think he had to go change his shorts."

"I guess I should watch my back, then."

"Nah. If my dad was going to take you down it would be in the chest. Or if he really wanted you to suffer, the gut."

"Now you *are* kidding," he said, but he sounded a little nervous.

She laughed. "Yeah, I'm kidding."

"So, you've been feeling okay?"

"I've been feeling great."

They eased into a conversation about her pregnancy, and he told her about the test he'd read of on the internet. They made plans to bring it up at her next appointment in three weeks. They ended up talking for almost an hour. She lay in bed later, replaying the conversation over and over, wishing things were different. Both anticipating and dreading her doctor appointment. Sometimes she missed Adam so much, the feeling sat like a stone in her chest. She knew seeing him face-to-face would only make it worse. Yet she longed to be close to him again. And she was terrified that if he got too close, if he wanted to make love again, she wouldn't be able to tell him no.

She tossed and turned all night and woke so late the next morning she missed breakfast, but Elvie kept some scrambled eggs and bacon warm for her. After she ate she went searching and found her mom in the chicken coop.

"Sorry I slept in."

"That's okay. Your body is changing. You need more rest than before. I used to get exhausted in my first few months."

"Is there anything you need me to do before I lock myself in the office?" It was her day to do the payroll and order supplies.

"Nothing I can think of."

Katy turned to leave and her mom added, "I talked with your dad last night."

Katy's heart gave a resounding thud. She had completely forgotten that she was going to break the news. "So, what did he say?"

"He said he sort of had the feeling something was up with the two of you," her father said from behind her. Katy swung around to find him leaning in the coop doorway. "And he said that while he'd prefer to see you married and settled down, a baby is a blessing. No matter whose it is."

"Thank you, Daddy," she said, and all of a sudden she was on the verge of tears.

Then he came over and hugged her and she did start crying.

She felt terrible for thinking he would be angry, and expecting the worst. As far as parents went, hers were pretty darned wonderful. It made her wonder, as she had so many times before, how could Becca have taken them for granted?

As long as she lived, it was a mistake she would never repeat.

The day of Katy's appointment couldn't come fast enough.

Adam told himself it was because he was eager to learn about the baby's progress, but the truth was, he'd missed her. Since their phone conversation, when he'd accused her of sleeping with her friend Willy, they'd been talking a lot more often. Usually in the evenings, after he left work and she finished her chores. He had never been much of a talker. He was more the silent-observer type, but that turned out not to be a problem, because Katy did enough talking for the both of them. And the more they talked, he found himself opening up to her.

It was astounding how different she and Becca really were. While Becca had been complex and at times intractable, Katy was so…uncomplicated. And honest. If she said something, she meant it. There were none of the games women seemed to like to play. He found himself calling more often, making up excuses to talk to her, just so he could hear her voice.

Though he'd known many women in his life, he'd never actually been friends with one. Sadly, he realized, not even Becca. They used to talk when they were first dating, but now he wondered if she was only telling him what she thought he wanted to hear. Katy in contrast didn't pull any punches. If she felt strongly about something, she wasn't afraid to speak her mind. At times quite passionately. But he liked that she challenged him. Because in all honesty, given his position of power in the corporate sector, not many people stood up to him.

He considered her more of an equal than most of his "rich" friends and colleagues.

The day of the appointment, when Reece pulled the limo into the lot at the fertility clinic and saw her truck already parked there, Adam experienced an anticipation that he'd not felt in a very long time. He didn't even wait for Reece to get out and open his door. And when he walked inside and saw her standing near the elevator, something deep inside of him seemed to… settle. Followed promptly by the yearning to pull her into his arms and hold her.

She smiled brightly when she saw him, her skin glowing with good health and happiness. Just the way he imagined a pregnant woman should look. She was dressed in her girls' clothes, and though she looked sexy as hell, he knew she would look even better wearing nothing at all. But the last thing either of them needed was to complicate this situation, and sleeping with her would do just that.

But damn, what he wouldn't give to take a quick nibble of her plump, rosy lips.

"Hi, stranger," she said as he approached her, rising up to give him a quick hug and a peck on the cheek. It took all his willpower not to turn his head so it was his lips she kissed instead. There was an energy that crackled between them. The same sensation of awareness he'd felt when they kissed the first time.

"You look fantastic," he said.

"Thanks. I feel great. My friend Missy is jealous because by this point in all four of her pregnancies she was sick as a dog."

The elevator opened and they stepped inside. He touched her back, to guide her, and electricity seemed to arc between them. And he knew, from the soft breathy sound she made, the slight widening of her eyes, that she felt it, too.

When they signed in at the doctor's office they were called back immediately to an exam room. Adam waited in the hall while she changed into a gown, and he was only in the room a minute or two when Dr. Meyer knocked.

"So how have you been feeling?" he asked Katy. "Any morning sickness?"

"None at all. I feel great. A little tired sometimes, but I just go to bed earlier."

The doctor smiled. "Sounds like a reasonable solution. You've been taking the vitamins I prescribed?"

"Every morning. And our cook has been filling me up on vegetables and whole grains."

"Excellent."

He asked her a few more questions, then took her blood pressure and pulse.

"I need to do an internal exam," he said, looking from Adam to Katy, as if he wasn't sure Adam would be staying or not. And frankly neither was Adam. But Katy smiled and said, "That's fine."

It wasn't as if he hadn't been up close and personal with every conceivable inch of her body anyway, but the doctor was still very discreet.

"Everything seems to be progressing well," he said

when he was finished. "Why don't you get dressed and meet me in my office."

After he stepped out of the room, Adam said, "Thanks for letting me stay."

"I'll bet seeing that makes you pretty happy to be a guy," she joked.

"Men have their own indignities to endure," he said, but spared her the gory details. "I'll wait in the hall for you."

Katy emerged a few minutes later and they walked down the hall to Dr. Meyer's office.

"Do you have any questions for me?" he asked when they were seated.

"We've been reading up on DNA testing," Adam told him, and asked about different options. His opinion was that if they wanted to do the test as soon as possible, the safest way would be through amnio.

"I have a question, too," Katie said. "My mom was telling me how fast her labors were, and since I'm two hours away, I'm wondering what that could mean for me. So far my pregnancy has been just like hers were. I'm afraid that if I go into labor and have to drive all the way to El Paso, I might give birth in the truck."

"I didn't realize you lived so far from here," the doctor said, looking concerned. "Do you have a regular ob-gyn closer to home you could see?"

"I've been seeing Dr. Hogue since I was twelve, and he delivered both me and my sister."

"I know Dr. Hogue. He's a very competent physician."

Adam wasn't sure he liked that. "Shouldn't she be seeing you?"

"Honestly, as long as her pregnancy remains

uneventful—and I have no reason to believe it won't—I see no reason why Katy shouldn't see her regular physician. I'm sure he'll have no problem keeping me apprised of her progress."

Meaning Adam would be driving to Peckins for her appointments instead of Katy coming here.

"Are you upset?" Katy asked him when they left the office and walked down the hall to the elevator.

"Not upset. I wish you would have discussed this with me first."

"I know, and I would have, but it was something my mom brought up this morning before I left. And while I like Dr. Meyer, I think I'll be more comfortable seeing Doc Hogue. He knows me."

Adam could object, and insist she see Meyer, but why? What was his justification?

It would be an inconvenience for him. Though no more than it was for her. And since she was the pregnant one, wasn't it safer if he did the traveling? And she had a valid point about getting to the hospital. "If that's what you want, then of course."

She took his hand and squeezed it, smiling up at him. "Thank you, Adam."

Their eyes met, then locked, and he felt it like a fist to his gut. His palm buzzed, then went hot where it touched hers. He wanted to kiss her. No, he *needed* to. And he was 99 percent sure she was thinking the same thing.

As if caught in a magnetic pull their bodies began to move in closer, her chin tipped upward, and his head dipped....

Then the damned elevator door slid open and people stepped out. Katy jerked back, breaking the spell.

He cursed silently as he followed her on and they rode it down to the first floor. They walked though the lobby and out the door. It was overcast, and thunder rumbled in the distance. The weathermen had been predicting rain.

"Sounds like there's a storm headed this way," he said.

"I better get going," Katy said. "So I beat it home."

"But you just got here. I thought we could spend some time together."

"I really have to go."

Reece pulled up to the curb to meet him, but Adam gestured for him to wait, and followed Katy to where her truck was parked.

"You could at least let me take you to lunch."

"I don't think so." She seemed in an awful hurry to leave, and she wouldn't look at him.

He took her by the arm and turned her to face him. "Katy, what's wrong?"

"I just really need to go."

"Why?"

She glanced around, like she worried someone might be listening. "Because you almost just kissed me, and if I stay, you *will* kiss me."

"Would that be so terrible?"

"Yes, because after you kiss me you'll make up some stupid excuse why I should come to your house, and I will, because at this point my brain will have completely shorted out. And we won't be there thirty seconds before we're naked and…well, you know the rest."

"Would *that* really be so terrible?"

"I'm not a yo-yo. You can't say one minute that it

would complicate things, then try to jump me the next. It's not fair."

She was right. He was sending mixed signals like crazy. He cared for her. More than any other woman he'd been involved with, maybe even Becca, but this relationship had no future. Not a romantic one anyway. To let himself love her, to care that much, would make it that much more unbearable if he ever lost her.

Though he wished it were possible, he couldn't give her what she wanted. What she deserved. A man who would love her, and marry her.

"You're right. I'm sorry."

A bolt of lightning arced across the sky to the south.

"I really have to go," she said.

"You'll call me and let me know when you make your appointment."

"Of course."

"And let me know that you got home safely."

"I will." She hesitated, then rose up to press a kiss to his cheek, lingering a second before she turned and climbed in the truck, and as he watched her back out and drive away, he could swear he saw tears in her eyes.

Fifteen

As soon as Katy got home from El Paso she called and made an appointment with Doc Hogue, then she texted Adam with the date and time, because frankly she was feeling too emotional to talk to him. It took everything in her not to sob all the way home. The way he looked at her...for a minute she let herself believe that he wanted her. As close as they had become lately, she thought he was going to tell her that he'd made a mistake, that he loved her.

Why did she keep doing this to herself? Even if he did love her, there was no rational way to make it work. They could try a long-distance relationship, but that would only last so long before they grew apart. She'd seen it happen before to friends who had boyfriends in the rodeo and the military.

When she chose to be with a man, she wanted be

with him. Not one hundred and fifty miles away. Not that she could be with a man who didn't want to be with her. But she was happy that she and the father of her child—if it *was* her child—would be good friends. Still, she was almost relieved when he called her a week before the doctor appointment to say that he had to fly out of the country and wouldn't make it back till two days after her appointment.

"It's imperative that I go," he told her.

"It's okay," she assured him. "Things happen. Besides, it's only my third month. I seriously doubt anything exciting will happen."

"I wanted to meet the doctor."

"So you'll meet him next month."

But next month didn't happen, either. Two days before her appointment Adam caught a nasty flu virus.

"You sound terrible," she said when he called to tell her, dousing her disappointment.

"I feel terrible," he croaked, his throat so raw and scratchy he could only speak in a coarse whisper.

"Do you have a fever?"

"One hundred and one. Celia won't let me out of bed and she's been force-feeding me chicken soup."

"Good. It sounds like what you need is rest."

"I'm sorry, Katy," he rasped.

"For what?"

"I feel terrible for missing another appointment. Not to mention the amnio. I wanted to be there with you."

And she had wanted him there. She didn't like feeling that she was in this alone. But he couldn't help that she was sick.

"I've heard it's really not that big of a deal. They'll numb me so I won't feel a thing. And, no offense, but I wouldn't want to go anywhere near you right now. The last thing I need is the flu. Just take care of yourself and you'll be better in time for the next appointment."

Her mom went with her to her appointment, and after her checkup, it was off to the hospital for the amnio—which really wasn't all that bad. Doc Hogue had already warned her that it usually took six to eight weeks to get the results—in some cases even longer, and she knew the waiting would be torture.

When she called Adam to tell him the test went well, he sounded relieved. "Nothing will stop me from making the next appointment. I promise."

She hoped that was true. And not just because she wanted to see him, but things were progressing faster than she'd anticipated. Her mom had always said that she started showing early in her pregnancies, so Katy shouldn't have been surprised when, in the last week of her fourth month, she woke up one morning and couldn't fasten her jeans.

"Isn't that supposed to happen?" Adam asked when she called him later that night to complain. "And didn't you tell me that you're not worried about the physical repercussions of pregnancy."

"I don't care about that," she told him. "But there's nothing more I hate than shopping!"

He laughed and called her "unique."

Delaying the inevitable, she wore her jeans with the button unfastened, but after a couple more weeks, when she couldn't get the zipper up more than an inch, and the buttons on her shirts were stretched to the limit, her mom dragged her to the maternity shop for a new wardrobe.

With her next appointment only a week away, Katy

felt torn in two. On one hand, she was anxious to see Adam, on the other, she was dreading it. They talked on the phone almost daily now, but seeing him face-to-face…she was afraid it would be a stark reminder of everything she couldn't have. Would *never* have. And though she had never come right out and told Adam how she felt, she was pretty sure he already knew. She also knew that if he was going to have a change of heart, he'd have had it by now. Losing his mother, then Becca, had done something to him. It had cut him so deeply she didn't think he would ever completely heal. He would never come right out and say it—he was too tough for that—but she knew he was afraid of being hurt again.

The Friday before her five-month checkup, Katy had finished up in the office for the day and was taking an afternoon nap when she woke to the sound of her mom's voice. She stood in the bedroom doorway.

"Wake up, honey. We have a visitor."

She sat up and yawned, rubbing her eyes. "Who?"

"Come down and see for yourself," she said, wearing a smile that made Katy suspect she was up to something.

Katy rolled out of bed and peeked out the window. There was a sporty little red car parked in front of the house. Who did they know who drove a sports car? She stretched to look out toward the barn and saw her father standing by the fence with a man Katy didn't recognize. Not from the back anyway at this distance. He was tall and broad-shouldered, wearing jeans, cowboy boots, a plaid flannel shirt and a black Stetson.

Puzzled, and anxious to meet the mystery man, she

quickly dragged a comb through her sleep-matted hair and brushed her teeth.

She grabbed a sweater and headed downstairs, and as she glanced in the family room on her way out the front door she noticed a duffel bag next to the sofa. Whoever it was, it looked as though they were there for an extended stay. Maybe it was some long-lost cousin or uncle that she didn't know about.

She stepped out onto the porch, checking the car out as she walked past. The plates were Texas, but the car looked totally unfamiliar. And very expensive.

So it was a *rich* long-lost relative.

She crossed the yard to where her father stood with the mystery man, and he must have heard her coming because he suddenly turned in her direction. "There you are, Katy! Look who came to visit."

The man beside him turned, his head lowered so that his face was hidden by the brim of his hat. Then he lifted his chin, and when his face came into view, her heart did a somersault with a triple twist.

"Hello, Katy," Adam said.

Her first instinct was to throw herself into his arms and just hold him, but she restrained herself. Especially with her dad standing there. "What are you doing here? Our appointment isn't until Tuesday."

"I figured if I came early I would be guaranteed not to miss it this time. And your mom is always telling me I should come and stay for a few days. So here I am."

"Well," her dad said, looking from her to Adam. She could tell he was wary of Adam's presence, but he restrained himself from butting in. "I better head in and…see how dinner is coming along."

They both knew that the only part of dinner he ever

participated in was eating it, and he was just making an excuse to leave them alone. But she was grateful.

When he was gone, Adam looked her up and down, eyes wide, and said, "Wow, you look..."

"Pregnant?" she finished for him.

He grinned, and it was so adorable her knees actually went weak. She'd missed seeing him smile. Missed everything about him. "I was going to say fantastic. Pregnancy definitely agrees with you."

She laid a hand on her rounded belly. "Doc Hogue said he's never had a patient who took to it so well. If it wasn't for my belly getting bigger, and the fact that some days I need an afternoon nap, I wouldn't even know that I was pregnant."

He nodded to her belly. "Can I feel?"

This was the part she dreaded. Well, one of the parts. He talked a lot about being anxious to touch her belly, and feel the baby move, and she knew darned well what happened when he put his hands on her. But she couldn't tell him no. Not when it meant so much to him.

"Sure," she said, trying to sound casual, when in reality her heart had begun to pound.

His hand was so big it practically dwarfed her tiny bump, and the warmth of his palm seeped through her shirt to warm her skin. "Have you felt the baby move?"

"Little flutters, but the book says those could just be muscle spasms. No kicks yet. But Doc Hogue said probably soon."

The feel of his hand on her belly was making her go all soft inside, and the energy building between them was reaching a critical level. She knew if she didn't back away soon she was going to do something really dumb, like throw her arms around his neck and kiss him, but Adam didn't give her a chance. His arms went around her, tentatively, as if he thought she might object to being held, and said, "I missed you, Katy."

She couldn't have fought it if she wanted to. She wrapped her arms around him and squeezed, tucking her head under his chin, breathing him in. "Me, too."

It was wonderful, and awful, because she managed to fall in love with him all over again. Not that she'd ever really stopped. But being apart for so long made her forget a little.

What if she *never* got over him?

The dinner bell started clanging and her mom called from the house, "Come on, you two. Time to eat!"

Though she didn't want to, Katy let go of Adam, and decided right then that there would be no more hugging and touching while he was here. It seemed he could turn his feelings on and off like a lightbulb, but for her it wasn't so easy. A few more days of this and her heart might never recover.

Something very weird was happening.

In the past, whenever Becca brought Adam over it was always awkward, the conversation stilted. Probably because Becca herself was so uncomfortable, as if being back home would rub off on her somehow and tarnish the new life she'd built with Adam. But now, everyone was happy and relaxed and seemed to genuinely enjoy each other's company.

After supper, while her dad took Adam out to the stables, Katy and her mom sat out on the porch swing.

"As much as I hate admitting I'm wrong," her mom said, "You were right about Adam. He's a good man.

Maybe if your sister had been more comfortable here, he would have been, too."

"I've given up on trying to figure out why Becca did the things she did. Maybe if she'd lived, she would have eventually come around."

"Maybe," her mom said. They were quiet for several minutes, then she said off-handedly, "I noticed Adam couldn't keep his eyes off of you at dinner."

Katy had noticed that, too. Adam sat across from her, and every time she looked up from her plate he was watching her. And each time their eyes met she would feel this funny zing through her nervous system, and her heart would skip a beat. She'd barely been able to choke her dinner down. "What are you suggesting?"

Her mom shrugged. "Only that a man doesn't look at a woman that way if he doesn't care about her."

Whether or not Adam cared about her wasn't in question. "But for me, that just isn't enough. I want the whole package. I deserve that. And, Adam, well, he's not available."

"Things change."

"Not this."

She might have argued further but Adam and her dad walked up, putting the conversation to an abrupt end.

They all sat out on the porch and watched the sunset until ten, when a chill set in the air. It was hard to believe it was fall already. The time seemed to fly by lately.

Her parents settled in front of the television to watch their favorite sitcom and her mom told Katy, "Why don't you get Adam settled in the blue room." When

Katy cut her eyes sharply her way, she added, "It's the nicer of the two."

It was also right next door to, and shared a bathroom with, her own room. The green room was at least across the hall. Although, if he were staying with the men in the bunkhouse it would be too close as far as she was concerned.

Her mom wasn't trying to set them up, was she? Did she think proximity would make Adam change his mind? She wanted Katy to be happy, but she was making her miserable instead.

"This way," she told Adam, leading him up the stairs. He grabbed his duffel and followed her up. The heavy thud of his boots on the steps seemed to vibrate up through the balls of her feet to twang every single one of her nerves.

As soon as she hit the top step Sylvester darted out from his hiding spot behind the artificial palm tree and tried to wrap himself around her legs, so she toed him out of the way.

"The homicidal cat," Adam said.

"Homicidal?"

"He did that to me the last time I was here. I almost fell down the stairs."

"He can't help it. He got kicked in the head by a horse a few years back and he hasn't been right since. He mostly just stays up here and hides."

"And opens doors," Adam said with a grin, and she didn't have to ask what he meant. If it hadn't been for Sylvester opening her bedroom door, Adam never would have seen her naked, and maybe this entire mess might have been avoided.

She doubted it, though. With sexual attraction like theirs, sleeping with him had been inevitable.

"Here it is," she said, stepping into the spare room. "I know it isn't the Ritz, but the linens are fresh and there are clean towels in the bathroom cabinet. But if you flush the toilet and it keeps running just jiggle the handle and that should fix it."

The door snapped shut behind her and she whirled around to find Adam leaning against it. He had a look in his eyes, as if he was about ten seconds from devouring her.

Oh, Lord, give me strength.

"Don't look at me like that," she said.

His duffel landed with a thud on the floor beside him. "Like what?"

"Like I'm the main course on the buffet table."

He grinned. "Is that how I look?"

"I can't, Adam." But she wanted to. She wanted to slide her hands under his T-shirt, up his wide, muscular chest. She wanted to feel his bare skin against hers.

He took a step closer and her heart started to hammer. "I was just going to ask if I could feel the baby, that's all."

She didn't believe him for a second. Once he got his hands on her, her belly wasn't the only thing he would touch. And she would probably let him, because she wanted him so much she could hardly see straight.

"Maybe tomorrow," she told him. "I'm going to turn in for the night."

"It's barely ten."

"And I have to be up at five."

"How about a kiss goodnight, then?"

Why was he doing this to her? "I don't think so."

"Why?"

At the end of her rope, she asked, "Adam, what do you want from me?"

He shrugged. "I just...*want* you."

Isn't that the way it always was? They wanted her... until they didn't any longer. Well, she wanted forever, and he wasn't a forever kind of man. Not anymore. "That's not enough for me."

His expression was grim. "You want more."

"I *deserve* it."

"You do. And I'm being selfish." He opened the bedroom door. "I'm sorry. I'll back off."

"Do you need anything before I turn in?"

He shook his head. But as she walked past him to the door he caught her arm and pulled her to him. And heaven help her, she couldn't resist wrapping her arms around him.

Though it was packed with emotion, there was nothing sexual about the embrace. He just held her, and she held him. But it wasn't any less heartbreaking.

"I wish I could be what you need," he whispered against her hair.

She nodded, because if she tried to speak she would probably start blubbering. Besides, they'd already said all they needed to say.

Since he'd popped in unannounced, Adam felt it was only fair to do his share of work while he was visiting, so when Gabe invited him to ride along while he repaired fence posts, he went with him. It was tiresome, backbreaking work, but it felt good to be out in the fresh air and not cooped up in an office behind a desk for a change. Since Becca's death he'd become something of a shut-in. Now he was even thinking it was time to start living again.

They had finished replacing several busted fence posts when Katy's mom brought them lunch on horseback. Thick barbequed beef sandwiches, a plastic bowl full of potato salad and cold sodas. They sat in the truck bed and ate. Adam was so famished he wolfed down two sandwiches and a huge pile of salad.

"Don't they feed you in El Paso?" Gabe asked with a wry grin.

"I don't get this hungry sitting behind a desk," he admitted.

"Out here you earn your appetite. When I think about sitting at a desk day in, day out…" He shook his head. "Being outdoors, that's my life."

"You never considered doing anything else?"

"Nope. I know every inch of this land. It's who I am."

"It sure is beautiful."

He pointed to the east. "See past that fence line? That's ten acres of prime land, some of the prettiest around here. It used to be a horse farm but it went belly-up last fall and the property went into foreclosure."

"I'm surprised no one was interested in buying it."

"Times are bad. I thought about purchasing it and expanding the east pasture, but with this economy it's too much of a gamble. It would be perfect for a young couple, though. Build a house, raise a family. Maybe keep a horse or two."

Adam couldn't help wondering if he was talking about Katy. Was it possible she was seeing someone? No, she would have told him. But realistically she wasn't going to stay single forever. She was going to find a good man. One willing to give her everything he couldn't. What she *deserved*.

"I understand you should be getting the DNA results soon," Gabe said, balling up the plastic from his sandwich and stuffing it in the paper sack from their lunch. "What do you plan to do if it's Katy's?"

The question put him on edge. Up until now they had avoided talking about Adam's relationship with Katy. But it was bound to come up. "I want to assure you that I'm going to take care of her and the baby. They won't ever want for anything."

"You know, it makes sense in a weird way. You fell in love with one of my daughters. I guess it's not so unusual you'd fall in love with the other one."

Love? Did he think…did he think Adam was going to *marry* Katy? "Katy and I…we don't have that kind of relationship."

"Is that why you two talk on the phone for hours practically every night?"

"Gabe—"

"And you can't keep your eyes off of her?"

"No disrespect to you or to Katy, sir, but I don't want to marry anyone."

"You've got something against marriage, son? I know Becca could be a handful, but—"

"Becca was a good wife. And the day I buried her, I swore it was something I would never do again."

Gabe took a swallow of his soda, then said, "So you'll spend your life alone instead? Sounds like a pretty miserable existence."

Not alone. He would have his child. "I don't see it that way."

Gabe shrugged, like it was no skin off his nose.

"We should get busy. We have a lot to get done before supper."

He didn't want Gabe, or Katy's mom, deluding themselves into thinking he was going to whisk Katy off her feet and carry her into the sunset. They would just have to get used to the idea of him and Katy being good friends.

Sixteen

Katy barely made it to three o'clock when she was so exhausted she had to lay down. And though she only planned on sleeping an hour or two, when she woke to the sound of the water running in the bathroom, it was almost six.

Her dad must have given Adam quite a workout if he needed a shower.

She knew she should get up, but she was so comfortable she didn't want to move. She curled in a ball, the tops of her thighs pressed against her belly. She was just starting to drift off when she felt it. A soft bump.

Her eyes flew open. Could that have been the baby kicking?

She lay there very still, waiting to see if it happened again. Then she felt it, a distinct kick. Maybe those flutters she'd been feeling had been the baby moving after all.

Nearly bursting with excitement, she rolled onto her back and pulled her shirt up so she could see her belly. It only took a few seconds before she felt another kick, and it was so hard this time she could actually see her stomach move!

She lay there frozen, afraid that if she moved the baby might stop, and she wanted Adam to feel it, too.

She heard the shower shut off and the sound of him tugging open the curtain.

"Adam! Get in here!" she called. "Hurry!"

Only a few seconds elapsed before the bathroom door swung open and Adam appeared, fastening a towel around his waist, hair mussed and still dripping. When he saw her lying there he must have thought the worst because all the color seemed to drain from his face. "What's wrong?"

"Nothing." She gestured him over. "Hurry, it's kicking."

He was across the room in a millisecond, and perched on the edge of the mattress. "Are you sure?"

"Just watch," she said. "Right below my navel."

They waited several seconds then there was another quick bump-bump. "Did you see that?"

Adam laughed. "Oh, my God! Can I feel?"

She nodded, and he very gently placed his hand over her belly. His hand was warm from his shower and still damp. And there it was again, a soft little jab, as if the baby was saying, "Hey, I'm in here!"

She had been trying so hard to stay disconnected, to not think of it as *her* baby. But in that instant, feeling the baby move, she fell hopelessly in love. And she wanted it to be hers, so badly her heart hurt.

"What does it feel like to you?" he asked.

"Just like you would think. Like someone is poking me, but from the inside. I should call my mom in here so she can feel it."

"She's not here. She and your dad went out. She said they were going to catch a film in town and they would be back late."

They hardly ever went to the movies, so odds were good they were just giving Katy and Adam some time alone. They both seemed to have it in their minds that Adam was going to have a change of heart and suddenly decide that he loved her. What she didn't think they realized, what she hadn't realized until last night, was that he *did* love her. Even if he couldn't say it, she could see it in his eyes. And knowing that made his rejection a little easier to swallow for some reason. She wasn't damaged Katy, whom no one could love. Someone finally did. It just sucked that he was afraid to acknowledge it.

"It stopped," he said, sounding disappointed, but he didn't take his hand from her belly. And the fact that she was lying in bed wearing nothing but a shirt and panties, and he was only wearing a towel, started to sink in. Suddenly she felt hot all over and her heart was beating double time.

She would never know what possessed her, but she put a hand on his bare knee.

Dark and dangerous, his eyes shot to hers. "That's *not* a good idea."

Probably not. But for all the energy she'd spent convincing herself that this was never going to happen again, it didn't take much to have a total change of heart. And though she knew it was a mistake, and she was asking for heartbreak, she wanted him so much she didn't care what the repercussions would be.

She stroked his knee, scratching lightly with her nails.

"You're sending some pretty serious mixed signals," he told her, his voice uneven.

"Then let me be 100 percent clear." She slid her hand under the towel and up the inside of his thigh. He groaned and closed his eyes.

"I can't let you do this," he said, but he wasn't making an effort to stop her. And when her fingertips brushed against the family jewels he sucked in a breath and said in a gravelly voice, "Katy, stop."

"I can't. I want you, Adam. Even if it's just for a night or two."

He still wasn't ready to give in, so she took his hand that was still resting on her belly and guided it downward, between her thighs. "Touch me," she pleaded, and that was his undoing. He leaned over and kissed her. And kissed her and *kissed* her, and it was so perfect, she wanted to cry. He tugged the towel off and slid under the covers beside her. She expected it to be urgent and frenzied, like the night after she found out she was pregnant, but Adam took his time, kissing and touching her, exploring all the changes to her body, telling her she was beautiful. She'd never felt so sexy, so attractive, in her life. And when he made love to her it was slow and tender.

Afterward they lay curled in each other's arms and talked. About work, and the baby, and the ranch—anything but their relationship.

Around ten she threw on her robe and went down to the kitchen to get them something to eat while Adam checked his phone messages. When she came back up with a plate of leftovers, Adam was dressed and shoving clothes into his duffel bag.

"You're leaving?" she asked.

"I'm sorry," he said. "I had a message from my COO. There's been an accident at the refinery."

"What kind of accident?"

"An explosion."

She sucked in a breath. "How bad?"

"Bad. At least a dozen men were hurt."

Katy's heart stalled. "How seriously?"

"Second- and third-degree burns."

"Oh, Adam, I'm so sorry."

"Since I took over, safety has been my number-one priority and we've had a near-spotless record. Not a single accident that required more than the need for a small bandage. Injured employees means negative press and lawsuits and OSHA investigations."

"So this could be bad?"

He nodded. "This could be very bad. But my main concern right now is making sure those men are being taken care of."

"What caused the explosion?" she asked.

"We're not sure yet." He sat on the bed to pull on his socks and boots. "They're still trying to put out the blaze. Jordan said they had just completed a maintenance cycle and were bringing everything back on line when something blew. Which makes no sense, because everything had just been thoroughly inspected." He rose from the bed and grabbed his duffel. "Katy, I am going to try like hell to be back in time for your appointment, but I just don't know if I can."

"Adam, don't even worry about that. If you can make it, fine, if not, there's always next month."

"Yes, but I've been saying that for two months now. I *want* to be there."

She smiled. "I know you do. That's why it's okay if you're not."

He dropped the duffel, gathered her up in his arms and planted a kiss on her that curled her toes and shorted out her brain. And if he didn't have to leave, man would he be in trouble.

"What was that for?" she asked when they came up for air.

"Because you're being so understanding."

"That's what you do when you love someone," she said.

It wasn't until she saw the stunned look on Adam's face, that she realized what she'd just said. How could she have just blurted it out like that?

And he obviously had no clue how to respond. It might have been amusing if she wasn't so mortified.

"Wow," she said, cheeks flaming with embarrassment. "I did not mean to just blurt that out."

"Katy—"

"Please," she said holding up a hand to stop him. "Anything you say at this point will only make it worse, and I'm humiliated enough. Just, please, let's pretend it never happened."

If there was any hope that he might have ever returned the sentiment, it died with his look of relief. "I really have to go."

"Go," she said, forcing a smile.

"We'll talk about this later." He gave her another quick kiss, then grabbed his duffel.

No, they wouldn't talk about it, she thought, as she listened to his heavy footfalls on the stairs, then the sound of the front door slamming. She resisted the urge to get up and watch him drive away. It would just be too hard, because it was a symbol. A symbol of the end of their relationship as she knew it. Not just their sexual relationship, but their friendship, as well.

Remaining friends after this would just be too… awkward. She didn't doubt that he knew she had strong feelings for him, maybe even loved him. But knowing it, and actually hearing the words were two very different things. He had no choice but to shut her out. She just hoped he would always be there for the baby.

And it occurred to her, as close as they had become these last few months, not only did she just lose her lover, but she'd also lost her best friend.

It never ceased to amaze Adam how, when his company did something positive, like adopting new and innovative environmentally friendly practices, he was lucky to get an inch on page twelve of the business section. But toss in a suspicious inferno, a few injured workers and an OSHA investigation and they'd made the front page of every national newspaper in the country. He personally had been hounded by the press at the office and even outside his home.

They had gone from being praised as having the most impressive safety record in the local industry to being labeled a deathtrap overnight.

Already they had been served with lawsuits by six of the thirteen injured men, the ones whose burns had been the most severe. The board, on the advice of their attorneys, had already agreed to settle the suits. It would set them back financially, but Adam was stead-fast in his belief that it was the right thing to do. He was just thankful that no one was left permanently disabled, or, God forbid, killed.

Since the refinery had been in maintenance mode, the number of men on the line had been reduced by nearly half. The majority of the damage had been to the infrastructure. And now, every day they had to remain off line while the equipment was checked and rechecked, they lost hundreds of thousands of dollars in revenue.

Monday afternoon Adam called an emergency executive meeting in his office. OSHA had begun their investigation and it was beginning to look like the accident really wasn't an accident after all. If they ruled that it had been a case of gross negligence on the part of the men on the rig, the company would be slapped with a hefty fine.

Jordan, loyal to the death to his men, refused to believe they could possibly be responsible.

"My men work damned hard," he said, wearing a bare spot in the oriental rug with his pacing. Unusual considering he was by far the most laid-back of the four. "I would trust most of them with my life. There's no way they would be so careless. Not to mention that the entire line in question had just been thoroughly inspected. It doesn't make sense."

"Something about this does smell fishy to me," Nathan said. He sat in the chair opposite Adam's desk, looking troubled.

"You suspect foul play?" Adam asked.

"I say we shouldn't rule anything out. It would have to be an inside job, though."

Jordan stopped pacing to glare at his brother. "Impossible. Our people are loyal."

"Who then?" Nathan asked.

Jordan looked as though he wanted to deck him. "*Not* one of mine."

Adam didn't like the idea that one of his own employees could be responsible, but they had to know for sure, before there was another accident. "I think we need to hire our own investigator."

"We'll have to keep it quiet," Emilio, who had been standing by the window quietly observing, finally said. "If it was sabotage, and someone on the line is responsible, if they find out we're digging, any possible evidence will disappear. If he thinks he got away with it, he may be careless."

"Nathan," Adam said. "I want you in charge of this one."

"Why him?" Jordan scoffed, outraged. "I'm the one who understands the day-to-day operations. Those men trust me."

"Which is exactly why I'm assigning it to Nathan. It's going to get out eventually and you should have a certain degree of deniability. Not to mention that you're biased."

Jordan knew he was right. "Fine. But I want to be kept in the loop."

"Of course. If we do have suspects, you'll be in the position to keep a close eye on them, so this doesn't happen again. And I suppose it goes without saying that until this is resolved, I won't be stepping down as CEO. However long that takes. But that does *not* mean I won't be watching all of you."

"How is the pregnancy going?" Nathan asked.

"Great. In fact, I have to be back in Peckins tonight. Katy has her five-month checkup tomorrow." And he and Katy were long overdue for a serious discussion about the future of their relationship.

"Wait a minute," Jordan said. "You're actually leaving town? After everything that just happened?"

"I'll only be gone a day or two."

"What if we need you here?"

Jordan's reaction was understandable. Six months ago Adam wouldn't have dreamed of leaving town during a crisis. Not for a couple days. Not for five minutes. But his priorities had changed. Hell, his whole life had changed, and he had Katy and her family to blame. Or thank.

He kept thinking about what Gabe said, about how spending his life alone would be a miserable existence. Well, Adam *had* been miserable. For three years now. Until he got tangled up with Katy, he had genuinely forgotten what it felt like to be happy. To have something to look forward to.

Calling and asking her to meet him was one of the smartest things he'd ever done.

"We'll manage," Emilio said, sending Jordan a sharp look. "Can you two give me and Adam a minute?"

Nathan and Jordan left, and Emilio sat on the corner of Adam's desk.

"Okay, what's up?"

"What do you mean?"

"Jordan is right. You never leave during a crisis."

Emilio was going to find out eventually, so why not tell him now. "Something happened the other day when I was in Peckins. Something...unexpected. When

I heard about the accident, I told Katy I had to leave, and said I might have to miss her appointment."

He winced. "You've missed two already."

"I know. And you know what she said?"

"I'm guessing it can't be good if it has you rushing back there."

"She said it was fine. That I could just go to the next one. She said knowing that I want to be there is good enough. And when I thanked her for being so understanding, she said that's what you do when you love someone."

Emilio's brow lifted. "She told you she loves you?"

He laughed. "Yeah, she just kind of blurted it out. And my first instinct, after I got over the surprise of her saying it, was that I love her, too."

"So did you tell her that?"

"I didn't get a chance. She got really embarrassed, and asked me to forget she said anything. I had to go. It didn't seem right to throw it out there, then leave."

"So you're going to tell her when you get there?"

"At this point, considering everything I've put her through, I don't think telling her is good enough, so I'm going to show her, too." Adam pulled the ring box out of his desk drawer and tossed it to Emilio.

Emilio laughed. "Is this what I think it is?"

Adam grinned.

He opened it and gave a low whistle. "I thought you were never getting married again, never taking the chance on burying another wife."

"It wasn't losing Becca that had made getting over her so hard. It was the regrets. The things we *didn't* say. And I can't go on pretending that we didn't have problems. Almost from the start."

"So why have kids?"

"I guess I thought that having a baby would fix everything. I thought it would bring us closer together. But honestly, it probably would have just made it worse. Neither one of us was very happy. If she hadn't gotten sick, I don't doubt we would be divorced by now."

He knew now that Celia was right, Becca *wasn't* his soul mate. She wasn't the love of his life, and he was pretty sure she sensed that.

"It's never easy admitting our mistakes," Emilio said.

"It's different with Katy. She's unlike anyone I've ever known. She couldn't care less about my money. And if she thinks I'm acting like an ass, she isn't shy about saying so. She's everything I could possibly want or need in a wife. I can't even imagine my life without her in it."

"So what are you still doing here?" Emilio asked, tossing the ring back to Adam.

"It's only three."

"Yes, but you have a long drive ahead of you. Besides, we can handle things without you."

Emilio didn't have to tell him twice.

They weren't expecting company, so when Katy pulled up the driveway after a quick trip to the bank, she was surprised to see a car there. Before she got a good look she thought it might be Adam, but this was a dark sedan. A Mercedes, or BMW or something similar. And she knew Adam drove a red and sporty car.

She parked by the barn, thinking maybe they really did have a rich uncle. But she didn't have time to worry about that. She had a letter in her jeans pocket that could very well change the rest of her life. She got out and walked to the house, wondering who it could be. She went through the kitchen, the scent of home-fried chicken making her mouth water.

"Smells delicious, Elvie."

"That man is here," she whispered.

"What man?"

She nodded to Katy's belly. "The baby's father."

"*Adam* is here?" Elvie had to be mistaken.

She nodded, wide-eyed, and crossed herself. She was convinced, because Adam was so tall and dark and handsome, that he was *el Diablo* in the flesh.

She pushed through the kitchen door to the great room, expecting to see some man who looked like Adam sitting there with her parents, but it actually *was* Adam. And the instant she saw him, she knew all that stuff about them not being friends anymore was just bull.

When they heard her come in everyone turned in her direction.

She thrust her hands on her hips and asked Adam, "Exactly how many cars do you own?"

He grinned at her, then turned back to her parents and said, "I think that about covers it."

The three of them stood and her dad shook Adam's hand. Why would he do that?

"What's going on?" Katy asked them.

"Let's take a drive," Adam said.

"Why?"

"So we can talk."

"But it's almost suppertime."

"We won't be long."

Whatever he had to say must have been pretty bad if they had to leave the ranch. "Where are we going?"

"Not far." He crossed over to where she stood and took her hand, leading her to the front door. She looked back at her parents, but their expressions didn't give anything away.

Would he hold her hand—and in front of her parents—if he was about to tell her something awful? Or did he think it would soften the blow?

He opened the passenger door for her and she slid into the soft leather seat. He walked around and got in the driver's side, saying, as he started the engine, "Buckle up."

He waited until she was fastened in, then put the car into gear. It felt a little weird being in a car with him while he was actually behind the wheel. In the past it was always Reece driving. Not that she expected him to be a terrible driver. It was just…different.

"How many cars do you own?" she asked as he made a left onto the road.

"Just the three."

They drove about a half a mile, then Adam made a sharp left and pulled up the road to the abandoned horse farm next door.

"What are we doing here?"

"I'll explain," he said cryptically.

The house and stables were in disrepair and the property overgrown, but it used to be a beautiful piece of land. And had the potential to be again someday. Her dad had talked about buying it, and she'd been disappointed when he changed his mind. Though she had never admitted it to anyone, she had even considered purchasing it. She had enough for a down payment in the bank. She just didn't like the idea of living alone.

Adam parked in a clearing by the stable and they got out. The sun was just beginning to set and there was a chill in the air.

"Are you warm enough?" he asked.

She nodded. He took her hand again and they walked slowly toward the stables. "Does this mean you're staying for my appointment tomorrow?"

The question seemed to surprise him. "Of course. Why would I drive all this way and not go?"

She shrugged.

"What do you think of this land?" he asked her.

"It's nice. Perfect for a small horse farm."

"What would you think if I said I bought it?"

She stopped in her tracks. "What? Why?"

He grinned. "So I could build a house here. And probably a new stable."

"You're serious?"

"Yep."

Well, if the baby was hers, and he was going to be visiting a lot, didn't it make sense that he had somewhere to stay? But they weren't even sure yet.

They started walking again, past the stables and along the corral fence, the overgrown grass and weeds grabbing at her pant legs. "I think that sounds like a good investment."

"So you wouldn't mind living here?"

Living here? He was going to build a house for *her*? Did he know something she didn't? Had the lab sent him a letter, too, and had he read it? After they agreed they would look at the results *together*.

"Adam, what's going on?"

They stopped where the corral turned, near an apple tree that had probably been there longer than the house. "This should do," Adam said.

"Do for what?"

"There are a few things I have to tell you, Katy."

She swallowed hard, bracing for the worst, her hands clammy she was so nervous.

"We had to launch an investigation into the accident at the refinery, and as soon as it's resolved, I'm leaving Western Oil."

For a full ten seconds she was too dumbfounded to speak. And when she found her voice, it was uncharacteristically high-pitched. "Leaving? As in quitting?"

"I'll still be on the board, but I'm stepping down as CEO."

"W-why?"

"It's time. I want to be around to see my child grow up."

"That's wonderful," she said, wondering what that meant for her, if it meant anything at all.

"Remember the other night, when you said you love me?"

She cringed, still mortified that she had actually done something so stupid. "I thought we agreed not to talk about that."

"You issued an order, and I didn't agree to anything."

It was obvious he wasn't willing to let it go. He was going to torture her. "Okay, what about it?"

"I'll admit I was a little stunned—"

"You were way more than stunned. And I don't blame you, Adam. It was wrong of me to put you on the spot like that."

He took a deep breath and exhaled. "Can I finish?"

She nodded, even though she knew she wasn't going to like what he had to say.

"I was in a hurry to leave, but if I'd had more than thirty seconds to think about it, I would have told you that I love you, too."

He heart climbed up into her throat. She had never expected him to admit it, to say it out loud.

"Aren't you going to say anything?" he asked.

"I…I don't know what to say."

"You could say that you love me, too."

Unable to look in his eyes, and see the sincerity there, she looked down at the ground instead. "You already know that."

"I *need* you, Katy."

For now. But what about a month from now? He didn't want to get married, and she couldn't accept any less than that.

She wanted forever.

Adam bent down on one knee in the weeds. She thought he was going to pick something up off the ground, then she saw that he already had something in his hand.

"What are you doing?"

"Something I should have done months ago." He opened his hand and sitting on his palm was a black velvet box. It actually took her several seconds to figure out what was happening. Then she started to tremble so hard she wasn't even sure her legs would hold her up.

Adam opened the box to reveal a stunning diamond solitaire ring. He looked up at her and grinned. "Marry me, Katy?"

"You're serious?"

"I've never been more sure of anything in my life."

"But...Becca—"

"Is gone. Becca was my wife, and I loved her, but I didn't need her the way I need you. You're my soul mate. I don't want to go another day, another minute, knowing you aren't going to be mine forever."

She'd imagined this moment so many times in her head, but none of her fantasies compared to the real thing, and she'd be damned if she was going to give him even a second to change his mind.

She threw herself in his arms so hard that they lost their balance and tumbled backward in the weeds.

He laughed and said, "Should I take that as a yes?"

"Definitely yes," she said, kissing him, wondering if this was a dream. Was it even possible to be *this* happy?

Adam sat them up and pulled her into his lap. "Would you like this now?" he asked, holding up the ring box.

She'd almost forgotten! "Will you put it on me?"

He took it from the box and slid it on her finger. It was a perfect fit. "I have *huge* fingers. How did you guess the size?"

"I didn't. I asked your mom."

"When?"

"Sunday morning."

Katy's mouth fell open. "She's known about this since *Sunday?*"

"I didn't tell her why I needed it, but I think she had a pretty good idea."

Suddenly it made sense why he was sitting there with her parents when she walked in, and why her dad shook his hand. "Oh, my gosh, did you ask my parents' *permission?*"

"I thought it would be a nice touch, since I kind of missed that step last time. I figured they deserved it."

She threw her arms around his neck and hugged him, the baby pressed between them. That's when she remembered the letter in her pocket. They were together now, and no matter whose baby it was, she would be raising it. But he deserved to know the truth.

"I have to show you something," she said, pulling the letter out. "This came in today's mail."

"The DNA results?"

She nodded.

He took the letter from her, and for a minute he just looked at it, then he looked up at her, shrugged and said, "I don't care."

"You don't care?"

He took her hands. "What difference do genetics make? This is *our* baby, Katy. Yours and mine. Either way, it's a miracle. So unless you really need to know—"

"I don't," she said. "Though I tried to be impartial, and not get attached, I've felt like this baby has been mine pretty much from the day it was conceived."

With a smile on his face, Adam ripped the envelope in two, then into fourths, then he kept on ripping until there was nothing left but scraps, then he tossed them in the air.

Katie couldn't help wondering, though…would she ever be curious? Someday would she want to know?

But the following spring, when Amanda Rebecca

Blair was born—a healthy eight pounds seven ounces—
and Katy held her daughter for the first time, she knew
without a doubt that it would never matter.

* * * * *

New Zealand born, to Dutch immigrant parents, *USA TODAY* bestselling author **Yvonne Lindsay** became an avid romance reader at the age of thirteen. Now, married to her "blind date" and with two children, she remains a firm believer in the power of romance. Yvonne feels privileged to bring to her readers the stories of her heart. In her spare time, when not writing, she can be found reading a book, reliving the power of love in all walks of life. She can be contacted via her website: yvonnelindsay.com.

Look for more books from Yvonne Lindsay in Harlequin Desire—the ultimate destination for powerful, passionate romance! There are six new Harlequin Desire titles available every month. Check one out today!

HONOR-BOUND GROOM
Yvonne Lindsay

This book is dedicated to all my wonderful readers, who make it possible for me to keep writing books. Thank you from the bottom of my heart.

Prologue

Isla Sagrado, three months ago...

"*Abuelo* is losing his marbles. He talked again of the curse today."

Alexander del Castillo leaned back in the deep and comfortable dark leather chair and gave his brother, Reynard, a chastising look.

"Our grandfather is not going mad, he is merely growing old. And he worries—for all of us." Alex's gaze encompassed his youngest brother, Benedict, also. "We have to do something about it—something drastic—and soon. This negative publicity about the curse is not just affecting him, it's affecting business, too."

"That's true. Revenue at the winery is down this quarter. More than anticipated," Benedict agreed, reaching for his glass of del Castillo Tempranillo and taking a sip. "It certainly isn't the quality of the wine that's doing it, if I say so myself."

"Put your ego back where it belongs and focus, would you?" Alex growled. "This is serious. Reynard, you're our head of publicity, what can we do for the family as a whole that will see talk about this stupid curse laid to rest once and for all?"

Reynard cast him a look of disbelief. "You actually want to lend credence to the curse?"

"If it means we can get things on an even keel again. We owe it to *Abuelo,* if not to ourselves. If we'd been more traditional in our ways then the issue would probably not have arisen."

"The del Castillos have never been renowned for their traditional outlook, *mi hermano,*" Reynard pointed out with a deprecating grin.

"And look where that has put us," Alex argued. "Three hundred years and the governess's curse would still appear to be upon us. Whether you believe in it or not, according to the legend, we're it—the last generation. If we don't get things right, the entire nation—including our grandfather—believes it will be the end of the del Castillo family. Do you want that on your conscience?" He stared his younger brother down before flicking his gaze to Benedict. "Do you?"

Reynard shook his head slightly, as if in disbelief. He seemed stunned that his eldest brother had joined their grandfather in the crazy belief that an age-old legend could be based in truth. And more, that it could be responsible for affecting their prosperity, indeed, threatening their very lives today.

Alex understood Reynard's skepticism. But what choice did they have? As long as the locals believed in the curse, bad publicity would affect the way the del Castillo family could do business. And as long as *Abuelo* believed, the paths he and his brothers chose could make or break the happiness of the man who had raised them all.

"No, Alex." Reynard sighed. "I do not want to be responsible for our family's demise any more than you do."

"So what do we do about it?" Benedict challenged with a humorless laugh. "It's not as if we can suddenly drum up loving brides so we can marry and live happily ever after."

"That's it!" Reynard declared with a shouted laugh and pushed himself up and out of his seat.

His abrupt movement and shout unsettled the dogs sleeping in front of the fire, sending them barking around his feet. A clipped command from Alex made them slink back to their rug and assume their drowsing state.

"That's what we need to do. It'll be a publicity exercise such as Isla Sagrado has never seen before."

"And you think *Abuelo* is losing his marbles?" Benedict asked and took another sip of his wine.

"No," Alex said, excitement beginning to build in his chest. "He's right. That's exactly what we must do. Remember the curse. If the ninth generation does not live by our family motto of honor, truth and love, in life and in marriage, the del Castillo name will die out forever. If we each marry and have families, well, for a start that will show the curse for the falsehood it is. People will put their trust in our name again rather than in fear and superstition."

Reynard sat back down. "You're serious," he said flatly.

"Never more so," Alex answered.

Whether he'd been kidding around or not, Reynard had hit on the very thing that would not only settle their grandfather's concerns but would be a massive boost to the del Castillo name. Its ongoing effect on the people of Isla Sagrado would increase prosperity across the entire island nation.

While Isla Sagrado was a minor republic in the Mediterranean, the del Castillo family had long held a large amount of influence on the island's affairs, whether commercial or political. As the family had prospered so, by natural process, did the people of Isla Sagrado.

Unfortunately, the reverse was also true.

"You expect each of us to simply marry the right woman and start families and then, hey, presto, all will be well?" Reynard's voice was saturated with disbelief.

"Exactly. How hard can it be?" Alex got up and patted him on the shoulder. "You're a good-looking guy. I'm sure you have plenty of candidates."

Benedict snorted. "Not the kind he'd bring home to *Abuelo,* I'd wager."

"You can talk," Reynard retorted. "You're too busy racing that new Aston Martin of yours along the cliff road to slow down long enough for a woman to catch you."

Alex walked over to the fireplace and leaned against the massive stone mantel that framed it. Carved from island rock, the hearth had seen generation after generation of his family sprawl in front of its warmth. He and his brothers would not be the last to do so. Not if he had anything to do with it.

"All joking aside, are you willing to at least try?" he asked, his eyes flicking from one brother to the next.

Of the two, Benedict looked most like him. In fact some days he felt as if he was looking into a mirror when he saw his brother's black hair and black-brown eyes. Reynard took after their French mother. Finer featured, perhaps more dramatic with his dark coloring because of it. Female attention had never been an issue for any of them, even from before they'd hit puberty. In fact, with only three years in total separating the brothers, they'd been pretty darn competitive in their playboy bachelorhood. They were all in their early thirties now and had mostly left that phase behind but the reputation still lingered, and it was that very lifestyle that had brought them to this current conundrum.

"It's all right for you, you're already engaged to your childhood sweetheart," Benedict teased him with a smirk, clearly still not prepared to take the matter seriously on any level.

"Hardly my sweetheart since she was only a baby when we were betrothed."

Twenty-five years ago their father had saved his best friend, Francois Dubois, from drowning after the latter had accepted a dare from their father to swim off Isla Sagrado's most dangerous beach below the castillo. In gratitude, Dubois had promised the hand of his infant daughter, Loren, to Raphael del Castillo's eldest son. In a modern society no one but the two men had ever really given any credence to the pledge. But the two men were old-school all the way back down their ancestral lines and they'd taken the matter very seriously indeed.

Alex had barely paid any attention at the time, despite the fact that, virtually from the day she could walk, Loren had followed him around like a faithful puppy. He'd been grateful when her parents had divorced and her mother had taken her away to New Zealand, clear on the other side of the world, when Loren had been fifteen. Twenty-three years old at the time, he'd found it unsettling to have a gangling, underdeveloped teenager telling his girlfriends that she was his fiancée.

Since then, the engagement had been a convenient excuse to avoid the state of matrimony. Until now, he hadn't even considered marriage, and certainly not in the context of Francois Dubois's promise to Raphael del Castillo. But what better way to continue to uphold his family's honor and position on Isla Sagrado than to fulfill the terms of the spoken contract between two best friends? He could see the headlines already. It would be a media coup that would not only benefit the del Castillo business empire, but the whole of Isla Sagrado, as well.

He thought briefly of the dalliance he'd begun with his personal assistant. He didn't normally choose to mix business with pleasure, especially from within his own immediate work environment. But Giselle's persistent attempts to seduce him had been entertaining and—once he'd given in—very satisfying.

A curvaceous blonde, Giselle enjoyed being escorted to the high spots of Sagradan society and entertainment. Certainly she was beautiful and talented—in more ways than one—but wife material? No. They'd both known that nothing long-term would ever have come of their relationship. No doubt she'd be philosophical and he knew she was sophisticated enough to accept his explanation that their intimacy could no longer continue. In fact, he'd put a stop to it right away. He needed to create some emotional space between now and when he brought Loren back to be his bride.

Alex made a mental note to source a particularly lovely piece of jewelry to placate Giselle and turned his mind back to the only current viable option for the position of his wife.

Loren Dubois.

She was from one of the oldest families here on Isla Sagrado, and had always taken great pride in her heritage. Even though she'd been gone for ten years, he'd wager she was still Sagradan to her marrow— and as devoted to her father's memory as she had been to the man during his lifetime. She wouldn't hesitate to honor the commitment made all those years ago. What's more, she'd understand what it meant to be a del Castillo bride, together with what that responsibility involved. And she would now be at the right age, and maturity, to marry and to help put the governess's curse to rest once and for all.

Alex smirked at his brothers. "So, that's me settled. What are you two going to do?"

"You have to be kidding us, right?" Benedict looked askance at Alex, as if he'd suddenly announced his intention to enter a monastery. "Lanky little Loren Dubois?"

"Maybe she's changed." Alex shrugged. It mattered little how she looked. Marrying her was his duty—his desires weren't relevant. With any luck she'd be pregnant with his child within the first year of their marriage and too busy thereafter with the baby to put any real demands upon him.

"But still, why would you choose her when you could have any woman alive as your wife?" Reynard entered the fray.

Alex sighed. Between them his brothers were as tenacious as a pair of wolves after a wounded beast.

"Why not? Marrying her will serve multiple purposes. Not only will it honor an agreement made between our late father and his friend, but it will also help relieve *Abuelo's* concerns. And that's not even mentioning what it will do for our public image. Let's face it. The media will lap it up, especially if you leak the original betrothal story as an appetizer. They'll make it read like a fairy tale."

"And what of *Abuelo's* concerns about the next generation?" Reynard asked, one eyebrow raised. "Do you think your bride will be so happy to ensure our longevity? For all you know she may already be married."

"She's not."

"And you know this because?"

"*Abuelo* had an investigator keep tabs on her after Francois died. Since his stroke last year, the reports have come to me."

"So you're serious about it then. You're really going to go through with a twenty-five-year-old engagement to a woman you don't even know anymore."

"I have to, unless you have any better suggestions. Rey?"

Reynard shook his head. A short sharp movement of his head that bore witness to the frustration they all felt at the position they were in.

"And you, Ben? Anything you can think of that will save our name and our fortunes, not to mention make *Abuelo's* final years with us happier ones?"

"You know there is nothing else," Benedict replied, resignation to their combined fates painting stark lines on his face.

"Then, my brothers, I'd like to propose a toast. To each of us and to the future del Castillo brides."

One

New Zealand, now...

"I have come to discuss the terms of our fathers' agreement. It is time we marry."

From the second his sleek gray Eurocopter had landed on the helipad close to the house she'd wondered what had brought Alexander del Castillo here. Now she knew. She could hardly believe it.

Loren Dubois studied the tall near stranger commanding the space of her mother's formal sitting room. Her eyes drank in the sight of him after so long. Dressed all in black, his dark hair pushed back from his forehead and his brown-black eyes fixed firmly on her face, he should have been intimidating but instead she wondered whether she'd conjured up an age-old dream.

Marry? Her heart jumped erratically in her chest

and she tried to force it back to its usual slow and steady rhythm. Years ago, she'd have leaped at the opportunity, but now? With age had come caution. She wasn't a love-struck teenager anymore. She'd seen firsthand what an unhappy alliance could do to a couple, as her parents' tempestuous marriage had attested. She and Alexander del Castillo didn't even know one another anymore. Yet, for some reason, the way he'd proposed marriage—in typical autocratic del Castillo fashion—made her go weak at the knees.

She gave herself a swift reality check. Who was she kidding? He hadn't proposed. He'd flat out told her, as if there was no question that she'd accept. It didn't help that every fiber in her body wanted to do just that.

Wait, she reminded herself. *Slow down.*

It had been ten years since she'd laid eyes on him. Ten years since her fifteen-year-old heart had been broken and she'd been dragged to New Zealand by her mother after the divorce. A long time not to hear from someone by any standards, let alone from the man she had been betrothed to from the cradle.

Even so, a part of her still wanted to leap at the suggestion. Loren took a steadying breath. Although their engagement had always been the stuff of fairy tales, she was determined to stay firmly rooted in the present.

"Marry?" she responded, drawing her chin up slightly as if it could give her that extra height and lessen Alex's dominance over her. "You arrive here with no prior warning—in fact, no contact at all since I left Isla Sagrado—and the first thing you say to me is that it's time we marry? That's a little precipitate, wouldn't you say?"

"Our betrothal has stood for a quarter of a century. I would say our marriage is past due."

There it was—that delicious hint of accent in his voice, characteristic of the Spanish-Franco blend of nationalities of their home country, Isla Sagrado. It was an accent she'd long since diluted with her time in New Zealand, yet from his lips the sound was like velvet stroking bare skin. Her body responded to the timbre of it even as she fought down the wave of longing that spiraled from her core. Had she missed him that much?

Of course she had. That much and more. But she was grown-up now. A woman, not a child, nor a displaced bratty teen. Loren attempted to inject a fine thread of steel into her voice.

"A betrothal that no one seriously expected to be fulfilled, surely."

Somehow she had to show him she wouldn't be such a pushover. In all the time since she'd left Isla Sagrado he'd made no contact whatsoever. Not so much as a card at Christmas or her birthday. His indifference had hurt.

"Are you saying that your father made such a gesture lightly when he offered your hand?"

Loren laughed, the sound of it hollow even to her ears. She still missed her father with a physical ache, even though he'd been dead these past seven years. With him had gone her last link to Isla Sagrado and, she'd believed, to Alex. But now Alex was very much here and she didn't know how to react. *Stay strong,* she told herself. *Above all, stay strong. That's the only way to earn the respect of a del Castillo.*

"A hand that was little more than three months old when it was promised to you—you yourself were only eight," she said with as much bravado as she could muster.

Alex moved a step toward her. She almost felt the air part to allow him passage; he had that kind of presence. Despite her inexperience with men of Alex's caliber, it was one she responded to instinctively.

Alex had always been magnetic, but the past ten years had seen a new maturity settle on his broad shoulders, together with a stronger and more determined line to his jaw. He looked older than the thirty-three years she knew him to be. Older and harder. Certainly not a man who took "no" for an answer.

"I'm not eight anymore. And you—" he paused and ran his eyes over her body "—you are most certainly no longer a child."

Loren's skin flared hot, as if he'd touched her with more than a glance. As if his long strong fingers had stroked her face, her throat, her breasts. She felt her nipples tighten and strain against the practical cotton of her bra. And the longing within her grew harder to resist.

"Alex," she said, her voice slightly breathless, "you don't know me anymore. I don't know you. For all you know I'm already married."

"I know you are not."

He knew? What else did he know about her, she wondered. Had he somehow kept tabs on her all this time?

"It would be foolish for us to marry. We don't even know if we're compatible."

"We have the rest of our lives to learn the details of what we can do to please one another."

Alex's voice was a low murmur and his eyes dropped

to her mouth. Please or pleasure? Which had he really meant, she thought, as she struggled against the urge to moisten her lips with her tongue. The longing sharpened and drew into a tight coil deep within her. Loren fought back a moan—the pure, visceral response to his mere gaze shocking her with its intensity.

Her lack of experience with men had never bothered her before this moment. All her dealings with guests and male staff here at her mother's family's sheep and cattle station had been platonic and she'd preferred it that way. It had been difficult enough to settle into the isolation of the farm without the complications of a relationship with someone directly involved with the day-to-day workings of the place. Besides, anything else would have felt like a betrayal—to her father's promise and to the lingering feelings she still bore for Alex.

Now, that lack of experience had come back to haunt her. A man like Alex del Castillo would certainly expect more than what she had to offer. Would demand it.

In her younger years, she'd adored Alex with the kind of hero worship that a child had for an attractive older person—and, oh yes, he'd been attractive from the moment he'd drawn his first breath. She'd seen the photos to prove it. She'd believed that adoration had deepened into love, love not dimmed by Alex's vague tolerance of the scrawny kid who followed him like a shadow around the castillo that had been his family home for centuries.

For as long as she could remember she'd plagued her father to repeat the story of how Alex's dad, Raphael, had saved him from drowning on the beach below the castillo after a crazy dare between friends had almost turned deadly. And she'd hung on his every word as he'd reached the part where, in deepest gratitude, he'd promised his newborn daughter in marriage to Raphael's eldest son.

But her childish dreams of happily ever after with her fairy-tale prince were quite different from the virile, masculine reality of the man in front of her. Every move he made showed that Alex had a degree of sensual knowledge and experience she couldn't even begin to imagine, much less match. It was exciting and intimidating all at once. Was she already in over her head?

"Besides," Alex said, his voice still low, pitched only for her ears, "it is time now that I marry and who better than the woman to whom I've been affianced all her life?"

Alex's dark brown eyes bored into hers, daring her to challenge him. But, surprisingly, beneath the dare, Loren saw something else reflected in their depths.

While he'd appeared so strong and self-assured from the moment he'd alighted from the helicopter and strode toward their sprawling schist rock home nestled near the base of the Southern Alps, there was now a hint of uncertainty in his gaze. As if he expected some resistance from Loren to the idea that they fulfill the bargain struck between two best friends so long ago.

The scent of his cologne wove softly around her like an ancient spell, invading her senses and scrambling her mind. Rational thought flew out the window as he took another step closer to her, as his hand reached for her chin and tilted her face up to his.

His fingers were gentle against her skin. Her breath stopped in her chest. He bent his head, bringing his lips to hers—their pressure warm, tender, coaxing. His hand slid from her jaw to cup the back of her neck.

Loren's head spun as she parted her lips beneath his and tasted the intimacy of his tongue as it gently swept the soft tissue of her lower lip. A groan rippled from her throat and suddenly she was in his arms, her body aligned tightly against the hard planes of his chest, his abdomen. Her arms curved around him, snaking under the fine wool of his jacket and across the silk of his shirt. The heat of his skin through the finely woven fabric seared her hands. She pressed her fingertips firmly into the strong muscles of his back.

She fit into the shape of his body as though she had indeed been born to the role, and as his lips plundered hers, all she could, or wanted to, think of was how it felt to finally be in his arms. Not a single one of her frustrated teenage fantasies had lived up to the reality.

This was more, so much more than she'd ever dreamed. The strength and power of him in her arms was overwhelming and she clung to him with the longing of a lifetime finally given substance. It barely seemed real but the solid presence of him, his skillful mouth, the sensation of his fingertips massaging the base of her scalp, all combined to be very, very real indeed.

Every nerve in her body was alive, gloriously alive, and begging for more. She'd never experienced such a depth of passion with another man and was certain she never would.

She knew to her very soul that this connection, this instant magnetic pull between them, was meant to be forever, just as their fathers had preordained. And, with this one embrace, she knew she wanted it all.

In the distance she heard the front door slam, its heavy wooden thud echoing down the hardwood floor of the main hallway. Reluctantly she loosened her grip and forced herself to draw away from Alex's embrace. The instant she did so, she almost sobbed. The loss of his warmth, his touch, was indescribable. Loren fought free of the sensual fog that infused her mind as her mother swept into the sitting room, the staccato tap of her swift footfall fading into silence as she stepped onto the heirloom Aubusson carpet.

"Loren! Whose is that helicopter out on the pad? Oh!" she said, displeasure twisting her patrician features. "It's you."

It was hardly the kind of welcome Naomi Simpson generally prided herself on, Loren noted with a trace of acerbity. As her mother's gaze darted between her and Alex, Loren fought not to smooth her hair and clothing, drawing instead on every ounce of her mother's training to appear aloof and in control—at least as far as her hammering heartbeat rendered her capable.

Alex remained close at her side, one arm now casually slung about her waist, his fingers gently stroking the top of her hip through her red merino wool sweater. Tiny sizzling tendrils of electricity feathered along her skin at his lazy touch and she found it hard to focus.

Her mother had no such difficulty.

"Loren? Would you care to explain?"

There was no entreaty in Naomi's words. Even phrased as a question she demanded answers and, if the frozen look of fury on her face was any indicator, she wanted those answers right now.

"Mother, you remember Alex del Castillo, don't you?"

"I do. I can't say I ever expected to see you here.

I'd hoped we were completely shot of Isla Sagrado the day we left."

With typical Gallic charm Alex nodded toward Naomi. "It is a pleasure to see you again, Madame Dubois."

"I wish I could say the same. And, just for the record, I go by Simpson now," Naomi answered. "Why are you here?"

"Mother!" Loren protested.

"Don't worry, Loren," Alex murmured into her ear. "I will deal with your mother."

The warmth of his breath against the shell of her ear sent a tiny tremor down her spine. He exaggerated the two syllables of her name, emphasizing the last to give it an exotic resonance totally at odds with her everyday existence here on the station.

"Nobody needs to deal with anyone," she replied. She cast a stern look at Naomi. "Mother, you are forgetting your manners. That is not the way we treat guests here at the Simpson Station."

"Guests are one thing. Ghosts from the past are quite another."

Naomi threw herself into the nearest chair and glared at Alex.

"I'm sorry, Alex, she's not normally so rude," Loren apologized. "Perhaps you should go."

"I think not. There are matters that need to be discussed," Alex answered, his attention firmly on Naomi's bristling presence.

He guided Loren to one of the richly upholstered sofas before settling his long frame at her side. A shiver of awareness rippled through her as his presence imprinted along her body.

"I believe you know why I'm here. It is time for Loren and me to fulfill our fathers' promise to one another."

Naomi's snort was at total odds with her elegant appearance.

"Promise? More like the ramblings of two crazy men who should have known better. No one in the developed world would sanction such an archaic suggestion."

"Archaic or not, I feel bound to honor my father's wish. Much as I imagine Loren does, also."

Loren felt that shiver again as Alex responded to her mother's derision. Naomi wasn't the kind of woman who liked to be contradicted. She ruled the station with an iron fist and a razor-sharp mind and was both respected and feared by her staff. Despite her designer chic wardrobe and her petite frame she was every bit as capable as any one of the staff here. A fact she had proven over and over again. But she was very much accustomed to being in charge, with her decrees accepted without question. The problem was, Alex was used to that, too. This confrontation could get messy, especially once her mother realized whose side Loren was on.

"Loren." Her mother turned to her with a stiff smile on her carefully tinted lips. "Surely you're not going to take this seriously. You have a life here, a job, responsibilities. Why on earth would you even consider this outrageous plan?"

Why indeed, Loren wondered as she looked around her. Yes, she had a life here. A life she'd been dragged to, kicking and screaming and full of sullen teenage pout. She'd never wanted to live with her mother but her father hadn't contested his wife's petition for full custody of their only child. Loren had later realized that had in part been because he'd never believed Naomi would actually go through with the divorce and relocate to the opposite side of the world. But his apparent indifference had hurt at the time and she'd arrived here at the Simpson Station feeling as though her entire world had been ripped apart. With that kind of beginning, it was hardly surprising that she'd learned to accept her place at the station, but she'd never learned to love it.

And as for her work here and her responsibilities? Well, it would only be Naomi who missed her, and then only for as long as it took to browbeat some other assistant into docile submission. No. Loren had nothing to hold her here. She and Naomi had never enjoyed the kind of mother-daughter relationship that Loren knew others had and she had learned very early that it was easier to accede to her mother's wishes than fight for her own. On Isla Sagrado, Loren had been almost solely her father's child, and Loren had always believed her mother had taken her from the island more as a punishment for Francois Dubois than out of any kind of maternal instinct.

She'd missed Isla Sagrado every day of the past ten years. Of course that pain of loss, the wrench of being repatriated, had dimmed a little over time, but it was still as real now as the man seated alongside her.

Seeing him again was as if he'd brought with him the heat and splendor and lush extravagance of Isla Sagrado. Not to mention the promise of the revival of a passion for living that had lain dormant within her since she'd left the country of her birth.

Yes, her initial reaction to Alex's arrival here had

been shock and disbelief. But it was clear he meant what he said. Why else would he have traveled half the world to come and see her?

Thoughts spun through her mind with lightning-fast speed. Her earlier objections, as weak as they were, had come reflexively—a direct result of surprise at the manifestation of the man who'd been a part of her dreams her entire life. She'd wanted—no, she'd *needed*—to hear him refute her doubts to her face. To tell her they belonged together as she'd always imagined, as she'd pretty much lost hope of imagining.

Now she knew what it was like to be in his arms, to feel truly alive for the first time she could remember, there was no way she was going to turn her back on her destiny with the only man she'd ever loved.

"Why would I consider marrying Alex? I would have thought that was quite straightforward," Loren responded with as much aplomb as she could muster under her mother's piercing gaze. "Inasmuch as Alex wishes to honor his father, so do I mine. I've always understood that this would be my future, Mother." She turned her face to look at Alex. "And it's what I've always wanted. I would be honored to be Alex's wife."

"How on earth could you know what you want?" Naomi demanded, pushing up out of her chair and pacing back and forth between them. "You've barely been off the station since we've lived here. You haven't experienced the world, other men, anything!"

"Is that what it really takes to make a person happy? Are *you* truly happy?" Loren held her mother's gaze as her questions unerringly hit their mark. Naomi gaped for a moment, clearly surprised to hear Loren fight back. But even Naomi couldn't deny the truth of what Loren had said.

Naomi's affairs were legend in New Zealand—her power and beauty made for a magnetically lethal combination—and yet, even though many had tried, no man had captured her heart. Loren knew she didn't want that life for herself.

"We're not talking about me. We're talking about you—your future, your life. Don't throw it away on a pledge made before you can even remember. You are worth so much more than that, Loren."

Loren felt the walls, her mother's walls, closing in around her and she pushed them back just as hard.

"Exactly, Mother." Loren sat up straighter, confidence coming from Alex's warmth against her side—confidence to speak her mind at last and say the words she'd locked down deep inside for too long. "I stayed here because I had nothing else to do. Growing up on Isla Sagrado, I believed I had a purpose, a direction. When you and Papa split up I lost that. You took me away from the only future I ever wanted."

"You were just a child—"

"Maybe then, yes. But I'm not a child any longer. We both know I've been marking time these past few years. You know my heart isn't in the station like yours is. You always felt displaced on Isla Sagrado. That's how I feel here. I want to go back.

"As you so correctly pointed out, we are talking about *my* future and *my* life—and I want that to be on Isla Sagrado, with Alex."

He could hardly believe it had been so easy. Alex savored the exhilaration that surged within him as

Loren's words hung on the air between mother and daughter.

His body continued to throb in reaction to the slightly built woman at his side, remembering how it felt to be pressed against her far more intimately. Yes, kissing her had been a risk, but he'd built his formidable business reputation on taking big risks and reaping even bigger rewards. This had definitely been a risk worth taking.

Just one look at her had been enough to prove the information he'd been given about her sheltered lifestyle. She appeared as untouched and protected as she'd been the day she left Isla Sagrado. But beneath that inexperienced exterior beat a sensual heart. Wakening that side of her would be a delight and would make the whole process of providing *Abuelo* with a great-grandchild, as proof the curse did not exist and laying it to rest once and for all, an absolute pleasure.

Alex tilted his head slightly to watch Loren as her mother began a tirade of reasons why she should not return to Isla Sagrado. He wasn't worried about Naomi's arguments. If there was one thing he remembered most clearly about Loren as a child it was that despite her quiet attitude, there was no matching her tenacity once she had made up her mind. The vast number of his girlfriends she'd scared off being a case in point.

Instead of following the argument, he took the time to fully take in the woman who would be his wife. Her long black hair, scraped back in a utilitarian ponytail, showcased the delicate structure of her face. And what a face—the child's features he remembered had matured into those of a beautiful young woman's. Her brows were still strong and delicately arched but the eyes beneath them, dark brown like his own, glowed with an inner fire, and her lips were full and lush. Fuller, perhaps, because of their recent kiss, and certainly something he wanted to taste and savor again.

Where had that gawky kid who'd followed him around incessantly disappeared to? In place of the slightly older version of her that he'd expected, he'd discovered a woman who, while she had every appearance of fragility and a vulnerable air about her that aroused his protective instincts, somehow had managed to develop a backbone of pure steel.

He was reminded of Audrey Hepburn as he looked at her now. The gamine features, matured into beauty—the delicate bone structure, intensely feminine. Something else roared to life from deep inside of him. Something ancient, almost feral. She was his— betrothed to him as a matter of honor between friends, but his nonetheless. And she'd stay that way. Nothing Naomi could say would ever change that.

Two

Despite the luxurious trappings of first class, Loren had been unable to sleep during the long journey from New Zealand. After a day and a half of travel and changeovers she felt weary and more than a little disoriented as she made her way through Sagradan customs and immigration. Nothing about the airport was familiar to her anymore. Still, she supposed as she hefted her cases from the luggage carousel and onto a trolley, it was only natural that change had come to Isla Sagrado in the ten years she'd been gone.

Even so, a pang for the old place she'd left behind lodged behind her heart. Loren shook her head. She was being fanciful if she expected to be able to walk back into her old life as if she'd never left. So much had changed. Her father was gone, her mother was now half a world away and here she was—engaged and preparing to reunite with her fiancé of only a few weeks.

It didn't seem real, Loren admitted to herself—and not for the first time. Everything had moved so fast from the moment she'd told her mother she was returning to the home of her birth. Well, at least once Naomi had recognized that she could not sway her only child's stubborn insistence that she would be marrying Alexander del Castillo.

Alex had taken control once her mother had ceased her objections and washed her hands of the matter, smoothing the way toward having Loren's expired Sagradan passport renewed and booking her flights to Isla Sagrado. Loren hadn't had to lift so much as a finger. Well used to taking care of such details for both her mother and for the overseas guests who visited the massive working sheep and cattle station, it had been a pleasure to have someone else take care of her for a change.

Once he'd had everything organized to his satisfaction, Alex had departed, but not before arranging a private dinner for just the two of them, off the station. They'd choppered to Queenstown, where they'd visited a restaurant on the edge of Lake Wakatipu. The late autumn evening had been clear and beautiful and the restaurant every bit as romantic as Loren had ever dreamed.

By the time they'd returned to the station she knew she was totally and irrevocably in love with him. Not the innocent adoration of a child nor the all-absorbing puppy love of an adolescent, but the deeper knowledge that, no matter what, he was her mate in this lifetime and any other.

He'd been solicitous and attentive all night and, before walking her to her small suite of rooms in the main house at the station, he'd kissed her again. Not with the heated, overwhelming rush of emotion that consumed her the day he'd arrived, but with a gentle, sure promise of greater things to come. Her body had quivered in response, eager to discover the depths of his silent promise right there, right then. But Alex had backed off, cupped her cheek with one warm strong hand, and told her he wanted to wait until their wedding night—it would make their union more special, more intimate.

It had only made her love him more and had served to leave her fraught with nerves the entire journey to Isla Sagrado. Nerves that now left her giddy with exhaustion and made battling the broken wheel on her luggage cart all the more taxing. Fighting the way the thing wanted to veer to the left all the time, Loren paid little attention to the sudden silence in the arrival hall as she came through the security doors after clearing customs.

A silence that was suddenly and overwhelmingly broken by the flash of camera bulbs and a barrage of questions flung at her from all directions and in at least three different languages.

One voice broke over all the rest to ask in Spanish, Isla Sagrado's dominant language, "Is it true you're here to marry Alexander del Castillo and break the curse?"

Loren blinked in surprise toward the man, even as a multitude of others around him continued with their own questions.

A movement at her side distracted her from answering. A tall and stunningly beautiful woman, wearing a startling red dress, hooked an arm around her and leaned forward, her long, honey-blond hair brushing Loren's arm like a swathe of silk.

"Don't answer them. Just smile and keep walking. I'm Giselle, Alex's personal assistant. I'm here to collect you," she murmured in a French-accented voice that was very un-assistantlike. Her emphasis on the word *personal* hinted strongly at things Loren herself had no experience of.

"Alex isn't here?" Loren blinked to fight back the sudden tears that sprang to her eyes as sharp points of disappointment cut through her.

Believing he'd be here to welcome her home at the end of her journey had been what had kept her going these past few hours. Now, she fought to keep her slender shoulders squared and her sagging spine upright. Struggled to keep placing one foot in front of the other.

Giselle put her free hand on the handle of the luggage cart and directed it, and Loren, toward the exit. Airport security had miraculously cleared a path and beckoned them toward the waiting limousine at the curbside.

"If he'd have come, the media circus would have been worse and we'd never have cleared the airport," Giselle said in her husky voice. "Besides, he's a very busy man."

Giselle's intimation that Alex had far more important things to attend to than collecting his fiancée from the airport pierced Loren's weariness, making her stumble slightly.

"Oh, dear," the other woman said, tightening her hold around Loren's waist. "You're a clumsy little thing, aren't you? You'll have to improve on that, you know, or the media are going to have a field day with you."

While Giselle's tone was light, Loren felt the invisible slap of disapproval behind her words. But there was no chance to respond right away. They were at the car at last. There, a uniformed chauffeur, who looked more like a bodyguard than a driver, hefted her cases into the voluminous trunk of the limo as if they weighed little more than matchsticks. Once that was taken care of, Loren took the opportunity to speak.

"I'm tired, that's all. It's been quite a trip," she responded as she slid over onto the broad backseat of the limousine, her voice a little sharp, earning her an equally sharp look from Giselle in return.

"Touchy, too, hmm?" Giselle narrowed her beautiful green eyes and gave Loren an assessing look. "Well, we'll see how you measure up. Since Reynard issued the press release about Alex's engagement, the whole drama of your father's near drowning and him giving you away afterwards has been front-page news. Goodness knows paparazzi will be crawling all over you to find out about you."

"I'm surprised. I thought Alex might have kept that quiet," Loren said, frowning at the thought of having to rehash the story of her and Alex's fathers' actions over and over again.

"Quiet? Hardly. With the way things are here they need all the strong publicity they can get. You must remember how the island's prosperity seems to be intrinsically linked with the del Castillos'. Whether there's any truth to the curse or not, everyone here is lapping up the story. Promises of happily ever after and all that. Honestly, they've made it all sound so sweet it's almost enough to give you cavities." Giselle finished with a high-pitched laugh that didn't quite ring true.

"So you don't believe in happily ever after?"

"Sweetie," Giselle replied with a smile stretching her generous lips into a wide curve of satisfaction, "what's more important is if Alex believes in it. And we both know he's far too pragmatic for that. Besides, it's not like you two are going to have a real marriage."

"Well, I certainly expect we'll have a real marriage. Why else would we even bother?"

"Oh, dear, you mean he hasn't said anything yet?"

Loren felt her already simmering temper begin to flare. "Said anything about what?" she asked through clenched teeth.

"About keeping up appearances, of course. Though perhaps he thought it would be clear. After all, if he'd had any interest in a *real* marriage he'd have wanted to have some say in the organization of the wedding ceremony and reception, wouldn't he? Instead, he gave me carte blanche. But don't you worry, I'll make sure you have a day to remember."

"Well, *I'd* like to go over the wedding details with you later on, when I'm more rested," Loren asserted, pausing for effect. "Then I'll more than happily take the arrangements off your hands. I'm sure you have far more important things to occupy yourself with."

Loren chose to ignore the rest of what the woman had said. She knew she and Alex had little time before their proposed wedding date only two weeks away, but surely he hadn't left everything to his assistant—his *personal* assistant, she corrected herself.

"Oh, but I have everything under control. Besides,

Alex has signed off on what I've done already. To change anything now would only cause problems."

The implication that Loren would bear disapproval from Alex for those problems sat very clearly between the two women. Loren took a steadying breath. She wasn't up to this right now but she knew what Giselle was doing. She'd probably taken one look at Loren and totally underestimated her. Clearly Giselle had some kind of bond with Alex that she didn't want to let go. Maybe she'd even harbored a notion of a relationship with him.

Whatever might have happened between Alex and Giselle before she had arrived home, Loren was his fiancée, and she'd prove she was no walkover. Her battle with her mother to come here in the first place had proven to her that she was anything but that.

"Well," she said, injecting a firm note into her voice, "we'll see about that once I've checked everything over and conferred with Alex." At the other woman's sharply indrawn breath she added, "It is *my* wedding, after all."

Loren settled back against the soft leather upholstery and gazed out the window of the speeding limousine, wondering if she had gone too far in establishing where she stood with Giselle. Perhaps she'd been oversensitive, worn out as she was with travel. But underneath Giselle's self-assuredness and apparent solicitude she sensed a vague but definite threat, as if she was stepping where she wasn't fully welcome by coming back to Isla Sagrado.

She stifled a sigh. She'd expected her homecoming to be different, sure, but when push came to shove she couldn't forget what—or more importantly, *who*—had brought her here.

Alex.

Just thinking about him created a swell of longing deep inside. Without thinking, she traced the outline of her lips with her fingertips, silently reliving their last kiss. If she tried hard enough she could still feel the pressure of his mouth against hers, still experience the heady joy of knowing he'd traveled to New Zealand to fulfill their fathers' bargain—that he'd seen her and still wanted *her*.

Loren let her hand drop back into her lap and stared out the passenger window, searching for familiar sign-posts and buildings. The landscape had changed so much that Isla Sagrado hardly felt like home anymore, she thought sadly as the unfamiliar roads and build-ings swept by them.

The soft trill of a cell phone startled Loren from her reveries. From the corner of her eye she saw Giselle lift a phone to her ear.

"Alex!" Giselle answered, her voice warm and sweet as honey.

Loren's stomach clenched in excitement and she waited for Giselle to hand the phone over to her so she could speak with him herself.

"Yes, I have your future bride here in the car. I ex-pect we'll be at the castillo in about half an hour." She cocked her head to one side and smiled as she listened. "Fine. Yes. I'll let her know."

Giselle flipped the phone shut and gave Loren a smile. "Alex sends his apologies but he won't be able to meet with you until this evening. Business, you un-derstand."

If Loren wasn't mistaken, there was a distinct hint of smugness in the other woman's glittering emerald gaze. She swallowed her disappointment. Not for anything would she yield so far as to display even one hint of weakness, no matter how bitter the pill that Alex couldn't spare even a few minutes to greet her on her first day here.

"Of course. I look forward to the opportunity to have a little rest and freshen up before I see him." Loren smiled in return, summoning a bravado she hoped she could pull off. "Besides, Alex and I have the rest of our lives together. What're a few more hours?"

Alex put down his office phone and stared out the window. It looked down and over the sprawling luxury waterfront resort that was his main concern in the management of the del Castillo financial empire. From his position, it looked beautiful and peaceful, but appearances could be deceiving.

A matter between two of his key management staff that he'd thought Giselle had settled weeks ago had flared up again today with no apparent warning. He sighed. There was no accounting for personalities and how people could either rub along together or end up rubbing one another entirely the wrong way. Add to that the constant harping on about the wretched governess's curse, both in the media and in the whispers among the staff—suffice it to say that the sooner this wedding was done and Loren was pregnant with his child, the better.

How a nation of well-educated and forward-thinking people could remain so superstitious defied belief. The legend of the governess and her curse on the del

Castillo family when she was spurned by her lover was just that. A legend. There was no proof. Even the media interest he himself had encouraged had turned into a two-headed beast he could barely tolerate. Giselle had been an enormous help, always stepping in to deflect questions away from him so she could handle them herself.

And she had come to his aid again today. In the face of the urgency in dealing with today's debacle, her calm suggestion that she collect Loren from the airport had been welcome. Giselle was a consummate professional. He knew she'd make Loren feel at home and get her comfortably settled at the castillo.

If he'd gone to get her, the press would never have let them leave. They'd still be there, posing for pictures, answering questions—wasting time that could be better spent letting Loren unwind after her flight and letting Alex get this administrative headache straightened out. It would be much better for Alex to spend time with her tonight, at the quiet family dinner he'd organized with his brothers and his grandfather, and no press around to badger them.

He allowed himself a small smile at the thought of his grandfather's excitement over their planned dinner. *Abuelo's* reaction when told that Loren would be returning to Isla Sagrado as his future bride had been worth the time away from the problems at the resort to visit with her.

He thought back to when he'd broken his brief liaison with Giselle. She'd pouted a little but had taken his decision, and the diamond tennis bracelet he'd bought her as a severance gift, with good grace and assured him her efficiency in her work would continue. And she'd reiterated her willingness to take up where they'd left off should he ever change his mind.

Until he'd seen Loren again, he'd given Giselle's offer some serious thought. After all, once he'd married and met *Abuelo's* concerns by ensuring the next del Castillo generation would be born, why shouldn't he have some fun? But, despite the clinical manner in which he'd imagined this alliance would go forth, from the second his lips had touched Loren's there had been something about her that had pushed Giselle's offer right out of his mind.

That Loren was unschooled in the ways of love was clear, but how unschooled? The thought that she might be a virgin both intrigued and enticed him. To be her first lover, to unlock the sensual creature he'd tasted in that first kiss? Oh yes, there were definitely aspects of his marriage to Loren Dubois that he found himself looking forward to far more than he'd anticipated. Now, if he was going to enjoy any time with Loren later today he needed to catch up with his work here at the resort. Fortunes didn't make themselves—legend or no.

By the time Giselle returned to the office he was entrenched in his work. He lifted his head only briefly when she came in with some papers.

"I hope Loren didn't mind I couldn't be there to greet her. Is she all settled now at the castillo?" he asked, scoring his signature across the letters she leaned over to place on his desk.

"Of course she minded you weren't there. Wouldn't any woman?"

Giselle laughed, but he noticed her smile did not quite reach her eyes.

Her fragrance, as heady and sensual as the woman

herself, wove around him. But rather than the usual re-action it evoked in him—an anticipation of pleasurable things to come—he was reminded instead of the contrast between his assistant's overt sexuality and Loren's more subtle blend of allure. For some perverse reason, the latter was now far more appealing.

"And yes, in answer to your question, I made sure she was completely comfortable in her suite," Giselle answered. "Although she did seem very weary from her travel."

"Too tired for the dinner with *Abuelo* tonight, do you think?"

"Well, obviously I can't speak for her but, yes, she did look rather shattered. I wouldn't be at all surprised if she slept all the way through until morning."

Alex furrowed his brow in a frown. Until morning? That wouldn't do. *Abuelo* was looking forward to re-newing his acquaintance with the daughter of the man who'd been his son's best friend for so many years. An edge of irritation slid under his skin at the thought that Loren would prefer to sleep rather than spend the eve-ning with him. Alex had planned to present her with the del Castillo betrothal ring tonight. The official seal of their engagement. He huffed out a breath.

"Well, she's just going to have to find her strength from somewhere. The dinner is far too important to postpone."

He missed the subtle curve of Giselle's mouth as he voiced his frustration.

"She probably will benefit from a few good meals, Alex. She does look rather…frail," Giselle commented as she collected the papers off his desk and turned to go back to her desk in the outer office.

"Frail?"

Alex frowned again. Certainly Loren was very slightly built, but in his arms he'd felt the strength and suppleness of her body. Plus, he'd witnessed firsthand her mental determination.

"Appearances can be deceptive," he concluded. "She will be fine, I'm sure."

"Would you like me to make sure she's ready for the dinner tonight?"

"No, Giselle, that won't be necessary, but thank you."

"No problem." His assistant smiled in return before closing his door behind her.

Alex sat staring at the door for some time, comparing the disparities between the two women. Aside from the obvious physical differences—Giselle's lush femininity versus Loren's more gamine appearance—they were worlds apart in other matters. While Giselle tended to be exactly what she appeared to be, and wasn't afraid to say exactly what she wanted, Loren had hidden strengths. The way she'd dealt with her mother's objections being a case in point. The phrase "still waters run deep" had been designed with someone like Loren in mind, he was sure.

Had he done the right thing? He pinched the bridge of his nose in an attempt to alleviate the throbbing headache that had begun behind his eyes. He had to have made the right choice. To have done anything else was unacceptable. Loren had all the credentials—from her bloodlines right down to her experience within the milieu where he moved socially. This marriage between them *would* work. She was everything he needed in a wife and he would do whatever he had to in order to be what she needed in a husband.

The late-afternoon sun slanted like a blush of color across the golden brick of the castillo as he approached. A wry smile tweaked at Alex's lips as he realized just how much he took for granted that the medieval stronghold, in his family for centuries, was indeed his home.

While still remaining true to the age-old architecture and the style so typical of the island, the interior had been modernized to make for very comfortable living. Several del Castillo families could, and had in the past, share the various apartments the castillo offered for private family living, if desired. Despite that, his brothers had chosen to make their own homes elsewhere on the island—Reynard in a luxurious city apartment overlooking the sparkling harbor of Isla Sagrado's main city, Puerto Seguro, and Benedict in a modern home clinging to the hillside overlooking the del Castillo vineyard and winery.

He understood why they each felt the need to carve out their own space but he still missed their presence around the castillo, for all the rare time he spent at home these days. Between himself and *Abuelo* there was a great deal of space to fill. A little more of the castillo had been filled today because Loren was inside right at that moment—waiting for him. Something about the thought of his bride-to-be newly settled in his home made it all abruptly real to Alex. After all the planning, she was finally here. In a few weeks, she would be his wife. And hopefully, in the not-too-distant future, the building would fill with the sounds

of children again. *His* children. The thought made
something deep inside him swell.

It would be good for *Abuelo* to be distracted from
the rigors of growing old by the prospect of amusing
the next generation of del Castillos. He had a wealth
of family history to share. It was only right he have the
opportunity to do so.

With that thought in the forefront of his mind, Alex
swept his sleek black Lamborghini through the elec-
tronic gates and inside the walls, toward the stables that
had been converted to a multicar garage thirty years
ago. In minutes he was on the large curved stone staircase leading to the next floor, which housed the private
suites of family rooms. Loren's was close to his own
and he hesitated at her door, his hand poised to knock.

Something stayed his hand, and he let his fingers
curl instead around the intricately carved heavy brass
handle of her door. It lifted smoothly, gaining him entrance. He would have to speak to her later about keeping her door locked. While the castillo's security was
advanced, paparazzi were not above masquerading as
one of the many staff, or even bribing them, in an attempt to get the latest scoop on the family.

Long silent strides on the thickly carpeted floor led
him to her bedroom. There, sprawled across the covers,
lay his future bride. Every nerve in his body surged
to life as he observed her, arms and limbs askew, hair
spread like a dark cloud around her head. There should
be a childlike innocence about her, he thought, yet instead there was only the lure of her female form.

Small breasts pressed in perfect mounds against
the fine cotton of the T-shirt she'd obviously chosen
to sleep in. And only the T-shirt, he observed, keep-

ing himself grimly in check even as he feasted on the sight of the faint outline of her nipples against the well-washed fabric. He tore his eyes from their gentle peaks and instead gazed upon the long slender length of her legs. Not one of his most sensible decisions, he thought as a heated pulse beat low in his groin.

One of her arms curved up and over her pillow, the other was flung out to one side, her unadorned hand curled like a delicate shell.

Alex dropped to his knees at her bedside and leaned over the mattress. He felt the warmth radiating from her, as if it were a tangible thing, as his lips hovered over the softness of her palm. Then he bent his head and pressed his lips against the fleshy mound at the base of her thumb, the tip of his tongue sweeping across its surface to taste her skin.

Loren's fingers curled to cup his cheek and he sensed the precise moment she emerged from her slumber. Heard the sharp intake of breath through her lush pink lips. Saw the awareness flare in her eyes as her lids flashed open.

"Alex?"

Her voice was drugged with the residue of sleep yet its huskiness sent a lance of pure heat cutting through his body, provoking him to full, aching arousal. Right now he wanted nothing more than to sink onto the soft mattress with her, to envelop her in his arms and to taste all the delights her body had to offer. But he'd already promised to wait until their wedding night and they would be expected amongst company very soon. He forced his unwilling flesh to cooperate and gently pulled away from her touch.

"I know you're tired, but you must begin to ready yourself for dinner tonight."

"Dinner?"

She sounded confused. Surely Giselle had informed her of this evening's expectations.

"Yes, dinner. My grandfather looks forward to welcoming you back home."

He averted his gaze as she pushed herself upright and sat with her legs crossed beneath her. The creamy skin of her thighs and the shadowed hollow he knew lay at their apex, just beyond the hem of her shirt, were pure torment as he imagined touching her softness and delving into the hidden flesh there.

Arousal flared anew, this time even more demanding than before. But Loren's next words, delivered with an unmistakable note of challenge, doused his ardor as quickly as it had flamed into searing life.

"And you? Do you also welcome me home, Alex?"

Three

He fought back the flare of irritation that swelled inside him at her words. Was she criticizing him for not having been at the airport to welcome her? Giselle's insinuation echoed in the back of his mind. He fought for an edge of control, reminding himself she was no doubt still overtired from her journey and perhaps still wearing her disappointment he wasn't there to welcome her in person.

"Ah, I see you are still upset I was not at the airport to greet you. I thought Giselle explained why I could not be there."

"Oh yes, she explained." Loren unfolded her legs, threw them over the edge of the bed and rose to her full height.

Barefoot, the top of her head barely even reached his shoulder, and dressed as she was she gave an almost childlike impression. But there was nothing childlike in her demeanor, nor in the very female brand of dissatisfaction reflected in her eyes. He was reminded of the times he'd upset his mother. Never one to raise her voice, she'd only needed a look such as this to put him in his place.

"I would have been there if I could." Alex softened his tone. He should have made more effort to be at the arrival hall. He realized that now. He'd tried to make things easier for both of them, but instead he'd made matters worse. Still, the situation wasn't beyond salvaging and now he was determined to recover as much ground as possible.

"I have been looking forward to seeing you this evening," he said, his voice low.

He saw pleasure light her eyes and felt an inner relief as her full lips curved into a smile.

"So have I," she said shyly, dropping her gaze.

"So, you will dress for dinner and come down to share our repast?"

"Of course I will. I'm sorry I was a bit cranky. I'm never at my best when I first wake."

Alex allowed his mouth to relax into a smile. "I'll make a special note to remember that for after we're married."

She laughed, a delicious liquid sound that penetrated the last remnants of his temper and scattered them to the corners of the room.

"It might pay to." She smiled. "Now, tonight. What time and where? I'm assuming your family still dresses for dinner?"

She must have been half-asleep already when Giselle told her, he decided.

"Yes, we change for dinner. We meet for drinks in the salon usually about eight and dine at nine. Late, I know, if you aren't used to it anymore."

"Oh, don't worry, I'll acclimate. Will you take me down?"

"You no longer remember where the salon is?" He cocked a brow at her.

"Of course, I don't imagine the castillo has changed all that much. I just…" She worried her lower lip with perfect white teeth. "No, don't worry. I'll meet you there at eight."

Alex dropped a chaste kiss on Loren's upturned face and moved away before the disappointment he sensed in her encouraged him to take more. Now that she was here and they were on the verge of achieving his goal of settling the governess's curse, there was no need to rush into anything. There would be plenty of time to kiss her the way he wanted—after they were married.

"Good girl. I'll see you there."

Loren watched her door close behind Alex's back and she fought the urge to stomp her foot in frustration. Now she was here he'd reverted to treating her like a child. Gone was the attentive lover who'd wooed her back in New Zealand. In his place was the old Alex she remembered so well. Slightly indulgent and full of the importance of his role as eldest son.

Well, she'd show him she was no infant to be coddled. Her body still hummed with her reaction to the soft kiss he'd pressed in her palm to wake her. Just one small caress and she'd shot to full wakefulness, her joy in seeing him only to be dashed by his reminder of her duty to be at some formal dinner tonight.

She knew they still adhered to the old ways, ways she'd taken for granted until moving to New Zealand with its more casual approach to lifestyle and mealtimes, but she'd hoped for a private dinner with her new fiancé. It wasn't so much to have expected, was it? Surely Alex's grandfather would have granted them this first night alone together?

There was nothing for it now, though, she reminded herself as the chime from an antique ormolu clock in her sitting room chimed the half hour. She had to fulfill Alex's expectations. At least she knew she'd have fun catching up with his brothers. As for Alex, well, maybe she'd punish him a little for not pressing to have kept her to himself tonight. She had just the perfect outfit in there. She'd bought it with Alex's reaction to her very firmly in mind.

She looked about her room for her suitcases and was surprised to see them gone. A quick look in her dressing room solved her problem as she espied her clothing already unpacked and hung neatly on hangers or folded away in the built-in drawers. She must have been totally out of it not to have heard the maid come in and see to her things.

She quickly filtered through the selection of dresses she'd bought, her hand settling on the rich red silk organza cocktail dress she wanted to wear tonight. The bodice was scattered with tiny faceted beads that caught the light and emphasized her small bust, while the layers of fabric that fell from the empire line below her breasts had a floating effect that made her feel as though she was the most elegant creature on the planet. Not a feeling she embraced often, Loren admitted silently.

She laid the dress on her bed and chose a pair of stiletto-heeled sandals in silver to wear with it.

"And if that's not dressed up enough for dinner, then nothing will do," she said out loud.

She made her way into her bathroom and took a moment to appreciate the elegant fixtures. The deep claw-foot bath beckoned to her but she knew she had little time left to get ready. She wondered briefly why Alex had acted as if she should have known all along about the dinner tonight. Perhaps Giselle had meant to tell her and had forgotten. Although Loren suspected that Giselle forgot very little indeed.

No, it must have been an oversight somewhere along the line. What with all the paparazzi at the airport, it was something that could easily have slipped Giselle's mind. She was prepared to be charitable. After all, she was finally *home*. Back on Isla Sagrado. Back with Alex.

She hummed happily to herself as she took a brief and refreshing shower. After toweling herself dry with a deliciously soft, fluffy bath sheet that virtually encased her from head to foot, she swept up her hair into a casual chignon and applied her makeup with a light hand. She studied her appearance for a moment then decided to emphasize her eyes a little more and to apply a slick of ruby-red gloss to match her dress. With the strength of color of her dress she'd disappear if she didn't vamp things up a bit, even if she normally only wore the bare minimum of cosmetics. Finally satisfied with her smoky eyes and glossy lips, she reached for a clean pair of panties and then slipped into her gown.

Loren loved the shimmer of the fabric as it brushed over her skin. The tiny shoestring straps and the low

back of the dress made it impossible to wear a bra, but
the beading hid any evidence that she was braless. She
slid her feet into the high-heeled sandals and bent to
do up the ankle straps before checking herself in the
antique cheval mirror in her room.

Yes, she'd do nicely for her first meal at home with
the del Castillo men, and for whoever else might be
joining them. She wondered whether either Reynard
or Benedict would have companions for the evening.
Both of Alex's brothers' eligible bachelor status led
them to be featured highly in magazines even as far
away as New Zealand, and she doubted either of them
would have far to look to find company.

A quick look at the clock on the bedroom man-
telpiece projected her through her suite and out the
main door into the corridor to the main stairs. She was
grateful for the ornate carpet runner because she had
no doubt her heels would have caught on the ancient
flagstones beneath it as she hurried down the stairs.

For a moment the sense of longevity about the castillo seeped through her. How many del Castillo brides
had traversed this very path to their betrothed over the
centuries, and how many of those marriages had been
as happy as she hoped hers and Alex's would be? She
shook her head a little, chiding herself for being fanciful as a sudden weight of expectation settled upon her
shoulders. A small chilled shudder ran down her spine,
as if she was being watched—judged, even.

Loren hesitated on the stairs and looked around her,
but of course there was nothing there but the gallery
of portraits of successive heads of the family over the
past many years. She injected a little more urgency

in her step as she reached the bottom of the staircase and headed to where she remembered the salon to be.

The murmur of deep male voices, punctuated by the sound of laughter, was comforting as she approached the room where Alex had said to meet. Loren quashed the lingering effects of the sense of disquiet that had hit her earlier and focused instead on the prospect of an evening with the man she'd loved for as long as she could remember. Nothing could go wrong now, nothing. Her life was finally what she'd always dreamed it would be.

With a smile on her face, she entered the salon and was treated to the impeccable manners of four gentlemen rising from their seats to welcome her. Loren nodded in greeting to Reynard and Benedict, each easily recognizable and, she noted with some surprise, unaccompanied by female adornments.

Alex stood a little to one side. His hair, still wet from a recent shower, was slicked back off his forehead, giving him a sartorial edge that went well with the black suit and shirt he'd donned for the evening. But the serious set to his mouth and his darkened jawline made him appear unapproachable.

His dark eyes caught hers and burned beneath slightly drawn brows. She felt her smile waver a little under his gaze, but then he smiled in return and it was as if another giant weight had been lifted from her.

"You look beautiful," he said, his eyes glowing in appreciation.

A flood of pleasure coursed through her at his words, warming her all the way to her toes.

"Come, say hello to *Abuelo*. He has been impatient to see you."

She crossed the room, straight toward the silver-haired figure nearest the fireplace. Despite the fact it was May, a fire roared in the cavernous depths, throwing heat into the room and adding a cheerful ambience that chased the last of the lingering shadows from Loren's mind.

From his proximity to the fire she deduced Alex's grandfather felt the chill far more than he used to, and she couldn't help noticing the slight droop to one side of his face and the way he leaned heavily on an ebony cane. It saddened her to see he'd aged so much since she'd left, but one look at the spark in his eyes showed her that *Abuelo* was still very much the patriarch and very much in control.

Her lips curved in genuine pleasure as she placed her hands in his gnarled ones and leaned in to kiss him on the cheeks.

"*Bienvenido a casa, mi niña,*" he murmured in his gruff voice. "It is past time you were back."

"It is so good to be home, *Abuelo,*" she replied, using the moniker he'd insisted she call him back when she was a child.

"Come, sit by me and tell me what foolishness has kept you from us for so long."

The old man settled back into his easy chair and gestured to the seat opposite.

"Now, *Abuelo,* you know that Loren's mother insisted she move to New Zealand with her," Alex said, coming to stand behind Loren's chair and resting one hand upon her shoulder. "Besides, you cannot monopolize her when she is here to see everyone."

Loren felt the heat from his palm against her bare

skin and leaned into his touch, relishing the sizzling contact.

"I do not see any ring upon her finger, Alexander. You cannot monopolize her while she is yet a free woman."

"Ah, but that is where you are wrong, *Abuelo,*" Alex teased in return. "Loren is most definitely mine."

A fierce pang of joy shot through her, catching her breath, at his words. If she'd had any doubts, they were now assuaged.

Loren felt Alex's hand slide down the length of her arm, to her left hand. Clasping it, he drew her upright to face him. Butterflies danced in her stomach as she saw the intensity in his dark eyes. Alex was a man who obviously thought deeply, not sharing those thoughts with many, but if the possessive fire she glimpsed burning bright in his gaze was any indicator, she had no doubt that he was about to stake his claim to her before his family.

Alex slipped his free hand into his jacket pocket and withdrew it again.

"This is a mere formality, as Loren has already consented to be my wife, but I want you, *mi familia,* to witness my pledge to marry her," Alex announced as he revealed the ring in his hand.

"That's if she hasn't taken one look at us and changed her mind," Reynard taunted his elder brother and was rewarded with a quelling glare.

"I h-haven't. I w-wouldn't," Loren stuttered slightly as she saw the exquisitely beautiful, smooth, oval ruby set in old gold.

"Then this is for you," Alex murmured, sliding the ring upon her engagement finger.

The gold felt warm against her skin and the ring fit as if it was made for her and her alone. She'd recognized it immediately when he'd drawn it from his pocket. The del Castillo betrothal ring, handed down from firstborn son to firstborn son, had been in the family for centuries. The last woman to wear it had been Alex's mother.

The gold filigree on each shoulder of the ring had been crafted into delicate heart shapes and the stone appeared to take on a new glow against her skin.

"It's beautiful, Alex. Thank you," she said, lifting her eyes to meet his. "I'm honored to accept this."

"No, Loren, you honor me by agreeing to become my wife."

"I've always loved you, Alex. It's no more than I've ever wanted."

The air between them stilled, solidified, almost becoming something corporeal before Benedict interrupted them with two glasses of champagne. He thrust one at each of them.

"This calls for a toast, yes?"

He passed another glass to their grandfather before raising one of his own.

"To Alex and Loren. May they have many happy years."

A look passed between the brothers, something unspoken that hovered in the air as they connected silently with one another, then as one lifted their glasses to drink. Whatever it was, it was soon gone as sibling rivalry and teasing took over the atmosphere, leading even *Abuelo* to laugh and admonish them gently, reminding them of the lady in their midst.

Now she really belonged, Loren thought as she

smiled and sipped the vintage French champagne, letting the bubbles dance along her tongue much as happiness danced through her veins. And, as the subtle lighting in the room caught the ruby on her finger, she knew that no matter how distant Alex had been today, everything was now perfect in her world.

Four

"I see he's given you that old thing."

Loren forced her shoulders to relax and her instincts not to bristle at Giselle's throwaway remark. It was three days after her arrival at the castillo and the first time she'd been forced back into Giselle's company. Days that had been filled with dress fittings and learning her responsibilities toward the staff at the castle. At least in the matter of her wedding dress she'd been able to choose for herself. As far as the wedding ceremony and reception went, Loren had been forced, with so little time left, to refrain from making any changes.

She chewed over Giselle's comment about the ruby. Clearly the woman wanted to belittle both her and Alex's gift, but she'd chosen the wrong target. What would the other woman know, or even begin to understand, of del Castillo tradition and the importance and validation behind having received the ring Alex had given her?

"I'd have asked for something more modern myself," the other woman continued.

Giselle lifted one hand from the steering wheel of the car in which she'd just picked Loren up from the castillo. Shafts of sunlight caught on the diamond tennis bracelet she wore on one wrist.

"Something more like this."

Loren merely smiled. "Your bracelet is beautiful, but I prefer knowing that there is only one of this ring and understanding the history behind it. I feel privileged to be chosen to wear it."

And she did feel privileged. Being given the family heirloom had cemented her place at Alex's side, no matter how emotionally and even physically distant he had remained since that night. She was confident that in time their emotional distance would close and eventually disappear altogether, especially if their reaction to one another was anything to go by. She closed her eyes and momentarily relived the pressure of his mouth against hers as he'd said good-night at the door to her suite on the night he'd given her the ruby. She'd all but ignited under his masterful lips and tongue.

She'd wanted to clutch at the fabric of his shirt and pull him toward her, to feel the length of his body imprint against hers as it had when he'd kissed her back in New Zealand. But he'd stepped away slightly—only allowing their lips to fuse, their tongues to duel ever so briefly, before pulling away and wishing her a good night's rest.

What would he have done, she wondered, if she'd taken him by the hand and pulled him into her suite and closed the door firmly behind them? Would he have taken her to her bed and finally taught her the physical delights of love that she'd only read about?

Her timidity frustrated her. What kind of woman was she, coming to marriage to a man of the world such as Alex with no experience beyond a few unsatisfying furtive fumblings and clumsy kisses? She was eager to learn from Alex, but anxious at the thought of disappointing him.

She cast a sideways glance at Giselle. No doubt she'd never faced such a conundrum. The woman looked as if she'd been born ready to take on the world and all its challenges. She also didn't look like the kind of woman to whom Loren could confide her insecurities.

She wondered who'd given Giselle the bracelet she wore so proudly. No doubt some man who'd found her particular brand of confidence and self-assurance as sexy as her lush figure and thick, cascading blond hair. She probably had an array of jewelry like it.

As if suddenly aware of her scrutiny, Giselle flicked her a glance.

"Where would you like to start today? Alex said you're to spare no expense on your trousseau. I imagine you were limited for choices where you lived in New Zealand."

"A little, yes, but aside from the usual imported labels we have access to our own wonderful designers, too. I just rarely had the necessity to dress up all that much."

Loren shifted in her seat, a little uncomfortable with the unspoken suggestion that her wardrobe lacked for anything. Had Alex said as much to Giselle? Did he even trust her to choose her own clothing? The answer was obviously no. Why else would he have insisted Giselle come with her today, when she'd already hinted she'd prefer to spend her time with him, not his assistant?

Besides, everything she owned was of excellent quality, even if the outfit she'd chosen today lacked the European flair of Giselle's tailored trousers and open-necked silk blouse.

"Well, that will all change as Alex's wife, you know. You'll need a good range of items that can take you through any occasion. We frequently entertain royalty and overseas celebrities at the resort and Alex likes us to keep a personal touch with those special guests."

Giselle's casually possessive use of the words *we* and *us* struck Loren as more than accidental. Was she hinting that she had acted at Alex's side in a role as something more than merely his employee? They'd certainly have made a striking couple—he with his dark good looks and she with her golden beauty. Loren silently chastised herself for the pang of envy she felt. Giselle was Alex's right-hand person—of course she'd have escorted him on company business.

She took a steadying breath before replying, "Yes, we pride ourselves on that level of care at the station, too. You'd be surprised at the caliber of guests we have entertained there. But that was nothing new to me. As you know, I grew up here and my father was also a prominent member of Sagradan society. I'm well used to moving among royalty and celebrity and I look forward to accompanying Alex in the same regard. Now, with the shops, I think we should start from the skin out, don't you? I love lingerie shopping."

"Good choice. I know just the right shop to start at and Alex already has an account there."

Loren stiffened. There was no avoiding it. Alex kept an account at a lingerie store, which meant he was well accustomed to purchasing women's lace and finery—from the skin out. Taking a deep breath, Loren reminded herself that there could be an innocent reason for why he kept such an account—perhaps for those special guests that Giselle had already alluded to. Luggage went missing, or was delayed, every day around the world, and things were occasionally lost or damaged in hotel laundries. It would make perfect sense for him to hold an account, Loren rationalized silently.

But in spite of the logic of that explanation, a bitter taste settled in her mouth. Yes, Alex probably used the account for business reasons—but she was a fool if she thought that was the extent of it. Of course he was a man of the world and had no doubt had multiple lovers. Even as a teenager, she'd noticed the way women flocked to him. At the time, she'd dealt with it by trying to scare them all off, but she hadn't been naive enough to believe that she'd succeeded. And now she had proof. She didn't have to like it but she was going to have to learn to live with it, one way or another.

Unconsciously she twisted the heavy ruby ring on her finger. She hadn't expected any words of love from him when he'd given it to her, even though she'd expressed them herself. How could he have learned to love the person she was now, anyway? She'd changed so much from the sometimes petulant and demanding child he remembered. But they had plenty of time for him to learn to love her. They were to be married and she was going to do everything in her power to make it a long and loving marriage.

At the lingerie store Loren was overwhelmed by the multiple arrays of delicate fabrics and colors on offer. She fingered a satin-and-lace nightgown of the sheerest oyster pink. There was a matching wrap that had an exquisitely detailed lace panel in the back. She knew she had to have it.

"Oh, that's pretty," Giselle commented over her shoulder. "But I wouldn't waste too much money on things like that. Alex isn't keen on night wear."

Loren stiffened again. And she'd know that snippet of information how? Okay, so maybe the other woman's earlier comments could have been misconstrued but there was no doubt that Giselle had ceased to be subtle about her allusions to things about which she appeared to have a very personal knowledge.

A needle of pain worked deep into Loren's chest. So, Alex had indulged in an affair with his beautiful assistant. May indeed still be doing so, for all she knew. Did he plan for it to continue even after their marriage? Loren swallowed against the bile that rose, sudden and foully bitter, in her throat.

Giselle still hovered at her side, her green eyes narrowed slightly as if gauging the result of her comment on Loren. Loren knew she had to say something—anything to get through the next few minutes—but she also knew that she dare not show any sign of weakness. A woman like Giselle would capitalize on that weakness and run with it and there was no way Loren was about to let that happen.

"Hmm," she murmured calmly, nodding slowly. "Good to know. Thanks, but I think I'll get it anyway."

She was rewarded with a sharp look from her companion, puzzlement followed swiftly by acceptance, as if Giselle realized that she'd made her point but had failed to rattle Loren as she'd so obviously intended.

It was a hollow victory.

The rest of the day stretched ahead interminably for Loren. The mere thought of absorbing and defusing more comments from Giselle extinguished every last moment of pleasure she'd anticipated in the day.

Loren suggested they take a break with a coffee at one of the harborside cafés. Once they were settled at their table and had placed their orders she sat back and let the warmth of the late spring sunshine seep into her body. She took a deep, steadying breath. She knew what she had to do.

"Giselle, look, I appreciate that you've taken time out of your day to help me with my shopping but I think I'd like a little time to myself and see if I can't catch up with some old school friends instead. You head back to the resort, I'm sure you have plenty of work you'd rather be doing. I'll just get a cab back to the castillo later today."

"Alex specifically asked me to assist you today. I can't leave you just like that," Giselle protested.

"Come on, let's be honest here. You don't want to spend time with me any more than I do with you. You've made it clear that you and Alex have a history. I accept that. But it is now very firmly in the past."

So back off, the unsaid words hung in the air between them.

Loren's heart hammered in her chest. She wasn't used to confrontation of any kind—avoided it like the plague on most occasions, to be honest. But when shoved hard enough she always stood her ground and right now she'd drawn her demarcation line.

"So you're sending me back to be with him? A bit risky, don't you think?"

The smile on Giselle's face was predatory.

"Risky? Well, it was me he traveled half the world to visit and asked to marry, wasn't it?"

Giselle snorted inelegantly. "Nothing more than the fulfillment of his duty to allay an old man's concerns and create some strong publicity for the del Castillo business empire. You can ask Alex about that yourself if you don't believe me." She bent and collected her handbag and rose gracefully from her chair. "Well, I can see I'm no longer wanted here. Far be it from *me* to stay where I don't belong."

Loren sat and watched Giselle walk away, the clear insult about Loren's presence on Isla Sagrado, in Alex's life, echoing in her ears.

But Giselle was wrong, Loren had no doubt about that. If anything, *Giselle* was the intruder here, not Loren. Not when Loren had been born and raised here. Not when Alex had brought her back. Her hands curled into tight fists in her lap. She did belong here, Loren repeated silently in her mind. She did.

When Alex returned to the castillo that night Loren half expected him to mention something about Giselle returning to the office early, or even insist that she avail herself of the other woman's expertise. She'd prepared at least a dozen responses to him by the time she'd finally returned home herself, her arms laden with parcels after a full afternoon of shopping on her own. Her feet ached with the miles she'd walked but inside she'd reached a state she could finally call happy. No matter what Alex said to her about Giselle, she wouldn't let it bring her down.

The number of people who'd recognized her, the old friends she'd indeed bumped into who had been excited to see her—all had made her feel so thoroughly welcomed back.

As it transpired, she hadn't needed a single one of her arguments. Alex was distracted all through the evening meal, letting *Abuelo* direct most of the conversation and listening to her tell him of all she'd seen and done during the day.

After their meal, Alex walked her to her suite as he did every night. As she unlocked the door he put out a hand to cover hers.

"Would you mind if I come in with you this evening?" His voice was deep and the sound caressed her ears like a lover's touch.

"Not at all," she answered with a smile as she swung the heavy door open and stepped inside. "Please, come in."

Loren's heart fluttered in her chest. Had Alex decided not to wait for their wedding night? Nerves, plaited with a silken thread of longing, pulsed deep inside, slowly stoking a furnace of heat within her. Her skin grew sensitive. So sensitive, even the newly bought gown she'd worn to dinner felt too heavy against her.

She turned to him, aware that her cheeks were warm and no doubt bore a flush of color quite at odds with the elegance of her appearance tonight. Her eyes raked over him. Ah, she never tired of drinking in the sight of his masculine beauty. Of the breadth of his shoulders as

they filled the designer suit he wore with such effortless grace and style. Of the press of his chest against
the crisp white cotton of his shirt. Even the way his
throat moved above the knot of his silver-and-black
striped silk tie mesmerized her.

Her mind filled with the prospect of placing her
lips to that very point where she could see the beat of
his pulse—of pressing her lips into his skin, allowing
her tongue to caress that spot and taste him, tasting
so much more.

She clenched her thighs against the sudden thrum
of energy that coiled there. But instead of lessening
the sensation, it only intensified it, sending a small
shock of pleasure through her and driving a tiny gasp
past her lips.

She felt as though she was poised on the balls of
her feet, ready to move into the shelter of his arms and
feel once more the press of his body against hers. Her
whole body was attuned to the man only a few short
feet away from her.

"There is something I need to discuss with you,"
Alex said, the abruptly businesslike tone of his voice
quelling her ardor as suddenly as if she'd been drenched
by a rogue wave on the rocky bay beneath the castle.

Was he now going to take her to task for her dis-
missal of Giselle today? Loren felt the lingering remnants of desire slowly flicker and die. She swallowed
and took a steadying breath.

"Well then, would you be more comfortable sitting
down? Perhaps I can pour you a drink?"

"Yes, thank you. A cognac I think. And pour one
for yourself, too."

Did he think she'd need it? Suddenly Loren wished

he had simply stuck with their usual routine. Even a noncommittal kiss at the door was bound to have been better than being castigated for rejecting his assistant's company. Not that she was going to take any criticism of her choice today without putting up a decent protest of her own. But was she ready to face the truth if she asked him about his relationship with Giselle?

She crossed the sitting room of her suite to the heavily carved dark wooden sideboard against one wall. She took two crystal snifters from within and then lifted the cut-crystal stopper from one of the decanters on the edged silver tray that sat on the polished surface. Alex's warm hand closed over hers.

"Here, let me pour, hmm?"

A fine tremor ran through her as his touch sent a sizzle of electricity coursing up her arm.

She pulled away from him and forced her suddenly uncooperative legs to take her over to one of the two-seater couches. She lowered herself onto the richly upholstered fabric, yet couldn't bring herself to sit back and relax against the cushioned back, instead perching on the edge.

Alex crossed the room and handed her one of the glasses. Loren bent her nose to the rim, taking a deep breath of the aroma of the dark amber liquid before lifting it to her lips and allowing the alcohol to trickle over her tongue and down her throat. She never normally drank hard spirits, but she had the distinct feeling that tonight she was going to need it.

She swallowed, welcoming the burn the distilled liquor left in its path, and watched as Alex sat down opposite her. He unbuttoned his jacket and reached inside, drawing out a folded paper packet. He carefully placed the packet on the coffee table between them, then took a sip of his cognac.

The liquid left a slight sheen upon his lips, capturing her gaze with the inevitability of a moth to a flame. He pressed his lips together, dissipating the residue, allowing her to look away.

"Is that what you want to discuss?" Loren pressed as he made no effort to explain the papers he'd laid before them.

"Yes. It's a legal document I need you to read and sign before we are married. Someone can take you into the notary's office tomorrow for it to be witnessed."

"What kind of legal document?" Loren asked, not even bothering to point out that she could quite capably make her own way into the city.

Alex's dark eyes bored into hers. "A prenuptial document."

"Well, that is only to be expected," Loren said matter-of-factly, even as she forced herself to quell the swell of disappointment that rose within her. Did he really find such a document necessary?

As far as she was concerned, this marriage was forever. She had no desire and no plans to ever leave Alex, nor, if such a heartbreaking event should occur, could she imagine she would ever make unreasonable financial demands against him.

"Perhaps it would be best if you read it first. If you have any questions I'm sure the notary will be able to answer them for you."

Alex put down his glass and rose from his seat. "I'd better get going. I have an early flight tomorrow."

"Flight?" Loren asked. "Where? May I come with you?"

"It is nothing but a business trip to Seville. You would be bored. Which reminds me, you will need to ask Reynard or Benedict to take you to the notary as Giselle will be accompanying me. Actually, best to call on Reynard. Benedict drives like a demented race-car driver at the best of times and I would hate for anything to happen to you before the wedding."

Loren fought back the bitter disappointment his words evoked in her. "I'll bear that in mind," she replied through stiff lips. "When will you be back?"

"In a couple of days, certainly no more than three."

Three days away with Giselle? Loren felt the news deep in her gut, as if it was a physical blow. Perhaps her earlier fears of today were true after all.

"Good night, then." Alex walked the couple of steps that brought him to her side and bent to kiss the top of her head before leaving the room.

As she watched the heavy door of her suite close behind him she blinked against the prick of tears that had begun behind her eyes. She would not cry. She would not.

Loren reached across the table, lifted up the legal packet and slid out the folded document. Her eyes scanned the information. As unaccustomed as she was to legal jargon it all seemed to make sense until she reached a paragraph headed up with the words *legal issue*.

She read the paragraph, then read it again to be certain she understood the terminology. If she was correct, to ensure the continuation of the del Castillo bloodline she and Alex must make love at the time when her body was at its most fertile, and to ensure the correct timing, her menstrual cycle was to be monitored.

Even the details of the clinic she would be monitored by were in the agreement.

Loren let the papers slide from suddenly nerveless fingers.

The legalese twirled around in her mind, sentences fragmenting before joining back together. Did this mean that she and Alex would *only* make love when she was ovulating? That was, what? A span of a few days at most in each month. And what if she got pregnant? Would he still share her bed, still make love with her as a husband did with his wife? Or would her job have been done, leaving him free to go back into Giselle's arms?

Just what kind of marriage was she entering?

Five

Loren heard the knock at the door to her suite and wondered if perhaps her maid had forgotten something. She'd only just sent her away, preferring to spend these last few moments before her wedding alone. She picked up her voluminous skirts and went to open the door.

"Giselle!" Loren stepped back, startled to see the blonde there. She let her skirts settle back down to the carpet beneath her, the ivory French taffeta giving a distinctive rustle.

"My, don't you look every inch the fairy-tale princess," Giselle remarked, coming into the sitting room.

Loren tolerated the woman's scrutiny of the dress that was the fulfillment of all her childhood dreams. Yes, she did feel like a fairy-tale princess in the strapless gown. Somehow the words from Giselle's glossy red lips made the idea more of an insult than a compliment.

"Was there something you wanted?" Loren asked coolly.

"No, Alex asked me to come up and check on you. He thought you might benefit from some female company since your mother isn't here."

Loren bit back the retort that immediately sprang to her lips. She would not fight, not with anyone, on her wedding day.

"That's lovely of him. But as you can see, I'm fine, thank you."

She waited for Giselle to leave but instead she settled herself on one of the couches. Loren had to admit, she looked beautiful. The woman certainly knew how to make the most of her features. The dress she wore would have looked vampish on anyone else, but on Giselle it was elegantly sensual.

"You know, I have to hand it to you. I thought you'd have given up by now," Giselle said.

"Given up?"

"Well, how many women would have signed that prenuptial agreement, for a start? I know I certainly wouldn't."

"Perhaps you would if you loved your fiancé enough," Loren commented quietly. "As I do."

Giselle waved her hand as if dismissing Loren's words, the very gesture making Loren's spine stiffen in irritation. She'd wanted this time alone to reflect on her coming marriage, and particularly on the terms of the prenuptial agreement that Giselle had mentioned. Clearly, the blonde knew all about it, and that fact rankled with Loren. It should have been a private matter. One between her and Alex alone.

This past week had been such a whirl of activity with a museum opening to attend along with several charity functions, all of which gave her a taste for what her duties would be like as a del Castillo bride. She and Alex, while together for much of their waking moments, had barely had a moment alone to talk. Whenever she'd tried to bring the subject of the prenuptial document up, Alex had brushed it off until later. Now, today, was about as late as it could get and Loren was still unsure of where she stood on the agreement she'd eventually signed.

"Well, whatever," Giselle continued, oblivious to Loren's obvious displeasure in her company. "You've really gone above and beyond the call of duty. It's either incredibly naive of you to stick with it or incredibly kind."

"Kind?"

"To agree to the terms just to help the company out and keep an old man happy."

"I don't know what you mean. I'm marrying Alex because I love him. Because I've always loved him," Loren stated as firmly as she was able.

"Surely you're aware that Alex is only marrying you because of the curse."

"The curse?" Surely she didn't mean the old governess's curse?

Loren knew well the story of the woman who'd been brought to Isla Sagrado from the south of France to educate the daughters of one of the original del Castillos on the island—a nobleman from Spain. The poor woman had fallen in love with her employer and entered into an affair that had lasted years.

Legend had it that she'd borne him three sons, but that in view of the fact his wife had only borne him daughters, he'd taken her boys from her and he'd raised them as his legitimate issue, paying her off with a ruby necklace from the del Castillo jewel collection. Paintings in the family gallery that predated the nobleman showed the necklace, known as *La Verdad del Corazon*—the Heart's Truth. It was a stunning piece of chased gold with a massive heart-shaped ruby at its center. Loren had always privately believed that it was more the type of gift a man gave to his one true love than as payment for services rendered.

When the nobleman's wife died, however, he'd married another woman—one from a high-ranking family. In her misery the governess was said to have interrupted the wedding, begging her beloved to take her back. When her lover—and her sons—turned their backs on her, she cursed the del Castillo family. If, in the next nine generations, the del Castillos did not learn to live by their family motto of honor, truth and love, the ninth generation would be the last. With that pronouncement, she cast both herself and the Heart's Truth from the cliffs behind the castle and into the savage ocean. Her body was later found, but the Heart's Truth had been lost ever since.

Loren had always found the story to be truly tragic and, as a child, had often imagined a happier ending for the governess and her lover.

If the curse was to be believed—not to mention previous generations' total disregard for its power— it was responsible for the steady diminishment of the family over the past nine generations. But to believe that Alex was marrying her in an attempt to break the curse, well, that was just ridiculous. What happened three hundred years ago had no bearing on life today.

"Surely you must know of it. You're from here, after all, and the papers have been full of it, especially since the announcement of your engagement. The boys are the ninth generation—the last of the line. Old Aston was starting to have concerns that they would stay that way. Alex is trying to downplay it but you know what his grandfather is like once he gets an idea into his head. He believes he's even seen the governess's ghost. Can you imagine it? Of course, Alex would move mountains to please the old man—especially if it also happened to be good for business.

"Anyway, they came up with this fabulous publicity drive where they'd all get married and have babies to prove to everyone, their grandfather especially, that the curse isn't real."

Giselle laughed but Loren was hard-pressed to quell the shiver that ran down her spine. Even more so when she weighed the truth in the other woman's words. If, as she'd said, *Abuelo* was genuinely concerned about the curse, Alex *would* do anything to alleviate those concerns. It was the kind of man he was and his loyalty and love for his family were unquestionable.

Would that loyalty and love extend to her, she wondered, or was Giselle right and was Loren merely the means to an end?

Giselle rose from her seat and brushed an imaginary fleck of dust from her dress.

"Well, I can see you don't need me. I'll go down to

Alex and let him know you're ready. The cars are waiting to take everyone to the cathedral."

"Thank you."

Loren forced the words past her lips and tried not to think too hard about the ceremony ahead.

She would much rather have married in the intimate private chapel that formed a part of the castillo's family history, but her wedding to Alex was to be quite a show. Visiting dignitaries from all over Europe would be in attendance along with the cream of Sagradan society. Hundreds of guests, if the lists she'd seen were any indication.

Hundreds of strangers.

As the door closed behind Giselle's retreating figure it struck Loren how alone she truly was. The few old school friends she'd managed to touch base with since her return all viewed her differently now. Sure, they were friendly, but it was as if there was an invisible wall between them. As if she was unreachable. Untouchable.

Well, untouchable certainly fit in well with how Alex had continued to treat her. Maybe he was saving himself, making sure he was locked and loaded for when they met the terms of their prenuptial agreement, she thought cynically. Or maybe he managed to sate his appetites elsewhere, a snide voice niggled from the back of her mind. She pushed the thought from her head but couldn't quite get rid of the bitter aftertaste in her mouth at the thought.

Loren crossed the sitting room to the large window that looked out past the castle's walls and over the landscape. The sun was hot and bright today, a portent of the burgeoning summer months ahead. The sky was a sharp clear blue, broken by slender drifts of cirrus cloud here and there. It was a perfect day to be married by any standard, so why then did she suddenly feel as if it was anything but?

Alex fidgeted with his cuff links for what felt like the umpteenth time today as he stood at the altar of the cathedral.

"Do that again and they'll fall off," Benedict cautioned from his side.

"Funny guy," Alex responded, but forced himself to relax.

He looked back across the rows and rows of guests, some faces he knew well, others hardly at all. The cathedral was packed. Today's ceremony would be the beginning of the new age of del Castillos that would lay old ghosts to rest, and everyone who was anyone wanted to be there to see it. He met *Abuelo's* stare from the front pew, the one carved with the del Castillo crest. The old man gave him a slow nod of approval and Alex felt his chest swell with pride. Any doubts he might have had about whether he was doing the right thing were nothing in the face of his grandfather's happiness.

"Do you know what the delay is?" Reynard asked. "Maybe she's got cold feet and has made a run for the airport."

Alex gave his brother a glare, but he felt a short sharp pang of concern. Loren had been different since he'd given her the prenup to read and sign. A little more distant and a little less eager to please. Had the agreement bothered her that much? Surely she could see the necessity for such an agreement without it affecting their marriage. The financial considerations of providing for her, should he die unexpectedly or should their marriage fail, aside, of primary importance was ensuring the next generation. Once that was out of the way then, well, they could take whatever came next at their leisure—a prospect that, he had to admit, filled him with pleasure. It had been hell keeping his hands off Loren these past two weeks, especially when she'd obviously been eager to take their relationship to an intimate level.

But tonight his wait would be rewarded. Granted, the timing of their union meant that their liaison to-night would not be part of the agreement they'd both signed. It would instead be the consummation of the promises they would make to one another before all these witnesses today.

The importance of those promises settled in his chest like a solid lump of lead, pressing down on his heart, his very honor. It didn't settle well with him to be pledging to love another for the rest of their days when, in truth, he didn't love her.

Love. It wasn't something he and Loren had dis-cussed. Hell, it wasn't even something Alex had con-sidered until she'd declared her feelings for him the night he'd given her the engagement ring.

When she'd first agreed to marry him back in New Zealand, he had assumed she cared for him, perhaps admired him a little the way she had when she was a child. He'd also *known* she was attracted to him—just as he was attracted to her. And she'd wanted to honor her father's memory, in much the same way that he'd wanted to ease his grandfather's mind. So Alex had been comfortable with the arrangement—with the idea of a marriage based on mutual regard, a healthy dose of desire and shared respect for family. Love had never been part of the plan.

But something about her sweetly serious declaration when she accepted his ring and gave him her heart had moved him unexpectedly, making him feel almost shamed. Was it fair to her to accept her love when he was not yet prepared to return it? A picture of his parents flashed through his memory. He wondered what they'd think of the choice he was making today.

They had known real love. It had been considered only fitting that if their light had to be extinguished so early that they die together. The avalanche that had taken them, while on a romantic skiing holiday together without their sons, had wiped out joy as the boys had known it up until that time. Yet they'd been lucky to have had *Abuelo,* who'd put his own grief aside to continue to guide and raise the three teenage boys whose anger at their parents' fate sought many outlets.

It had been *Abuelo's* steady love and firm hand that had brought them through. Love they reciprocated. Taking another look at his grandfather's beaming face, Alex knew that while he would not be telling the truth as he made his vows to Loren today, the gift of hope it would give his grandfather was worth far too much for him to give in to second thoughts now.

"Last chance to back out," Benedict said under his breath. Before Alex could respond, a sudden hush spread through the cathedral. The centuries-old organ, which had been delivering a steady medley of music, halted. The lump of lead in Alex's chest shifted, forming a fist around his lungs as all eyes turned to the main doors. They swung slowly open and a burst of sunlight filled the doorway, bathing the vestibule with its golden glow. And then, within the glow of light, a lone figure appeared.

The fist squeezed tighter as Alex realized how difficult this must be for Loren. In the face of her mother's blank refusal to attend their nuptials, he should have insisted she be accompanied on her journey down the center aisle of the cathedral—past the many assessing eyes of the glitterati and politically powerful. But she'd refused all offers from his brothers and *Abuelo*.

"My father will be with me in spirit," she'd said, holding that determined, fine-boned chin of hers firmly in the air, daring him to challenge her wishes. "I need no one else."

He'd had to accede to her wish. After all, it was the only thing on which she had insisted in all the matters pertaining to the ceremony.

The powerful organ began again and as Loren began to glide down the aisle toward him, Alex realized he'd misjudged his bride's strength and fortitude.

Pride suffused every cell in his body as she walked toward him with effortless grace—her bare shoulders squared and her spine straight, her slender neck holding her head high. Loren's skin gleamed against the strapless ivory gown that hugged her torso and exposed the gentle swell of her breasts before spreading into a bloom of fabric around and behind her. For the first time in his memory, Alex was speechless. Beneath the gossamer-fine veil that covered her head and shoulders and drifted down to her waist he caught glimpses of light striking the diamond tiara that had once been his mother's. The matching necklace, its design the inverted image of the tiara, settled against her luminous skin at the base of her throat and spilled in a gentle V over her collarbone.

Her face was composed behind her veil, her eyes avoiding contact with his, focused instead on the altar behind him. As she drew closer he could hear the swish of the fabric of her gown as it swept across the floor, could see the fine tremors that shook the opulent bouquet of early summer blooms she carried.

"Looks like lanky little Loren Dubois has really grown up, hmm?"

Reynard's voice in his ear snapped Alex from his trance.

"For once in your life could you just shut up?" he hissed at his brother through teeth clenched so tight his jaw ached, earning a glare of disapproval from the priest in the process.

Reynard's next words, however, shocked him in a way he never expected.

"Don't hurt her, Alex. Whatever you do, don't *ever* hurt her."

"Noted," Alex replied with a swift nod.

He met his brother's eyes briefly. There was no doubting Reynard meant what he said. For some strange reason it made him feel better that Loren had a champion. That it should have been him was not wasted on him at all, but given what he'd agreed to do to save the del Castillo family and fortunes, it was only fitting it be one of his brothers. Both, if the look on Benedict's face was any indicator.

A savage rush of possession roared through his veins. They could look, certainly, they could warn him as much as they liked, but essentially, Loren was his.

As she joined him on the steps in front of the altar that knowledge gave him the ultimate satisfaction.

When it came time to say their vows, Loren looked at him, truly looked at him, for the first time that day. And as she pledged to love him, he found he had to look away. Her words carried such surety, such conviction. She deserved more than empty promises in return. Her voice wobbled slightly on the last word of the formal ceremony they'd chosen. No, he corrected himself, the ceremony Giselle had chosen. Shame scored him. This was Loren's wedding day. He should have given her more say in how the day was to go.

He'd approached this all wrong. He already had her love and loyalty and he'd walked roughshod over both in the execution of *his* goals and *his* needs. Loren was more than a means to an end, she was a vital, living, breathing woman.

He would make it up to her, he promised himself silently. As soon as they'd fulfilled the first part of the prenuptial agreement, he would definitely make it up to her.

Loren had barely spoken half a dozen words directly to him since they'd exchanged their vows. In the car from the wedding reception it was no different. Alex found the uncharacteristic silence challenging. Normally Loren found something, anything, to talk to him about—it was one of the things he found so engaging about her.

But something had changed inside her today; he could sense it in the way she held herself, the way she'd spoken to others. As if she was playing a part and was not really totally involved in what she was doing.

As their car swung through the gate of the outer wall and drew up to the entrance of the castillo it finally occurred to Alex why she was so quiet. She had to be nervous about tonight. He would make sure their first time was one she would remember forever. A special night. A memory to be treasured.

Dios, but she looked exquisitely beautiful. He could almost taste the satin softness of her skin already. Almost feel the shiver of desire ripple across her skin.

As the driver opened his door he gave a short command to the man to allow Alex himself to escort his new wife from the vehicle. He walked around to her side of the car and pulled open her door, offering her his hand.

"Come, Loren. Let me help you inside."

"Thank you," she said softly.

The voluminous skirts and sweep of the train of her dress was a confection of fabric about her, yet she handled the garment with the grace of a swan. Another definite plus in her favor—no matter the situation, she handled it with aplomb. In spite of his concerns, he knew he'd chosen well when he'd decided to marry her. She would be a marvelous asset to him in so very many ways.

"You were wonderful today, I was so proud of you," he bent to murmur in her ear as they approached the arched entrance of their home.

"It was an—" she hesitated a moment before continuing "—interesting day."

"Interesting?" Alex forced himself to laugh softly. Surely she hadn't picked up on his unease during the ceremony—or had she? Well regardless, he'd have to put her mind at ease. "It was a great success. All of Isla

Sagrado knows you are now my beautiful bride and their blessings upon us will reflect back upon them. I imagine, though, it must have been difficult for you."

"Difficult?"

"Without your family to support you."

"Yes, it was difficult, but it was what my father would have expected of me."

There was a note to her voice that sounded off-key but Alex pushed the thought aside. She was obviously weary after the pomp and ceremony of the day and the obligations she'd fulfilled at the lavish reception.

Alex guided Loren up the stairs and toward the shared suite he'd ordered their effects delivered to today—the suite that had been his parents'. As they swept inside he nodded in approval at the sensual soft lighting provided by the plethora of candles he'd requested be lit before their arrival.

The heady scents of rose and sandalwood drifted on the air, feminine and masculine, yin and yang.

"Would you like to be alone while you change? Or perhaps I should call your maid to assist with your gown?"

"No, it's all right. I can manage the lacing myself," Loren replied.

Again there was that slight discordance. Again he shrugged it away.

"I'll leave you to change then."

She merely inclined her head and moved gracefully across the room to her private chamber. Alex watched as she drew the door closed behind her then wasted no time getting to his private en suite bathroom and divesting himself of his clothing before stepping under the hot steam of a quick shower. A few swift swipes of his towel later and he was dry. Naked, he padded through to his dressing room where he reached for midnight blue, satin pajama bottoms and a matching robe.

Would her touch be as soft as the fabric that caressed his skin, he wondered. No, it would be softer, he was certain. His body coiled tight in anticipation of what lay ahead.

Before he realized it, he was at the door to her rooms, his hand twisting the handle and thrusting open the door. Candles had been lit in here, too. The large pedestal bed, swathed in cream-and-gold draperies, stood invitingly empty.

Empty?

A sound drew his attention as his bride came from her bathroom. Her satin nightgown skimmed her slender form enticingly, cascading over her gentle curves much as his hands now itched to, also. A small frown puckered her brow as she worked a brush through her hair.

"Here, let me," Alex said as she crossed the room. He took the brush from her fingers. "Sit down on the bed."

Loren did as he requested and Alex stood a little behind her and forced himself to focus on her hair and only her hair as he reached to stroke the brush through her tresses, easing out the knots and occasional forgotten hairpin.

"Ah." She sighed. "That feels wonderful."

Liquid fire pooled in his groin at her words. He planned to make her feel so much more wonderful very soon. Now that the brush flowed more smoothly through her hair he allowed himself to focus on the deliciously smooth, bare shoulders she presented to him.

Palest pink straps of satin were all that held her nightgown up. Straps that with the slightest breath could slide down those shoulders and farther, down her slender arms, exposing her back. He'd never found the prospect of observing a woman's back so enticing before. But then again, with Loren everything was different. Everything felt new.

He couldn't help himself, he had to taste her. He gathered her hair in one fist and gently drew it away from the nape of her neck then bent to kiss her, allowing his tongue to stroke across her skin in a private caress.

He felt her response ripple down her spine. Smiling to himself, he kissed her again—this time sucking gently—and was rewarded with the soft sound of her gasp. Alex let the hairbrush drop to the floor and placed both his hands upon her shoulders, coaxing her upright to turn and face him.

Her face, clean of the makeup she'd worn today, appeared flushed in the candlelight—her eyes luminous, their pupils dilated so far they almost appeared to consume the dark velvet brown of her irises. Her lips were moist and remained slightly parted. His gaze dropped to her breasts, to the clearly delineated pinpoints of her nipples as they thrust against the satin with her each and every rapid breath.

Something knotted tight and low in Alex's belly. Something possessive. Something wild. Every instinct within him roared that he plunder her lips, that he drag the delicate fabric of her nightgown from her body and expose her to him, allowing him to feast on her feminine glory. To rush her to dizzying heights she had no experience of.

To mark her as his own.

She is inexperienced, he reminded himself sternly, forcing himself to hold back, to slow down.

He let his hands skim across her shoulders and gently cup the back of her neck, tilting her head to him. He lowered his face, his eyes locked upon hers. His entire body rigid with the need to take this as gently as humanly possible.

His lips were only millimeters from hers. Already he could feel her breath against him, smell the sweetness of her breath.

"Alex, wait!"

Through the cloud of passion that controlled him he heard the plea in her voice. He closed his eyes for a moment and drew in a shuddering breath, constraining his desire.

"You are frightened. I'm rushing you. Do not worry, Loren. I will make tonight one you will never forget."

"No, it's not that," she said, pulling out of his arms, creating a short distance between them.

Already his body cried out for her. Craving her slender frame against his, aching for her warmth to envelop him.

"Then what is it?" he asked, fighting back the edge of frustration that threatened to spill over into his voice. He didn't want to frighten her more with his hunger.

"It's about us. Our marriage."

"Us?"

A cold finger of caution traced a chilly path down his spine. What was she speaking of? They were married. Tonight would see the consummation of that marriage.

"Yes, Alex, us. I love you. I've always loved you

one way or another. I accept that you don't return my feelings in the same way."

"You know I care for you, Loren," he asserted, determined to salve her concerns as quickly as possible.

"I know you do, but more as a brother would a sister."

"Believe me, my feelings toward you are most definitely not brotherly."

"Be that as it may." She waved her hand to disregard his words. "Even knowing you don't love me, I agreed to marry you in part because of my feelings for you, but also to honor my father and his promise to yours." She lifted her eyes to him. Eyes that glistened in the candlelight with unshed tears. "Can you honestly tell me that you have done the same?"

Tell her he'd married her to fulfill their fathers' vow to one another? No, not even he could lie about that. Not after the lies he'd already told before his grandfather in the church today. Lies that still coated his tongue with a tang of unpleasantness. The old promise was the reason he'd chosen to seek her out rather than find a bride on Isla Sagrado, but it was not the sole reason he'd decided to marry.

"No," he responded, his voice flat and tinged now with the anger he bore toward himself more than to her. "But you have asked me to be honest. If you do not like my truth then you have only yourself to blame."

"But you have married me with the intention of producing an heir, is that true?"

She stood upright before him, holding her chin high, her shoulders straight, demanding his response.

"Of course."

"To dispel the governess's curse?"

Words failed him momentarily.

"The curse is nothing but an overstated legend. It has no bearing on us or on our marriage."

"So you didn't suddenly decide to travel all the way to New Zealand and then to marry me to put *Abuelo's* mind to rest? To prove that the curse wasn't real? Can you truly say that if it hadn't been for the curse you would *ever* have followed through with our fathers' wishes?"

He couldn't answer, to answer truthfully would damn him forever in her eyes—to tell a lie was impossible on top of the abomination of falsehoods he'd committed already.

"I see," Loren continued. "Well, then. It appears that we are at an impasse. I could have accepted almost anything from you, Alex, but I will not accept deception. You brought me here under false pretences."

"You say you love me, and you did sign the prenuptial agreement," Alex reminded her, the words like gravel on his tongue. "You cannot back out now."

"I will meet the expectations of that agreement. You will have your heir, Alexander del Castillo, but I see no reason why we should enter into a physical marriage." A sharp note of bitterness crept into her voice. "In this day and age of technology why would you even want to consider the hassle and inconvenience, or indeed even the inconsistency, of making *love?*

"After all, if the act is to be as clinical and bereft of mutual affection as I imagine it will be, surely a petri dish will do, as well."

Loren's words hung like icicles in the air between them. Anger welled and rolled within him, much like the violent surf they could hear from the beach below through her open casement windows.

"You are refusing me your bed?" he finally managed through a jaw clenched so tight he thought his teeth might shatter.

"No. I am refusing you my body."

Six

Loren barely dared draw breath.

Alex stood before her, magnificent in his anger. Were she less determined about her decision she would have quailed in the face of his fury. To be honest, were she less determined she would have given in to the rush of longing that had drawn through her body like a fine silken thread as he'd touched her.

All her life she'd waited for the day that Alex would turn to her and welcome her into his life, and into his arms. Too bad that when that day had finally come she'd been forced to spurn him. She had never believed it would matter so much to her that he had hidden from her his true reasons for entering into their marriage.

In the lead-up to the wedding it had been enough for her to believe, however misguidedly, that they stood a chance of making their marriage work. But in the stark face of what she'd learned today, it was clear that Alex hadn't been above using her to get what he wanted. That it was for his family didn't assuage the hurt deep inside her. Nor the anger she bore at herself for having been such a blind and love-struck fool where Alex was concerned.

That she loved Alex with a passion that went soul deep was undeniable. But now she realized it most definitely wasn't enough. In her naïveté she'd thought she could change his perception of her as a child to that of a woman. A woman capable of great passion and unswerving loyalty.

Clearly she was still that naive child to have thought she could make a difference—make him begin to love her. He'd taken advantage of the promise made between her father and his and, shamefully, she'd let him. She was no innocent in this. She should have known and understood what was at stake. She should have asked questions, demanded answers.

But, no. She'd been focused on fulfilling a childhood dream. Of returning to the land of her birth and of being his bride. She'd allowed herself to be duped— heck, allowed? She'd been a fully willing participant into a marriage that stood no chance of being real right from the beginning.

Well, now he had his bride. He had his baby-making machine. That didn't mean she needed to debase herself any further by pandering to his machinations. Whatever the scheme he'd hatched with his brothers, she would do no more than her duty. She would give him the baby he required, but she'd find a way to live through this with what was left of her dignity intact.

"I think you'd better leave," she said, her voice

breaking on the last words as she struggled to hold back the tremors that threatened to turn her into a quivering wreck.

Alex's eyes narrowed as he continued to stare at her in silence.

"P-please, Alex. Go."

"This is not over, Loren. I am not a man who likes to be thwarted."

Loren didn't answer, instead turning her back even as her chest throbbed with the pain of rejecting him and her eyes burned with the tears she refused to shed in his presence. She had what was left of her pride and she would not let that go. Not for anything. Not for anyone. Not even the man she loved with every heart-wrenchingly pain-filled breath in her body.

Behind her, Loren heard her chamber door close with a gentle sound. The fact he hadn't slammed the door behind him spoke volumes to the measure of his control. Control he would no doubt have been exerting over her behind the filmy curtains of her pedestal bed right now, had she let him.

Something twisted deep inside her, something sharp and raw, and her inner muscles clenched on the emptiness. She looked at the bed now and knew she would not sleep there tonight. She could not.

Loren crossed to the deep-set casement window that had been flung open to the velvet night. Despite the warm night air that coursed past her to fill the room, Loren was suddenly beset by a chill that went to her very bones.

Without a doubt spurning Alex tonight was the hardest thing she'd ever had to do in her life—the hardest decision she'd ever had to make.

Her fingers gripped the age-old stone of the window ledge so tight they became numb, and she stared out at the night sky wishing things could have been so very different.

The sound of gentle knocking at her bedroom door woke Loren from the fitful slumber she'd finally fallen into around dawn. She straightened from the chaise longue she'd eventually sought rest upon and quickly threw her pillows and the comforter back onto the bed. Everyone knew how servants gossiped and, despite their loyalty to the del Castillo family, the staff here were no different.

She crossed the room to unlock the door and took a rapid step back when she saw it was not her maid, but Alex standing on the other side.

"*Buenos días,* Loren. I trust you slept well?"

He was absolutely the last person she expected to see this morning. She'd anticipated being totally left to her own devices after her rejection of him last night. Instead, here he was, looking and smelling divine. As if what had transpired between them had never happened. As if she'd never rejected him.

"As charming as your nightgown is, you will need to change for our excursion today."

"Change?"

"Of course, unless you want to be seen out and about Isla Sagrado in your night wear."

"We…we're going out? I thought—"

"Yes, I'm sure you thought that after last night I would not want to be near you. You underestimate me, Loren. We are newly married. We are expected to be seen together. Do you honestly believe that after everything I've put in place to make our marriage happen that I would just dissolve into the castle walls because you have decided we are not to sleep together?"

There was a dangerous edge to his voice. A hint of a reined-in temper simmering just beneath the surface of his urbane exterior.

"Of course not. I don't know what I thought, to be honest." Loren dragged in a breath, her senses instantly on alert as his fragrance infiltrated her confused mind and sent her pulse hammering in her veins. "When do you want me to be ready?"

"Our first appointment is in about half an hour, near Puerto Seguro, so about five minutes ago would be ideal."

"Appointment?"

"Yes, a tradition in my family when someone marries."

Thinking it was to be with the family lawyer, Loren spun away and yanked open her wardrobe, choosing a slim-fitting ice-blue suit. Her arm was stayed by Alex's hand upon her. She couldn't help it, she flinched, and didn't miss the frown that descended over Alex's features. He pointedly withdrew his hand from her bare skin before speaking.

"That's too formal. Wear something comfortable but smart."

Without any further information he spun on his heel and left her room. For a moment she just watched him. Her eyes drinking in the beauty of his movement, the breadth of his shoulders beneath the lightweight cream shirt he wore teamed with dark caramel-colored trousers. The way those trousers skimmed the cheeks of his buttocks.

She forced herself to blink, to break the spell he'd unwittingly woven about her, enticing her. She shoved the suit back into the wardrobe and flicked through her hangers, finally settling upon a black sundress with an abstract white print patterned upon it, relieving the starkness of the background. A mid-heeled pair of strappy sandals would hopefully give the outfit just the right balance Alex had specified.

Gathering her dress and a fistful of clean underwear, Loren swept into her bathroom. She wanted nothing more than to wash her hair but she doubted time would allow it. She swept its length into a shower cap and stepped beneath the stinging spray of the shower before the water had even reached temperature, gasping slightly against the cold.

She reached for the shower gel and liberally lathered it over her body. Had things been different, she wondered, would it be Alex's hands sliding over her skin now? Her nipples beaded into tight buds at the thought. Shaking her head at herself, Loren quickly rinsed off and stepped out of the shower cubicle and reached for a towel to dry off.

It only took a moment to dress and spritz a light spray of perfume on her pulse points. Her hair she brushed into a fiercely controlled ponytail, which she then braided and pinned in a spiral against the back of her head, all the while trying to forget how it had felt last night as Alex had brushed her hair. He'd shown her a tenderness she knew he'd have brought to his love-making—had she let things get that far.

Her reflection, however, definitely gave her pause. The sleepless night had left dark shadows beneath her eyes. It would take everything she had in her cosmetic arsenal to restore some semblance of the dewy bride Isla Sagrado had seen yesterday.

It took her a further ten minutes but by the time Loren met Alex in their communal sitting room she was satisfied that she could cope with anything the day brought.

"Where are we going?" she asked as she checked her handbag for her sunglasses.

"You'll see when we get there," Alex responded enigmatically.

"What about breakfast?"

"Breakfast was a couple of hours ago but there will be a morning tea where we are going. Can you wait until then?"

Loren hazarded a look at her husband from under her lashes as she pretended to search in her bag for something else. *Her husband!* The solid truth of those two words rammed into her chest and clutched at her heart with a sudden twist. At her sharply indrawn breath, Alex gave her a look.

"Is everything all right?" he asked.

"Fine, I'm fine," Loren hastened to assure him. "And yes, I can wait for something to eat."

"Then we should be on our way."

He held the door to their suite open and escorted her along the wide corridor and down the sweeping stairs to the front entrance of the castillo. There, in the massive entrance hall, the staff had all assembled in a line, some bearing small gifts, others with nothing to give but the warmth in their hearts and the smiles on their faces.

How could she have forgotten the age-old Sagradan custom? It was tradition that the staff celebrate the master's marriage with offerings. On that occasion, the master and mistress of the property would also give the staff a small monetary gift.

"Have you—" she started to ask in a whisper.

"I have it under control," Alex assured her as one by one they greeted the people who worked tirelessly behind the scenes in the castillo.

As she went forward to accept each small gift—some traditional in the old ways, such as the symbol of fertility that was pressed into her hand by the cook, and some modern—Alex in turn gave each staff member an envelope.

By the time they reached his waiting Lamborghini outside, Loren's arms were full of the tokens bestowed upon them. She made it into the car without dropping a one, and once settled she allowed them to tumble gently into her lap. Alex reached behind her seat to extricate a box and passed it to her before turning the key in the ignition and easing the car into gear and out through the castle gates.

Loren gently placed each token into the box, her fingers lingering on the Sagradan symbol of fertility, an intricately carved egg, before placing it inside and closing the lid.

"That was lovely," she commented, her hands firmly holding the box on her lap as they drove along the coastal road toward Puerto Seguro.

"You think so?" Alex asked, raising one dark brow. "I wouldn't have thought you'd have cared."

"Of course I care. Why would you think I wouldn't?" Surprise brought a defensive tone to her voice.

Alex merely shrugged and Loren felt herself bristle at his nonchalance.

"Don't judge me by your other women," she said quietly, but with a strong hint of steel.

"Don't worry, I wouldn't dream of it," Alex replied. "You are nothing like them."

Unable to come up with a suitable response, Loren lapsed into silence. She watched the road ahead of them through burning eyes and wished things could have been different. Of course she was nothing like his other women. If the tabloids had carried even an ounce of truth, those women had been confident, sophisticated and unerringly beautiful. Women like Giselle, for example.

For what felt like the umpteenth time, Loren castigated herself for having hoped for anything else from Alex other than what she'd ended up with. She knew better than most that life was no bed of roses. The only child of parents who'd loved passionately and fought bitterly, she'd seen what a push-me-pull-you state marriage could be. And she'd experienced firsthand the pain that ensued when such a marriage irrevocably broke down.

But at least her parents had enjoyed many years together before the cracks had started to show. It was more than what her immediate future held, unless she was fortunate enough for a fertilization procedure to work on the first attempt. If she could fill her life with a child then she could quite possibly manage to be happy.

Loren was unfamiliar with the building they now approached. A cluster of paparazzi was waiting at the entrance. Of fairly recent style, it was a large sprawling construction set in lush gardens and toward the back she caught a glimpse of what looked like playing fields. Was this some kind of school? She wondered what del

Castillo family tradition called for a bride and groom to visit a school the morning after their wedding.

She recognized the family coat of arms carved into the lintel above the door but aside from that one claim of ownership there was nothing about the building to tell her of its purpose. At least not until they set foot inside. Muffled giggles and shushing sounds came from behind closed doors.

Children? At school on a weekend?

Alex laced his fingers through hers and Loren closed her eyes briefly in an attempt to quell the sudden surge of electricity that flared across her skin at his touch. The double doors ahead of them opened and, as they walked into what appeared to be a small auditorium followed closely by the media contingent, the air filled with the sound of children's voices in song.

Loren couldn't hold back a smile as the pure notes swirled joyfully around them.

"Who are they?" she whispered to Alex.

"Orphans, for the most part. Some are from families who cannot afford to feed and clothe them. They are the lucky ones for at least they have someone."

As the song drew to a close, one little girl separated from the bunch. In her hands she clutched a colorful bouquet of flowers. The caregiver behind her gave an encouraging little push in Loren's direction, but as the child drew closer a barrage of camera flashes filled the air and she tripped and started to fall forward. Loren reached out and caught the little girl before she could face-plant on the hard wooden floor. Some of the flowers, however, did not fare as well and when the child saw their snapped-off heads her lower lip began to wobble.

"Are these for me?" Loren asked, setting the child on her feet and kneeling down in front of her, ignoring the rapid-fire clicks and whirs of the shutters of the cameras trained on them.

The girl nodded shyly, one tear spilling from her lower lid and tracking slowly down a chubby cheek.

"Thank you, they're beautiful." Loren bent forward and kissed her on the forehead. "And look, here's a flower just for you."

Placing the bouquet gently on the floor beside her, Loren pinched off one of the damaged blooms and tucked it behind the little girl's ear, securing it there with one of the pins from her own hair.

With both disaster, and further tears, averted, the little girl happily scampered back to her group.

"Nicely done," Alex murmured in her ear as he helped Loren rise to her feet.

She hoped he didn't see how his praise affected her, and that he missed the fine tremor that shook the bouquet she now held in her hands as if it was her most precious possession.

The rest of the morning passed uneventfully as she and Alex shared tea with the children and sat through a delightful series of performances. They were then led on a tour of the orphanage and Loren felt her heart break as she was shown the nurseries and the babies there. Under Alex's silent gaze, she took the time to cuddle each one and spent several minutes discussing their welfare with the nurses charged with their care.

By the time they took their leave and got back into his car Loren was shattered. Her arms still ached to hold the parentless children, as if by doing so she could somehow alleviate the harsh blow life had dealt them.

"You did well," Alex commented as they pulled away.

"It was nothing. I adore children, I always have."

"Especially the very young ones."

"Yes, especially them. They've had little opportunity to know love and of anyone they probably deserve it the most." Loren sighed and gently stroked the petals on the now rather tired-looking bouquet she'd been given. "What happens to them?"

"The babies or all the children?"

"All of them."

"Those that can be, are fostered with families on the island. We try and keep extended family involved wherever possible. Sometimes that's not an option, however. Others, like the babies and the toddlers, are usually adopted within months of their arrival at the orphanage. For the ones who remain, they are provided with schooling and, given their aptitude, they have the opportunity to earn scholarships to train in their chosen fields. Of the nurses and teachers there, at least half are returning children."

Loren nodded. She could understand why. The atmosphere there had been one of a strong sense of community and home, as far as they could manage on such a scale.

"Does the orphanage have a patron?"

"Not officially, not since my mother died. It has always traditionally been a del Castillo bride who becomes the orphanage's patroness. Between *Abuelo* and myself we have done what we can but some things definitely require a woman's touch."

"I'd like to take that on."

"You don't have to."

"No, I know that. But I want to, if that's okay."

Loren turned to look at Alex and saw him nod slowly.

"Then it looks as if tradition will live on, hmm?"

"Yes," she said emphatically. "It will."

Loren noticed they were now driving away from the city but not toward the castillo.

"Are we expected somewhere else today?"

"Yes," Alex responded, his eyes on the road ahead.

"Well, are you going to tell me where?" Loren demanded, suddenly feeling decidedly snippy.

The emotional toll of the orphanage visit, on top of the demands of their wedding day only yesterday and the distress of last night were all making themselves felt. She wanted nothing more right now than some peace and quiet.

"Look, I'm not up to any more of your cloak-and-dagger stuff. If you won't say where we're going you may as well let me out of the car right now and I'll find my own way home."

Alex still didn't respond.

"Stop the car," Loren demanded.

"We're almost there."

"Almost where?"

Loren looked around her but all she could see were fields and trees. Then, just in the distance, she caught sight of a series of domed buildings and a fluorescent wind sock on a tall pole.

"An airfield?" she asked. "Why are we going to an airfield?"

"Because our plane leaves in a short while."

"Our plane?" Loren felt as if all she could do was dumbly question everything that came from Alex's mouth.

"Yes, our plane."

She clenched her fists in frustration. Getting information from him was like getting blood from a stone.

"And where would this plane be taking us?" she inquired acerbically, fighting the urge to shout.

"On our honeymoon, of course."

Seven

"Honeymoon?"

Loren's voice reached a pitch that should have made Alex's ears ring. He turned to his new wife and smiled.

"It is usual for a newly married couple, and it is expected of us."

"But my things?"

"Await you on the plane."

"But what about…"

As Loren's voice trailed off he allowed himself a moment of satisfaction. She may have won the first round but this one was definitely his. Until her refusal of his attentions he would have been happy to remain at home on Isla Sagrado with her for their honeymoon as he'd originally planned. But she'd laid down a gauntlet when she'd spurned him last night. He was unaccustomed to anyone saying no to him—least of all

the woman who had become his wife. He had serious
ground to recover if this marriage was to work.

Her words had plagued him until dawn this morning, when he'd realized what he would have to do. It
would be too easy for Loren to avoid him if they stayed
at the castillo, or even if they'd gone to avail themselves of one of the luxury holiday homes on the other
side of the island. No, he had to take her away, get her
wholly to himself.

During their trip to the orphanage it was a simple
matter to have her maid pack her things and have them
delivered to the private airfield. Her passport and other
papers were already in his possession, having been
necessary for the legal paperwork of their marriage.
A short call to a friend who owned a private holiday
villa in Dubrovnik, a mere two-hour flight away on the
Croatian coast of the Adriatic Sea, and his plan was in
action. Only five minutes out of Dubrovnik old town,
the two-bedroom stone cottage was a fifteenth-century
delight. Private, fully modernized and the perfect setting for the seduction of his wife.

"Loren, you have nothing to worry about. Trust me."

"Trust you?" She snorted inelegantly. "That's rich,
coming from the man who lied to marry me. The man
who played on my own sense of values to get what he
wanted."

A burr of irritation settled under Alex's skin, aimed
more at himself than at her. He couldn't deny that she
was painfully right.

"And what did you want, *mi querida?*" he asked, not
bothering to hold back the cynicism that laced his en-
dearment. "Don't tell me that you, for your own part,
didn't use me a little, also?"

"I never lied to you," she answered quietly, her eyes impossibly somber as they met his.

For a few seconds the air between them thickened with the pain of the emotions he saw reflected in her gaze, and for a brief moment he tasted the bitterness of shame on his tongue. But he could not afford to dwell on his wrongdoing. They were now married and that was final. How successful would their marriage be? Well, that would no doubt depend on the next two weeks.

According to Loren's doctor at the clinic, based on her normal cycle, she would be entering her most fertile time soon. If his plans remained on track there would be no need for the detached methods she'd insisted were the only way she'd get pregnant with his child.

"Come," Alex said, getting out the car and going around to the passenger side to open her door. "The pilot is waiting."

"Where are we going?"

Sensing she'd had enough of secrets, Alex didn't beat around the bush. "Dubrovnik. We can be alone there."

He felt her shrink away from him as the words sank in.

"I hope they have a good selection of reading material," she commented tartly.

Alex laughed out loud, the humor in it startling even himself. If he knew his friend, any reading material would be eclectic and with a heavy emphasis on both cooking and eroticism. Suddenly he couldn't wait to get there.

The flight in the chartered jet was smooth and over within two hours, and it took very little time to clear customs and immigration. The midafternoon sun was bright and hot as they made their way to the waiting car outside the terminal building. Through it all, Loren maintained an icy silence. A silence that Alex looked forward to thawing, one icicle at a time.

The water in the little bay, fifty yards below where the cottage perched on the hillside, was a clear crystal blue. So clear you could even see the rocks and pebbles on the seafloor. Steps had been hewn from the rocky face leading down to the private beach. The cottage itself was a delight. Despite its aged appearance from the outside, Alex had been reassured to discover the interior was comfortably appointed and supplied with everything they would need for the duration of their stay.

He'd asked that the refrigerator-freezer and pantries all be fully stocked, and had stipulated that the cleaners were only to come when he could ensure they were away from the property. He wanted no interruptions to this idyll.

Loren was outside now, on the rear terrace, gazing out at the calm seas, a light breeze tugging at the severe hairdo she'd worn since this morning. Alex's fingers itched to take her hair down and to see her relax. As tense as she was now it would take days for her to unwind. He left the narrow kitchen area and walked across the tiled open-plan living area to where she stood.

"How about a swim before we have an early dinner?" he asked, coming out onto the terrace.

"An early dinner and bed sounds good to me."

"What, not game to tackle the steps?" Alex teased, reaching out a hand to caress her bare shoulder.

She stepped out of reach and sighed. "No, Alex, I'm not game to tackle the steps. In fact I'm not game for anything right now but something to eat and a decent night's sleep."

He gave her a thorough look. She did indeed look washed-out, with the pale strain of tiredness about her eyes more visible now than earlier. He gave a small nod.

"Okay," he said softly. "It's been a busy couple of days. Why don't you shower and change into something comfortable and I'll prepare something for us to eat."

"What? You? Cook?"

Ah, so she was not so tired that she couldn't insult him. That at least was mildly promising.

"I cook very well, as you'll soon discover. Now, you'll find the bedrooms downstairs. If you don't like the one where your cases are, we can swap."

Her eyes widened. "We have separate rooms?"

"Of course. Separate rooms, separate bathrooms. Unless, of course, you'd rather share?"

"No! I mean, no, that's fine. I thought…"

Alex knew exactly what she thought, but he was prepared to bide his time.

"Go on. Freshen up. Take your time, hmm? I want to shower and change myself before starting our meal."

He watched as she walked back inside the cottage and made for the stairs that led to the two bedrooms on the lower level. Yes, he was prepared to bide his time—for now. But he would not wait forever for his recalcitrant bride to accept the very real attraction that lay between them, nor the pleasure he was certain they would find together when she did.

* * *

"Loren, wake up. Dinner is ready."

Alex's voice pierced the uneasy slumber Loren had fallen into after taking her shower. The wide expanse of bed, with its pale blue coverlet and fresh cotton pillow slips, had proven too much of an enticement. She stretched as she stirred, forcing her eyes open.

The sun was much lower in the sky now, its light sparkling across the water visible through the floor-length windows like a thousand diamonds skipping across the waves.

Loren pushed herself upright, then snatched at her robe as she felt it slide away from her, exposing her nakedness beneath.

"If you'll give me five minutes, I'll be with you," she said as coolly as she could, hyperconscious of the hot flare of interest in Alex's dark eyes as she gathered the fine silk about her.

His lips had parted, as if he was about to say something but the words had frozen on his tongue. His stare intensified, dropping to the pinpoints of her nipples where they peaked against the soft blush-colored fabric. Her breath caught in her throat, she could almost feel his gaze as if it was a touch against her skin.

She shifted on the bed, untangling her legs and pushing them over the side of the mattress, the movement making her robe slide across her nakedness like a caress. Heat built everywhere—her cheeks, her chest and deeper darker places she didn't want to acknowledge with Alex standing there, staring hungrily at her as if she was to be his appetizer before the evening meal.

"Alex?" Loren asked, finally getting to her feet and

welcoming the feel of her robe settling like a cloak about her, hiding her.

"Okay, five minutes. Come out onto the terrace."

He pushed one hand through his hair, the vulnerability of that action striking her square in the chest, before turning for the staircase leading back up to the main floor. Loren took a steadying breath. She hadn't meant to fall asleep but weariness had dragged at every inch of her body. To be woken by him had reminded her starkly of the day she'd arrived at the castillo. Of how he'd kissed the palm of her hand, of how she'd believed their marriage to be so full of promise at that moment.

Even now, her body still thrummed in reaction to Alex's presence, and he hadn't so much as touched her this time. It had only been a look, but it had set her senses on fire despite how angry she was with both him and herself for the debacle they now found themselves in.

Coming here had been a terrible idea. She should have resisted. Should have demanded he take her back to the castillo. She could have avoided him there for most of the time at least. Thrown herself into her duties as patroness of the orphanage. Something. Anything but time in this isolated beauty alone together.

Loren spun on her bare foot and skittered across the floor to where she'd found her suitcase. She hadn't bothered to check its contents before her shower, only grabbing at the first thing she could find at the time, her robe. But now she wondered just what she had to wear. She certainly hoped her maid had covered all possibilities.

She flipped open the lid of the case and rummaged through the layers of swimwear with matching wraps and night wear Bella had packed for her, tossing it all to one side. Finally, thankfully, her fingers closed around some basic cotton T-shirts. Loren lifted them out and put them on the bed behind her before searching through her case again. A small gasp of relief escaped her as she found a batik wraparound skirt her mother had brought back for her from Indonesia a couple of years ago.

All she needed now was clean underwear. Loren pulled open a drawer of the dresser in her room and swiftly put away the things she'd already taken from the case, then methodically unpacked the rest—her frustration rising by degrees until the case was completely empty.

What on earth had her maid been thinking? No underwear? Not even a pair of cotton panties? She prayed that Bella had perhaps run out of room in her case and had packed her underthings with Alex's, but a rapid check of his room showed no sign of anything of hers.

The chime of a clock upstairs reminded her that she'd told Alex she'd only be five minutes. Sliding her robe off, Loren picked up the underwear she'd worn all day. The idea of wearing them again, against clean skin, just felt wrong. She'd have to make sure she rinsed them out before bed tonight and bought some more lingerie tomorrow.

Loren chose the thickest of her T-shirts and pulled it on, then swiftly wrapped the skirt about her waist and slid her feet into flat leather mules.

The cotton of the batik skirt was soft against her buttocks and she was acutely conscious of the brush of fabric caressing her bare skin as she walked up the stairs. Maybe going commando hadn't been such a clever idea after all.

Out on the terrace Alex had set a small round table with a clutch of flowers and had lit a large squat candle that flickered in the gentle evening breeze. Knives, forks and two colorful serviettes completed the setting.

"I'll have to buy you a watch, I think," Alex said as he walked toward her holding a flute of champagne in each hand.

Loren took one and smiled in return. Not for anything would she admit what had delayed her.

"I thought it was a woman's prerogative to be late."

"When she is as lovely as you, then she's always worth waiting for."

"Even ten years?"

Loren couldn't help it. The words had popped into her mind and past her lips before she could think. Alex tipped the rim of his glass against hers.

"Especially then," he said, a tone to his voice she couldn't quite put her finger on. "To a better beginning, hmm?"

"If you say so," she replied, and took a long delicious sip of the bubbling golden liquid.

She was certain the alcohol bypassed her stomach and went straight to her legs, because all of a sudden they felt tingly, the muscles weak.

"I think I'd better have something to eat. That feels as if it'll have me on my ear if I keep it up."

"Here, try the antipasto."

Alex crossed the few short steps to a stone bench next to the outdoor grill. He picked up a platter and offered it to her, watching again with those velvet black eyes as she selected a sliver of artichoke heart and popped it into her mouth.

"How is that?" he asked as she chewed and swallowed.

"Good. Here, try some."

Without thinking, Loren picked up another piece and proffered it to him. He paused a moment before opening his lips. She held the morsel, startled as his lips closed around the tips of her fingers, their moist warmth and softness sending a jolt of need rocketing down her arm.

"You're right," Alex said after he'd swallowed and taken another sip of wine. "That was very good. Give me something else."

Her hand shook slightly as she chose a stuffed olive and held it before him. He bent his head and slowly took the fruit into his mouth, his tongue hotly sweeping between the pads of her forefinger and thumb as he did so. If she'd thought the wine had made her legs weak, the caress of his tongue made them doubly so.

"Don't!" she cried.

"Don't do what?"

"That. What you just did. Just…don't."

"It disturbs you, my touch?"

Oh, far more than he could ever imagine, but she certainly wasn't going to let him know that painful truth.

"No, I just don't like it. That's all. Here, let me put the platter on the table, then we can help ourselves."

Loren relieved him of the platter and set it on the table next to the candle then settled herself on one of the wrought iron chairs before her legs gave way completely.

The warmth of the sun-heated metal seeped through the thin cotton of her skirt—heating other, more sensitive places. Loren shifted slightly but the motion only enhanced the sensation.

"Uncomfortable out here? Perhaps you'd rather sit indoors," Alex suggested as he topped off their glasses before sitting down opposite her.

"No, it's okay. I'm fine," Loren assured him, all the while forcing her body to relax.

Maybe it was the wine, or perhaps it was merely the exquisitely beautiful setting, but Loren felt herself begin to relax by degrees. By the time Alex rose to bake fillets of fish, garnished with herbs and lemon and wrapped in foil, on the outdoor grill she was feeling decidedly mellow. She rose from the table and took the near-empty antipasto platter through to the kitchen indoors.

The kitchen was very compact and narrow—a long row of cupboards down one side and the bench top and stove running parallel, with little more than a few feet between them. Loren searched the cupboards for a small dish to put the leftover antipasto into, and then the drawers for some cling wrap to cover it. She'd found a space for the dish in the heavily stocked fridge and was just about to rinse off the platter when Alex came through from the terrace.

He squeezed behind her, far more closely than necessary, she decided with a ripple of irritation.

"The fish is just about done. Can you grab the salad from the fridge? I'll get our plates."

He was so close his breath stirred the hair against the nape of her neck. She could feel the solid heat of his body as he pressed up against her buttocks and reached past her to grab the jug of vinaigrette dressing from the bench top.

She would not react to him; she would not. Loren clenched her hands into fists on the countertop, fighting against the urge to allow her body to lean back into the strength of his. It was almost a physical impossibility in the close confines of the kitchen.

Thankfully, Alex appeared to be oblivious to the racing emotions that swirled inside her. He propped the jug on top of the two dinner plates he'd taken from the crockery pantry behind her and was already on his way back outside.

She took a deep, steadying breath before opening the fridge again and lifting out the bowl of salad he'd obviously prepared while she slept. The crisp salad greens, interspersed with feta, olives and succulent freshly cut tomatoes looked mouthwateringly tempting, but nowhere near as appetizing as the man who was currently walking away from her.

No matter how idyllic this setting, the next two weeks would be absolute hell on earth.

Eight

To her surprise, over the next few days, Loren began to relax in a way she hadn't managed in some time. Yet beneath the surface a simmering tension lay between her and Alex.

As yet, he'd made no overtures to force their relationship onto a physical level. By day she was eternally grateful for that, but every night as she lay tangled in her sheets aching for the man who slept only a corridor width away from her room, she wondered whether she had indeed made the right decision in denying him her body.

He lied to you, she reminded herself. *He appealed to you on an emotional level he knew you could not refuse. He manipulated you for his own ends.*

But he hadn't done so for personal gain, she argued back silently as the moon traversed the sky and she wriggled against her mattress and stared out through the glass doors that led onto a small balcony off her room. He'd done it for his grandfather, to assuage the old man's sudden and irrational fears about the family's longevity.

It doesn't matter, she argued back again, thumping her pillow in frustration as she tried to get comfortable. He should have told her the truth from the start. How on earth did he expect to embark upon a marriage without even honesty between them? Without truth, they had nothing, because they certainly didn't have love. At least, not a love that was reciprocated.

Giving up on sleep, Loren rose from her bed and walked over to the French doors. She pushed them open and stepped out onto the balcony. The night air was balmy and still, enveloping her in a myriad of scents and sounds. She looked up at the clear night sky, observing the constellations so different to how they appeared back in New Zealand, and suddenly she was struck with a sense of loneliness that brought sudden tears to her eyes.

A tiny sob pushed up from her chest and ejected into the darkness. She gripped the iron balcony railing tight beneath her hands, but no matter how hard she squeezed she could not stop the flow of tears down her cheeks.

This wasn't how she imagined her life would be. She'd expected happiness. A mutual respect between herself and Alex. Respect that would hopefully grow to become more. Loren dragged a shaking breath into her aching lungs and blinked against the moisture that continued to well in her eyes. It seemed that now she'd started to cry, she was incapable of stopping.

The air beside her shifted and she turned her head to see Alex standing on the balcony beside her. Wearing only a pair of silken pajama pants, he looked like some god risen from the sea in the moonlight. Silver beams caressed the muscled width of his chest and shoulders, throwing the lean, defined strength into shadowed relief.

"What's wrong?"

"I…" Loren shook her head, averting her eyes, both unwilling and unable to verbalize what ailed her.

Warm, strong arms closed around her in comfort, drawing her against the smooth plane of his chest.

At first she resisted—she didn't trust him, she couldn't—but his arms tightened around her and for just that moment she wanted to forget all her dashed hopes and give in to his silent support. She let her cheek settle against his chest, her gulped sobs calming as her breathing adjusted to his, her heartbeat slowing to his strong steady rhythm.

She felt Alex's chin drop to the top of her head, felt the slight tug of the bristles of his beard in her hair. She nestled in closer, relishing the feel of his body against hers. His masculine form felt unfamiliar to her and yet instantly recognizable—as if this was where she had belonged all her life, safe within the circle of his arms.

Fresh tears sprang to her eyes at the foolishly irrational thought. She may have thought she belonged with him, but the truth couldn't be more converse.

"Hush, Loren," he whispered against her hair. "We will work this out."

"I don't think we can, Alex."

"One way or another, we will work it out."

With a powerful sweep of muscle, Alex lifted her

into his arms and took her back into her room. Still holding her to him he settled onto the mattress and leaned back against the padded headrest. Loren's head rested against his shoulder, her legs across his lap. She struggled to sit up and tried to push him away. With her defenses as weak as they were right now she couldn't afford to give him any leeway.

"Relax, I'm not going to try and force you into anything. You're upset. Let me comfort you."

She hesitated a moment before allowing the slow circular motion of his hand across her back to soothe her. Eventually her eyes slid closed and she allowed her senses to be filled with the gentleness of his touch, the steadiness of his breathing and the delicious warmth and scent of his bare skin.

Alex felt Loren relax by degrees until she finally drifted back off into sleep. Inside, his thoughts were in turmoil. Each day that passed saw them spending practically every waking moment together, yet each day she seemed to withdraw from him more and more. So much so that tonight she hadn't even felt as if she could accept his comfort.

Ironically, that had hurt more than the days they'd spent together so far, where he'd fought to keep his libido firmly under control, and far more than the nights where he'd lain on his bed, wondering if a quick dip in the Adriatic Sea would help diminish the fire raging under his skin.

He remembered back to a time when she'd been just a toddler. Her parents had been visiting his and for one reason or another she'd taken a tumble. Rather than seek consolation from either her father or mother, she'd tottered toward him, past them both, and offered her grazed palms for his inspection and reassurance that she was okay.

His brothers had teased him mercilessly. He'd been all of ten or eleven years old and they'd thought it hilarious that Loren had come to him. But now, in the moonlit night, with her slumbering in his arms, he remembered how it had secretly made him feel. Remembered the sense of responsibility and duty he had to protect her and keep her safe from all harm.

And here he was now, having harmed her in the worst way possible. He'd betrayed her trust and brought her back to a world that was no longer familiar to her, to people whose only memories of her were as a child and not as a woman with hopes and dreams of her own.

Anger curled a tight fist deep in his gut. He should never have interrupted her life. Never have brought her back. She'd had a new world in New Zealand yet she'd eschewed all of that to return to the old one she'd left behind. For him. He owed it to her to somehow make up for that wrong.

He knew that he still had to fulfill his duty to his grandfather and the people of Isla Sagrado. But for the first time, he admitted to himself that duty to family extended beyond his brothers and *Abuelo*. He was a married man now. His wife came first.

Bright bursts of morning light stabbed at Loren's eyes, dragging her to full consciousness. Beneath her, her bed had grown increasingly lumpy as she stretched and squirmed awake.

Lumpy? Realization and remembrance dawned with a rush. That lump was her husband; in fact, it was one particular part of her husband. Sometime during the night Alex had slid them both down onto the mattress and, as unaccustomed as she was to sharing a bed with anyone—let alone her husband—Loren had remained sprawled halfway across his body.

Even now the delicious scent of his skin, that blend of spice and citrus tang combined with the heat of his own special smell, teased at her nostrils and warmed her in places that made her squirm again.

"Loren, you will have to stop doing that or I cannot be answerable for my actions."

"Oh!" she exclaimed, springing away from him as if he'd delivered a high-voltage current directly to her.

She jumped up off the bed and kept her eyes averted from his prone form, from the irrefutable evidence that her actions had not left him unaffected.

"I'm sorry, I didn't mean to."

Alex sighed. She heard him stretch on the sheets and fought the urge to turn her eyes to him, to drink in the sight of his male beauty.

"Yes, I am sure you didn't mean to."

He sounded so tired and a pang of remorse plucked at her conscience. He'd come to her in the night when she was at her most vulnerable and he'd offered solace. No questions asked.

"I'm sorry, Alex. Truly. And I..." She pressed her lips together, looking for the right words. "Thank you for last night."

"*De nada.* It is what couples do, after all, is it not? Offer one another ease?"

Her eyes flew to his. She hadn't misunderstood the double entendre in his remark if the look on his face was anything to go by.

"Yes, well, I appreciate it." She shifted her weight from one foot to the other, unsure of what else to say or do.

"Go and have your shower, Loren. You are perfectly safe walking past me. As I said last night, I am not going to force you into anything."

"Anything else, you mean."

Alex sat up and swung his legs over the side of the bed. He stood and Loren's gaze was inexorably drawn to his torso, to his taut stomach and the fine scattering of dark hair that arrowed down from his belly button to the waistband of his pajama pants.

There was a thread of steel in his voice when he spoke, a thread that warned he was barely holding on to his temper.

"Remarks like that are unbecoming to a woman of your intelligence. Whatever my sins, I did not force you into marrying me."

Loren dropped her head in shame. He was right. She had to stop treating him as if he was solely to blame for their position. He made a sound of disgust and she heard him walk past her and leave the room, his own bedroom door slamming shut behind him.

She should apologize. Before she could change her mind, Loren followed him and knocked tentatively on his door. At his response she slowly opened it and stepped inside.

"I shouldn't have said what I did. I'm sorry."

Alex gave her a hard look but the small frown lines that bracketed his mouth eased a little. He gave her a small nod.

"Apology accepted."

"Thank you." Unsure of what to do next, Loren

started to close the door again. "I'll leave you to get dressed."

"Loren?"

"Yes?"

"I am not such an ogre, you know. I am merely a man. A man with responsibilities and needs."

There was something in the tone of his voice that spoke of a deep-seated longing that struck straight to her core. She felt the inexorable pull of it even as she started to move across the room.

He stood still and watched her as she came toward him, his stance proud. There was a frankness in his eyes that spoke straight to Loren's heart. In all of this she hadn't stopped to consider what this marriage had cost him. He hadn't married her for his own gain but for that of the people of Isla Sagrado and for the sake of his grandfather's fears. Whether Alex himself believed in the curse was irrelevant. He'd married her out of his respect and love for *Abuelo* and in determination to do whatever it took to lift the spirits of the people who looked to the del Castillo family for so much.

Loren lifted one hand and raised it to Alex's cheek, her fingers gently cupping his whisker-rough skin. She slowly rose on her tiptoes and pressed her lips to his. Softly, shyly, she kissed him. To her chagrin, his lips remained unresponsive beneath hers. Uncertain, she started to pull her hand away, but Alex's hand shot up to hold it there and to press it against his face, his long fingers covering hers.

"Don't play with me, Loren. Even I have limits."

"I...I'm not playing, Alex."

She reached up to kiss him again, this time feeling a zing of power as she felt his lips tremble beneath hers. She traced the seam of his mouth with the tip of her tongue, feeling suddenly bolder than she'd ever felt before. He was a man who had everything and wanted for nothing. This was all she could give him. Her love.

Alex's arms wrapped around her, pulling her against his hard male form, showing her in no uncertain terms that he was more than prepared to accept what she offered. Loren stroked her hands across his shoulders, loving the feel of his leashed strength beneath her fingertips. His body burned into hers, making the light summer tank top and cotton shorts she'd worn to bed feel as if they were too much against her skin.

She strained against him, wanting more, yet not quite fully understanding what it was she needed. Alex's strong hands skimmed down her back and over the mounds of her buttocks, cupping them and pulling her up higher against him. Angling the part of her body that ached with a demanding throb against his arousal. A shock of pleasure radiated through her at the pressure of his sex against her. She felt herself grow damp and hot.

He pulled her to him again and flexed his hips against her, starting a rhythm that made her whole body pulse with need. Loren slid her hands up the cords of his neck and knotted her fingers in his short dark hair, pulling his face down to hers, wanting to absorb every part of him any way she could.

"Lift your legs and put them around my waist," Alex commanded, his voice vibrating with desire.

Through the haze of passion that focused her senses only on the touch and taste of the man in her arms, she managed to comply. Alex walked them to the bed and laid her down on the sheets, still rumpled from last night. Without losing physical contact, he lay down with her, their bodies aligning perfectly, his legs cradled between hers.

Loren's breasts ached and swelled against the soft cotton of her top, her nipples pressing like twin points against Alex's chest. At this moment she hated the barrier that stood between them. As if he read her mind, Alex shifted his weight slightly, then his hands were at the hem of her top, pushing it up and over her head and exposing her small round breasts with their blush-colored peaks.

"So perfect," he murmured as he traced the outline of first one dusky pink nipple, then the other, with the tip of his finger.

She watched, unable to speak, unable to move, as he moistened his finger with his tongue then retraced the shape of her again. A shudder rippled through her, bringing a small smile of intent to Alex's face. Then he brought his lips to a tight bud, his tongue flicking out to mimic what his finger had been doing only seconds before.

Another shudder spread through her body, this one bringing a swell of pleasure with it, a swell that ballooned as Alex's lips closed over her nipple and sucked hard. She nearly leapt off the bed, her body arching into him, wanting all he could give her. His hips held her pinned against the mattress and she hooked her legs around his, running her feet over his calves, the slippery fabric of his pajamas soft and sensual against her soles.

His body felt so different from her own. Stronger, firmer and with an energy vibrating from deep inside of him that excited her both mentally and physically.

She knew what was yet to come, knew that there would be discomfort, possibly even pain, but she also knew to the depths of her soul that this was totally right. That out of anyone, Alex was the only man she could ever be this intimate with.

She gasped aloud as he scraped his teeth over her nipple before lavishing more of the same attention to its twin. She thought she would go mad with the sensations he wrung from her body. He was trailing his tongue along the curve of her breast, sending a rash of goose bumps to pepper her skin as, one by one, he traced each rib, lower and lower.

Despite the warm air she felt a shiver flow across her skin. His hands were at the drawstring tie of her shorts, she felt the bow loosen, the fabric begin to give way. Alex pulled himself up onto his knees and tugged her shorts away from her, exposing her body's deepest intimacy to his scorching gaze.

She felt wanton under the power of his stare and she squirmed against the sheets, relishing the feel of high-thread-count cotton softness against the bare skin of her buttocks. Her movement caused a flush to deepen high on Alex's cheekbones, made his eyes darken even more. He reached for her, his broad hands holding her hips firmly, his fingers splayed across her skin as he lowered his face to the V at the apex of her thighs.

Loren tensed, unsure of what to expect. All tension flowed from her as he pressed his lips with unerring accuracy at the central spot that was the heart of the sensations pouring through her. She felt his tongue gently glide over her sensitized nerves and lost all sense of reality. Again and again his tongue swept over her, gentle at first then firmer until, when she thought she could bear it no longer, he closed his mouth over that spot and suckled as he had done with her nipples only moments ago.

Sensation splintered through her body, at first sharp and then in increasing undulating waves of sheer pleasure reaching a crescendo of feeling she'd never dreamed herself capable of. Her entire body tensed, taut like a bow, before she collapsed back against the bed, weak, spent. Sated.

She sensed Alex's movement, heard the slither of fabric as he shucked off his pajama bottoms. She opened her eyes as he knelt between her splayed legs, watched as he stroked his hand from base to tip of his erection. He positioned himself at her entrance and she felt the hot, blunt probe of his flesh.

A sudden shaft of fear shot through her. "I haven't… I mean, I've never…"

"Shh," Alex said soothingly. "I know. I will take care of you, Loren. Trust me."

She locked her gaze with his, searching for any hint that he could be untrue to her, even now as they lay together with nothing but their past between them.

"I do. I trust you, Alex," she whispered.

"That's my girl," he replied.

He leaned down and kissed her, his tongue sweeping inside her mouth to tangle with hers. She welcomed his invasion, letting her senses focus on the thrust and parry of his kiss, and the blend of her essence and the flavor that was all his.

She felt his hips slowly push against hers, felt him slide within her body. She stiffened involuntarily, unsure how she would accommodate him, but then he withdrew and did the same thing again, this time probing a little farther, waiting a little longer. Her body stretched and molded around him, at first uncomfortable and then not. Tremors racked his frame as he held himself partially within her. The next time he moved, she pressed back, taking him inside her a little farther.

A new sensation began to build inside her, one that demanded more, demanded him, so much so that when he thrust all the way inside her on his next stroke she ignored the sharp tear of pain and clutched at his hips, urging him to continue. With no barrier impeding him, Alex deepened his strokes, propelling her once more toward the growing pleasure whose epicenter lay hidden within her.

He gathered momentum and Loren found her body meeting him stroke for stroke, both of them reaching for the shadowy pinnacle of their desire. And then it burst upon her. Wave after wave. Bigger than before, deeper than before. A cry of sheer delight broke on her lips as Alex shuddered in release against her, before collapsing, spent, against her body.

In the aftermath of their lovemaking Loren gave herself over to the delicious lassitude that spread through her body. She knew of physical pleasure, but she'd never dreamed it could be like this. She trailed her fingers up and down the length of Alex's sweat-dampened spine and in that moment she loved him more than she ever had before.

Alex watched his wife as she slept naked in his arms. His heart still hammered in his chest. Coming down from the high of their first physical union had taken its time. Even now he still felt twinges of pleasure, aftershocks of satisfaction that seemed endless in their reach.

It had never been like this before, with anyone. Somehow the knowledge that he was Loren's husband and her first lover had lent a different note to the act itself. He'd always prided himself on being a considerate lover but it had become even more important to him to ensure that her first time be special than he'd believed possible.

And in giving he'd also received. The climax that had wrung his body dry had been spectacular. He rested one hand on her smooth, flat belly. Perhaps even now he'd managed to achieve his goal.

He had scarcely been able to believe his luck when she'd followed him to his room. After last night he'd hoped they'd gained a new high ground together, but her reaction to him this morning had dashed that hope. Until he'd heard that gentle knock at his bedroom door.

Alex dropped his head back against the pillow. He'd made that first time special for her. No matter what came after, she would always have that. Somehow that truth didn't help assuage the kernel of guilt that had nestled somewhere in his chest. She deserved to have her first time with someone who loved her. But whatever she deserved, Alex was what she had—what she *would* have for the rest of her life, since he had no intention of ever letting her go.

She stirred against him, her slender body curling around his as naturally as if they'd always slept together. He'd had enough of thinking, enough of trying to justify his decisions. Action came more naturally.

Pushing aside thoughts that could only plague him, Alex gathered Loren closer to him and began to stroke her with long sweeps of his hand. He was already hard for her again. Mindful that she might be tender, he decided this time to take things even slower.

She woke as he dragged his fingertips along the inner curve of her hip. A tremulous smile pulled at her lips, soon to be lost in a moan that tore from her throat as he slid one hand between her legs to gently stroke her soft folds.

"Too much? Too soon?" he asked, watching her face carefully, hoping against hope that she would say no to his inquiry.

"Oh!" she cried as he brushed over her clitoris. "No, not too much. Not too soon."

"Good." He smiled in return and focused on the task at hand.

She had so much still to learn about the pleasure they could give one another, and he thanked his lucky stars she was such an eager pupil.

Her legs began to quake in what he recognized as the precursor to her climax and he slowed his touch, drawing out the pleasure for her as far as he was able. When he himself could hold on no longer he pulled her beneath him and sank inside her, the action sending her skyrocketing over the edge. Just like that he was with her, his body pulsing, spilling his seed, his mind filled with nothing more than wave after wave of ecstasy and the overwhelming sense of rightness that consumed him with Loren in his arms.

Nine

While Loren loved living at the castillo she adored the compactness of this stone cottage perched on the hillside. The small kitchen that had so tormented her with its closeness when she and Alex had first arrived was now a teasing adventure. And, even though they had neighbors in abundance, with the mature trees and the staggered terrace style of building around them, she felt as if she and Alex were totally isolated. There was a delightful sense of freedom in knowing that she could do whatever she wished.

It had been one glorious week since the morning they'd first made love. A week filled with discovery as she'd learned to bring the strong man she'd married exquisite physical delight and receive the same in return. Her one regret was that while they grew closer physically with each encounter, Alex continued to maintain an emotional distance between them she couldn't seem to break through.

They'd done all the tourist things available in the area, enjoying the food and the countryside almost as much as they enjoyed one another in the close confines of the cottage. Going back to the castillo would be difficult but she had very definite plans for her and Alex to plan more time alone together.

A smile pulled at her lips as she heard Alex come up the stairs from the pebble beach below where they'd been swimming together. Only the knowledge that they'd been visible to some of their neighbors while in the water had held them back from making love as they'd floated together. But now, her smile deepened, now they were in their own cocoon of privacy again and she could do what she wished.

Alex lowered his body onto one of the sun loungers on the terrace, the white-and-navy striped cushion beneath him accenting the depth of his tan. Black swim trunks clung to him, outlining his hips and the tops of his thighs. Loren's mouth watered at the prospect of what lay hidden beneath the dark fabric.

Her hands gripped the edges of the tray she'd brought through from the kitchen and she put it down on the terrace table, none too gently, and grabbed at one of the highball glasses before it toppled over. Even after all they'd shared he continued to have the power to rattle her senses. Just thinking about him had her heart racing, her lower body flushed and eager for his touch.

She forced her hands to still so she could grab the pitcher of iced tea and pour two glasses. She took one over to Alex, aware of his eyes watching every step she took toward him.

"Cool drink?" she said, offering him a glass.

"After that swim I think I need more than a cool drink."

He took the proffered drink and drained the glass with a series of long, slow pulls. Loren watched, mesmerized by the play of muscles working in his throat. Alex put his glass down on the terrace beside him, the unmelted blocks of ice tinkling in the bottom, and gestured to Loren to join him on the lounger.

"Here, come and sit with me."

"There's no room," Loren half protested.

"So use your imagination." Alex smiled in return.

Loren lifted the folds of the emerald green sarong that matched her bikini and straddled the lounger, settling on Alex's strong thighs.

"Like this?" she said, her voice a husky rasp as she felt the hairs on his legs tickle the already sensitive flesh of her inner thighs.

"Oh yes, exactly like that."

Alex pushed the flimsy sarong aside, baring her legs completely and exposing the shadowed area of her body at the apex of her thighs. He traced the outside edge of her bikini bottoms, from the tie at her hip to her inner thigh and back again.

Heat and moisture flooded to her lower regions and she drew in a sharp breath as one finger slipped inside the edge of her bikini pants to brush lightly over her inner folds. Back and forth he stroked, until finally he slid one finger inside her. She clenched her inner muscles against him, tilting her pelvis forward and rocking slightly against his palm.

"You like that?" he asked, his voice deep and low.

"You know I do," she whispered back and gasped anew as he slid another finger inside her.

With his free hand, Alex tugged at the bows that held her bikini bottoms together and pulled the fabric away, dropping it beside the lounger, exposing her and what he was doing to her.

Loren looked down and felt another sharp jolt of pleasure rock through her body as she watched him. She ached for release, wanted to rush toward the starburst of pleasure she knew was just around the corner, yet conversely wanted to make it last as long as she could. When Alex's thumb settled against the hooded bud of nerve endings at her core she nearly lost it, but she clenched against him, harder, tighter, determined to remain in control.

"Come for me," Alex commanded, his voice guttural now, his eyes molten with desire.

He started a gentle circular motion with his thumb, slowly increasing and releasing pressure with each stroke. She was near mindless when she felt the first flutters of her orgasm begin to wash over her. Finally, she could hold back no more. She tilted her hips some more, leaning into his hand, and let his magical touch send her flying over the edge.

Loren slowly returned to her surroundings, to the man who lay beneath her. A beautiful sensual smile pulled at his lips and she felt herself smile back in return.

"You're beautiful when you climax, did you know that?" he said.

Loren felt the heat of a blush stain her cheeks. Even after what they'd just done she still felt embarrassed when he spoke to her like that. In lieu of a response she leaned forward and captured his lips with hers. He tasted of a delicious combination of sunshine, tea and a hint of mint.

She broke off the kiss and pulled free from his arms.

"It seems to me that things are a little unbalanced here," she said.

"Unbalanced?"

Loren traced the prominent outline of his erection through his swim trunks with her fingernails.

"You heard me."

"Hmm, you could be right," Alex said, his speech thickening as she continued to tease his length. "It's always important for things to be balanced, of course."

"I was thinking the exact same thing," Loren said and rose from the lounger in a fluid movement.

She undid the knot of her sarong and let it drop to the terrace floor, and then undid her bikini top, allowing it to fall on top of the puddle of emerald green fabric. Her nipples tightened in anticipation in spite of the warm air as she bent toward her husband.

"Lift your hips," she said.

As he did, she eased his trunks down, exposing him to her hungry gaze and her eager hands. She tossed the shorts behind her, uncaring of where they fell.

"Now, spread your legs," she requested. She knelt between them on the striped cushion as he silently obeyed.

Loren leaned forward and took his erection in her hand, curling her fingers around the velvet hard length and stroking firmly from base to tip and back again. Bending down, she swirled her tongue around the tip of him. Again and again, before gently rasping her teeth over the smooth head. She smiled as a harsh groan tore from Alex's lips.

"Too much? Do you want me to stop?" she teased. She knew what his answer would be before he could even verbalize it.

"Stop now and I may have to punish you severely," Alex said through gritted teeth.

Loren laughed softly and took him in her mouth. She loved that she could do this to him, for him. Just a few months ago, she would never have dreamed she could be so bold, so forward, but he'd taught her much in this past week. Most importantly, he'd taught her how to give him pleasure and how to draw that pleasure out until he finally let go of the iron control with which he held himself.

She looked up at his face. His head was thrown back against the chair cushion, his eyes squeezed closed. He'd flung his arms back and his hands gripped the back of the lounger. Loren took him deeper into her mouth, suckled more firmly at his tip, relished the hot salty taste of him as he fought to hold back.

Then she stopped, releasing him to the warm air around them. Alex tilted his head back up, his eyes narrowed as he watched her rise and spread her legs before lowering herself back down. She guided his shaft to her with unerring accuracy.

His hands let go of the lounger, finding a new home cupping her breasts as she took his length inside her body. She leaned against the strength of his arms as she started a rhythm guaranteed to bring them both to completion. Beneath her she could feel Alex's body tremble with the sheer force of his indomitable will.

She knew he would not allow himself the freedom of his climax unless he knew she too was near.

But this time she wanted to drive him over the edge. This time she wanted to show him that love was not all about control or always about giving. Sometimes it was about taking what you needed, when it was offered. And she was offering herself. Everything. Her heart, her body, her soul.

She knew the second she'd overcome his resistance. Felt the moment his body began to let go. Intense joy flooded her mind. Hard on the heels of that sense of elation, her own orgasm shuddered through her.

Loren collapsed against Alex's body, both of them slicked with sweat, and lay against his chest, listening to the rapid thud of his heartbeat.

"I love you, Alexander del Castillo," she whispered.

In answer he wrapped his arms around her and pulled her even closer—but the words she wished to hear, more than any other from his mouth, remained unsaid.

They'd been back from Dubrovnik for nearly a week. Already their time together seemed as if it was a distant memory. Alex had disappeared back into his work as if nothing else existed. Apparently bookings at the resort were on the increase. The publicity surrounding their marriage had seemed to have done the trick as far as lifting the profile of Isla Sagrado in the media. Once again the island nation was becoming a popular holiday destination for the moneyed and famous.

Loren was pleased for Alex that things were improving so steadily although she sometimes wished the demands of his work were less so they could recapture some of the wonder of their honeymoon again. It was rare that Alex arrived home before she went to bed anymore, and he hadn't been to her room or in her bed since their first night back.

She'd believed they'd built a foundation for their future together in those exquisite days and nights at the cottage, yet now she was no longer so certain. This morning a courier had delivered her a copy of their prenuptial agreement for her records. It served as a sobering reminder of the parameters under which she and Alex had married.

Had he encouraged their intimacy, their discovery of one another, purely to make the child he was so determined to produce? Before the wedding, he'd gone with her to the doctor where she'd had a physical check and the doctor had discussed her cycle. Alex had known when she should have been most fertile. That that time had coincided so soon after their wedding was fortuitous, he'd said, as they'd driven back from the clinic.

Was that why he'd been so patient with her? So passionate? Had making a baby been the sole object of their lovemaking?

Her period had been due a few days ago but as yet hadn't made its appearance. She placed a hand on her stomach, wondering if Alex would have his wish after all. As much as she desired to bear his child, she wanted more from their marriage before she felt ready to bring a child into it. Especially now she knew just what it would be like to share a life with him.

Unless, of course, their honeymoon had been a farce—nothing but a means to an end for Alex.

"Señora?"

Loren turned from the flowers she'd been arranging

for the dining table tonight and greeted the maid who'd brought a cordless phone on a silver tray.

"A call for me?" she said, picking up the handset.

"*Sí,* it is *Señor* del Castillo."

Loren felt an instant rush of elation and hit the hold button, saying "hello" before the maid had even left the room.

"Loren, I left some papers in my office at home and I can't spare Giselle to come to the castillo to collect them. Would you be able to bring them to the resort?"

Hard on the heels of disappointment that he didn't so much as ask how she was feeling, she found herself agreeing to do so.

"Sure, I can do that. I'm expected at the orphanage at lunchtime for a concert with the children. I can stop in to your office on my way through."

"Thanks, I appreciate it. You'll find them in the blue folder on my desk."

Without waiting for her to say goodbye, Alex disconnected the call. He'd treated her as no more than one of his staff. Loren felt a bubble of anger rise in her throat. Anger mixed with another emotion she didn't want to examine too closely for fear it would bring her to tears.

She swallowed hard against the obstruction in her throat and squared her shoulders. She would tell him what she thought of his manner when she saw him. If he thought he could treat her like that and get away with it, well, he had another think coming.

Half an hour later Loren drove her new Alfa Romeo Spider—a belated wedding gift surprise from Alex when they'd arrived home—toward the resort's main offices and pulled into the visitor parking lot outside.

She looked around for Alex's Lamborghini but it was nowhere to be seen. Strange, but then perhaps he'd used a driver today.

She collected the blue folder he'd requested from the passenger seat and walked with clipped, sure steps toward the office door. Inside, with a wave to the receptionist, Loren made her way directly to Alex's office.

Even as hurt and angry as she was, her heart lifted at the prospect of seeing him like this in the middle of the day. Perhaps she'd even be able to persuade him to come with her to the lunchtime concert.

Her hopes were dashed, however, as she was greeted by Giselle at Alex's office door.

"Oh, thanks. You finally brought them, did you?" Giselle said, unfolding her elegant long legs from behind her desk and coming to relieve Loren of the folder.

"I'd like to give this directly to Alex myself, if you don't mind," Loren stated, holding firmly on to the cardboard packet.

"Oh, he's not here."

"He's not? Where—"

"Didn't he tell you? Of course, obviously not. He had a meeting in Puerto Seguro with some potential investors for the resort expansion. I'll take these with me as I'm headed that way now."

Loren let go of the documents. As she did so she was assailed with a sense of dizziness. Giselle was quick to react, putting a hand under Loren's elbow and guiding her to sit on a large sofa against one wall.

"Are you okay?" Giselle asked. "You've gone awfully pale."

"It's nothing. I skipped breakfast this morning and I shouldn't have."

"Are you sure that's all it is? After all, Alex is a very—" Giselle paused for a moment, her face suddenly reflective "—virile man. And you've just had a couple of weeks at the cottage in Dubrovnik, yes? It's so beautiful there. So deliciously private and romantic, don't you think?"

Giselle spoke so knowingly—indeed, with such familiarity—that nausea pitched through Loren's body. Oblivious to Loren's discomfort, the other woman continued.

"Alex will be pleased if you've fallen pregnant so soon." She patted Loren's hand. "That would mean he'd be able to go back to normal so much sooner than he'd planned."

What exactly was Giselle referring to? It wasn't as if subtlety was the woman's strong point. She had to be referring to Alex and her resuming their relationship.

"Back to normal?" Loren asked, hoping against hope that her suspicions were ridiculous.

"I'm sure you know exactly what I mean." Giselle smiled in return but there was little humor in the cold glitter of her eyes. Instead, the proprietary nature of the curve of her lips said it all.

"Oh, dear, look at the time. I'd better get these to Alex before he comes bellowing on the phone, demanding to know where I am. I'll let you see yourself out. You look as though you could do with a few minutes to yourself."

Within seconds Loren was left alone with nothing but the slightly cloying scent of Giselle's perfume in the air around her.

She shook her head slowly. No. What Giselle had said couldn't be true. Go back to his old life and ways?

Alex wasn't that kind of man, surely. Not the Alex she thought she knew, anyway. Before their marriage his playboy lifestyle had been well represented in the media, but months before he'd come to New Zealand he'd all but dropped out of circulation. She'd noted it at the time, long before she'd had any reason to believe his new and uncharacteristic circumspection might have anything to do with her.

Loren leaned against the big square cushion of the couch. Had it all been part of his carefully orchestrated plan to prove to everyone that he could break the curse? Even *Abuelo* would have had a hard time believing that Alex would have gone directly from playboy bachelorhood to married. But what would happen now? Once their PR campaign of a marriage had served its purpose and they'd fulfilled the terms of the prenuptial agreement, would Alex revert back to his old social life, leaving her to sit at home with the children?

Children? Oh, Lord. What if she *was* pregnant? There was no way she'd raise a child here with him if he was going to have affairs behind her back—or even in front of her, if it came to that.

One thing was certain, Loren thought. If she was pregnant, Alex would be the last person she'd be telling until she knew exactly what kind of father he planned to be.

Ten

Loren had a pounding headache by the time she left the orphanage after the children's concert. As had become her habit, she had spent an extra couple of hours in the babies' nursery. Two had already been fostered, with a view to full adoption once all the paperwork had been processed, but a newborn had been admitted, sadly undernourished and displaying all the signs of fetal alcohol syndrome.

It broke her heart to think that a child could be abused so poorly, even before birth, and she spent extra time with the wee mite.

She drove back to the castillo slowly, her mind on the children she'd just been with and the prospect of a child of her own. That it would satisfy Alex was a given, but what of the child? Would Alex even be able to spend any time with the baby? He already worked excessively long hours. So much so that since their return they'd barely seen one another, let alone shared a bed.

Was that to be the tenor of their marriage? Passionate couplings to bring forth an heir and nothing in between?

It wasn't what she'd expected of marriage. As difficult as her parents' relationship had been, they had truly loved each other at the beginning. And even when it started to fall apart and the arguments began, they'd been together until her mother—in a fit of pique at her husband—had taken things a step too far with a mutual friend and had betrayed her marriage vows.

Naomi had admitted to Loren, when she'd been about twenty, that she'd regretted forcing Loren's father's hand to divorce her that way, but she hadn't seen any other way out. He'd insisted he still loved her, a fact Loren truly believed, but for Naomi that love had sputtered and died like a guttered candle in the face of the arguments that had become habitual between them.

Loren felt a sharp ache in her chest at the memories, still vivid, of frozen silences between her parents. Silences that would be periodically broken by vicious arguments late into the night when she was supposed to be sleeping.

She'd been about ten years old the first time she became aware of how contentious her parents' marriage had become. Back then she'd hidden under her bedcovers until things had grown silent. By the time she was in her teens she'd sit at the top of the stairs and listen as they threw accusations back and forth.

She could still hear every venomous word of the final exchange that had led to the divorce—of her mother's admission of infidelity, of her father's sobs later after her mother had withdrawn to bed.

Loren swallowed against the sudden lump in her throat and blinked back burning tears. She didn't want that for her child or children. In all conscience she could not bring a child into an unhappy and unstable relationship right from the very start.

But she'd agreed to give Alex the heir he'd stipulated in the prenup. She was honor bound to do so. It was a difficult predicament she found herself in—especially when she wanted so much more.

Only a week ago she'd almost begun to believe her husband might even be beginning to share her feelings for him. That he might be starting to fall a little in love with her, too. But the cold distance he'd maintained since their return had dashed her hopes.

Suddenly the prospect of returning to the castillo held no appeal. She pulled over to the shoulder of the road, then executed a U-turn and headed back in the direction of Puerto Seguro. She needed to be around other people, people who didn't have an agenda as far as she was concerned.

Alex looked up from his seat at the head of the boardroom table in Rey's offices, where he'd arranged to meet with potential investors today. As Giselle approached, he was relieved to see the folder he'd requested from Loren in his PA's hand. A burst of gratitude toward his wife filled him, accompanied by a deep sense of regret that he hadn't been able to spend more time with her lately. He missed her and their nights together with a physical ache, but the negotiations he was in the process of finalizing were vitally important and required all of his attention. Besides, he'd decided it would be selfish to wake her when he arrived home every night after midnight. Alex silently resolved to make it up to Loren once the deal was signed.

Giselle sidled up next to him, one breast brushing not so subtly against his shoulder as she leaned across and put the folder in front of him. There was a time when her actions might have been welcome. That time was well past. He drew away from her touch and noted the tiny crease on her forehead as her brows pulled together in a silent query.

"That will be all, thank you, Giselle."

"All?" She smiled, giving him the sloe-eyed look he'd once found so attractive. "Well, if you're quite sure…"

"Absolutely certain. I am a married man. I shouldn't have to remind you of that."

A married man who'd been neglecting his duties to his wife shamefully. His conscience pricked again.

"Loren looked a little peaked today," Giselle remarked nonchalantly as she finally moved away from his side.

A sudden swell of concern surged through him. "Peaked?" he asked. "What makes you say that?"

"She had a bit of a turn when she brought the papers in from the castillo. Perhaps you've been keeping her up a little too late at night. After all, as we both know, a man of your appetites—"

"That's quite enough," Alex interrupted before she could finish her sentence.

"I was only saying. Anyway, she told me she hadn't eaten breakfast this morning but I couldn't help but wonder if a little del Castillo isn't already making his presence felt. You did want her pregnant, didn't you?"

Pregnant? It was most definitely what he wanted.

The possibility that Giselle spoke the truth bloomed in his mind, overtaking rational thought. Loren, pregnant with his child? All legalities and legends aside, he hadn't given enough credence to how he'd feel when such an event became a reality. The prospect that his son or daughter could even now be growing in Loren's womb caused an unexpected tightness to coil around his heart. A tightness intermingled with an overwhelming urge to discard his responsibilities to his business and race to Loren's side. To cherish her and share the wonder that they could already be on the way to being parents.

Alex gathered his thoughts together. Despite what his heart wanted, he had duties to fulfill, no matter how inconvenient to him. He looked up and found Giselle watching him carefully, as if waiting for him to confirm or deny her suspicions.

"That would be a matter between my wife and myself. You can head back to the office now, Giselle," he said with finality and looked pointedly at the door.

Giselle made her way out of the boardroom, but her words had left their mark upon him. Try as he might, Alex couldn't ignore his resentment toward the matters of business that had kept him from home so late each night, and that were now an unwelcome barrier between him and the answers he so desperately wanted from his wife.

Loren couldn't say what had drawn her to the graveyard afterward. She'd gone to the city with the determination to lose herself in some shopping, perhaps a meal out, and then to return to the castillo much later. But somehow she'd found herself driving toward the old church on the coast, with its eclectic mix of centuries-old headstones blended with those of more modern times in the burial grounds.

Locking her car in the car park, she pushed through the old wooden gate and picked her way through the headstones until she reached the Dubois family plot. It wasn't difficult to find her father's grave. The stone was the newest and brightest marble amongst the others. Loren knelt down in the grass surrounding the grave and cleared a few of the weeds that had pushed through around the base of his headstone.

"Oh, Papa, did you ever imagine what would come from the pact you and Raphael made all those years ago?" she said, a sudden gust of wind snatching her words and casting them away.

She still missed him so much. By the time her mother had imparted the news that Francois had died of complications after a bout of pneumonia, he'd already been buried. Loren had never had a chance to say goodbye.

The last time she'd spoken to him, though, on one of his frequent phone calls, he'd made her reiterate the one promise he'd asked of her when she'd left Isla Sagrado. Even now she could hear the deep baritone of his voice as he'd spoken across the long-distance telephone lines.

"Loren, mi hija, *you must always follow the truth of your heart. Always. Promise me."*

"Yes, Papa, I promise." Loren now spoke the words

out loud. "But it's not so easy when the man of my heart does not feel the same way toward me."

She closed her eyes and bent her head, willing some of her father's wisdom and love to help her with her decision. Did she accept that she had to fulfill the conditions of the prenup, or did she tell Alex she refused to give him the child he had asked for?

Follow the truth of her heart. What was that truth anymore? All her life she'd believed in one thing, that she was Alex's mate for life. She now accepted how naive that had been. The problem was that truth— her love for Alex—had not diminished. Yes, it had changed. It had grown from childish adoration and infatuation to something she knew was as intrinsic to her being as air was necessary for her to breathe.

So what now, she wondered. Did she accept a marriage as hollow and barren as her parents' marriage had become, or did she fight for what she wanted—what she was due as Alex's wife?

Loren kissed her fingertips and touched them to her father's headstone.

"I love you, Papa. I always will."

Never stop. His automatic response to her words echoed in her heart.

Never stop. Never give up.

And suddenly it was clear what she had to do. If she wanted her husband to *be* her husband, she had to fight for him. Had to fight for what was her right as his partner and as the potential mother of his children. Surely it would not be too much to expect of him that he remain faithful to her, especially not when they were already so obviously compatible. If she could only persuade him to give them a chance, she knew they could make their marriage work.

She straightened up onto her feet and squared her shoulders before resolutely walking back to the car. She would lay her demands on the table to her husband tonight. One way or another, she would have her answer.

And if that answer is no, a small voice in the back of her mind questioned, *what then?*

Loren shook her head as if she could dislodge the thought before it took hold. She couldn't afford to fail in this. Not when her heart's truth was on the line.

Back at the castillo, Loren was pleased to hear from the housekeeper that Alex would be dining with her and *Abuelo* that evening; in fact, both his brothers would also be there. Knowing that time with his brothers was bound to put Alex in a good mood put a spring in her step as she ascended the stairs to their suite.

And she would make an extra effort with her appearance tonight. Somehow she knew she'd need all the additional armor she could gather around her. She looked at her wristwatch. Yes, she had plenty of time to prepare for the night's success.

In her room, she searched out the candles that had so romantically lit the atmosphere on her disastrous wedding night. She wanted to re-create that golden glow of hope when she and Alex retired to their rooms after dinner. Then she'd show her husband, with her words and with her body, what she expected of him and their marriage.

Satisfied with the placement of the candles, Loren spent a good half hour choosing what to wear for the evening. She didn't want to be too obviously seductive, after all she had a dinner to attend with the four del Castillo men before she would even have so much as an opportunity to have her husband alone. Eventually, she decided upon a simple strapless white gown that skimmed to her knees with flirtatious layers of organza. The bodice was slightly gathered, the scalloped top edge giving a soft and feminine line, while the boned built-in corset meant she could get away with the bare minimum of underwear.

She smiled, remembering her lack of underwear on their honeymoon. It was ironic that even though she'd bought replacement garments on the first day after their arrival, once she and Alex had consummated their marriage she'd had very little need, or opportunity, to wear any.

The fact that the physical side of their marriage had stopped upon their return meant that the memory left a bittersweet taste in her mouth. She pushed the niggle of doubt about her success for tonight to the very back of her mind.

She decided to team the dress with an elegant pair of gold high-heeled pumps and chose a pair of ruby drop earrings that *Abuelo* had given her on their return from their honeymoon. Given the style and shape of the stones, she believed they were probably equally as old as the heirloom engagement ring she wore on her ring finger. They'd be the perfect complement to the gown. A light cobwebby gold shawl to cover her shoulders was the perfect finishing touch.

Her spirits bolstered, she ran herself a deliciously deep bubble bath and set about her preparations.

As she had been the first time she'd descended the stairs alone at the castillo, Loren was aware of the murmur of male voices from the salon off the main entrance hall. And uncannily, as she had that very first time, she felt the weight of generations of del Castillo brides settle upon her shoulders. She knew, historically, that most marriages in the del Castillo family in the past had been structured to gain both political and financial advantage. Even Alex's parents' marriage had brought with it the alliance between his mother's family's vineyards and winery that formed part of the del Castillo brand today. They had, by the time of their marriage, been very truly in love, but they had also been not unaware of the advantages of their union. A union that in all likelihood would not have taken place if the financial gains had not been there in the first place.

That her marriage had been predestined was a fact of life in a family such as this. But a marriage based solely on duty and honor would not be enough to satisfy her. Tonight would establish whether she would finally be able to achieve the kind of marriage she wanted.

A frisson of something cold trickled down her spine and she increased her pace to get to the salon, suddenly eager to see her husband.

She slowed her steps as she drew nearer the salon. Unseemly haste would spoil the image of sensual elegance she'd worked so hard to create tonight. She paused in front of a massive gilt-edged mirror just outside the salon and checked that the somewhat austere hairdo she'd finally settled on, knowing how much Alex loved to tug it loose, remained intact.

Her hand stilled in the air as she heard her husband's voice raised with a thread of anger in it.

"Don't be a fool, Reynard. Marriage is a serious

business. I know we all agreed to do our part but I can tell you up front that I regret having done what I have. In fact, I think I may have made the biggest mistake of my life."

Cold shock settled like ice in the pit of Loren's stomach.

"We all know Reynard won't go ahead with actually marrying this girl. The engagement is merely a front to keep *Abuelo* happy as we all agreed." Benedict's voice filtered through the air. "But you needn't worry that I plan on doing anything so stupid as marrying someone I don't love."

"No, we all know you'd marry your car if you could," Reynard jeered. "I pity the poor woman you do eventually settle down with."

"Well, I pity Loren," Benedict continued. "She didn't ask for any of this."

Loren felt her knees grow weak, her legs unstable beneath her. She had to move, had to get out of there before one of them realized she'd overheard their discussion.

She forced her feet to carry her to immediate refuge in a downstairs guest bathroom and locked the door firmly behind her. Not daring to let go of the breath she was holding in so tight she thought her lungs might burst, she gripped the scallop-shaped marble pedestal basin. Right now it was the only thing keeping her vertical. She was afraid if she let go that she'd sink to the ground and never want to get up again.

The biggest mistake of my life.

Alex's words echoed, over and over, in her mind. Was that how he saw her? Saw their marriage? On the heels of the hope and determination she'd returned home with today, his words were like a death knell to her dreams.

Black spots danced before her eyes and a roaring sound rushed through her head. She forced herself to let go of the breath she'd been holding and dragged in a new breath. The spots began to recede but the pain in her heart only grew with her every inhalation.

Biggest mistake. Biggest mistake.

That she had his brothers' pity was no salve to her wounded soul. She couldn't bear to be the object of any man's pity. Not when all she wanted was Alex's love.

Somehow she had to gather the courage to go in there and face him.

Loren twisted the cold tap on and let the cool water run over her wrists. As she did so an all-too-familiar ache started in the pit of her belly. An ache that always functioned as a precursor to her period.

Hot tears sprang to her eyes as she realized her fears that she might have been pregnant, and her concerns about Alex's presence as a father, were far outweighed by her desire to have had a part of Alex that would be her own.

She dried off her hands quickly. As she did so, the overhead light caught the bloodred of her ruby engagement ring, the color uncannily symbolic of the end of her expectations.

Alex looked up as Loren joined them in the salon. He allowed a small frown to crease his forehead. He'd expected her much earlier. Mind you, given the slant of the conversation he and his brothers had indulged in, it was just as well she was a little tardy. Reynard's announcement that he'd asked some stranger to be his wife had momentarily knocked his judgment for a loop. It was lucky that Loren had not interrupted their discussion of Rey's news.

She looked beautiful tonight, almost bridal, and for the umpteenth time this week he rued that work had kept him away from her. He'd become quite addicted to his wife in their time in Dubrovnik. Addicted in ways he'd never imagined.

Leaving her to sleep alone in her bed each night after he'd crawled in from working late had been hell, but he was conscious of the need to ensure she remained well. Replenishing the rest she'd missed during their sojourn was one way of doing that.

A flood of heat hit his groin as he remembered the highlights of that sojourn. Right now he wanted to do nothing more than lead her from the salon and take her back upstairs to their suite and into bed. It seemed it was about the only place they could be honest with one another.

Honest? He cringed internally. Their marriage hadn't started with much honesty. But that was something he was now very keen to put right. While it was true he still wanted the heir he'd demanded of her, he wanted so much more besides. And he wanted to give more, too.

He had not only made the biggest mistake of his life in marrying Loren the way he had, he'd done her a major disservice. She deserved to be cherished, to be loved.

The taste of what their marriage could be had made him hungry for more. More of what made a union real and binding.

A union based on love.

His fingers curled tight around the base of his glass as he finally acknowledged his feelings toward his wife. He loved her. Now all he had to do was convince her of the fact. He crossed the room toward her and dropped a kiss to her cool lips. Instantly he was enveloped in the subtle fragrance she used as her signature perfume. Inhaling her scent made him rock hard in seconds.

"I've missed you this week," he said.

"You've been busy. I understand."

Her response wasn't what he'd hoped for. Where was the passionate, teasing lover he'd come to enjoy so much while they were away?

"You're more understanding than most wives, I'll wager."

"But then I'm not *most wives,* am I?"

Her cryptic answer made him study her face more carefully. She was pale beneath her makeup and there were fine lines of tension about her eyes.

Since their return home, the hope that they'd made a child together during their honeymoon had burned inside of him. That Loren looked somewhat frail this evening gave a hint of truth to the bombshell Giselle had dropped on him this afternoon and made him want to ask Loren outright if she was expecting his baby.

He'd played Giselle's words over in his mind again and again ever since she'd told him about Loren's dizzy spell at the office earlier today. Through all the meetings this afternoon and the interminable legal jargon he'd been forced to wade through, he'd had to fight to keep his focus on the business at hand.

Now that focus was very firmly on the woman before him. His wife. The woman he loved. The woman who now, hopefully, carried their child.

"Are you feeling all right?" he asked, searching her eyes for any hint of a lie.

He raised a hand to her chin and was surprised when she subtly moved clear of his touch.

"I'm fine."

She dismissed his concern with a brittle smile that didn't fool him for a second. Every instinct in him urged him to gather her up in his arms and take her back upstairs. To tie her to the bed, if necessary, until he knew the truth of what lay behind the fragile exterior she exhibited.

"Loren," Reynard interrupted them, bringing Loren a glass of champagne.

Alex was about to intercept it, to tell his brother she wouldn't be drinking tonight or any night for the next several months, but Loren forestalled him by accepting the drink.

Reynard tipped his glass to hers. "You should congratulate me. I'm engaged."

"Engaged? Really? And who is the lucky lady? I had no idea you were even seeing anyone on a regular basis."

There was a slightly wistful note to her voice that pulled at something in Alex's chest.

"Her name is Sara Woodville. She's a Kiwi girl, actually. You might have heard of her. She was here riding for New Zealand in the equestrian trials we sponsored recently."

"And she'd only been on Isla Sagrado for about five minutes before being snapped up by Reynard," Benedict commented drolly. "You've got to hand it to him, he can sure spot an opportunity."

"Well, at least he didn't wait twenty-five years," Loren said, raising her glass to Reynard. "Congratulations, Rey, I hope the two of you will be very happy."

Alex laughed at her comment along with his brothers, but he sensed the thread of bitterness behind her words even if they didn't.

"Well, we can certainly recommend a lovely spot for a honeymoon, can't we?" Alex said, hooking his arm around Loren's slender waist and drawing her against his side.

She stiffened but didn't immediately pull away.

"Oh, yes, I understand that cottage comes very highly recommended."

Again, that hint of double entendre slid like a stiletto through the air. Loren looked across to where *Abuelo* usually sat.

"Is your grandfather not joining us?" she asked.

"No," Alex responded. "His valet sent down a note to say that he wasn't feeling a hundred percent."

"That's not like him. Should I go and check to make sure he's okay?" Loren offered.

If he hadn't thought she would use the opportunity as an excuse to get away from him he would have encouraged her to go. Instead, given how distant she'd been since her arrival this evening, he feared she'd use the visit to his grandfather's rooms as a reason to stay with the old man and not to return—and right now he wanted her here, by his side.

"That won't be necessary. Javier is quite capable of seeing to his needs. Besides, you know how much *Abuelo* hates to be fussed over."

"By you perhaps, but he's never turned away a pretty face—especially Loren's," Benedict noted.

"Be that as it may, Loren can grace us with her company tonight instead. After all, it's the first evening I've had home with her all week."

"Well, don't think you won't have to share her with us. Surely the honeymoon is over by now," Reynard said with a smile designed to needle his older brother even as he hooked an arm in Loren's and drew her away to one side. "Please tell me you are tired of my brother's attentions and we can have our old Loren back again."

Loren laughed, a genuine sound that sent a thrill of longing through Alex. Something untamed knotted deep inside. Logically he knew that his brother was only teasing him, doing what brothers do best when it comes to yanking one another's chain, but he suddenly wished they lived in older times. Times where he could realistically secure Loren away in the castillo's tower rooms and force her to remain only unto him.

He had no doubt that if he answered his instincts and lay claim to her here and now by dragging her from Reynard's clasp that she would find nothing about the action appealing. Besides, forcing her into anything wasn't what he really desired. Truth be told, he simply wanted to hear her laugh—and, more importantly, to be the one who caused her such joy.

Envy didn't sit comfortably on Alex's shoulders. If anything he was the one whose life was coveted by others. That said, he would find some way to remind Reynard of his place.

"Tell us about your new fiancée, Sara, and why you didn't bring her along to meet us this evening," he said pointedly. "Worried she might take one look and decide she's chosen the wrong brother?"

And so the evening rolled on. By the time they took to the massive dining table, with each of the chairs ornately carved with the del Castillo family crest, Alex had firmly reasserted his dominance over his younger siblings. His dominance over his new wife, however, was another matter entirely. She wouldn't so much as meet his eyes and the knowledge definitely set his teeth on edge.

They had just finished their desserts and Reynard was discussing a new publicity drive for the vineyard with Benedict when the castillo's majordomo all but ran into the room. Alex was up and out of his chair before the man came to a halt.

"Qué pasa?" Alex demanded.

"It is *Señor* Aston, he is very ill. Javier, he asks for your help."

"Call for the doctor and an ambulance at once!" Alex barked.

"Already done, *señor.*"

An elevator had been installed for *Abuelo* after his stroke when he'd refused to relocate to a suite downstairs, but Alex eschewed it in favor of the stairs that led to the old man's suite. His grandfather's words, insisting he'd die in the rooms he'd always lived in before anyone could convince him to move, rang loud and clear in Alex's ears. Suddenly the prospect that the elderly head of their family could possibly fulfill that prophecy was frighteningly real.

When Alex arrived in his grandfather's room he was shocked to find the old man lying on the floor, propped up by his manservant and covered with the coverlet from his bed. There was a gray tinge to his features and the muscles on the already weakened side of his face sagged more than usual.

"What happened?" he asked as he knelt to take his grandfather's hand. To feel for himself that the old man's lifeblood still flowed through his body.

"He said he had a headache and preferred to take his evening meal here in his rooms. When I came to take his tray away I found him here, on the floor. I called the doctor straight away and asked Armando to let you know."

Alex heard his brothers enter the room behind him.

"Should we move him onto the bed?" Reynard asked, kneeling down next to Alex.

"No, he is comfortable for now. We'll wait for the doctor and see what he recommends."

Alex felt his grandfather's fingers curl in his, the gnarled digits nowhere near as strong as they should have been. He leaned forward and murmured in Spanish.

"Relax, *Abuelo,* the doctor is coming."

But the old man struggled against him, tugging on Alex's hand as much as he was able. Alex bent closer, trying to make sense of the garbled words coming from his grandfather's mouth. His skin prickled with an icy chill as he finally understood what the old man was saying.

"It is the governess. She was here. It is the curse."

Eleven

"What's he saying?" Benedict asked.

"Nothing," Alex replied, his answer clipped. "He's rambling."

It was always the damn curse. Even now his grandfather wouldn't let go of it. Anger and frustration warred with concern for the old man. He'd done everything he could to put *Abuelo's* mind at ease. He'd married Loren. He believed she was now carrying his baby. But without conclusive proof she was pregnant he couldn't divulge that information to his grandfather.

Or could he? It might be the difference between the old man fighting what appeared to be another stroke or giving up entirely.

Alex gripped his grandfather's hand more tightly. Willing his strength into the old man's failing body.

"It is too late," Aston said, his voice growing weaker. "She has won, hasn't she, the governess?"

"No, *Abuelo,* she hasn't won. The curse, it is broken." Alex forced the words from his lips, prepared to do anything to hold his grandfather to the world around them for as long as he could.

"Broken? Are you certain?" Aston del Castillo's voice grew ever so slightly stronger.

"*Sí,* I am certain."

Just then the doctor arrived at the door, followed closely behind by an emergency paramedic team. In the subsequent bustle of activity as Aston was checked and deemed safe to move to the waiting ambulance downstairs, Alex noticed Loren hovering just inside the doorway.

How long had she been there? Had she heard the exchange between him and his grandfather? No, probably not, he consoled himself. Even Reynard and Benedict who had been at his side could barely hear his grandfather's words.

He looked at her again, studied her drawn features, the concern painted so starkly in her eyes and he knew that she would give him the answer he sought tonight.

"*Señor* del Castillo?"

Alex and his brothers all turned toward the doctor.

"I believe your grandfather has suffered another stroke. I will admit him to hospital immediately. We will need to do a CT scan and possibly an MRI as soon as possible."

"Whatever it takes, Doctor," Alex said, his voice suddenly thick with emotion. "Just make sure he can come back home again."

"We will do everything in our power. I will travel

in the ambulance with your grandfather. Perhaps one of you could follow in my car?"

"We will all come to the hospital," Reynard said.

Alex cast Loren a glance. In response she gave a small nod.

"Fine," he said. "Loren and I will bring one of the estate cars and you and Benedict can travel in the doctor's vehicle. That way we all have transport back home."

He could see that Loren wanted to protest, perhaps even to suggest that she'd travel with Reynard or Benedict, but thankfully she merely acceded to his suggestion.

They completed the drive to the hospital, on the outskirts of Puerto Seguro, in silence. Alex had no need for casual conversation when all he wanted right now was to see his grandfather safely settled in the hospital and to hear a promising prognosis for his future from the neurological specialist on call.

They were pulling up outside the hospital when he placed a hand on Loren's arm and squeezed lightly.

"Thank you," he said.

"What for? I've done nothing tonight."

"For coming with me."

He meant it, too. It would reassure his grandfather to see Loren with him. Would help underline his promise that the curse was well and truly broken. That there was a power of hope ahead for the del Castillo family.

"Alex, you know I would do anything for your grandfather."

Anything for his grandfather but not for him? Alex bit back the question before he could give it voice.

"I am grateful for that," he finally managed through a throat that had suddenly grown thick with emotion.

"He's strong, Alex. He'll be okay."

Loren placed her free hand over his and pressed firmly, as if trying to underline her words and make them a reality.

He could only nod. Drawing in a deep breath, he pulled away from her, missing the contact instantly.

"Come, let's go into the emergency department."

He helped her from the car and was relieved when she didn't pull away from him as he draped one arm around her shoulders and pulled her close against his side. Where she belonged, he reminded himself. No matter what this strange distant game she had played tonight, she was his wife and she belonged with him. Always.

It was nearly two in the morning when they made it back to the castillo. Alex's grandfather was comfortably settled in a private room at the hospital, his neurologist hopeful that because of Javier's quick call for help that they had been successful in halting any additional damage as a result of the ischemic stroke he'd suffered. They'd been able to medicate as soon as the scan results had confirmed their suspicions, falling just within the window of time vital to ensure a strong chance of survival and recovery.

Alex had taken a moment to thank Javier as they'd arrived home. The manservant had been awaiting their arrival and broke into unashamed sobs of relief when given the news that his master would in all likelihood pull through with minimal permanent damage.

Reynard and Benedict had chosen to take taxis to

their homes directly from the hospital, rather than return to the castillo for their vehicles or stay over at their old family home. The next day would be soon enough to work out the logistics of recovering their vehicles. Besides, they would undoubtedly cross over with one another at the hospital as each planned to be there with their grandfather for as much time as their work commitments permitted.

Loren left Alex with Javier and went up the stairs to their rooms, feeling more than twice her age as she let herself into her bedroom and kicked off her shoes.

She looked around the room, feeling as if it had been days since she'd been here, rather than the hours it had actually been. Her eyes fell on the fragrant candles she'd set around the room in an effort to create the right atmosphere in which to seduce her husband. A seduction she'd planned before she'd heard what she suspected was the first excruciating shred of complete honesty from him in all her time back here.

In the drama surrounding *Abuelo's* stroke, the earlier events of the evening had been pushed aside, but now every word she'd overhead came rushing back in a painful remembrance.

She quickly gathered the candles up and dropped them into the wastebasket near her escritoire. She stood there, shaking with anger. How dare he have played with her life like that and then call it a mistake?

"Loren?" Alex spoke from the entrance to her bedroom. "Are you all right?"

A short, sharp sound burst from her throat. It should have been a laugh but there was far too much bitterness behind it to even mimic humor. Alex covered the distance toward her and tried to take her in his arms, but she pulled free and took two steps back from him.

"Don't! Don't touch me."

She had to keep some distance between them; it was the only way she could keep her anger in the forefront of her mind when all her body wanted to do was meld with his and find again the ecstasy they'd shared for all too brief a time. She knew it took more than a physical connection to keep a marriage alive.

"Don't touch you? What is wrong? I've barely seen you all week and we've had a very distressing evening. I need to touch you. I need *you*."

"No." She shook her head.

The bleak weariness that had been on Alex's face earlier was now replaced by sharp intellect and a satisfied nod of understanding. "You are emotional. It is only to be expected. Giselle told me today you might be pregnant."

Loren couldn't believe her ears. "Giselle *what?*"

Alex continued, "Don't you think that you should perhaps have given me the news yourself?"

"And when would I have had the opportunity? You've been away from the castillo all week—not even home at night until very late and then gone early in the morning. Even today, on the telephone, you treated me as no more than a private messenger service." She cut the air between them with a sweep of her hand. "Whatever, as it happens, your assistant's conjecture is premature. My cycle was obviously out of sync. Whether it was from the travel or the stress of the wedding, it matters little. Tomorrow I will have my period."

"And you know this for sure because?" he growled.

"Because I know my own body, and I know I'm not pregnant."

Alex blew out a breath and closed his eyes, his features suddenly contorted with disappointment. When he opened his eyes she was struck by the raw regret mirrored there. She decided to ignore it. She was no doubt as wrong about his feelings on this as she'd been about so many things to do with Alexander del Castillo. If he had any regrets it would only be that he had to continue with this total charade of a marriage to get the heir he so desperately wanted.

"I've given the matter of our prenuptial agreement further thought," she continued. "I believe it would be best for us to go back to my original request for an assisted pregnancy. In fact, I'd prefer it."

"Prefer it?" Alex echoed.

"Yes. Intercourse between us is clearly going to be a hit-and-miss affair. After all, it's not as if we didn't try hard enough before. To be honest with you, I'm not keen to resume that side of our marriage."

"Not keen." His voice was flat, his jaw rock hard.

She clenched her hands into fists at her sides, her fingernails digging small crescents.

"That's right. Plus, I believe you also wish to get on with things yourself."

"Things? Would you care to define exactly what those things are?"

Loren chewed her lower lip for a second. Did she dare acknowledge that she knew of his affair with Giselle, that she was aware he'd been biding his time to pick up again where they'd left off? She lifted her chin and met his gaze squarely.

"I think you know what I'm referring to. We both

know this marriage between us was a mistake. In fact I heard you say the very thing yourself tonight."

"You heard me say that?" His voice was deadpan, as was the expression in his eyes.

Alex stepped in closer, filling her senses with his presence. Loren stood her ground. He knew very well what he'd said and now he knew she'd overheard him.

"Alex, as I said before, I will fulfill my duties to you under our legal agreement. That means I must deliver you a child. There was nothing in there about how I am to achieve that goal so I elect to use the clinical facility here on the island. Now, if that is all, it has been an extremely long and demanding day and I would like to get some sleep."

"There was also nothing in there about you being the one to elect how you should fall pregnant," Alex said.

Loren felt her heart stutter in her chest before resuming a rapid rhythm. "Are you suggesting you would force me?"

"Force? No, I doubt that would be necessary. Not when I know I can do this and have you willing in my arms."

He snaked one arm around her waist and drew her against his body, molding her hips to his lower body, widening his stance to cradle her there. Instantly Loren felt the answering call of her body to his, the intensity of awareness, the heated flow of blood through her veins.

When Alex bent his head to hers and caught her lips in a possessive kiss she found herself answering in kind. Allowing her anger an outlet, showing him he may be able to dominate her physically but he would never dominate her will.

They were both panting, their breathing discordant and harsh in the air between them, when Alex broke away.

"Out of respect for your oncoming *condition*," he said, his fingers splaying across her hip and lower belly, "I will not continue, but I believe my point has been made. You cannot refuse me, Loren. Your own body makes a lie of that."

As she watched him leave the bedroom and pull her door closed behind him she forced herself to acknowledge he was painfully right. She'd adored him as a child, been infatuated with him as a teen. Now she loved him with every cell in her body as a woman. Even knowing he would still choose another did not assuage the loss she felt as he'd walked away.

Was this how her father had felt when he'd learned of her mother's infidelity? This frantic sense of hurt and betrayal, the urgent desire to turn back the clock and start over—to get things right next time?

Her mother had once, and only once, alluded to the fact that she'd chosen to do something totally against her nature to force her husband to finally let her go. That the passionate highs and desperate lows of their rocky marriage had been as destructive as they'd been exhilarating and that she'd been incapable of bearing them any longer.

The fact that Naomi had been unfaithful to Francois Dubois to break free of her marriage had been a cop-out as far as Loren was concerned. She'd always believed that if they had loved one another enough they could have made things work. Not all marriages were always sailed on an even keel. Some people, some relationships, were just not cut out to be like that. That didn't mean they had to fall apart.

But the one thing Loren did know for certain was that when one partner loved less, or not at all, that marriage was doomed to failure.

When Loren woke the next morning with her period she was torn between relief that she wasn't yet forced to bring a baby into a loveless marriage and sorrow that the intimacy they'd shared in so much happier times, no matter how orchestrated, had not resulted in a child to love. After taking care of her needs she carried on through into the sitting room of their suite. Her maid usually ensured a tray was sent up for Loren each morning with her preference of cereal and yogurt for breakfast together with freshly squeezed orange juice. Loren usually took this quiet time in the morning to review the papers and plan her day.

She was surprised, however, to see Alex pacing the carpet when she pushed open her chamber door.

"*Abuelo?*" she asked, one hand to her throat. "Is everything all right?"

"*Sí,* he is resting comfortably. That is not why I'm here."

"Oh? What is it, then?" Loren went instantly on the defensive. "Ready to go for round two in the baby debate?"

"There is no debate," Alex responded, his voice harsh.

"Well, there certainly is no debate today. I have my period. You can go and carry on with whatever it is you're supposed to be doing today."

"Are you certain?"

Loren just stared at him. She knew she looked anything but her usual self this morning. The cramps had started in earnest shortly after she'd gone to bed and had kept her awake for the rest of the night. Her reflection in the mirror had shown her cheeks were pale, her eyes dark and shadowed.

"I will contact the doctor today and find out what is necessary to instigate the procedure."

Alex rubbed one hand across his eyes and sighed.

"Loren, it doesn't have to be like this."

"Yes, Alex, it does. We wouldn't want there to be any further *mistakes,* now would we?"

"You have taken my words out of context," he argued back.

"Just how out of context?"

Alex felt a swirl of helplessness eddy within him in the growing whirlpool of frustration he'd been feeling since the previous night. If only he could convince her to listen to what he'd really meant. Caution warned him that today was probably not the best time to broach the subject of his innermost thoughts. She was unlikely to believe him if he declared his love for her right now, and given how he'd dissembled to her already he could hardly blame her.

Just seeing her like this, looking bruised and fragile, made him want to sweep her into his arms and tuck her back into her bed. To force her to relax and regain her strength. To be the vibrant young woman he'd reintroduced himself to in New Zealand.

"I do not wish to banter with you about something as important as this when you are clearly not at your best. Perhaps when you are feeling better and more amenable to discussion—"

"This is not just some passing mood, Alex! I'm serious. As far as I am concerned, until we are discussing the creation of our child, we have nothing else to say to one another."

"Fine," he said in clipped tones, not wanting to acknowledge the hurt her words had inflicted upon his hopes. "You contact the clinic. Let me know when and where I'm needed or if you happen to change your mind from this ridiculous insistence of yours."

Alex drove to his office in a fury, barely even noticing the summer glory of the countryside that led to the resort's location.

The fact Loren was totally unwilling to resume the physical side of their marriage completely baffled him. They had been perfect together. So she'd overhead him saying he'd made a mistake. He had. He was man enough to admit that. But her adamant refusal to enter into discussions with him unless they were discussing their child caused a pain inside him that was physical as much as it was emotional. A pain he was totally unaccustomed to feeling. If this was love, no wonder his ancestors had primarily chosen to marry for any other reason but that. Anything was better than giving someone else the power to make you hurt inside the way he hurt right now.

He thought fleetingly of the situation that had brought about his marriage to Loren. The governess's curse may not be real, but it had certainly made an impact on his life, and not one he was happy to accede to.

The three supposed edicts of the governess as she'd cursed his ancestor played back in his head—honor, truth and love. Well, he had both honored and continued to love his grandfather, and he'd tried to love his wife. Tried, and failed. It was a failure he wanted to put behind him as quickly and effectively as he could.

As he pressed the accelerator down a little harder, sending his car flying along the resort road, he vowed Loren would come back into his arms, and into his bed, on his terms or no terms at all.

Twelve

It had been two weeks since their last civil conversation beyond the frozen politeness they displayed to everyone at mealtimes at the castillo. At least those mealtimes when Alex deigned to come home.

His grandfather had been moved from the hospital, protestingly, into convalescent care. That he would be allowed back home when he met the rehabilitation markers set by his doctors was of no consolation to him. Loren had spent most of her days divided between keeping him company, preventing him from being cheerfully murdered by the staff at the facility where he was staying and performing her duties at the orphanage.

Each time she held the babies, she ached a little more for the child she did not carry. But, she told herself, that need would soon be assuaged by the procedures she would soon commence. Her doctor had agreed to begin the necessary treatments once both she and Alex were fully apprised of the information relating to them.

Now she finally had all that information to hand and she was determined to start whatever was necessary as soon as possible—which meant ensuring Alex was equally informed.

The prospect of undergoing injections to ensure she produced multiple viable eggs was something she didn't look forward to, but she was prepared to endure whatever she had to. She'd promised, legally and personally, to carry out her end of the agreement. She was her father's daughter. She did not renege on anything.

Loren checked her reflection before grabbing the file of papers the doctor and his nurse had given her. She smoothed her straight dark hair with one hand before straightening her shoulders and giving herself a small nod of approval. She was ready to go to Alex's office.

The dark blue shift she wore tapered to her slender form perfectly, and her matching sling-back shoes confirmed her businesslike appearance. And that's all this was. A business transaction. The execution of a plan.

At the resort, the receptionist waved Loren through to Alex's offices. At his door she paused, her hand curled, knuckles ready to rap on the smooth wooden surface. But then she decided against it. She was his wife, after all. There had to be some advantages to it.

She reached for the polished steel handle, pushed open the door and stepped inside only to come to a rapid halt at the sight before her.

Giselle was all but straddling Alex's lap—her hair

a golden tumble down her back, her hand covering his own as it pushed up the hem of her skirt, her other arm draped around his neck and his head bent into the curve of hers.

Loren gave a startled gasp and spun on her heel before stopping and forcing herself to face the couple who were now apart. Giselle quickly stood beside Alex's chair and slowly rearranged her clothing. Her face wore a distinct look of sly satisfaction—Alex's, however, wore one of dark fury.

Loren looked from one to the other, suddenly overwhelmed with a determination that would brook no denial. She would not tolerate this. If Alex wanted a child in this marriage then he'd have to play by her rules and her rules demanded no infidelity.

It was time she grew a spine and fought back. Adrenaline coursed through her body. Suddenly she could begin to understand why people took scary risks. The sense of exhilaration was both terrifying and electrifying at the same time.

She pointed one finger at Giselle. "You. Get out."

"I beg to differ," Giselle drawled. "I believe you're the one out of place here."

"You can beg all you like, but you will be doing it elsewhere from now on. Get out, now, and stay the hell away from my husband."

"Alex!" The other woman appealed to the silent male figure at her side. "You can't let her talk to me like that. You have to tell her about us."

"What's it to be, Alex?" Loren challenged.

"Leave us," he said, his voice calm and level.

"Surely you don't expect me—" Giselle protested.

Loren smiled at her, although it was more a baring

of teeth than a signal of pleasure. "I believe my husband asked you to leave."

With a sniff of disdain Giselle collected her bag, then with a hand trailing the side of Alex's face she said, "Should you change your mind, you know where to reach me."

Loren watched as Giselle sashayed out of the office and went to close the door firmly behind her. Then she crossed back over to Alex's desk and dropped the clinic folder onto his desk in front of him.

"If you want to go ahead and have a baby with me then there have to be some boundaries. The most important is that you keep your hands off other women or you can consider our marriage over."

He gave a short laugh. "Marriage? You think what we have is a marriage?"

"We have what approximates a marriage, but we'll have what is most definitely a divorce if you so much as touch another woman again."

Alex leaned back in his leather executive chair and steepled his fingers. Giselle's move on him had taken him by surprise. He'd made it more than clear, both before he'd traveled to New Zealand and since his return and subsequent marriage to Loren, that anything he and Giselle had shared was well and truly over.

At first she'd been subtle—well, subtle for Giselle anyway. In recent weeks, her overtures had been more blatant, but nothing like today's blitzkrieg. He'd been on the verge of pushing her away—off his lap and out of his employ—when Loren had entered his office. He'd half expected Loren to simply leave again, but even then his little wife had surprised him.

Despite keeping her distance from him it was patently clear she was not prepared to share her toys, either. The knowledge gave him a surge of satisfaction. Perhaps now she would listen to reason.

He reached forward and flicked open the file she'd dropped on his desk with one finger. His eyes skimmed the first page of details and everything inside him rebelled. No way would he accede to this barbaric coercion of nature when for them, in all likelihood, it was not even necessary.

"No other women, you say?" he asked, arching one brow and allowing his lips to relax into a smile.

"You heard me."

His wife stood opposite him, standing her ground like a sentinel.

"Hmm." Alex pursed his lips in consideration. "Yet you do not plan to share your bed with me like a dutiful wife ought?"

"We've been over this, Alex. You don't love me, yet you want a baby with me. Some people might be able to separate emotion from their physical behavior but I am not one of them. I won't share my bed with you if your only purpose in coming to me is to conceive a child."

There was a tiny break in her voice. A break that gave him the leverage he was looking for. She had not stopped loving him, he was sure of it. And if she hadn't, then he could press home his advantage and use this as an opportunity to win her back. To make their marriage the genuine article.

"I see. Well, then there is nothing for it but for me to agree to your condition that I not touch another woman."

"Thank you," she said, her breath escaping in a rush.

He raised a hand. "I haven't finished. I do agree to

your condition, on a condition of my own. I refuse to allow you to submit to this process, Loren. We will conceive our child the old-fashioned way."

"No."

"Then I'm sorry. Because on this I refuse to negotiate."

"And I refuse to take another woman's leavings. Our marriage is over."

Before he could stop her Loren had turned and left his office. Over? Surely she didn't mean it. Shock reverberated through his body. Shock followed rapidly by a determination to stop her in her tracks. To somehow make her retract her statement, to admit her love for him, to allow him to admit his for her. He would not let her go, not like this, not ever. Galvanized by a combination of fear and resolve, he shot from his chair and out of his office.

By the time he reached the reception area he was just in time to see his wife's sleek convertible spin out of the parking lot and up the driveway leading to the main road. He felt his jacket pocket for his keys and cursed that he'd left them in his briefcase instead. There was no time to waste. Alex turned and zeroed in on his receptionist.

"Your car keys, give them to me now."

Flustered, the woman withdrew her handbag from a file drawer and extracted her keys.

"It's the Fiat, at the end of the staff car park," she said with wide eyes.

"*Gracias,* you'll find my keys in the case beside my desk. Take my car tonight."

"The Lamborghini?"

But Alex barely heard her. He had to reach Loren before she did something stupid, like leave him for good.

She could barely see through the tears that spilled from her eyes and down her cheeks as she grabbed clothes indiscriminately from her wardrobe and drawers and jammed them into her suitcase.

Was it so unreasonable to expect him not to have affairs?

Perhaps it was if *she* wasn't prepared to give him the surcease his male body obviously demanded. But what of her needs? What of the pleasures he'd taught her to receive and, in turn, to give? If she didn't have him, she didn't want anybody else and she most definitely wasn't prepared to share him.

Besides, he didn't want *her*. Not really. He only wanted her to create the heir he so desperately needed to provide to prove to *Abuelo* that the curse was nothing but hearsay on the tail of a three-hundred-year-old legend. She certainly had to admire the lengths he was prepared to go to set his grandfather's mind at rest, but the cost wasn't something she was prepared to pay. Not anymore. Not when beneath it all he still thought marrying her had been a mistake.

Loren bit back a sob as she shoved the swimwear and the sarongs she'd taken to Dubrovnik into the case and dashed the tears from her cheeks. A sound behind her made her pause. Before she could return to her task, she was spun around. The articles of clothing she still held were plucked from her hands and cast to the floor at her feet.

Alex stood before her, his strong hands holding her upper arms firmly so she couldn't pull away.

"I am no woman's leavings," he ground out in a harsh breath. "Unless, of course, you really are planning to leave me?"

"Of course I'm leaving you. I can't do this anymore, Alex. I can't."

"Why? Tell me." His fingers curled into her arms, pulling her closer to him.

"I can't share you. I refuse to share you. You know I love you, I always have—stupidly, now more than ever. I accepted when I married you that you didn't love me. I could live with that. But I cannot live with you taking your pleasure from other women. I lived through that with my parents. My mother's infidelity drove them both insane. I will not fall victim to that kind of desperate dependence. Not even for you."

"But you have no need to share me. I have never been unfaithful to you, Loren. Please, believe me."

She yanked herself free from his grasp and a choked laugh erupted from her throat.

"Don't treat me like a fool. From the second I arrived here Giselle has made it perfectly clear that you were only biding time with me until I provided you with an heir. Even you yourself did nothing to disabuse me of that belief."

"And our honeymoon? Did that mean nothing to you?"

"Mean nothing? It meant *everything* to me when we could finally be a couple. Yet the second we returned everything went back to how it was before. Including your relationship with your assistant."

"My relationship with Giselle has been nothing but professional for several months."

"How can you expect me to believe that? All those

late nights and early mornings? I never saw you, you never spoke to me. And what about what I interrupted today?"

"I admit, I was involved with Giselle for a short period before I came to New Zealand, but once I'd decided to marry you I broke things off with her. Today was Giselle's desperate attempt to reignite a flame that never went beyond a distant flicker. What we shared was well and truly over before I asked you into my life, Loren. It's only ever been you since then."

Loren just shook her head. She wished she could accept his words as the truth but she hurt too much.

"Why should I believe you, Alex? Why should I believe my husband when he thinks our whole marriage is a mistake?"

"Because I love you!"

"Don't lie to me about that, Alex. Not now, not ever!"

She spun away from him and clutched her arms around her body as if she could somehow assuage the empty pain that filled her chest in the place of her heart and the death of her dreams.

He turned her back to face him and cupped his hands around her face, tilting it up so her eyes would meet his.

"Loren, I love *you*. I didn't plan to. To be totally honest, I didn't even want to. I thought we could marry, and that our feelings for each other would never go beyond companionship at best. How wrong I was!" He shook his head at his own foolishness. "I didn't count on falling in love with you, but from the moment you stood up to your mother, you started to inveigle your way into my heart. Day by day, week by week, I've learned to respect you and to love you.

"That's what I meant when I told my brothers I had made a mistake marrying you the way I had. It was wrong to rush into marriage merely to disprove some stupid curse that has no bearing on our lives today no matter what my grandfather believes. It was wrong to use you that way. But I do not regret marrying you, Loren. I will never regret that. If I had this time over again I would still have brought you back to Isla Sagrado, back home, but I would have taken the time to woo you, to learn about the woman you are now, to acknowledge that love is not something to be spurned or used to a man's advantage." He pressed a kiss to her forehead. "Loren, please, give me another chance. Give *us* another chance."

Confusion swirled inside her. Half of her wanted to believe him, to have faith in his words and hold them to her forever. But the other half still hurt, deeply and most painfully. Her trust in him had been broken, her pride dashed. Deep down, she didn't want to lay herself open for any more hurt.

"I don't know if I can," she whispered. "I don't know if I even want to try again."

His dark eyes deepened to darkest black as she saw her own pain reflected in their depths.

"Then go. Return to New Zealand. I will not hold you to a marriage that you no longer can commit to. I will see to our dissolution, to your freedom. I'm sorry, Loren. I never thought things would come to this. As much as it breaks my heart, I would rather see you free to go than be trapped here with me, even as much as I need you by my side."

"You would do that? You'd let me just leave? What about the curse? What about *Abuelo?*"

"Don't you understand? Without your love, without you, I will forever be cursed. If you cannot love me then who am I to hold you here? I can only beg your forgiveness for being such a fool and for using you the way I did.

"Losing you has taught me a valuable life lesson. There is more to honoring a parent's wish and a family's expectations than just going through the motions. Without love, it means nothing."

He let her go and Loren rocked slightly on her feet as he did so. The confusion that had so clouded her mind only moments ago began to solidify into one clear thought.

Alexander del Castillo loved her.

Finally, this tall, proud man was hers.

Relief coursed through her veins followed by a bubbling rush of exhilaration. She drew in a deep breath.

"Alex," she said, in as level a tone as she could manage, "would you do one final thing for me?"

"Anything."

"Would you bring my suitcase?"

She saw his features settle into a frozen mask, but to his credit he said nothing. Merely zipped up the case and hefted it off the bed with one hand.

"Thank you," she said, and started walking through their suite and into his bedchamber.

"What are you doing?" he asked, his voice thick as if his throat was constricted.

"I don't want to be apart from you anymore—not even in separate rooms."

"Then you're staying?"

"You couldn't get rid of me now for anything."

Loren looked at him now, face-to-face, surprised to see the sheen of tears reflected in his eyes. That this powerful man was reduced to tears by the fact that she'd chosen to remain with him said it all.

"Love me, Alex."

"Forever, *mi querida*."

His arms closed around her, making her feel as if she'd finally come home. After their clothing had been torn from their bodies and they came together on his massive pedestal bed Loren knew she was home forever.

Past hurts dissolved into distant memories as his hands caressed her body with a new reverence. Fears about the future disappeared as she welcomed him inside her, not only physically but, finally, wholly and emotionally, as well.

It was late and the castillo silent and brooding in the darkness as Alex led Loren down the stairs.

"Where are you taking me?" Loren asked in a whisper.

"There is one more thing we need to do. Trust me."

He felt his heart swell as her slender fingers tightened in his. That small silent communication meant so much. To finally have her trust and to know he honestly returned it was one of the greatest gifts he'd ever received.

Their slippered feet made no sound as they crossed the great hall toward the small private chapel that formed part of the castillo's ancient history. The well-tended chapel door swung open silently beneath his touch.

"Wait here a moment," he instructed before moving swiftly down the center aisle of the centuries-old place of worship.

Moonlight gave eerie illumination to the stained-glass windows that had been fitted by successive generations of del Castillos. At the altar Alex lit the thick candles in their squat candelabra, letting their golden glow chase the shadows of the past to the corners of the chapel.

He turned back to Loren, covering the short distance back to the door, to his bride, in seconds. Taking her hand again, he led her to the altar.

"I should have done this right the first time. I owed you that," he said, stroking the side of her face softly before letting his hands reach down to take both of hers in his own.

"It's all right, Alex. We survived anyway."

Her smile was bittersweet and Alex made a silent vow to ensure that the last of their ghosts were banished from this moment.

"We may have survived but you deserve more than that. This time I don't want there to be any doubt.

"Loren, I love you for your strength in the face of adversity, for your pride and incredible sense of honor and for the gift of your love to me, even when I didn't deserve it. From this day forward, you will never again be lonely for I will always be at your side to give you comfort and to support you in whatever you do for all of our lives together.

"I promise you, I will always be your rock, I will always honor you, remain true only to you and I will always love you—today and forever."

He lifted her hand and placed a kiss on her ring finger, sealing a brand upon her skin where his rings already claimed her as his by law. He rested their clasped hands against his chest as Loren took a deep breath and started to speak, her voice low and clear in the air between them.

"Alex, I have always loved you for your principles, for your direction and your love for your family. I am honored to be your wife, to be your partner for life and to be the one to support you and love you through whatever comes our way in the future. I treasure your love for me and will always do everything in my power to protect and nurture that love.

"Together I know we can weather any storm and be safe in the knowledge that it will only bring us closer and will only serve to help me love you more. I can't wait to have children with you, to watch them grow with your guidance and strength behind them and I promise that I will always be there for you and always love you."

She reached up and kissed him, sealing their vows to one another with a hunger and a pledge that promised a happier future.

As one, they bent to blow out the candles, then left the chapel to return to their chamber, oblivious to the fading apparition in the far reaches of the shadows—a woman in eighteenth-century dress—smiling.

* * * * *

We hope you enjoyed reading this
special collection from Harlequin® books.

If you liked reading these stories, then you
will love **Harlequin® Desire** books.

You want to leave behind the everyday.
Harlequin Desire stories feature sexy,
romantic heroes who have it all: wealth, status,
incredible good looks…everything but the
right woman. Add some secrets, maybe a
scandal, and start turning pages!

Enjoy six *new* stories from
Harlequin Desire every month.

Available wherever books and
ebooks are sold.

COMING NEXT MONTH FROM

HARLEQUIN

Desire

Available February 3, 2015

#2353 HER FORBIDDEN COWBOY
Moonlight Beach Bachelors • by Charlene Sands
When his late wife's younger sister needs a place to heal after being jilted at the altar, country-and-western star Zane Williams offers comfort at his beachfront mansion. But when he takes her in his arms, they enter forbidden territory...

#2354 HIS LOST AND FOUND FAMILY
Texas Cattleman's Club: After the Storm
by Sarah M. Anderson
Tracking down his estranged wife to their hometown hospital, entrepreneur Jake Holt discovers she's lost her memory—and had his baby. Will their renewed love stand the test when she remembers what drove them apart?

#2355 THE BLACKSTONE HEIR
Billionaires and Babies • by Dani Wade
Mill owner Jacob Blackstone is all business; bartender KC Gatlin goes with the flow. But her baby secret is about to shake things up as these two very different people come together for their child's future...and their own.

#2356 THIRTY DAYS TO WIN HIS WIFE
Brides and Belles • by Andrea Laurence
Thinking twice after a reckless Vegas elopement, two best friends find their divorce plans derailed by a surprise pregnancy. Will a relationship trial run prove they might be perfect partners, after all?

#2357 THE TEXAN'S ROYAL M.D.
Duchess Diaries • by Merline Lovelace
When a sexy doctor from a royal bloodline saves the nephew of a Texas billionaire, she loses her heart in the process. But secrets from her past may keep her from the man she loves...

#2358 TERMS OF A TEXAS MARRIAGE
by Lauren Canan
The fine print of a hundred-year-old land lease will dictate Shea Hardin's fate: she must marry a bully or lose it all. But what happens when she falls for her fake husband...hard?

HDCNM0115

SPECIAL EXCERPT FROM

HARLEQUIN®

Desire

Here's a sneak peek at the next
TEXAS CATTLEMAN'S CLUB:
AFTER THE STORM installment,
HIS LOST AND FOUND FAMILY
by *Sarah M. Anderson*

*Separated and on the verge of divorce, Jake Holt is
determined to confront his wife. But when he arrives
in Royal, Texas, he finds that Skye has been keeping
secrets…*

Jake had spent the past four years pointedly not caring
about what his family was doing. They'd wanted him to
put the family above his wife. Nothing had been more
important to him than Skye.

He was not staying in Royal long. Just enough to get
Skye back on her feet and figure out where they stood.

Just then, the baby made a little hiccup-sigh noise that
pulled at his heartstrings.

Jake's brother picked the baby up so smoothly that
Jake was jealous.

"Grace, honey—this is your daddy," Keaton said as he
rubbed her back. Then, to Jake, he added, "You ready?"

Not really—but Jake wasn't going to admit that to
Keaton. He tried to cradle his arms in the right way. Then
Keaton laid the baby in them.

The world seemed to tilt off its axis as Jake looked
down into his daughter's eyes. They were a pale blue—

just like her mother's. Up close now, he could see that Grace had wispy hairs on her head that were so white and fine they were almost see-through.

She didn't start bawling, which he took as a good sign. Instead, she waved her tiny hands around, so of course he had to offer her one of his fingers. When she latched on to it, he felt lost and yet *not* lost at the same time.

He was responsible for this little girl from this moment until the day he drew his last breath. The weight of it hit him so hard that if he hadn't already been sitting, his knees would have buckled.

This was his daughter. He and Skye had created this little person.

God, he wished Skye was here with him. That things between them had been different. That he'd been different.

But he couldn't change the past, not when his present—and his future—was gripping his little finger with surprising strength.

Don't miss what happens next in
HIS LOST AND FOUND FAMILY
by Sarah M. Anderson!

Available February 2015,
wherever Harlequin® Desire books and ebooks are sold.

HARLEQUIN®

A *Romance* FOR EVERY MOOD™

JUST CAN'T GET ENOUGH?

Join our social communities
and talk to us online.

You will have access to the latest
news on upcoming titles and special
promotions, but most importantly,
you can talk to other fans about your
favorite Harlequin reads.

Harlequin.com/Community

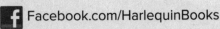

Facebook.com/HarlequinBooks

Twitter.com/HarlequinBooks

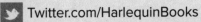

Pinterest.com/HarlequinBooks

HARLEQUIN®

A *Romance* FOR EVERY MOOD™

**Stay up-to-date on all your
romance-reading news with the
Harlequin Shopping Guide,
featuring bestselling authors, exciting new
miniseries, books to watch and more!**

The newest issue will be delivered right to you
with our compliments! There are 4 each year.

Signing up is easy.

EMAIL

ShoppingGuide@Harlequin.ca

WRITE TO US

HARLEQUIN BOOKS
Attention: Customer Service Department
P.O. Box 9057, Buffalo, NY 14269-9057

OR PHONE

1-800-873-8635 in the United States
1-888-343-9777 in Canada

Please allow 4-6 weeks for delivery of the first issue by mail.

Love the Harlequin book you just read?

Your opinion matters.

Review this book on your favorite book site, review site, blog or your own social media properties and share your opinion with other readers!

Be sure to connect with us at:
Harlequin.com/Newsletters
Facebook.com/HarlequinBooks
Twitter.com/HarlequinBooks